D0645289

FOR EVERY SOLUTION, A PROBLEM

Also by Kerstin Gier

Ruby Red
Sapphire Blue
Emerald Green

FOR EVERY SOLUTION, A PROBLEM

Kerstin Gier

Translated by Erik J. Macki

amazon crossing

Text copyright © 2007 by Verlagsgruppe Lübbe GmbH & Co. KG
English translation copyright © 2013 Erik J. Macki

All rights reserved.
Printed in the United States of America

No part of this book may be reproduced, or stored in a retrieval system, or transmitted in any form or by any means, electronic, mechanical, photocopying, recording, or otherwise, without express written permission of the publisher.

For Every Solution, a Problem by Kerstin Gier was first published in 2007 by Verlagsgruppe Lübbe GmbH & Co. KG in Bergisch Gladbach, Germany, as *Für jede Lösung ein Problem*.

Translated from the German by Erik J. Macki.
First published in English in 2013 by AmazonCrossing.

Published by AmazonCrossing
P.O. Box 400818
Las Vegas, NV 89140

ISBN-13: 9781477809860
ISBN-10: 1477809864
Library of Congress Control Number: 2013910362

For Renate and Biggi and our big plans

Jede Lösung eines Problems ist ein neues Problem.
(Every solution to a problem is a new problem.)

—Johann Wolfgang von Goethe

To the Editors of *BILD* Magazine:

It just occurred to me that you'll probably be reporting on my suicide, but when you do, you'll probably also ignore my true motives and invent your own: EVERY MONTH SHE WROTE ABOUT TRUE LOVE, BUT SHE COULD NEVER EXPERIENCE IT FOR HERSELF . . . WHY MORE AND MORE HOT SINGLES ARE COMMITTING SUICIDE IN GERMANY.

I suppose there is a kernel of truth in a teaser like that. Plus, maybe you can save it for the next slow news cycle. So go ahead and write whatever you want—just don't quote my mother. No matter what she says, it wasn't because of my hair color! Brunettes have just as much fun as blondes.

Just not *me*.

Sincerely yours,
Gerri T.,
The mysterious dead woman from that luxury suite

P.S. In the event that you need pictures of me naked to flesh out the story, which I presume you'll be running on page 1, as any self-respecting tabloid would, I recommend you use a photo montage with my face (see enclosed photos) cropped onto the body of Giselle Bündchen. The naked pictures of me that a certain Ulrich M. may offer you have been Photoshopped in a pathetic attempt to steal the spotlight for himself.

ONE

Could you please hand me the small Tupperware Wonderlier bowl from the cabinet, Lu—Ti—Ri—," my mother said. The leftovers from supper included one new potato, a razor-thin slice of pot roast, and a tablespoon of braised red cabbage with apple, which my mother simply couldn't bear to throw out. "It's the perfect portion for one," she said.

My name is not Lutiri, of course. I have three elder sisters, and my mother has always had trouble keeping our names straight. Our names are Tina, Lulu, Rika, and Gerri, but my mother just called us all Lutiri, Gerluti, Riluger, and so on—mathematically there are infinite combinations, extending even into the four-syllable range.

Anyway, I'm Gerri, the youngest. And the only one who lives alone and is thus somehow expected to subsist on one measly potato, a meager sliver of meat, and a scant spoonful of cabbage. As though someone automatically has less appetite if she's single.

"That's not the Wonderlier, that's the Servalier," my mother said. I put the plastic bowl back into the cupboard and handed her another one. I had shown up for Sunday supper at my parents' house to avoid drawing any unnecessary attention. However, my plan was for this to be our last meal together.

"That's the seven-cup FridgeSmart," my mother said, looking at me annoyed. "Much too big. Stop pretending to be dumber than you are."

All right, then. On to the next one.

My mother sighed. "That's the CrystalWave, but that'll work, too—hand it over."

It was weird that my mother was somehow unable to call her own children by name but had no such problem with Tupperware bowls. To say nothing of the fact that I would have far, *far* preferred a name like Crystal to Gerda. But that's how it is: Not only did almost everybody have prettier names than I did, so did most kitchenware.

But at least my sisters were similarly afflicted with names as unattractive as mine. This was because we were all supposed to have been boys: After each birth produced an unexpected girl, my parents basically just girlified the boys' names they had already selected. Tina, short for Martina, was supposed to have been Martin; Rika, short for Erika, was supposed to have been Erik; Lulu, short for Ludwiga, was supposed to have been Ludwig; and I was supposed to have been Gerd. Tina had the least to complain about; her main criticism was that Martina was so common. And then to make matters worse, she married a guy named Frank Meier, who was just as dissatisfied at how common both of his names were in Germany. So that's why their kids all had names that *no* one else had (and would not likely want, either, if you ask me). Their names are Chisola, Arsenius, and Habakkuk.

Chisola, Arsenius, and Habakkuk Meier.

Chisola was twelve and didn't talk much, which Tina blamed on Chisola's braces, but I blamed on Chisola's little brothers, who were four years younger. The boys were twins and never stopped making noise or mess.

As had been the case at supper just now.

It turned out I didn't needed to worry that anyone might detect something off with me. As always, all attention went to the twins. No one would have noticed me anyway, even if I'd been carrying my head under my arm.

Habakkuk kept mashing his cabbage and potatoes together, then trying to suck the pulpy mixture, jaws closed, through the gap in his front teeth. Arsenius kept clanking his utensils on the edge of his plate, chanting "Habakkuk! Chuck up that guck! Habakkuk! Chuck up that guck!" And after a little while, Habakkuk did so: He spit his pulp back out onto his plate, complete with gagging sounds.

"Habi," my mother said with mild disapproval. "What will Patrick think of us?"

"I don't care what he thinks," Habakkuk said, scraping a little piece of red cabbage out of his teeth with his fingernail.

Patrick was my sister Lulu's new boyfriend. I was flabbergasted when Lulu had brought him to Sunday supper for the first time a few weeks ago. Because Patrick looked exactly like someone I used to know.

Well, *know* might be a bit of an exaggeration. He looked like the guy from DatingCafé.de whom I'd gone out with once, *rockinhard12*. My memory of this meeting was not particularly fond, which is why at first I just stared at Patrick aghast. But Patrick didn't show the slightest sign of recognizing me. Nor did he wince when Lulu introduced me and I shook his hand, saying, "It is so rockin' hard to meet you." Even though I normally have a good memory for people and their faces, I quickly realized I was mistaken. Patrick and *rockinhard12* just looked like twins, is all. Patrick was good-looking, down to the pointy little goatee—and, unlike *rockinhard12*, he came off as more or less normal. Although Patrick was fairly secretive about his job.

"Now, Patrick, what do you do for a living?" my father had asked the first time he joined us for Sunday supper, and Patrick had vaguely answered, "IT."

This was now the third time he had been to my parents' house, and they still didn't quite get what kind of career "IT" was—but dared not ask the same question again. I did notice how my mother had taken Lulu aside before supper tonight, however.

"Now, what *exactly* does Patrick do for a living again, sweetheart?"

And Lulu answered, "IT, Mama. He told you that the last two times he was here."

My mother was still none the wiser. But I was pretty sure my sister was telling her girlfriends that her new boyfriend was "a really nice guy" and earned a lot of money in "eye tea." And that she hoped it was serious this time.

It was hard to guess what Patrick thought of us, though. His face didn't give much away.

"I'm sure Patrick knows that boys can be a little wild sometimes," Tina said. "He used to be a little rascal like that himself, I have no doubt."

"Before he went into IT," I said.

"But a well-behaved little rascal," my sister Lulu said, patting Patrick's arm.

"Well," Patrick began, "my dad always did emphasize the importance of good table manners."

"Are you suggesting our children aren't well behaved?" Tina asked, exchanging an angry look with her husband, Frank.

"Can I have some more apple juice?" Arsenius asked.

"*May* I," my mother said. "We say, '*May* I have some more apple juice?'"

"And *please*," I said. "'May I *please* have some more apple juice?'"

"I want apple juice *now*!" Arsenius said. "To wash this revolting taste out of my mouth."

"I want juice, too, please," Chisola whispered.

"Not well behaved at all, in fact," Lulu said.

"What are you trying to say about my kids? You have some kids of your own someday, and then maybe I'll be interested in your input," Tina said.

"I have a doctorate in child development and education, Tina," Lulu said. "I've been working closely with kids for more than six years. I think I'm *already* more than qualified to discuss child rearing."

"Girls!" my mother said, pouring apple juice for Arsenius and Habakkuk and setting the bottle back on the sideboard. "Not the same conversation every Sunday. What will Patrick think of us?"

Patrick still had on that neutral face. As he chewed a piece of pork, his gaze came to rest on the life-size porcelain leopard standing on the low, wide marble window ledge among some yucca palms in gold-and-white cachepots. This ensemble was framed by cotton drapes in gold-and-white metallic checks, gathered up at either side of the picture window and held in place by two chubby little decorative cherubim. If Patrick was thinking anything about us, it was likely something along the lines of *This is the tackiest dining room I've ever eaten in.*

And he would surely have been right.

My mother's penchant for fat little angels and the colors white and gold was evident everywhere in the room. As was her love of leopards. My mother was particularly fond of these great cats: Her favorite piece in the whole house was a floor lamp whose base was shaped like a sitting leopard.

"Doesn't he look real?" she used to ask—and she was right: If the leopard hadn't had a gold-and-white lampshade screwed onto his head, anyone would have taken him for the real thing, since he had genuine fur and whiskers.

Our family would convene every Sunday inside this cage filled with predatory felines. The only absentee was Rika, my second-eldest sister; she lived with her husband, Claudius, and daughter in Venezuela. Even my mother—who is a complete dimwit when it comes to geography—had managed to grasp that one cannot come to Sunday supper at one's parents' home in the Dellbrück neighborhood of Cologne, Germany, all the way from Venezuela.

"The Venezuela in South America," she would occasionally explain to acquaintances. "Not the one in Italy."

Like I said, a complete dimwit. But her pork roast was excellent. I had three slices, in fact; Habakkuk had four. He had stopped kneading his pulp of red cabbage and potatoes. At the end of the meal Tina did her routine swap of Frank's empty plate with the kids' plates, and without batting an eye Frank finished up whatever was left, even if it had already been chewed. Once last year during just such a leftover-disposal operation, Arsenius had started screeching when Frank downed the baby tooth that Arsenius had just lost and set on the edge of his plate. I still get sick to my stomach thinking about it.

The discussion of child rearing started to ebb.

"Oh, whatever," Tina was saying. "You have no kids and yet you're always trying to butt in about how I raise mine!"

I poured some apple juice for Chisola and myself.

"Thank you," Chisola whispered.

"Grandma, Gerri is drinking up all our juice," Habakkuk shouted.

"Grandpa will go get some more from the basement," my mother said, glaring at me. My father stood and then disappeared into the basement.

When he came back upstairs with the apple juice, he handed me an envelope. "Some mail came here for you, Gerri," he said, stroking my cheek lightly. "You look a bit pale today."

"Because she never gets any fresh air," my mother immediately chimed in.

"Since when does my mail get delivered to your house?" I asked. I noted that the envelope had been preopened for me; how considerate. I looked at the return address. K. Köhler-Kopuski. "Never heard of him."

"Of course you know Klaus!" my mother said, irritated. "Klaus Köhler. He's inviting you to your class reunion."

"Really? He has a hyphenated last name now?" I asked.

"That's how modern men do it these days," my mother said.

"Not when their wife's last name is Ko*poops*ki," I said.

Arsenius and Habakkuk burst out laughing, spitting apple juice all over the tablecloth.

"If only *you* had gone to senior prom with him, then Klaus's last name would be Köhler-*Thaler* now," my mother said, lost in thought. This was one of her favorite fantasies.

"No, I'll bet he just wanted as many *K*s as he could have," Tina said. "What did he do for a living again? The keyboard king?"

"Keg keeper?" I suggested. "That would suit him, too."

The twins crowed with excitement and chipped in "kangaroo killer" and "klutzy klepto."

"Klaus has a really good job," my mother insisted. "I've told you all about it before. He's raking it in. Hannah doesn't even have to work; she can stay home and take care of the kids. And Annemarie is so happy with her daughter-in-law and grandchildren."

Hannah Kopuski, aka Kopoopski, was the same year in school as Klaus and I were. But unlike me, and for reasons that would remain eternally inexplicable, she found Klaus fun, she dated him, and she eventually procreated with him. *Ew.*

"Well, *are* you going to go to the reunion?" Lulu asked.

I shrugged. "We'll see." In reality I had firmly resolved that there was absolutely no chance I would show my face there, other than as a crazy person wielding a gun or something. I've known about the reunion for a few weeks now because my best friend Charly had forwarded me an e-mail about it from Britt Emke.

Hello Former Partners in Crime!

As you may know, last year was the ten-year anniversary of our graduation (already!). Since we didn't have a party last year, Klaus Köhler and I, as your former class presidents, were thinking it would be nice to see everyone again at the eleven-year anniversary this year. This will give everyone a chance to find out what we've all been up to and chat about old times.

What on earth was that supposed to mean—"chat about old times" with Britt Emke? Britt, do you remember how you raised your hand that one time in history? "Mr. Miller, if you give Gerri a B, that's totally unfair to Kathrin. Gerri hardly said anything all semester, and she never took notes. She spent every period copying Charlotte's chemistry homework or playing Battleship on graph paper with her neighbors."

Britt the Tattletale had also included a short summary of what she had been up to, just in case anyone reading her e-mail was interested.

After getting my degree in special education, I worked for a year helping children with physical and cognitive challenges before my husband, Baron Ferdinand von Falkenhain, and I moved to a large estate in Lower Saxony. Our daughter Louise is already in kindergarten, and our son-and-heir Friedrich was born last year. We are very happy.

Warmest wishes to you all,
Baroness Britt von Falkenhain

Britt's little summary, however fairy-tale-like, was the sad proof we were no longer living in the good old days of high school, when making wishes still did some good. Because if Charly's and my wishes had come true, Britt would be working the cash register at the drugstore now, returning home every night to a musty basement apartment in a public housing complex to greet an unemployed alcoholic and a pit bull with bladder control problems.

And *I* would be married to Baron Ferdinand von Falkenhain, whoever he was.

"I wouldn't go if I were you," Lulu said. "Everyone will just be bragging about their fabulous husbands, houses, and kids, their awesome jobs, their pricey cars, their vacations, and their PhDs. You'll feel awful. I mean, you don't even have a boyfriend!"

"Well, thank you so much for the pep talk," I said.

"Plus, you've put on weight since graduation," Tina pointed out.

"Nine pounds," I said. (Ten at most!)

"And she looks pale," my father said again. I shot him an astonished look. Really? Was no one here going to notice that something was off with me?

"No one will notice the weight," my mother said. "And they're not *all* married. Boys, or men, don't even want to start settling down until they're around this age. Ti— Lu— Gerri could just say that she's an editor. Or a bookseller."

"Why would I do that?" I asked. "I have no reason to be embarrassed about my job. On the contrary, many people envy me."

"What does she do again?" Patrick asked Lulu.

"I'm an auth—"

"She writes pulp fiction," Lulu said. "Medical romances, tearjerkers, and the like. You know, schlock like you pick up in the grocery store waiting to check out."

"Ah! My grandma always used to read stuff like that," Patrick said. "And you can earn a living doing that?"

"Sure," I said. "Plus, th—"

"I don't know if I'd go that far," my father said.

"I get by," I said. Until three days ago, in any case. "Actual—"

"But she has no way to properly save for retirement, and she has no husband to make up for that," my father said, interrupting me. I was just trying to explain to stupid Patrick that *young* women were actually reading novels as well. "And now you're already thirty!" my father added.

Why did everybody insist on coming back to that number?

"Thirty really isn't that old," Lulu said. "I mean, I didn't meet Patrick until I was thirty-two, after all." That was only two months ago! I hadn't asked them yet where they'd met. But definitely not online, because one time when I mentioned DatingCafé.de to Lulu, she wrinkled up her nose in contempt and said, "Only psychos who never get any in real life lurk around on a site like that."

That would include *rockinhard12*.

"It's different for you," my father told Lulu. "You're a teacher with tenure. You'll get a generous civil servant's pension from the German government. You can afford to wait a bit before getting married."

"Besides, you're blonde," my mother said to Lulu. "How is Tiluri ever going to meet anyone with brown hair like *hers*, when, to top it off, she spends all her time up in her apartment hunched over a computer, writing?"

"Mama, I—"

"She should go to the reunion in any case," my mother said. "It's a good chance to see whatever became of the boys she used to know in school." She added with concern, "Otherwise, all she'll have left is to take out an ad in the *personals*."

"Oh, she tried that ages ago, Mama," Tina said. She had met Frank in a grocery store.

"What?" my mother said, honestly shocked. "She's already sunk so low? My daughter took out an ad in the personals! Don't you dare let even one word of that slip at Alexa's silver-anniversary party! I would melt onto the floor in shame."

"Don't worry," I said. I was as unlikely to appear at my aunt Alexa's party as I was at the reunion.

Chisola then knocked over her glass of apple juice, helpfully stanching that line of conversation. Habakkuk's pants got wet, which resulted in murderous screeching that did not stop until my mother served dessert.

After supper everyone else said good-bye, but I had to stay and help clean up.

My mother pressed the Tupperware bowl named Crystal into my hand. "Would you mind dropping this off at the pharmacy for me sometime this week?" she asked, setting a shoebox on top of the Tupperware I was holding.

"Shoes? To the pharmacy?"

"Don't be ridiculous," my mother said. "The box is full of old prescriptions, but your father won't let me just throw them in the trash. He says they're hazardous waste. The pharmacy collects old drugs for poor people in the Third World." She paused. "You didn't *really* take out a personal ad, did you?"

"No. But I responded to one." I gently lifted the lid to see what was inside. "Um, Mama?" I said, pulling a package out of the shoebox. "People in the Third World don't need nose drops with an expiration date of July 2004."

"There are other things in there, too," my mother said dismissively. "Never look a gift horse in the mouth. They'll be glad to have these at the pharmacy." She sighed. "I never thought one of my daughters would resort to the personals to find a man. But you always were my problem child."

I pulled another package out of the shoebox to inspect. "Dalmane," my mother said. "Sleeping pills." As I held that package, I was honestly stunned—this couldn't be a coincidence. My pulse quickened slightly.

"Every year in the run-up to Christmas I end up getting a prescription for these," my mother said. "But then when your father retired, I ended up needing them year-round, and so did he." She rolled her eyes at the memory.

"This package is still sealed," I said. My hands started trembling, but my mother didn't notice.

"Of course," she said, frowning. "Have you read the side effects for drugs like that? You can get addicted to them very quickly. I would *never* take something like that, nor would your father."

"But why did you both get prescriptions then?" I asked.

"What do you mean?" my mother said. "I just explained it to you: We couldn't sleep! For years and years we couldn't sleep a wink all night! Work, children, retirement . . . That's no way to live. Sleep is vital. It's no joking matter."

"But you just said you would never take something like that," I said. Oh God, she had dozens of boxes, all unopened.

"Medication isn't the answer to everything," my mother said. "And if you absolutely must take something to sleep, then there's always good old-fashioned valerian; I swear by it."

"But—" I began.

"Why does every sentence you say start with the word *but*?" my mother asked. "You've always been like that, nothing but talking back. That's why you have so much trouble with men, you know. Now, will you make yourself useful and drop this stuff off at the pharmacy for me or not?"

I gave up trying to solve the apparent oxymoron of my parents' drug use. "I don't mind," I said. "But I doubt the Third World is really itching for sleeping pills."

"Yet another *but*," my mother sighed, kissing my cheek as she pushed me toward the front door. "I *really* wish you'd start thinking more positively." She ran her hand through my hair. "You'll get your hair done before Alexa's party, right? I'm sure a few highlights would look good on you. Say good-bye to Tirilu, honey," she shouted over her shoulder toward my father.

"Bye, Gerri," my father called from the living room.

"Well, *I'm* not so sure," I muttered, but my mother had already closed the door behind me.

I took the shoebox home with me. There was no one to forbid *me* from trashing the stuff, not even my guilty conscience. I mean, come on. Contaminating a landfill with nose drops and sleeping pills? When there was a *nuclear waste repository* only a few hours away?

I had no intention of disposing of the pills. They were the answer to all the questions that had occupied my mind the past two days. Fate had brought me this shoebox, and just when I most needed it.

It was kind of like that time I wanted to buy a laptop computer. At a flea market I came across a signed first edition of Thomas Mann's *Buddenbrooks* for only fifty eurocents because, as the vendor said, "There isn't a bastard alive who can still read the old blackletter script it's printed in. And it's been scribbled in, too."

I was not particularly keen on Thomas Mann, and I had a policy of reading paragraph-long sentences of convoluted German printed in prewar blackletter script *only* when I absolutely had to. Which is why I listed the book on eBay, and a used-book seller in Hamburg bought it for two and a half thousand euros. Thus removing the last obstacle to my acquisition of a laptop.

Normally I'm not so lucky.

Never, actually.

I carefully sorted through the shoebox, and by the time I was done I had set aside no fewer than thirteen packets. Thirteen pristine packets of sleeping pills. I stacked and restacked them in new formations on my kitchen table; I couldn't take my eyes off them. They had pretty names like Loramet, Remestan, Rohypnol, and Lendormin. Some of them weren't even past their expiration dates.

There were so many pills that the only difficulty would lie in getting the last one swallowed before the first one took effect. But I had full confidence that I could manage it: Eating fast had never been a problem for me; indeed, eating fast is a skill that truly sets me apart from others.

I got a very pleasant case of goose bumps as I stared at the boxes of pills.

I had already spent the past two days running through everything in my head, but each time there was some kind of snag. I had to rule out most of my imagined scenarios because of logistical or technical requirements I just couldn't meet. For instance, slashing my wrists was out because I can't stand the sight of blood; plus, it's not that easy for beginners to find the arteries in the wrists.

But *I* could manage sleeping pills. Easy peasy.

Dear Mama,

Thank you very much for the impeccably sorted collection of sleeping pills; you really saved me a lot of annoying and potentially illegal work.

You were quite right, of course, when you told me, "Medication isn't the answer to everything." But it would really be a shame to let the pills go to waste. They're the perfect portion for one, it turns out.

No, all joking aside: I apologize for the trouble I'm causing you with the pills, but before you get angry, please remember all the future disappointments that I'm sparing you this way.

I'm honestly sorry I've been nothing but a disappointment to you so far. Starting with my birth when you noticed that I wasn't a Gerd but a Gerda. And that I was a brunette instead of a blonde. But believe me when I say I suffered at least as much as you when Aunt Alexa wanted only blonde flower girls at her wedding and when all my sisters and cousins got to scatter flower petals down the aisle, and I did not. I spent practically that whole party under the table. Well, fine. Maybe I shouldn't have tied Grandpa Rodenkirchen's shoelaces to Waldi's collar, but how could I have known that a little dachshund could have enough horsepower to pull Grandpa Rodenkirchen, the tablecloths, all the cakes, and Grandma Rodenkirchen's Meissen porcelain down onto the floor?

I also apologize that I refused to go to prom with Klaus Köhler, even though he's the son of your dear friend Annemarie and even though you assured me that zits, BO, and his being all full of himself were normal symptoms of adolescence that would go away on their own. Even now hardly a day goes by that you fail to mention what a successful and attractive man Klaus has become and how fortunate Hannah Kopuski is that he went to prom with her instead of me.

Believe me—there have been days *I've* regretted not going with him. But at fifteen I had no idea I would have been happy at thirty to have landed someone like Klaus. Because, had I known that, I would undoubtedly already have started collecting sleeping pills on my own.

Love,
Gerri

P.S. Even though I didn't end up becoming a teacher, there's no reason why you should keep how I earned my money secret from your friends and relatives. That's why I've just mailed out fourteen copies of *Claudia the Night Nurse: On Suspicion* along with a nice letter to all the people whom you've been telling for years that "our youngest girl runs a little transcription service" when they ask about my job. I also sent a copy to Klaus's parents and to Our Rich Aunt Hulda.

P.P.S. There are two cities in Italy named Verona and Venice; Venezuela is a country in the northern part of South America. But because you probably don't believe me, I hereby bequeath my old school atlas to you so that you can verify it all.

TWO

I am a Virgo, and we Virgos are pragmatic, orderly, and reliable people. Whenever we have problems, we keep a cool head and approach the solution systematically. As a rule, then, our lives are much more under control than are the lives of sensitive Pisces, cautious Cancers, or indecisive Libras, to cite just a few examples.

So our lives really have to be going down the tubes before we Virgos come to see suicide as the best solution to a problem. I mention that just to make it clear that we don't bail at the first little sign of trouble.

I had divided my problems into three categories, being the orderly person that I was.

1. Love life
2. Work life
3. Other life

My love life sucked. Or rather, it was nonexistent. It had been four and a half years since my last relationship, and although that relationship had been quite a disaster for me (by the end, I gotten into the habit of freely lobbing dishes and other objects in my reach at him), I certainly had no intention of staying single for more than a couple of months.

That's why a year after that relationship ended I set out systematically in search of a partner, leaving no possibility unexplored. I signed up with online dating services, answered personal ads, and had one of my girlfriends set me up with an old school buddy of her husband's. Which resulted in my meeting a fair number of men: men like *rockinhard12*; *shuttlecock007*; and *Max, 29, 6'3", NS/ND, shy but up for any kind of fun.*

I met twenty-four men in total. That was a pretty meager yield when you consider the hundreds of men I exchanged e-mails with via online personals and the some three dozen I talked to on the phone. But the pool of potential candidates really totaled only twenty-four: men under forty who were *not* roofers or married and who *were* interested in a woman like me (older than twenty-five, not blonde, A cups). Also, men who had a greater or lesser command of language and who did not write things like "Please send a ful-boddy shot of u as soon as posible."

When you meet these guys in person, however, you realize such considerations should not constitute your *only* criteria in selecting a potential partner.

Take *rockinhard12*, for instance, who looked like Lulu's new boyfriend, Patrick. *Rockinhard12* really just wanted to expose me as quickly as possible to the "little" rock-hard pal in his pants that had inspired his user ID. Preferably right then and there, in broad daylight, in the café where we were sitting. While I was trying to find out what he thought of old Katharine Hepburn movies and children and pets, he kept trying to take my hand and press it into his lap.

"Twelve is not my *age*, you know," he murmured. "If you get my drift."

"Oh, is it your apartment number, then?" I said, trying to play dumb while keeping my hands as far away from him as possible. By putting them to my head. In horror. But the waitress thought I was waving for her and called out, "I'll be right there."

"H-have you seen *The African Queen?*" I stuttered, trying to change topics.

"My drumstick," said *rockinhard12.* "My rockin' hard drumstick is twelve inches long, exactly. Go on, take a feel."

"Oh no," I said, turning beet red. "There must be some kind of misunderstanding. Unfortunately, I'm just not interested in percussion instruments, no matter how hard or rockin'."

The air hissed out of *rockinhard12,* like from a tire with a hole in it. "God, I knew it the minute I saw you walk in that door. Frigid cow! None of the other girls have complained. You don't know what you're missing." Then he stood and left the café without paying for his cappuccino.

"What can I do for you?" the waitress asked. My hands were still helplessly flailing around in the air.

"Check, please," I sighed.

I was a little more careful after that experience. I always picked a café with a back door I could disappear through before getting stuck with the check. We Virgos are thrifty characters, you see, and we like to hold on to our money. So when I met *shuttlecock007,* I slipped out the back when I noticed he was suffering from some mysterious obsessive-compulsive tics. He was evidently compelled to pour patterns of sugar onto the tablecloth so he could dab the sugar back up with a wet fingertip and lick it clean. After watching fifteen minutes of this, I realized his user ID might have been a reference to a pecking chicken rather than to a fondness for badminton and British spy movies, as I'd assumed.

Unfortunately *Max, 29, 6'3", NS/ND, shy but up for any kind of fun* was also a complete loser. His real name was Dietmar, first of all; he was 39 and not 29; and he was no taller than I was—which meant he was pretty short. Also, he was not the least bit shy. At our first meeting he explained that he had chosen "Max," shaved ten years off his age, and tacked eight inches onto his height because in his experience the right women wouldn't have responded to his ad otherwise. He was entirely correct, of course; I was a textbook example of his hypothesis. I was not even remotely up for *this* kind of fun, however, so I vanished through the tried and tested back door.

Things continued in that mode for years.

The nicest guy had been Ole, whom my friends Caroline and Bert had set me up with. Even though it should have sent up big red flags when they told me he had just broken up with his girlfriend of many years. At first glance everything about Ole was right. He had a really nice smile, fine blond hair that no amount of combing could keep off his forehead, and no recognizable neuroses. Plus, he liked the same things I did: old Katharine Hepburn movies, Italian food, and Tom Waits. Ole was a dentist and was in the process of opening his own private practice. We went out a couple of times, and I liked him better and better each time. But just as I started to admit that to myself, his ex-girlfriend,

Mia, showed up again, and eight weeks later the two of them were married. I pretended to be glad for Ole, but in reality I wasn't the least bit glad.

On the whole I was having more and more trouble feeling glad for other people, which segued perfectly to problem category number three: Other life.

I never planned to still be single at thirty. To be honest, I expected to be married to the man of my dreams by twenty-eight and to have my first child by twenty-nine, with at least one apple tree planted inside the white picket fence around my yard.

And yet somehow almost everyone but me was married. All my sisters, cousins, and friends. Even Klaus Köhler and Britt Emke from high school. They were all having babies, building houses, and planting apple trees in yards with white picket fences, while I was ducking out of cafés through back doors. My cousin Volker and his wife Hilla, Tina and Frank, Rika and Claudius, Caroline and Bert, Marta and Marius, Charly and Ulrich, Ole and Mia, Lulu and Patrick—everywhere you looked, nothing but happy couples.

As a single woman among all these couples, my Other Life was also looking pretty bleak. Especially true since my friends had started having kids. If my friends had any free time at all to spend with me, they inevitably fell asleep during the movie, reeked of sour milk, or spent all their time talking about how hard it was to score a spot at a good preschool or how challenging it was to handcraft a proper, traditional German first-day-of-kindergarten paper cone full of treats and school supplies—ideally, bigger and fancier than the school cones the other parents made.

Even so, it's not like I didn't want to turn into just that sort of bore myself. I just needed the right man.

"You're way too fussy," Ulrich always said. "That's your problem—you're looking for a man who doesn't exist."

Ulrich was my ex-boyfriend—the one I had lobbed Grandma Thaler's antique porcelain milk pitcher at, among other items, although Ulrich had ducked, so the pitcher shattered against the bathroom door. It was the only piece of china that had survived the Cataclysmic Meissen Porcelain Disaster at my aunt Alexa's wedding. It's not like that old milk pitcher was going to fund my retirement or anything, but I would never have hurled it if I hadn't been so furious at him. Ulrich always managed to drive me insane with his unique way of just not doing . . . anything.

During our three-year relationship, Ulrich had done nothing but lie around—on the carpet, on the couch, in the bathtub, in the bed. And everything that Ulrich owned or used also lay around everywhere. Clothes, socks, underwear, plates, silverware, pizza boxes, beer bottles, dumbbells, papers, books, and garbage. My apartment was small, which is why his constant lying around bothered me so much. I stumbled at every step over Ulrich and all his crap. But because he was paying half the rent, he assumed he could just "be himself," as he put it. That included taking mud-and-sea-salt baths, after which he never scrubbed the brown crust off the tub. That included eating all the yogurt but never buying more. That included taking the milk out of the fridge but never putting it back in. That included eating candy and dropping the wrappers on the floor.

Although Ulrich greatly valued personal hygiene and was always scrupulously clean and kempt himself, the apartment eventually began to stink. Of Ulrich's socks, sneakers, and the food remnants he left to rot everywhere. No matter what I tried, no matter what argument I raised, Ulrich wanted "to be himself"—and to continue leaving everything lying around, including himself.

"If it bugs you, then clean it up yourself" was his standard reply whenever I would ask for help, so I started throwing objects at him ranging from sneakers and yogurt cups to commercial-law textbooks. The Meissen milk pitcher had been a mistake.

At some point I no longer loved Ulrich; his good qualities had gotten completely lost in all the filth. When I finally kicked him out and had the apartment back to myself, I spent weeks simply enjoying the relief. Ulrich and I even managed to stay friends, and it was nice to see him without screaming at him or pelting him with household objects. I might have fallen back in love with him, too, but then he got together with my best and oldest friend, Charly, and moved in with her.

I'll admit it pained me a little to think of Ulrich lying around in Charly's apartment, although I had to bite my tongue fairly often any time Charly moaned about his socks on the coffee table, the crusty mud-and-sea-salt rings in the bathtub, and the empty yogurt containers behind the couch. But it didn't really, *really* hurt until after Ulrich finished law school (while supine—well done!) and abruptly stopped "being himself." His new self wore a suit and left the apartment punctually every morning at eight o'clock to go and earn piles of dough. With this money—and here's the real kicker—Ulrich paid for a cleaning lady, who came to the apartment twice a week. I'm sure that now and again he would still let candy wrappers flutter through the air to the floor, but all in all this Ulrich was unrecognizable from his old self. And so was his apartment. Ulrich and Charly got married last year. I was one of the bridesmaids, so I had to pretend I was happy for them.

Of course, I sometimes wondered whether I was being too fussy in my search for a boyfriend. But was it really *my* fault that someone like *rockinhard12* didn't exactly inspire my hormones to dance a jig?

Now as I think back, I realize it was a hard lesson learning to accept that you just can't plan some things—no matter how systematically you approach them.

Speaking of which, last week, exactly three days before my mother gave me the sleeping pills, Charly called to let me know I was going to be a godmother. It took me a while to grasp what she meant.

"*You're pregnant!*" I exclaimed.

"Ye-e-es!" Charly bubbled. "Isn't it freaking wonderful?"

Wow! Now there was a leading question. The news was without a doubt wonderful. For Charly and Ulrich. For me it was pretty awful; in fact, it surprised me *how* awful it felt.

I only just managed to force out a lame attempt at congratulations before claiming some milk was boiling over on the stove and I had to hang up.

Then I broke down, crying at the kitchen table and no longer understanding the world. What had become of me? A malevolent monster green with envy who couldn't even be glad about the most beautiful thing in the world: My best friend was having a child. But here I was, wanting only to die.

Yes, really. I would rather have been dead.

Shocked that I'd had that thought, I stopped crying, and—like a typical Virgo—I started thinking about how to stave off such thoughts. The first thing I did was search online for *suicidal thoughts,* and then I diagnosed myself with depression.

There are tons of Web sites on this topic. And evidently there are tons of people suffering from depression. I needn't have felt so weird. We depressives formed the foundation of an entire and very lucrative industry.

There are two distinct groups of us, namely, endogenous and reactive depressives. (We're actually supposed to be called "people *with* depression," so that we're not defined by our condition, but I don't mind being defined by my condition.) People with endogenous depression are melancholy from the inside out; those with reactive depression are reacting to adverse external events. A little relieved that there was some explanation for the way I was feeling, I decided I belonged in the latter group.

On another Web page, I found reactive depression categorized further into neurotic, psychotic, somatogenic, and cyclothymic types. And after thoroughly studying the symptoms, I decided, reluctantly, that I had neurotic depression. Also known as dysthymia. You know, that would also have made a nicer-sounding name than Gerda: *Dysthymia.*

And there really is no need to exaggerate how unhappy I was with this diagnosis. This was only going to make my search for a boyfriend that much harder.

"Hi, my name is Gerri Thaler, and I'm neurotic. A depressed reactive neurotic, to be precise. What's your name?"

But it isn't until you accept the consequences of your neurosis that you can stop caring what other people think. Though at that point, I still lacked the understanding or resolve to do anything about my condition. When the phone rang again, I winced. I was betting it was Charly again, wondering why I hadn't called back after saving my made-up milk from burning.

But it was a stranger's voice instead. "Is this Gerda Thaler?"

"Yes," I said hesitantly. I almost expected the unknown woman to say, "Aren't you even the least bit ashamed that you've sunk into a depression because your best friend is pregnant?"

But she said something altogether different. She said, "Congratulations! You're a winner."

I sighed with relief. Until quite recently I'd had to resort to time-consuming methods to ditch these "You're a winner!" people. No idea where they kept getting my number from, but almost every week someone would call me, claiming that I was a winner. Or, rather, that I was "as good as a winner." All I had to do was buy a subscription for a weekly ticket to some overseas lottery, and then I'd be a millionaire—or, at least, as good as one. If I declined, they always asked me the same thing: "What? Don't you want to be a millionaire?" They had probably all taken the same telemarketing seminar that had pounded one thing into their heads above all else: *Never let them shake you off—not even when the person you're talking to has some milk boiling over on the stove.*

That's why Charly always just hung up on them, right away. Sometimes, if she was actually expecting another call, she'd even say something mean before hanging up, such as "Get a new job, you loser!" or "Fuck off!" (Charly had no manners at all.)

By contrast, every time I tried to do the same—including the rude comments—I just couldn't pull it off. It always seemed unfair to slam down the receiver on these poor, friendly people without first having the courtesy to hear them out. Not everyone can afford to be choosy about his or her job, after all. Although I had in fact already bought an overseas lottery ticket subscription and had neither received the promised microwave nor become a millionaire, I felt guilty every time they called if I didn't buy *another* ticket. Unlike Charly, I needed a compelling reason to justify hanging up on them; otherwise, I knew the rest of the day wouldn't go well for me.

Boundless disappointment was a compelling reason, for example. Using that, the conversation would go more or less like this:

"Congratulations, you're a winner, Gerda! You are in the final drawing for a beautiful Beetle, Gerda, and you—"

"What, *really?*" I would say, interrupting the friendly woman or man with great enthusiasm. "A *Beatle*, which one? Paul McCartney? Or Ringo Starr? Well, I suppose your interpretation of *beautiful* may be slightly different from mine, but—no matter! How long can I keep him? Do you think he'll do housework?"

"Ha-ha-ha, I'm talking about the *car*, of course! A beautiful VW Beetle convertible. Wouldn't that be nice for the summer, Gerda? Can you picture it? And soon you'll not only be the proud owner of this Beetle but, with a bit of luck, a *millionaire*! Because we have reserved a priority ticket subscription for you. If you decide to subscribe now, then you'll be entered for a chance to win 2.5 million euros! Isn't that something? The cost is a mere six euros a week!"

And that was when I invoked my reason to hang up. Boundless disappointment, as I mentioned.

"Well, now, that's not very nice of you," I would start, preparing to vigorously depress the hang-up button on my phone. "First you get me drooling about Paul McCartney, and then you think a car is going to do something for me? Could you please explain to me how a *car* is supposed to help me around the house? Hmm? And a convertible! I'm so sensitive to drafts! Never call here again!"

At least with that technique, I would be rid of the caller, although I still always had a guilty conscience. Because, once again, I had not bought the weekly subscription.

But today, thanks to my online self-diagnosis, I didn't have that problem at all. You won't believe how fast even superbly trained telemarketing pros hang up on you when you tell them that you're suffering from neurotic depression. Certainly by the time you try to explain the difference between neurotic and psychotic depression. And when they hang up on you, it obviates the need to feel guilty about not buying anything!

So after I had gotten rid of the latest "You're a winner!" woman, with surprising ease, I might add, I glued myself back to my laptop screen to learn more about myself and my depression. Reading about depression was really depressing as I learned about the symptoms that we neurotic depressives confront. The symptoms weren't all that complicated, and to some extent they were even understandable—unlike the symptoms of people with *psychotic* depression. Neurotic depression is apparently often triggered by some kind of one-time conflict.

No kidding!

But I had to wonder what kind of person would even take the time to notice or feel empathy for someone who was stuck in some kind of conflict? I mean, I could imagine someone feeling empathy for me and understanding why I was depressed if, say, an avalanche had just buried my whole family alive. But surely no one would understand why I wanted to die just because my best friend was expecting a baby.

I myself didn't understand it.

"Stop whining and start thinking positive thoughts"—I have hated that advice ever since I was a child. My mother said that to me almost every day of my life.

I had spent years feeling disgruntled with myself because I just couldn't make myself think positive thoughts. About Klaus Köhler, for example. Or about *shuttlecock007*. If I could just have had positive thoughts about people who lick sugar off the tablecloth, for instance, I would never have needed to run out so many rear exits. If you think about it that way, positive thinking is an absolutely foolproof problem-solving method, even when logic holds there is no solution to a problem—however illogical that sounds. For an analytical person like me, having the solution to my problem sitting in a shoebox right in front of me but not being able to use it was awful. Now that I was reading up on things online, I finally understood why these things had always bothered me: "Positive thinking" is definitely not in the repertoire of a person with neurotic depression.

I realized I must have been like this even when I was little, because as I read I recalled the Chocolate Easter Bunny Incident. I was eight years old at the time and had grown very fond of him, that Easter bunny. So fond that I decided not to eat him. We would grow old together instead.

But that pig of a sister of mine, Lulu, had already polished off all her own Easter candy, and now she was eyeing Ralph!

My mother had been on a health food kick at the time, and candy was a rare commodity in our household, and mainly only at Christmas and Easter. Whenever we had visitors to the house who brought us chocolate or M&M's or whatever, my mother would confiscate the treats and then gradually dole them out later, one by one. Sometimes we would buy candy with our allowance, which was strictly forbidden—and then we would have to wolf down all of it in secret outside the house to avoid being caught. None of that was very fun. We envied the kids whose families let them have free access to a snack cupboard, and we tended to become closer friends with those kids than with others. Charly and I probably became best friends just because she was allowed to eat as much Kinder Chocolate as she wanted, which is why she had no problems sharing so much with me.

When my sisters and I complained that the only sweet thing we got all day was raisins in our morning muesli, my mother would say, "You girls will thank me one day." As far as I knew, none of us had thanked her yet.

Lulu was the one who suffered the most from our acute chocolate deficit, and she searched high and low for Ralph. She even offered to let me read her diary if I would just show her where I was hiding him. But I stood by Ralph.

After a couple of days, Lulu found him inside a shoebox high up in the closet, where I had imagined he could hide safely under a layer of Barbie dresses. Murderous screaming and bawling exploded from me when I came home and found the only part left of Ralph was the little bell he had worn around his neck.

Lulu was grounded for two days and had to apologize to me.

"I'm sorry I ate him," she said, dabbing a bit of chocolate from the corner of her mouth. "But he was about to start getting moldy anyway."

I sobbed.

Lulu was forced to reimburse me from her allowance for Ralph's monetary value. She grudgingly set two coins on my nightstand.

"So now you can stop making such a fuss," my mother said to me. "Everything is resolved."

But naturally, nothing was resolved, because—as I now know—I am hardwired to have neurotic depression. Based on the information I found online, my mother should have had empathy and understanding for me and the hair-trigger situation I was in. But she did not.

"Why are you still crying?" she asked.

"Because I want Ralph back," I said between sobs.

Lulu said, "I could stick my fingers down my throat and get him back for you that way," and everyone laughed—except me.

"It was just a silly chocolate bunny," my mother said. "Now stop with the crying. Look outside. The sun is shining, and it's a lovely day."

But I just couldn't see anything positive in that situation.

After a while, my mother completely lost patience with me. "Aren't you even the least bit embarrassed to be making such a fuss about a chocolate bunny? There are children starving to death in Africa who don't even know what chocolate tastes like! If you do not stop crying this instant, you will be grounded as well."

Had I been born under some other sign of the zodiac, suicide probably would have occurred to me much earlier.

But no, as a true Virgo, I analyzed the problem objectively. I recognized that I was facing an unsolvable problem: I wanted Ralph back, but Ralph was irretrievably lost and gone forever. Even if I could have come up with another chocolate Easter bunny of the same kind (by then it was mid-May), that Easter bunny would not have been Ralph.

The token money and Lulu's house arrest were nowhere near enough to make up for my feelings of loss. And to top it all off, my mother had been mean to *me*—although I was clearly the victim and not the perpetrator in the whole affair.

Because I was eight years old, I could think of only one thing to do, and I still feel guilty about it today.

Dear Lulu,

Do you remember when you were in fourth grade and woke up one morning as Bart Simpson? All these years you thought it was Rika who gave you that spiky haircut, right? And Rika still thinks to this day that she did it while sleepwalking. But she didn't. It was me, and I was wide-awake! I just wanted you to look stupid in your school picture. And you did, too. You earned that haircut: You know full well what you did to Ralph (the chocolate Easter bunny) and how sad that made me. Waiting a couple of weeks to exact my revenge only intensified my grudge. But apparently you guys had already forgotten about Ralph; otherwise, I might have expected to attract at least a shadow of suspicion. But once again, this shows how little the members of this family ever thought about what shape I was in.

Well, anyway, I'm really sorry for the whole thing now. I had no way of knowing the chain reaction I was about to set in motion. First, Rika woke up that next morning with her own Bart Simpson haircut, then she shaved off your eyebrows, and you Krazy Glued her ear to the pillow. Who knows where this would have led if Mama hadn't locked you both in different rooms each night. And, well, you and Rika have never been able to stand each other since. And to think that without my childish act of revenge, you two would probably have been the best of friends. Maybe Rika and you can take the opportunity of my funeral to make up with each other. You will each need someone to bitch to about Tina and Frank and their ideas of child rearing once I'm gone.

I sincerely wish you a beautiful life, at least to the extent that I am capable of wishing this, what with my neurotic depression.

As far as Patrick is concerned: There is a chance that he and I went out once. If he's the same guy, we met through the online personals, where he was using the name *rockinhard12*. We spent most of our first date engaged in a detailed conservation in which he tried to impress upon me, literally, the quality and dimensions of his rock hardness. As I said, there's *a chance*. And even if Patrick and *rockinhard12* are in fact the same person, this should in no way rob you of the pleasure of being newly in love. Just because he may previously have spent a period of his life trying to impress every possible woman he could with his command of sexual innuendo using musical metaphors, this does not necessarily make him a bad guy. Plus, you have mastered the art of "positive thinking" nearly as well as Mama.

Your loving sister,
Gerri

P.S. Please make sure that Chisola gets my pearl necklace, laptop, and MP3 player. Under no circumstances should you allow Mama and Tina to convince you that's unfair to the twins. To you I leave all my books, CDs, and DVDs. If you end up with two copies of anything, sell the extras for a good cause or donate them to the library.

THREE

My inability to master the art of "positive thinking" or develop anything more than a catastrophic love life did not mean my life lacked anything that made me happy: There was my job. I remembered that right off when I read on www.depressed-so-what.de that a person with depression takes no pleasure in anything.

This immediately gave me some hope: Maybe I wasn't depressed after all! Or maybe only a little.

I may have hated my life, but I loved my job. I looked forward to getting to work every day. Most atypical for a depressive.

I had figured out that I was born to be a romance novelist during my first semester at the university, where I was majoring in German literature. Presumably as a deterrent, we had to read and analyze a hospital romance novel, and unlike my classmates, I was totally fascinated by the brilliant love story, carefully orchestrated over eighty easy-to-understand pages. So instead of a research paper about "The Position and Significance of the 'Trashy' Novel in World Literature," I wrote my own hospital romance. I was surprised I was actually able to do it—it was almost as though some supernatural force had dictated the story about a curly-haired, ash blonde children's nurse named Angela to me. Angela's character was so pure and her hands were so talented that both the taciturn but kindhearted head of medicine and the despicable but dazzlingly handsome chief resident succumbed to her innocent charm. Even Alexandra, the bitchy redheaded nurse, ultimately had to admit both that she envied Angela and that her own machinations would always be doomed to failure in the face of Angela's true goodness. At the end of the story as the chief resident gazed deeply into Angela's eyes and convincingly reassured her of his eternal love, I was overcome by a kind of satisfaction that I had never known before. Yes, *this* is how the world should feel—exactly like this, and no other way. It wasn't trivial; it was . . . *existential.* I felt like lightning had struck, like someone who had untangled a really big secret, the way Einstein must have felt when he put forward his theory of general relativity.

That same night, I mailed the *Angela the Children's Nurse* manuscript to Aurora Publishing, and I wasn't surprised in the least when they got in touch a few days later saying they in fact wanted to publish my manuscript.

Plus, they wanted more.

My family was fairly shocked that I was dropping out of school to devote myself entirely from then on to writing romance novels under the pseudonyms of Juliane Mark and Diane Dollar. But I didn't care. I had found something that was fun for me and that I was really good at—so why should I keep going to school?

But the job wasn't easy.

Aurora published comics and inexpensive mass-market paperbacks ranging from fantasy, science fiction, action, crime, mystery, and Westerns to romance. Their romance line was subdivided into categories called Hearthstone, Healing Touch, Princes and Princesses, Nanette, and Norina. Each of the other lines had its own categories as well. Most people pretended they had never heard of Aurora Publishing. But that was always a lie. Everyone had read at least *something* that Aurora published.

Twice a year I wrote a novel for the Paging Dr. Poulsen series; otherwise, I focused wholly on the Norina series. The Norina novels were similar to the Healing Touch books, except that the Norina protagonists could have professions outside of medicine.

No one got rich writing grocery store romances, even though rumors of riches routinely raced through the industry. I had to write two novels a month to cover my (very modest) cost of living. So every two weeks I had a deadline that could not be postponed. I would usually spend the last forty-eight hours before the deadline writing nonstop, day and night. The publisher would not accept any excuse: No sickness, no personal problem was more important than turning a manuscript in on time. I wasn't even sure if they would accept death as an excuse.

And every week, our loyal readers could pick up a new Norina novel at the corner newsstand or in the checkout line at the grocery store; the supply of new titles had to be inexorable and unbroken. I didn't know how many other authors were working on the Norina series, actually, but it couldn't have been that many because at this point every other Norina novel was being penned by me. And I was very proud of that fact.

There was only one difference between the Norina and Nanette series: Norina was rated G; Nanette was not. The difference is better explained by way of example: In the Norina books, after a few misunderstandings the man was permitted to take his finger and gently draw the lowered jaw of the shy woman up until she was looking into his eyes, and in her eyes he would see the twinkling of her love for him. And that would be the end of the Norina story.

In the same situation in the Nanette books, by contrast, the man would passionately draw the woman to him so that she felt his throbbing manhood against her thigh, and then she would begin to tremble in excitement. And this was not the end of the story in the Nanette books. This was only the beginning.

I had been able to earn a living as a writer for ten years, and I still thought it was fun. Every two weeks, once I had printed out the finished manuscript and slid it into an envelope, I was overcome by the same feeling of happiness and contentment that I had first experienced with *Angela the Children's Nurse*—the feeling of having set the world right again, at least in a novel. There were no men like *rockinhard12* and *shuttlecock007* there. The men in my books had broad shoulders, good manners, and did not discuss their . . . instruments. Even the bad guys had a touch of that certain something. And there weren't any thirty-year-old single women in my books, either. I married off every woman before her thirtieth birthday.

I never treated myself to a break between books: Before getting down to work on the next novel, I always developed the plot outline for the novel I'd write *after* the next one. If you want to earn a living writing, you have to be organized—and I was. My perfectly thought-out work routine had never failed, not even once in the past ten years. Even when I was on vacation I just kept on writing; I had gotten the laptop specifically for this purpose. And I was not about to let a touch of silly suicidal ideation keep me from working now!

With a vigorous click, I put my laptop to sleep and took a deep breath. Things weren't that bad. My death wish was surely just some kind of shock in response to Charly's pregnancy news. In a couple of days I would probably muster up the strength to cope. Until then, I would just have to do what I loved doing most: work.

My current plot outline was titled *Leah's Path: A woman overcomes her terminal illness and finds love*, and my jangled nerves relaxed noticeably as I proofread the manuscript, tracing Leah's path from the leukemia ward into the strong arms of the anonymous bone marrow donor. I changed a word here and there as I read.

I was being serenaded from the apartment below by the sounds of Xavier Naidoo, who was bemoaning the perilous path *he* had trodden, or at least an R&B version of it. I furrowed my brow in irritation. This guy would have done well to take a cue from the plucky Leah: Her path really *had* been perilous, but you didn't see her moaning about it! It would never have occurred to her to unload on other people with monotonous songs.

Hilla, who also lived downstairs, used her collection of Xavier Naidoo CDs to soothe her while she did dishes. She had four kids and no dishwasher, so one meal's worth of pots and plates might certainly seem like a perilous path.

For my part, I couldn't imagine music helping me accomplish any activity more efficiently, which is why I always put in the earbuds to my MP3 player while Hilla was washing so I could listen to something else. But this time my phone rang again before I got that far.

I hesitated to answer. What if it was Charly calling back and she got me bawling again with more chat about her joyful news? And just as I had regained my inner balance by finishing my latest manuscript.

But it wasn't Charly; it was Licorice, my editor at Aurora.

"Well, isn't this a coincidence," I said. "I'm working on the plot outline for *Leah's Path* right now. If I drop it into the mail today, you'll have it tomorrow."

"Why don't you bring the outline by tomorrow morning; then we can discuss it in person," Licorice said.

I thought I must have misheard her, which is why I said, "Huh?"

"I'd like to introduce you to our new editor in chief," Licorice continued unflappably. "Could you stop by around ten thirty?"

Licorice's real name was Lily Karisch, and she was in charge of the Norina series. I'd never met her before in my life. Usually we interacted only by e-mail, and every now and again we spoke on the phone. She mailed me my contracts, and I signed them and mailed them back to her. We did the same thing with the manuscripts. In all the years I'd worked for Aurora, no one had ever wanted to meet me face-to-face.

"Gerri? Are you still there?" Licorice asked.

"Yeah . . ." I said hesitantly. "So, you want me to come to your office tomorrow?"

"It's not out of your way, is it?" Licorice asked. "You are local, right?"

"Yes, yes, just around the corner, so to speak," I said. Aurora Publishing and I were in the same city: I lived in my uncle's converted loft studio, with its paper-thin walls, and Aurora was headquartered in a prestigious-looking four-story building on the other side of the Rhine in downtown Cologne.

"We'll see you tomorrow morning, then," Licorice said, hanging up before I could ask any more questions.

What could that mean? Why would they want me to bring my plot outline by in person? I had been delivering my novels as punctually as clockwork for ten years, and they were obviously satisfied with my work. Perhaps that sounds immodest, but I knew I was good. They had never rejected a single one of my plot proposals; and only once did I have to replace my protagonist's Namibian mother with an Irish one so that her latte-brown complexion became fair and freckly. But we handled all that without a hitch by e-mail.

Why in the hell would the folks at Aurora suddenly want to change the procedure and *get to know me*? I came up with two theories as I printed out the plot summary. First: They want to offer me higher royalties for my ten-year anniversary with them. Or maybe offer me some kind of award with the Aurora logo on it. Or both. Second: The tax office had done an audit and determined I had never in fact had a business meal with an L. Karisch, Editor, and thus could not deduct three such meals from my taxes every year. Maybe a tax auditor would be waiting for me tomorrow in Licorice's office, poised to lead me away in handcuffs.

The latter possibility seemed rather unlikely, however.

It was more plausible that my hard work had paid off. With that thought, the belt that had started tightening around my chest, which started impeding my breathing the moment I heard Charly's news, slackened considerably. First, I resolved not to be neurotic or depressed when I met with Licorice; instead I would "just be going through a rough patch, personally speaking," as I would say. Because obviously things were looking up professionally. It would do me good to just focus on my job for a while. At least that would be something that I could count on.

I was already feeling better.

I even managed to call Charly back and reassure her, credibly, that I was totally excited about her pregnancy and honored by the idea of being the godmother.

Although that wasn't exactly the truth—yet—I had firmly resolved to work on my attitude. Certainly by the time the kid was born I would be a well-balanced, contented person. Charly wasn't the least bit angry that I hadn't called her back after taking the milk off the stove, either. To the contrary, she actually apologized to me.

"You must have been trying to call back all afternoon," she said. "But I was calling people all over the country to tell them our good news. I'm so sorry."

"It's fine," I said.

"I'm just totally beside myself," Charly said.

"Me too," I said.

"I could hug everyone in the whole freaking world," Charly said.

I rolled my eyes. Like I said, I'm still working on my attitude.

"I'm even finally growing breasts!" Charly said. "Can you imagine? Real boobs! You've got to feel these—they're awesome!"

"Uh, yeah, I'll take your word for it."

"I can't tell you how much I'm looking forward to the reunion. Britt Emke, that stupid cow, won't be the only one there showing off her firstborn son—and I'll have a belly to show off by then. God, it's hard to believe that her flat ass has a noble title on it now. You know, I googled that Ferdinand von Falkenhain guy she married, and do you know what? He's fifty-five years old! Britt Emke is following in the footsteps of Anna Nicole Smith! Who'd have thought?"

"I thought we didn't want to go to the reunion?" I said.

"Now I do," Charly said. "Now I've got a firstborn of my own in my belly and a pair of real boobs in my bra. Come on, it'll be fun. I'm sure there'll be a couple of teachers there, too. We'll get plastered and go around telling people off."

"Charly, you're pregnant. You can't get plastered."

"Oh yeah, that's right," Charly said. "No matter. It'll still be fun. Imagine being able to say right to that asshole Mr. Rothe's face that he's an asshole, and he won't be able to do anything about it because you graduated years ago."

"First of all, I don't think I can drink enough to muster up that level of courage. Second of all, while he can't give me a bad grade anymore, he could sue me for defamation. And third of all . . ."

"Oh, Gerri. Don't always be so negative! We're going, and we're going to stir things up good, and you're going to get plastered, and I'll go around telling people off and showing everyone my boobs. It'll be a blast!"

"Yeah, sure," I said, involuntarily grabbing my own breasts. Small as ever, but at least my butt was bigger . . . Whatever! No reason to be depressed! After all, I still had my job, and the size of my bust really didn't matter there.

The next morning I punctually made my way to the offices of Aurora Publishing. The impressive, gigantic entryway and lobby were entirely marble, which showed how lucrative the romance novel business was. I automatically squared my shoulders when I realized that *my* novels had contributed to this wealth. Perhaps my contribution had paid for the beautiful inlaid work on the columns in front. Or the polished marble counter, behind which sat a severe-looking lady who was scrutinizing me over the rims of her glasses. Well, given my contribution to Aurora's success, the polished marble counter was sort of at least partially mine.

"Gerri Thaler," I cheerfully said to the receptionist. "I have an appointment with Ms. Karisch."

The woman squinted at me with mistrust. "With Ms. Karisch?" she asked.

"That's right," I said, resting a hand on *my* counter.

The receptionist politely asked me to take a seat, said someone would be down to escort me up, and then called Ms. Karisch to inform her of my arrival. I looked around at all the glass display cases, searching in vain for one of my Norina novels. But all I saw everywhere were copies of *Gary Peyton: Ghost Hunter* and *Maggie the Demon Bride,* plus stacks and stacks of Westerns with ugly cowboys and shriveled cactuses on the covers.

Who read stuff like that? Probably the same people who watched those ancient Westerns that Channel 4 was always rerunning.

A fifty-something woman stepped out of the elevator. She had dark hair in a pixie cut and was wearing eyeglasses and a striped blouse. I knew immediately she was Licorice. I had imagined her exactly this way. But she gave me only a cursory glance as she scanned the rest of the lobby, which was devoid of other people.

"Did Ms. Thaler leave?" she asked the receptionist.

"That's her over there," the receptionist said.

Licorice looked at me, taken aback.

"Hello," I said, extending her my hand. "It's nice to meet you in person."

Licorice took my hand hesitantly. "Was Gerri unable to come?"

I tried to laugh, but all I managed was to clear my throat. "Were you expecting someone else?"

Licorice made a sound like "mmyezz," and looked me up and down, squinting. "Well, I—how old are you then, for goodness' sake?"

"Thirty," I said with a bit of bitterness. That number always caught in my throat. Why did she want to know that? Did she think I looked older? I probably shouldn't have worn my black sweater, even though it was made of cashmere and was the only piece in my whole wardrobe that was elegant and casual at the same time.

"Thirty," Licorice repeated. "That means you started with us when you were practically still a child."

"I was twenty," I said.

Licorice stared at me for a while, shaking her head. Finally she smiled slightly and said, "And here I always assumed you were about my age."

"No one ever asked me my age," I said. My social security number and my tax ID number and my bank account number, yes, but never my age. And was Licorice trying to say that my voice, which she had heard often enough all these years on the phone, made me sound like a fellow semicentenarian? I was a little insulted. It was probably because of my name, which came across as so old-fashioned. I was pretty much the only Gerda in my whole generation; I was confident I could win any bet on that claim. Thanks, Mama!

"Would it have changed anything if you had known my age?"

"Oh, my dear child," Licorice said. "If I had known how young you were, I would have encouraged you to pursue a *respectable* prof—" She fell silent and looked over at the receptionist. "Come with me—we're going upstairs," she said, taking my arm. "First we'll stop by my office, where we can talk in private. And then Mr. Adrian is expecting us at eleven."

"Is it a tax audit?" I asked softly.

"Not exactly," Licorice said, suddenly giggling. "Mr. Adrian is our new editor in chief. I can hardly wait to see his face. He thinks he has to break some bad news as gently as possible to an actual nurse on the verge of retirement."

"What bad news?" I asked with alarm. "And why a nurse?"

"A lot of our authors are former nurses. A nursing background is especially helpful when writing hospital romances for the Healing Touch series." Licorice looked over at the receptionist again and guided me to the elevator. Once the doors closed behind us, she continued speaking. "There are about to be a few changes in-house that you will need to be made aware of. That's why I've asked you here."

"Please, no," I whispered.

But Licorice continued single-mindedly. "As you may have read in the paper, Aurora has been swallowed up by a large publishing group, one with numerous successful mass-market series of its own. It's called Lauros."

"Oh, don't they do the Corinna books?" I asked, wrinkling my nose.

"Exactly," Licorice said. "Lauros has bought Aurora."

"That doesn't sound good," I said.

"No, it's not," Licorice said. The elevator doors opened, and we stepped out into the fourth-floor hallway. "I don't want to beat around the bush: They're shutting down the entire romance novel line, including Nanette."

"But I thought business was good?" I said.

"It is," Licorice replied. "But the Lauros folks have their own romance novel lines and don't want ours competing with theirs. They're hoping that all the Norina readers will

jump over to their Corinna series. And instead of our Mül-
lerthal Mountain Lodge series, they want readers to start
buying their Ranger Rüdiger books. Of course, I doubt their
plan will work."

"What about the Paging Dr. Poulsen series?"

"Discontinued," Licorice said. "Even though our Paging Dr. Poulsen series has been dramatically outselling their
Dr. Martin: Code Blue series." She snorted. "Instead, we are
supposed to expand our horror and action novel lines. The
editor of our Country Love line will be taking over a new
vampire line next month. She called in sick yesterday: nervous breakdown. Her husband says it happened when she
was mincing garlic while making dinner."

I was on the verge of a nervous breakdown myself. My
knees were so wobbly I couldn't keep walking. Licorice
pushed me through a doorway into a bright office with lots
of potted plants and pressed me down into a chair.

"I know this is devastating news," she said. "But I also
know we will find a solution. You're still so young, after
all. First let's have a little glass of champagne to steady our
nerves. And then we can get to know each other personally
a bit." She uncorked a bottle of champagne with a soft *plop*
and poured two glasses.

"To better times," she said. "We're all in the same boat,
if that's any consolation."

"I think I would have preferred a tax audit," I said, taking
a couple of hasty gulps. "Couldn't I just start writing books
for the Dr. Martin and Corinna series then? I'm good!"

"Yes, you really are," Licorice said. "The only problem is
that Lauros already has all the authors it needs for its series.

I'm sure they would have room to squeeze an extra manuscript or two in, but if you want to live off of it . . . What do you actually do for a living, Gerri? I've never asked you that."

"I'm a writer," I said.

"Yes, but what did you study in school? I mean, what did you earn your money doing before you started writing?"

"I've never earned any money other than by writing," I said.

"I see," Licorice said, topping off my champagne, which I immediately downed like water. "You were only twenty, of course. Well, there will certainly be some kind of opportunity for you. The way I see it, when one door closes, another opens somewhere. . . ."

"I could also write erotic novels for the Nanette series," I said. "I'd just have to do a bit more, uh, research . . . maybe online."

"Unfortunately, we have a surplus of authors for Nanette," Licorice said. "Apparently many people have a need to write about their own sexual experiences. But as I said, sometimes an abrupt career change like this can even be—"

"But I need this work!" I said, interrupting her. "I love writing! You see, I've recently determined that I'm a neuro—that I'd be seriously up a creek without this job."

Licorice didn't say anything for a while. Then she said, "A more-secure and better-paying job—that's what I would hope for you. Fortunately, you're young enough to re-create yourself."

"But I don't want to do anything else! Plus, you yourself said I'm good. Writing is my calling."

"You are without question *very* good," Licorice said. "But my coworker, the one who had the nervous breakdown, is also truly excellent at her job. Being good is of precious little help to us in times like these. We all have to eat, you know? Maybe you can keep your writing going for a while on the side, as a hobby."

"On the side, as a hobby . . ." I slumped unhappily in my chair.

"Have another drink," Licorice said empathetically as she filled my glass again and emptied her own in one gulp. I did the same. "All of us here have been in a state of shock since it became obvious how many jobs were on the chopping block. It's already clear to me that the new vampire line is going to be foisted off on me if my coworker with the nervous breakdown doesn't come back to work. I'm sure the new management hopes some of us will quit voluntarily, but none of us will be doing them that courtesy. I have only three more years to go until retirement, and I'm going to have to find a way to tide myself over one way or another."

"I have another thirty-five years until retirement!" I exclaimed.

"You'll find a solution." Licorice emptied the rest of the champagne into my glass and went to the little refrigerator to pull out another bottle.

"Sure," I whispered. After all, I was already well acquainted with this concept. "All I have to do is start thinking positively."

Dear Charly,

I just checked: Twenty-three years exactly have passed since the day my mother said for the first time that you were not the right kind of person for me to be hanging out with.

She was right: You stuffed me full of chocolate, talked me into smoking my first cigarette, and taught me to chew my nails. It was through you that I became acquainted with alcohol, Wonderbras, swear words, and hair dye. And the first and only time I ever got caught skipping school, I was with you.

To this day my mother still calls you "that harlot Charlotte." "Just because that harlot Charlotte has a pierced belly button does not mean you would look good with one, too." (It did look good on me; it's just the ugly infection afterward that didn't look so great. "Rust is antiseptic," you claimed. *Not!*) "Just because that harlot Charlotte is dropping out of school doesn't mean you should do it, too!" (In many ways, you and I have taken parallel paths in life, huh?) "I cannot believe that harlot Charlotte stole your boyfriend and she's still your friend." (My mother just cannot grasp why I would have kicked Ulrich out, while I just cannot grasp Ulrich's newfound ability to put matching pairs of socks into the washing machine himself, let alone hang an air freshener in his closet.)

But the truth is that my life would have been even sadder without you, harlot Charlotte, than it already is. You were the first person who made it clear to me that brown (or red or blue or purple) hair is just as worthy as blonde hair and that parents and teachers aren't always right. You stood by me when my mother wanted to hook me up with Klaus Köhler, and even today you're the only person who takes my profession seriously and immediately buys and devours my novels the moment they go on sale at the newsstand. I've never had as much fun with any other person as I've had with you.

If you end up having a girl, I hope she has a "harlot Charlotte" for a friend someday, too, because there isn't anything better.

With all my thanks and love,
Gerri

P.S. You really shouldn't have dropped out of college for your so-called singing career. Even if you passionately love singing, you absolutely can't sing. No one has had the courage to tell you that so far. Ask Ulrich, if you don't believe me. He really loves you, but he's always said, "I'd rather have a root canal without anesthesia than listen to Charly singing 'Over the Rainbow.'" Which is why you should please refrain from singing "Ave Maria" or something at my funeral. Under no circumstances do I want to give people a reason to laugh as they are standing beside my grave.

P.P.S. I immediately bequeath to you all my earrings and those rose-pattern pillows you love so much. There is also a brand-new package of hair dye in my bathroom, Indian Summer, which will look good on you. And don't worry: You will be a wonderful mother.

FOUR

Champagne makes me sentimental.

It feels as though the world is ending, I thought. *As though the ground were being ripped from under my feet. As though I've made it to the last stop . . .*

"Sorry?" Licorice asked. Apparently I had been mumbling aloud.

"I don't think champagne and I get along very well," I said. "I'm all dizzy."

"Me too," Licorice said. "But that's what's great about it." She looked at the clock. "We can head over to Mr. Adrian's office now."

"What for, actually?" I asked. "I already know what's going on."

"Yes, but he's new here, and we don't want him to think that we're going to do all his work for him. Especially not the unpleasant things. I'd like to watch him squirm his way through robbing you of your livelihood."

"All right then," I said. I swayed a little as I stood. Whoa! "Normallallally I don't drink during the day. And normallallally I can pronounce the word *normallallally* better than that. I should go home."

"Here," Licorice said, handing me a peppermint. She slid one into her own mouth, too. "We don't want the poor boy to think we drown our sorrows in alcohol."

"What poor boy?"

"Well, Mr. Adrian. He's a bit green still. Lauros kind of plunked him in here to handle the 'reorg,' as they're calling it. If you ask me, he wasn't exactly jumping up and down to get the job. He tries to play cool, but he's in way over his head. He's been banging his head into a brick wall with us old-timers; he hasn't been able to get us to pay much attention to him yet. We've got an office pool going about whether he'll leave before the end of the quarter, even though he's sleeping with our program manager."

The office of this Mr. Adrian was only two doors down from Licorice's. I managed to walk this great distance, more or less, by bracing my hands alternately on the left and right walls of the corridor.

"It's not actually an office," Licorice explained with some schadenfreude. "It's our old storage room. The poor boy hasn't even been able to come up with a proper office for himself so far. He's just not manager material." She knocked and simultaneously opened the door.

The former storage room was extremely small and packed to the brim with crooked old bookshelves all the way around. In the middle was a desk, which had also seen better days, and sitting cramped behind it with his back to the tiny window was the new editor in chief.

He wasn't quite as young as Licorice had said; I estimated him to be in his midthirties. I couldn't tell if he was that green, either, but his eyes definitely were. His eyes were the first thing that I noticed about him. Until that moment I had encountered eyes like his only in my own novels: *His eyes were framed by unusually thick, black eyelashes and were reminiscent of the color of dark, polished jade. His intense gaze sent small, warm shivers shooting down her back, and she was unsure why.*

"Let me introduce our new editor in chief, Gregor Adrian. Mr. Adrian, this is one of our authors of many years, Gerri Thaler," Licorice said, closing the door behind us.

"Come in," Mr. Adrian said. He sounded a bit resigned.

His name was Gregor. What a coincidence. I had christened the anonymous bone marrow donor in *Leah's Path* Gregor as well. *He knit his dark eyebrows and seemed to be wrestling with himself about whether or not he should vent the displeasure clearly painted across his face. Finally he overcame his hesitation, drew his mouth into a polite smile, stood, and extended his hand to her.*

"It's a pleasure to meet you, Ms. Thaler," he said. He looked as though he had spent the morning tugging at his dark, slightly wavy hair, which was already thinning a bit at the temples and was in urgent need of a cut. And a comb. I liked men who looked like Wild Things.

And then there was his handshake. I had a hard time keeping my balance, it was so powerful.

"Meased to pleet you, too," I mumbled. "I'm . . ." My voice cut out again because I had forgotten what I wanted to say. *Gregor's handshake was powerful; his hand was warm and dry. She enjoyed the physical contact—she would have liked to feel his hand in hers even longer, but courtesy compelled her to let go. Could he feel the magnetic attraction, too? His face gave no indication.*

God, was I drunk. Using *feel* two sentences in a row; I would never have done that if I were sober.

"Gerri is still rather shocked about the news," Licorice said. "She's been working with us on the Norina and Paging Dr. Poulsen series."

Yes, and she will be falling over in a moment if no one asks her to sit down, I thought. I was feeling the champagne first and foremost in my legs. But unfortunately there wasn't any room in this tiny "office" for extra chairs. I carefully leaned back against a bookshelf. *Ah, much better.* Now all I needed was to untangle my tongue.

"I understand," Mr. Adrian said. "Then the changes will impact you directly."

I nodded. "I'll have to spend the brinter living under a widge," I said.

"Sorry?" Mr. Adrian asked.

"I'm sure you understand," I said impatiently. "I've been lying to the writers' guild about my income just to save a couple of euros on my unemployment insurance. The result is that I'm going to receive only a hundred fifty euros a month in unemployment benefits. The only place I'll be able to afford is a spot with the bums under a bridge."

Amazing that such complicated sentences were passing so effortlessly from my lips. Mr. Adrian also seemed surprised by my eloquence.

"Of course the reorganization at Aurora is an unpleasant development for contract writers, but the publisher is making every effort to consider alternatives," he said.

Licorice managed to simultaneously clear her throat and make an extraordinarily snide-sounding "uh-huh" grunt.

"Even though we needn't make such efforts at all, since contract writers are always exposed to a certain level of risk," Mr. Adrian continued with raised eyebrows. "This is why at Lauros we advise our authors not to give up their bread-and-butter jobs under any circumstances."

"What is a bread-and-butter job?" I asked. Was he trying to tell me that Lauros novels were written only by women who worked the bakery counter? I supposed it was possible, actually; I'd read a couple of those Lauros titles.

"A bread-and-butter job is a job you do to earn a living," Licorice explained. "Aurora, of course, has traditionally preferred working more with professional authors than with hobby writers. But quality isn't always what counts most in life." She sighed.

"You don't have a day job?" Mr. Adrian asked, pretending he hadn't heard Licorice.

"Of course I have a jay dob!" I yelled, swaying so much that a couple of books fell off the bookshelf I was leaning against. "I'm a *writer*."

"One of our very best," Licorice added. "If not *the* best!"

"How wou—" Mr. Adrian said.

"There is one other option," I said. I had just thought of an alternative to sleeping under the bridge. "I could move back in with my parents." I intentionally slammed the back of my head against a shelf. "Or into an institution. Either option would be about the same."

Mr. Adrian studied me for a few moments, speechless. Then he asked, "Are you married or otherwise seeing someone?"

I blinked at him in confusion. *The question was indiscreet, but his interest flattered her. She couldn't help but blush, and lowered her gaze.*

"No, and you?"

Mr. Adrian blinked back with equal confusion. "I apologize. I only meant . . . I ask just because, uh, . . . during an, uh, transition period, it can be helpful to have someone else who can pay the rent."

"I beg your pardon?" I was getting angry.

"Lauros recommends that its contract writers take the precautionary measure of finding someone to pay their rent," Licorice explained. "Apparently here at Aurora we have failed to do that so far."

"Ms. Karisch, I find your sarcastic comments unhelpful at the moment," Mr. Adrian said. "I'm simply trying to help Ms. Thaler."

"Well, then do that," I said. "I could write for the Corinna series, or for that Code Blue shit whatchamacallit series," I said. "*Please!* Otherwise I'll come down with narcotic depression and won't be responsible for my actions! Neurotic deactive repression, I mean," I said, shaking my head to try to smooth out my tongue. "Oh, just look it up online."

Now Mr. Adrian was staring at me as though he could no longer trust his eyes or ears. I knew I wasn't making any sense, but I was desperate.

"Unfortunately we do not currently need any new contract writers at Lauros," Mr. Adrian said. "But as you may be aware, Aurora is expanding its action and horror lines. You could consider applying your talents to those areas in the future."

"That would be *horrific*," I said, folding my arms in front of my chest.

"Wonderful! We have a completely new Vampire Countess series going to press in June, so I suggest you send in a plot proposal as soon as possible."

"Vampire Countess?" I repeated. "I don't even know what that is."

"No one does," Licorice mumbled.

"Vampires are undead beings who have supernatural powers and who nourish themselves with blood," Mr. Adrian said in all seriousness. "They get ahold of blood either using hospital-style units of blood, of which most vampires have a considerable stockpile, or by biting a human being's carotid artery, which I'm sure you're familiar with."

I squinted and looked at him in disbelief. But there was no trace of irony in his voice.

"Vampires can move between the worlds of the living and the dead, so they can materialize from one location on the earth to another within a fraction of a second," he continued. "There are two types of vampires, born and transformed. Contrary to legend, vampires tolerate daylight perfectly well, even if they don't particularly enjoy it, but they in no way disintegrate into dust if a ray of sunlight strikes them. They are masters of the martial arts and archaic weaponry; they can read minds and can wield certain magical abilities, which grow more powerful the older they get. Their characteristic vampire fangs grow only when they feel a thirst for blood; otherwise, they cannot be distinguished from mortals by their appearance. Their history extends far back in time and is closely tied to that of the elves, the fay, the world of magic, and its beings of light and darkness. In principle, vampires and werewolves are not evil beings per se, even though there are some exceptions." He paused and looked at me expectantly.

I seriously fought back the urge to leap over the desk, seize the man by the collar, and shake him. *"Listen to me, Green Eyes, I'm going to dematerialize you right into the underworld if you don't stop with your inane blathering this instant!"* But to do that, my back would have had to detach from the bookshelf that was holding me up, and then presumably I would have merely toppled facedown onto the desk.

"Obviously not everyone bitten by a vampire becomes a vampire," Mr. Adrian added. "Transformation is an extremely complicated matter. Incidentally, vampires don't actually sleep in coffins—that's just something made up for movies and TV."

"Uh-huh," I said. "So what you're telling me here is pure fact, or what?"

"Uh, yes," Mr. Adrian said, turning slightly red. "That's just the background on vampires from the research we've done for the Vampire Countess series. Vampires are absolutely on the rise; they are scary, supernatural, and sexy—exactly what our readers want."

"I didn't quite catch what's sexy about them," I said. "This is the biggest piece of sh—"

"Is the garlic thing also made up for movies and TV, or does it really help?" Licorice asked, interrupting me.

"No," Mr. Adrian said. "Only if the garlic is integrated into a protective amulet with the help of some magic."

"Oh my God, please stop," I said with true anger. "Protective amulet? You have got to be kidding me!"

"This is all quite interesting," Licorice said, "but come on, Gerri. We don't want to bother Mr. Adrian any longer."

"How fast can you write up a plot proposal?" Mr. Adrian asked.

"About a person who practices kung fu, sucks blood, and sets out on erotic adventures in the world between the living and the dead?" I asked. "I'm certain that I could nev—"

"Not before next Friday," Licorice said, again interrupting me and pulling me by the elbow out into the hallway. "Ms. Thaler is a pro; she'll settle into the new subject matter as fast as lightning."

"Then I'm looking forward to your ideas," Mr. Adrian said. "It was nice to meet you."

"You, too," I said, but Licorice had already closed the door behind us.

And with that, my last bulwark against depression had fallen. My job, the only light that had shone in the darkness of my life, had just collapsed into a big black hole. Now there was nothing else standing in the way of serious suicidal tendencies. Once I was dead, they would probably all finally understand that there is a limit to the suffering any one person can endure.

As of that moment, my limit had been met.

I wanted only to head home and search the Internet for the best way to commit suicide. Preferably a way involving the least amount of blood possible.

"That didn't go so badly at all," Licorice said. "The Boy is always happy when he gets to talk about vampires. He's kind of an expert on them; he wrote the pilot novel for the Vampire Countess Ronina series personally."

"I would never write such garbage in my whole life!" I said. "I'm going to go back in there and tell him he should bake himself a protective garlic omelet as fast as possible, because otherwise I'm going to bite his neck myself." The idea brought me temporarily out of my rage, which is why I finished my thought on a somewhat lame note: "And then, uh, I'm going home. . . ."

"Not so fast," Licorice said. "First of all, a vampire book would be a great way to tide you over this financial bottleneck. You have to take what you can get. At least when it comes to work. That rule doesn't apply to one's personal life, but nowadays you can afford to turn an offer down only if you already have a better one lined up. So, you *will* be writing those vampire novels."

"What? But I can't do something like that," I said. "I didn't understand a single word coming out of his mouth all about different worlds and transvestite werewolves or whatever."

"Of course you can do it," Licorice said. "You just have to familiarize yourself with the material."

I shook my head. "Unfortunately, for someone with chaotic reactionary depression like me, that is quite impossible. Not even if there were such a thing as vegetarian vampires."

"Nonsense," Licorice said. "I think you're just drunk—and that's my fault. I should have realized you're too young to drink so much."

Once back in her office, she had me sit in a chair while she started packing mass-market paperbacks with bats and grotesque faces on the covers into a canvas bag. I watched her woozily as I gave some consideration to the pros and cons of vomiting. But I had been dealt a bad hand: The trash can in Licorice's office was one of those metal waste-paper bins full of holes.

As I stared at it, I gave further consideration to what Mr. Adrian must think of me. I hadn't behaved in a particularly exemplary or intelligent way. Here I'd finally met a good-looking man, and I was drunk as a skunk.

And why a skunk, of all things? Are skunks somehow more prone to intoxication? I urgently needed to research that on the Internet.

Someone entered the office without knocking.

It was a dark-haired woman dressed all in black, with a strikingly pale face.

"The Vampire Countess!" I whispered. So it was true: Vampires were able to move about freely in the daylight without disintegrating into dust.

The Vampire Countess didn't give me so much as a glance. "I've just been told by the personnel department that Ms., uh, whatever her name is, has just taken sick leave for two months, that hypochondriac bitch," she muttered. "So you are going to have to take over the, uh, whatever that series is, Ms., uh, whatever your name is."

"Karisch," Licorice said. "I assumed as much and have already started working on it. Since you're here, allow me to introduce you to our new Ronina author. This is Gerri

Thaler. Gerri, this is Marianne Schneider, Aurora's program manager."

"Oh! *The* program manager," I said, extending my hand to the Vampire Countess, brimming with interest. So this was the type of woman that Mr. Adrian liked. All she needed was the pointy fangs. "It's nice to meet you. Would you happen to know why skunks are so drunk?"

"So they don't have to smell themselves, I'd wager," the program manager said without skipping a beat, briefly shaking my hand but quickly pulling hers back. Although her pale skin was extraordinarily free of wrinkles, I estimated that she had been in her late thirties, maybe early forties, when she was transformed. So. Mr. Adrian liked older woman. Interesting. Interesting. "Or maybe to compensate for a deficiency in their diet. Are we playing *Who Wants to Be a Millionaire* here, or are we working?"

"It's research I'm doing for a book," I said, intimidated. She was a silly goose, wasn't she? *Or maybe to compensate for a deficiency in their diet.* Don't make me laugh.

The Vampire Countess turned back to Licorice. "Don't you even contemplate taking sick leave as well, Ms., uh, whatever your name is, because that will backfire," she said. "And don't tell me those are champagne bottles back there! You're not hosting a happy hour at work, are you, Ms., uh, whatever your name is?"

"Karisch," Licorice said calmly. "No. I'm using the bottles as flower vases."

"Good. Because even if you've been working here for a hundred years, that doesn't mean you can't be fired during your second hundred years. Please be sure to share that with any other colleagues who may be pretending to be zombies and shirking their work," the woman said, turning on the tips of her black vampire stilettos and leaving the office with as little courtesy as when she had entered.

"Ooh, she is definitely in the running for most popular manager of the year," I said.

"She really is an uncommonly annoying bitch," Licorice said, rankled for the first time today. "I cannot understand what The Boy sees in her."

"He's probably into S-M," I said. "And waists as narrow as my neck. And she has C cups to boot—some people have all the luck."

"None of it's real," Licorice said. "Silicone in her breasts, Botox in her brow, and her teeth are all crowns. But let's not let her totally bring us down." She handed me a three-ring binder titled Ronina: The Adventures of a Vampire Countess. "Please, Gerri. This dark future is the only future for the two of us now."

I stared at the binder and opened it up; the title of the pilot novel listed on the first page was *Ronina: Huntress in the Dark.*

"This is really outrageous," I said as I started to browse further. "Ronina is nothing but our Norina, only she's been bitten and transformed into this vampire countess. For God's sake, their names are even anagrams."

"You're right. Now that you point that out I can see it, too," Licorice said. "What a ridiculous coincidence." She pressed the handle to the canvas bag full of paperbacks into my hand. "So, now you have ample research material. You go and show that greenhorn! Write one hell of a vampire novel. And take two aspirin. I'll call you on Monday."

I stood up, swaying. "And what about *Leah's Path*?" I asked.

"Well, if you still want to write it, *Leah's Path* will likely have the dubious honor of being the last Norina novel ever," Licorice said.

"Over my dead body," I said.

To Aurora Publishing
Attn. Mr. Adrian
- confidential -

Dear Gregor,

Yes, I know we're not on a first-name basis, but under the circumstances we can probably just overlook the normal rules of workplace etiquette. Especially since I'll already have passed from the world of the living to the world of the dead by the time you read this letter. Ha-ha, just a little joke—I'm Catholic, so I'm going to heaven, because up until this suicide business I've actually never done anything wrong. Apart maybe from cutting my sister Lulu's hair. Everything else was either unintentional or self-defense.

Before I start chewing you out, Mr. Adrian—Gregor, I mean—I would like to tell you that you are really a very good-looking man, and sexy to boot. I'm saying that only because I was completely sloshed when we were introduced, but I still think those things, although now I'm completely sloshed again. You see, I'm practicing my ability to hold liquor a little before I have to rinse the sleeping pills down with the stuff. You can't prepare too much for a suicide like mine.

Where was I? Oh, right. I was talking about you. *Gregor*. If I say that you're sexy, I mean it—because when it comes to men, I'm very, very discerning. Just ask anyone. Say, do you wear colored contact lenses?

Nothing would ever have come of things between us, of course, because (a) I'm dead now and (b) you are in a relationship with that Schneider woman. But then you know that as well as I do. Although I also think you're being a little unwise, since surely you don't want to lose the respect of your new coworkers before you've even earned their respect, do you? That woman is not good for you—she got the position as program manager only because she schemed with the new management against the old program manager. Which is all the more incendiary when you consider that she had been in a relationship with the old program manager for many years. Plus, she has silicone breast implants—I'm sure you've already noticed. I know that first-hand, although I can't name my sources. Because if I did, you might decide to fire Licorice.

But, now, as far as *Ronina: Huntress in the Dark* goes. You can shove your amicably intended offer up your sexy ass. (I believe that it's sexy, anyway; unfortunately you were sitting on it the whole time I was in your office.) If you had made any effort to read one of my novels, you would know there is a vast qualitative difference between my oeuvre and that bloodsucker trash. I have honestly never read anything worse. Quite apart from various stylistic weaknesses, the whole plot stinks to high heaven.

Why does that stupid Kimberley take a shortcut on a night with a full moon through the exact same park where a renegade vampire sucked her best friend dry only a month before? And what on earth is this sentence supposed to mean: "Her breasts rose and fell breathlessly." Breathless breasts? HELLO? God, I was really rooting for the *renegade* to put an end to Kimberley's pointless existence, but, no—right when things were going well, the literally and figuratively soul-destroying Ronina leaps out from the underworld and ruins everything.

Why are Ronina and her bloodthirsty friends somehow always able to open portals from the underworld with nothing but the power of their minds, such that they can materialize from Peru to Paris in the blink of an eye, but they can't do this when the Army of Renegades appears with their poisoned cutlasses to engage in dubious kung fu battles? The whole time I was reading I was waiting for the erotic story to materialize, but this was evidently in vain—or were Kimberley's respiratory breasts supposed to cover that?

I'm sorry, but much as I'd like to, I could never write something so lousy and empty and bereft of meaning. I also don't think you are going to find readers for fare like that. Even people with a weakness for cutlass fights would still prefer to read about authentic feelings and true love, right? And a heroine with superpowers is interesting only if she also has some kind of weakness herself (apart from her culinary habits, that is). Otherwise, where is the excitement and suspense?

I could pile on a great deal more feedback, but I've got a tight schedule this week: I still have to finish all my other good-bye letters, and I wanted to get in a visit to the hairstylist, too.

So that brings me to a hasty but no less heartfelt end to this letter.

Sincerely,
Gerri Thaler

P.S. I just did the famous pencil test. You know: The more pencils you can hold under your breasts, the sooner you need to start saving for silicone. I expect that you won't care in the least, but my breasts couldn't even hold a single pencil.

P.P.S. Enclosed please find a farewell gift, a manuscript titled *Leah's Path to the World of Darkness*, which for time reasons I was unfortunately unable to edit any further. In it, Ronina's mortal sister Leah comes down with leukemia—at least, that's the doctor's diagnosis. But Ronina recognizes that Leah has been bitten by a renegade vampire and that her blood was contaminated with an insidious poison. Only Leah's brother by blood and soul, who lives in the underworld, can save her life now. But the powerful, embittered vampire Gregor . . . Well. Just read it for yourself. *This* story is actually erotic, at least!

FIVE

When I got home, the fire escape stairs leading up to my apartment were blocked by a child's red pedal car.

"Ge-ah-rri—hi? Know wha-hat? I got a new sticker."

"Hey, Johannes Paul. Unfortunately I don't have any time right now," I said. Oh, God, why did this kid always drone on and on so dreadfully like that?

"Lookit," Johannes Paul said, turning his Bobby-Car around 180 degrees.

I'M IN THE JESUS GANG, the sticker read.

"That's really great, Johannes Paul," I said. "But now you've got to let me by, OK? I'm really in a major rush to commit suicide."

"Theresa got a new sticker, too-oo." Johannes Paul turned his pedal car around to face me. "Do you want to read it, too?"

"I'll check it out from my window upstairs," I said. "But now you've got to let me by, OK?"

"Mama got a new sticker on her car, too," Johannes Paul said. "Know what it says?"

"'Droning kids onboard'?" I asked.

"No-ho," Johannes Paul said. "It says: JESUS IS MY COPILOT."

"Aha," I said. That did fit well with Hilla's other bumper sticker, which said, Give CONTROL of Your Life to Jesus. Hilla had a weakness for stickers like that. The sign on her mailbox didn't read No Ads Please but rather: Marriage Is a Gift from God. I'd never mustered the courage to find out why she put up that particular message, but I suspect it was intended for the mail carrier to dissuade him from getting a divorce. When I first met Hilla, I thought she was a Jehovah's Witness, what with all her stickers. But she was just a regular Catholic, if a rather zealous one.

Johannes Paul was the son of my cousin Volker, who was married to Hilla. That presumably made Johannes Paul my second cousin, or first cousin once removed. Or maybe my nephew once removed, or my nephew-cousin—in any case, he was related to me by only a couple of degrees of separation, as were most of the people living on the right bank of the Rhine in Cologne. I was renting my apartment from my aunt Evelyn and uncle Korbmacher (that's his last name; over the years I've actually forgotten his first name). It was just one neighborhood away from Dellbrück, where my parents lived, and had mainly single-family homes and small apartment buildings—as well as many, many garages. Which are extremely uncommon in large German cities. I didn't have any statistics about it, but another symptom of the local obsession with cars was that the people in no other place else on earth wash their cars as often as people did here. And apart from the seventy-five-year-old woman living kitty-corner across the street from me, I think I had to be the only single person over twenty within a twenty-block radius.

I had planned for many years to move to the hipper *left* bank of the Rhine, which bisects Cologne, and live somewhere with fewer relatives, fewer garages, and more movie theaters, shops, and restaurants. But the rents over there were shocking; plus, my current rent was a bargain even for the right bank. But no bargain comes without strings, so I had to spend three hours a week downstairs in my aunt Evelyn's apartment, cleaning her marble floors and vacuuming her Persian rugs. Sometimes Aunt Evelyn even had me use a toothbrush to clean the fixtures in the bathroom. Ah, the things one does to save a couple of euros . . .

"You probably have some tendency toward masochism," Charly always said.

"It's not as bad as that," I would reply. The main thing was that my apartment was *quiet*—a characteristic that cannot be undervalued when one works from home. Apart from the occasional Xavier Naidoo attacks, it was as quiet as the grave around here. Aunt Evelyn and Uncle Korbmacher lived on the ground floor; my cousin Volker and Hilla lived on the second floor with their four kids—Peter, Theresa, Johannes Paul, and Bernadette, who were amazingly quiet for children their ages. If there were even the slightest signs they were about to get into a fight, Hilla would tell them fighting makes Jesus very sad, and because making Jesus sad was the very last thing children should want to do, they should stop fighting immediately.

On the third floor under the building's sloped tile roof, there used to be two loft apartments, one big and one small. I lived in the small one, and Volker had converted the big one so that it was part of their second-floor apartment, to accommodate all the kids. The original stairwell had fallen victim to his conversion project: He screwed my former apartment door shut, and ever since I've had to clamber up the spiral steel staircase that had been mounted on the exterior of the building as a fire escape to get into my apartment. On frosty winter days this was a slippery affair, and last January I fell and hurt myself, developing an unsavory bruise on my tailbone. But last summer they added a balcony, so now I could sit out in the sun and watch all my neighbors washing their cars.

All in all, my living situation was entirely . . . adequate.

Charly did not agree, however. She thought my aunt and uncle were holier-than-thou, uptight, middle-class assholes; she thought my cousin Volker was weird; and she thought Hilla and their kids were "totally bananas." Well, they were possibly a *little* bananas, actually. The last time Charly had been over to visit, the kids had been playing "walking on water" in their sandbox outside.

"What do you have in your ba-ha-ag?" Johannes Paul asked me.

"Vampire Countess Ronina," I said, climbing over him toward the fire escape stairs.

"What's a va-ham-pie counta-hiss?" Johannes Paul asked behind me.

"You should go read about it in your children's Bible," I said. Normally I wasn't so mean to the kid, but today all the questions were getting on my nerves. I hurried upstairs, shut my apartment door behind me, and flung my purse and canvas bag into a corner. If I'd had a PLEASE DO NOT DIS-TURB sign, I would have hung it on my door handle. I just wanted everybody to leave me alone. I didn't want anything other than to spend a couple of days searching for a suitable way to die. Was that asking too much?

Thorough as I was, I had read on my depression Web sites that suicide wasn't the only way out of depression. There was medication, for example. But I seriously doubted the existence of any pharmaceutical preparation that could repaint the current state of my life in rosy colors. Plus, all the psychiatric drugs they listed seemed to have serious side effects: One of them made your hair fall out. I mean, how many tablets would you need to swallow so you could cope not only with your totally screwed-up life but also with your thinning hair?

To be honest, I would have much preferred some kind of serious hypnosis or something, the kind that makes you think you're a chicken, and you walk around jerking your neck, clucking, and trying to lay an egg. But hypnotists with that level of skill are quite rare. All you ever really encounter out there are people calling themselves hypnotists whose only goal is to con you out of a ton of money while they tell you thirty times, "You hate cigarettes; you get sick at the mere sight of them." Charly had been to one of those once, and, well, she still smokes.

And as far as seeing a therapist goes, it would take years upon years for him or her to learn everything about me. I just couldn't hold out that long at all.

I was fed up.

The tap was finally dry.

Empty. Done. *Finito.* I didn't want any more.

No one would miss me anyway.

And if they did, then they should have worried about me sooner.

"You've got mail," my computer told me.

"I don't care," I said to the computer. But then I peeked. Maybe I was getting the "You're a Winner" calls by e-mail now, too. But there were only messages from Britt Emke, now Baroness von Falkenstein, and from my cousin Harry.

"Dear Dellbrück Graduates," Britt's e-mail began. I was going to have to have a word with Charly, because she had obviously given my e-mail address to Britt. Presumably, Britt would now start cc'ing me on her year-end e-mail cards featuring her noble children wearing Santa hats. But that problem was now irrelevant because I would have been long gone by Christmas.

"The date for our class reunion is coming up fast," her e-mail continued. "We've tentatively reserved a space for June 3. So far we have six confirmed yeses and fourteen confirmed nos; I'm sad to report that one of our former classmates has died. And there are ninety-eight RSVPs still unaccounted for. So please get in touch as soon as possible so that Klaus and I can finalize the arrangements."

I'm sad to report one of our classmates has died? Who? And what did he/she die of? And why didn't Britt let us know his/her name, and why was she making a secret of his/her sex? It was probably just a cheap trick to lure us all to the reunion, though.

What would Britt send out by e-mail to the world when she learned about my suicide? *I'm sad to report that another of our classmates has died. If you want to find who he/she was, please come to the reunion on June 3.*

Maybe I should time my little undertaking so that the reunion and my funeral are the same day?

I looked at the calendar. No, I couldn't hold out that long. It was already the end of April, and I desperately wanted to get this over with as quickly as possible. I was going to need one to two weeks for the basic prep work—no more. I didn't have any time to lose, either; without a job, I would be out of money by mid-June.

Plus, Aunt Alexa's silver-anniversary party was going to be the first weekend in May, and under no circumstances did I want to still be around for that. There was a plan in the works for every member of the family to take turns standing up to sing solo in front of the party. We were each supposed to compose a four-line rhyming verse set to the tune of "Horch, was kommt von draußen rein," a nineteenth-century folk song from the Heidelberg area about unrequited love. Every children's choir in Germany has performed it at some point, as have most pop singers—from Roy Black to Nena. For our version, however, we would be accompanied on the piano by Cousin Harry. I hadn't been able to think of anything so far, beyond:

> Uncle Fred smells like bass
> holla hee holla hoe
> Man, that guy's a stupid ass
> holla hee-ahoe

But Uncle Fred was really nice; of the two of them, Aunt Alexa was the stupid ass. And neither of them smelled like bass.

Family reunions on my mother's side were always dreadful. There was a herd of white-haired great-aunts who all looked the same and always asked if you hadn't grown "a bit plump." Then the great-uncles at their sides would always say, "But you carry it well," and smack your butt as though that were some kind of normal familial ritual for great-uncles. The cousins with kids would always have some comment about my biological clock ticking, and my mother would continuously hiss at me to "stand up straight!" whenever she was within earshot.

Even the best caterer in the world couldn't make up for the psychological torture of attending such a party. Not to mention that Aunt Alexa's original wedding twenty-five years ago was not the finest memory for me, either.

Aunt Alexa was the youngest of Mama's four sisters, so her wedding had been a grand event—with two hundred guests in the park surrounding the Castle Hotel. There were magnificent fabric tents, a string orchestra, and the extended family's antique Meissen porcelain collection and actual-silver silverware; all the pieces had been specially reunited from the far corners of Germany just for that occasion. All of my blonde sisters and cousins got to wear pink-satin dresses, custom made for them, and they got to wear garlands of flowers in their hair and hold fabric-lined baskets full of fresh rose petals.

But I had to spend the whole wedding standing next to my parents, wearing my stupid dark blue dress, because otherwise my dark hair would have blemished the "sea of blonde flower girls' heads" in the wedding photos if I had been among them, as Aunt Alexa explained.

Even my mother thought that was extreme, but Aunt Alexa wouldn't budge. "I'm only getting married once in my life, after all. I want everything to be perfect," she said. "Plus, Gerri's still so little, she won't understand anyway."

My ass. To this day, every last detail of that wedding has stuck, branded into my memory. I even recall how my father mixed tiny pebbles into the rice for me to throw at the newlyweds in front of the church. And how one of the two doves set free as they left the church shit on my uncle Gustav's bald head. The wedding had been anything but perfect. Still, it might have proceeded without any major incident if only Aunt Alexa hadn't made so much fuss about the color of my hair. If someone had sewn *me* a pink-satin dress and let me scatter flower petals, I would never have crept under the table in a huff, where Grandpa's dachshund was sleeping. (Yes, old people bring their dogs to weddings in Germany sometimes.) I also would never have thought to cure my boredom by tying the laces of Grandpa's shoes to Waldi's collar. And if *I* had gotten to play princess with the flower girls, I would never have tossed Waldi's favorite ball out onto the lawn, and Waldi would never have yanked Grandpa off his chair, and Grandpa would never have grabbed onto the tablecloth for dear life, and all the porcelain would never have crashed to the ground, where it smashed into a thousand pieces. And I would not be known today as "Dorothea's youngest, the one responsible for the Meissen porcelain debacle." Although lately my epithet had expanded to "Dorothea's youngest, the one responsible for the Meissen porcelain debacle, who still isn't married."

"Dear Gerri," my cousin Harry had e-mailed. "The deadline for sending in your verse for the song at my parents' anniversary party was yesterday. Since I want to print out all the verses and present the song to them as a memento in a bound booklet, please send me your contribution as soon as possible. The verses will be listed in alphabetical order by name, so yours will come between Cousin Franziska's and Uncle Gustav's. And I'll be playing the song in D major, in case that's helpful when you practice singing beforehand."

"Still so young and way too dumb, holla hee holla hoe," I sang, although likely not in D major. "To hell with you and up yours, too, holla hee-ahoe." God, and he wanted us to *practice* singing this shit, too—but yet again, that was typical. Harry had attached his own poetic bilge as an "inspiration and motivating example." So helpful. I was struck by how he had perverted the meter and twisted the syntax of every line so each would end in *ing*, to rhyme.

> Awful poems Harry's writing
> holla hee holla hoe
> Which you, too, must now be trying
> holla hee-ahoe

I clicked away from Harry's e-mail and opened a new document. Critical To-Do Items Before My Death, I typed, and then:

(1) Write will.

(2) Give some thought to Harry's stupid song; otherwise that idiot is going to show up knocking at my door.

(3) Clean the apartment and remove all embarrassing items.

(4) Write good-bye letters—see separate list.

(5) RSVP no to the class reunion with my regrets.

(6) Hairstylist.

A will is important. Grandma hadn't written one; she had left behind only the oral instruction that her jewelry be distributed among her granddaughters.

"Each girl can pick something out," she had said. "Each in turn, starting with the youngest." That was of course a lovely idea, in principle, but after she watched all the in-fighting over her crown jewels from her cloud in heaven, I'm certain she realized it would have been better to write a will.

Aunt Evelyn, who had had only boys and thus was to-tally excluded from the "granddaughter" rule, stood in the corner of the room with her arms folded, grumbling; by contrast, my mother had been extremely pleased, what with her four daughters. I suspect that was the only time in my mother's life when she wasn't put out none of us had been boys.

"Take the *sapphire*, the *sapphire*," Aunt Alexa whispered to my then-three-year-old cousin Claudia. But Claudia, who had no idea what a sapphire looked like, chose a coral neck-lace on her first turn, and on her second she chose the am-ber pendant with a mosquito inside. Aunt Alexa burst into tears. Then our cousins Diana, Franziska, Miriam, and Betty each went in turn for the imitation pearls, the silver figurine pendants, the garnet pieces, and the rose quartz necklaces, while their mothers banged their heads against the wall. But

Tina, Rika, Lulu, and I all left the cheap plunder where it lay and instead went for the really good stuff. Tina got the sapphire choker; Rika got the diamond studs; Lulu, a delicate diamond and platinum watch; and I picked a ring with a giant gem-cut aquamarine.

When I slid it onto my pudgy little finger, Aunt Alexa sighed aloud, and Aunt Evelyn mumbled, "Changeling . . ."

"You would do well to bite your tongue," my mother said to her. "You've already walked off with all the antiques and porcelain."

"What porcelain would that be?" Aunt Evelyn yelled. "Your youngest is responsible for smashing the good Meissen porcelain."

"That's true," Aunt Alexa said. "By all rights she should be excluded from the inheritance."

But my grandma had said nothing about that on her deathbed.

Even on the second round—"Not *those* red earrings, Diana, the other red earrings!!!"—my sisters and I instinctively picked the most valuable pieces: Rika, the pendant with the boulder opal; Tina, the emerald ring; Lulu, the ruby earrings; and I, the pearl necklace with the diamond clasp. My mother had been so proud of us.

Apart from the jewelry, I really didn't own any items of value now, but all the same I didn't want the few things I did have to land in the wrong hands, such as my collection of old and antique children's books, my iPod, and my laptop. Spontaneously I reached for the receiver to my landline, about to call my mother to say, "I don't want you to funnel everything to Arsenius and Habakkuk, do you hear?" But I realized in time that calling her and uttering such things would have been rather imprudent. Until the day of my death, I was going to have to remain as inconspicuous as possible and act "normally," otherwise someone might figure out my plans and lock me up in the psych ward.

I wanted to approach the matter systematically, as I did everything in my life. I had already explained the why. The next issue I had to deal with was the how. My method would have to be as painless as possible, and not at all complicated. Not the least bit *unsavory*, under any circumstances. If possible, I wanted to look as good in death as in life. I had to consider the people who would find me, after all.

But it really wasn't that simple.

As I was getting ready for my Saturday-night cooking party with friends, I was still brooding over how I should do "it."

On www.depressed-so-what.de, I took an online psychological test called "What Suicide Type Are You?" and determined that I was clearly the Marilyn Monroe type and not the Anna Karenina type or the hara-kiri type. Honestly, that sounded about right. I couldn't find the right Marilyn Monroe–style sleeping pills anywhere, though, without a prescription. I could find only one company online that offered "brand-name pharmaceuticals of all types without original packaging" at a price of 50 eurocents per pill. Should I just order a couple of pounds of tablets from them, down them all, and see what happened? But with my luck, they'd end up sending Viagra and vitamin C tablets. Or pills so old they had grown mustaches of mold.

I pulled on my ancient green sweater, my jeans, and my favorite earrings with the Frog King on them. I checked in the mirror to see whether I was wearing my suicide plans on my face somehow and found that the corners of my mouth were most inappropriately attempting a smile.

They always did that. It was a purely anatomical fact. In our family, all the women had the same wide, upwardly curved, eternally smiling duckbills.

"Sensuous lips," Ulrich had always said about them.

"Gaping frog's mouth," Britt Emke had always called it, dating back to sixth grade. For that, Charly and I had tucked a bookmark inside her Latin book made of a flattened road-kill frog—so that she could see an *authentic* gaping frog's mouth. My God, how she had screamed.

As I clambered down the fire escape, Volker, Hilla, and their kids were already having their dinner.

"...and these, Thy gifts, which we are about to receive..." I heard them saying in chorus. Their window was ajar, and their dining room smelled deliciously of roasted meat. I suddenly realized that I had eaten practically nothing all day, so I hurried on down and to the streetcar stop.

Our cooking parties used to be a lot of fun. We used to cook challenging, often exotic dishes, pouring pricey apéritifs and wines, gorging ourselves, and talking late into the night. But ever since my friends had started having babies, they had lost all taste for exotic fare. Suddenly things like raw-milk cheese, alcohol, and tandoori were "dangerous." Despite the original ground rules we had established when we started the cooking parties, there always ended up being at least one kid along—"The babysitter canceled last minute," "She just wanted to come so much," "He's teeth-ing"—so we never made our own *nigiri* anymore, since kids don't like sushi.

And as expensive filets of halibut devolved into easy-to-hold fish sticks (to which ketchup and tartar sauce were inevitably added), the kids would play chase around the kitchen island. Later on, at least one of the kids present would fall asleep in my lap, and I dared not move even though my legs were falling asleep and I was having trouble staying awake myself, lulled into a stupor by the meandering conversation about kid-friendly hotels and preschool tuition. And if *I* didn't actually fall asleep, then at least one other adult did—which would signal that the party was over, typically well before eleven o'clock.

Ole and Mia were the only ones without kids, apart from Charly and Ulrich, and me, but they had recently started skipping the parties, offering suspiciously repetitive excuses of the flu or some other communicable disease. I suspected they were just enjoying pleasant Saturday nights out seeing movies together. Or maybe they were cooking up something spicy, raw, or unpuréed in their own kitchen.

And now that Charly and Ulrich were pregnant, I wouldn't have anyone to make fun of the rest of the parents to anymore.

We used to take turns hosting—even I hosted everyone in my tiny kitchen—and sometimes we'd meet at the park with a gas grill and a wok. But now we always met at Caroline and Bert's place because they had the largest kitchen, the quietest dishwasher, the biggest brood, and the most unreli-able babysitter. They lived in a townhouse that was tastefully furnished, if you could see past all the toys and other kids' stuff lying around everywhere.

Caroline welcomed me with a warm hug while kicking a Lego car and tiny pink cardigan out of the way, saying, "You're the first one, on time as always, come on in, I told Florina that you'd be up to tell her good night, you know she loves you, wow, is that a new sweater, you look great, really, you remind me of that actress, what's her name again, you know, the one who got caught shoplifting, do you think it's bad we bought pork tenderloins instead of saddle of lamb, you know lamb stew has to cook at low heat for so many hours, and tenderloins fry up quick in the pan, that would—oh, Bert, honey? Did you see that the day after tomorrow is our PTA meeting, I'm telling you now while I'm thinking of it that you're coming with me this time—oh, it's terrible, the last time they almost elected me treasurer, even though I'm terrible at math and our account is always overdrawn . . . —wow, is that a new sweater, it's totally cute on you . . ."

At some point between the arrivals of her second and third children, Caroline had lost her ability to utilize sentence-final punctuation. She just kept blathering until she ran out of breath. And she often repeated herself.

"Hi there, Gerri!" Bert said with a warm smile. He was carrying the baby, Severin, in his arm and kissed me on the cheek. Severin grabbed for my Frog King earring.

"I'm not going to the PTA meeting," Bert said.

"Well, I'm not, either," Caroline said. "I've been the last five times to listen to all their issues, no human being can take it, they take all those secret-ballot votes, and they always run late . . ."

Severin tried to rip the Frog King through my earlobe. He had the strength of a bear, and I'm certain he would have succeeded had I not intervened. When I pulled his fingers off it, he pouted. I rubbed my earlobe.

"Well, then neither of us will go," Bert said. Severin thrashed about angrily in his arms because he couldn't get at my earring anymore.

"I'll head upstairs and tell Flo good night," I said.

"Yes, that's sweet, I'll get started rinsing the vegetables," Caroline said. "I didn't pick up any chervil, but watercress is good, too, right? If neither of us goes, then they'll decide behind our backs to allow Nutella on toast for school breakfasts, or they'll decide to hold a pet day and all the kids will bring their chinchillas to class . . ."

"It doesn't matter," Bert said.

"It does to me," Caroline said. "I'm the one juggling whining kids all day, who would *love* to have chinchillas or Nutella or—"

"You act like I'm never home," Bert said.

"You're not."

Severin started bawling as I climbed the stairs.

"Oh look, how sweet," Caroline said. "He loves you, all our kids just love you, Gerri, is that a new sweater? It looks great on you. Doesn't Gerri look great in it, honey? Like that actress who got caught shoplifting . . ."

Flo was still lying awake in her bed when I came in. Her brother Gereon was already sound asleep in the bunk above her. That was good, since I had brought a present only for

Flo: my old musical clock with the dancer who turned when you lifted the lid.

"What is that tune?" Flo asked.

"'The Blue Danube,'" I said.

"And you're really *giving* it to me? Not just a loan?"

"Yes, it's yours now."

"Oh, thank you! You're really the best, Gerri. Gerri? When you were a little girl, did you have a pet?"

"We had a cat," I said. "But I had to share her with my three sisters. And since I was the youngest, the only part of the cat I ever got was her tail."

"Better than no pet at all," Flo said. "Can you give me a bunny rabbit for my birthday, Gerri? Mama and Papa won't be able to give it away if it's from you."

"We'll see. Maybe," I said, suddenly choking up. Flo's birthday was in July, and I wouldn't be around anymore. She was my goddaughter, and I had to admit that I loved her much more than Habakkuk, even though his parents talked me into being his godmother as well.

"It would be really nice to have a bunny rabbit," Flo said. Then, as she did every Saturday, she asked, "Did you meet any nice guys this week, Gerri?"

"Yes," I said, thinking of Gregor Adrian. "He has green eyes and a nice last name."

"And? Could you feel your heart thumping?"

"Yes," I said. "But he's already spoken for. By a *vampire countess!*"

"The good ones are always already spoken for," Flo sighed. "Give me a hug," she said, wrapping her arms around my neck and hugging me tight. "Mmm, you smell good."

"It's called Pampelune," I said. "I'll leave it to you, if you want."

"I'd much rather have a bunny rabbit," Flo said.

Dear Aunt Evelyn and Uncle Korbmacher,

This letter is notice that I will be vacating my apartment.

Unfortunately, I will not be able to meet the one-month notice requirement in my lease because I have to kill myself next Friday. But I'm sure you'll find another renter quickly, maybe an elderly lady from church or a religious exchange student from Korea. The exchange student would be better, if you ask me, because an elderly lady might slip on the fire escape and sue you.

It would also benefit your next renter immensely if you could buy Hilla a dishwasher. And instead of sticking pamphlets titled "Invite Jesus into Your Life" into Volker and Hilla's mailbox, maybe you could invite them down to *your* apartment for dinner once in a while.

Aunt Evelyn, you may think I was too young to understand it at the time, but I want you to know I have a perfect recollection of each time you called me a changeling behind my back when I was little. I remember as though it were yesterday how you and Aunt Alexa used to speculate about how I must have been switched at birth at the hospital, or how I must actually be the mailman's daughter because of the color of my hair, and how you would always giggle. At the time I thought you were just being mean, but later when we studied genetics in biology at school I realized what you were getting at.

But allow me to reassure you: I am my father's daughter. He gave me his dark hair and brown eyes; it's a little complicated to explain since he has light brown hair, but anyone can understand it if you just study Mendel's diagrams closely. Even you. This is why I left my old biology textbook in your mailbox, so you can peruse chapter 5 (pp. 146 ff) at your leisure. Given our parents, my sisters and I are an interesting collision of genes: Tina is blonde with brown eyes; Rika is blonde with blue eyes; Lulu is blonde with green eyes; and I'm a brunette with brown eyes. But eye and hair color are not mixed and passed on at random; this is where the concepts of dominant and recessive come into play.

According to Mendel, it's genetically *impossible* for a blue-eyed woman (such as you) and a blue-eyed man (such as Uncle Korbmacher) to have a brown-eyed child (such as Volker).

But you can go and read all about it in the textbook on your own. It's a really interesting topic, and the more you read about it, the more intensely you'll look people in the eyes.

Give my love to Volker, Hilla, Johannes Paul, Petrus, Theresa, and Bernadette. I suppose it couldn't hurt to pray for me.

Your niece,
Gerri

SIX

When I came back downstairs from saying good night to Flo, the others had already arrived: Marta and Marius, Ulrich and Charly, even Ole and Mia for once. Unusually, Marta and Marius didn't have a child in tow for a change—apart from the child in Marta's belly. Given the size of her belly, however, that supposed child could well be a small elephant instead.

Charly was totally psyched. "I haven't smoked a cigarette for three days now!" she said. "Without any hypnosis. Isn't that great? Plus, I'm actually craving salad! But the best part is these boobs! I don't need a Wonderbra anymore. Take a feel—they're real!"

Marius immediately reached out, but Marta swatted his hand down.

"Charly's only joking," she said. Marta's own breasts were the size of prize-winning Halloween pumpkins, and they made Charly's breasts look like mere oranges. But compared to the eight-months-pregnant belly jutting out below them, even Marta's breasts looked microscopic.

"No, I'm dead serious," Charly said. "Everybody needs to feel this! Come on! Don't be shy." She reminded me a little of *rockinhard12* that time in the café: "Go and take a feel, it's totally rockin' hard."

"What, no communicable disease today?" I asked as Ole welcomed me with a hug. His hair was as unruly as ever; it just wouldn't stay combed down. Very sexy guy, though. I was still sorry he had married another woman, even though he smelled a little like dentist, no matter how freshly showered he was.

"Pff," he said, laughing. "We ran out of excuses. Plus, I love Provençal lamb stew."

"Hope you like it without the lamb," I said, "because Caro bought pork tenderloins."

"Oh, that bites!" Ole said, looking over at his wife, whom Charly had already coerced into feeling her breasts. "Hey, Mia. You're driving—it's my turn to get drunk tonight."

"No, it's *my* turn," Mia said. She was a rather pretty redhead with enviably long legs. She worked as an assistant front-desk manager at the upscale Lexington Hotel downtown, where Aunt Alexa's silver-anniversary party was, coincidentally, going to be held. It cost 2,500 euros to rent the exclusive Hall of Mirrors, not including catering and waitstaff; I'd had Mia inquire about it for my mother. For some reason, the Hall of Mirrors was a thorn in my mother's side. Presumably because she had to hold her own silver-anniversary party in the Hall of Leopards and Angels, aka our living room, which Aunt Alexa had turned her nose up at.

"Alexa can dish out two and a half thousand euros to rent a space, but she complains to Aunt Hulda about her financial woes," my mother had said the moment I had put the receiver of my phone to my ear. Great-Aunt Hulda was also known in the extended family as Our Rich Aunt because she didn't have any children of her own but did have a large fortune. She lived in a magnificent mansion in the hills outside town. My mother and her sisters had each started at a very young age doing everything they could to become, and remain, Our Rich Aunt's favorite niece. This included regularly tattling on their competition.

"You got to drink the last time," Mia told Ole. "Hi, Gerri. It's nice to see you. You're not pregnant now, too, are you?"

"No," I said. "As you may remember, I'm single."

"And none of us understands why," Ole said. He always worked in some nice, harmless flirting with me, just enough to make me feel good without giving me false hope. Ole was my type. Sometimes—but only rarely—I allowed myself to imagine what it would be like if there weren't any Mia.

Caroline hugged me again as though I had just arrived.

"Is that a new sweater?" she asked. "It looks great on you, isn't that right. Ole? Gerri looks terrific, a bit like that actress who got caught shoplifting."

"Winona Ryder," Ole said.

"Exactly," Caroline said. "Gerri looks just like Winona Ryder."

Mia chuckled, and Caroline flashed her an angry look. She didn't like Mia; she had never forgiven Ole for getting back together with her after she and Bert had tried to set Ole up with me.

"Gerri is definitely a Winona Ryder type, with those big brown eyes, the dark curls . . ." Caroline said.

"The fat ass," Mia added.

"If Gerri has a fat ass, then what's mine?" Caroline asked, turning around to show off her butt.

"Even fatter," Mia said.

"Actually, I'm a Marilyn Monroe type," I quickly said to keep Caroline from going off on Mia.

"No way, baby," Charly said, butting in and playfully plastering each of my cheeks with affectionate kisses. "Marilyn was blonde and had big boobies. Like mine! Feel these, would you!"

"Well, enjoy them while you can," Caroline said. "Remind me to show you my stretch marks this summer at the beach."

Mia rolled her eyes. "OK, Ole. If you haven't felt up Charly's boobs yet, please get it over with. Otherwise she'll keep pestering us all night."

"Now, now, don't be jealous," Charly said. "Say, Gerri, did you get an e-mail from Britt Emke this week, too? Can you believe somebody from our class died? Who do you think it was? And what did he die of? God, I'm glad I quit smoking. Life is so short. We're getting to that age when you have to pay more attention to your health."

Ulrich swatted my shoulder. "Hey, old buddy!" he said. Ever since he'd started dating Charly, Ulrich had treated me as though we were old drinking buddies who had never dated. "So did you hear our big news?"

"Yes, I did—and congratulations," I said.

"Yes, congratulations," Mia said. "Really awesome boobs there."

"Sorry about the lamb, folks," Bert said. "We'll do the lamb next Saturday—promise."

"Unfortunately I can't make it next Saturday," Mia said. "I've got another continuing ed class for work down in Stuttgart that weekend."

"I may not be here next week, either," I said.

"What are you up to?" Caro asked.

"I . . . uh . . ." I stuttered. Dammit! Now I'd given something away. Fortunately, my embarrassment pointed in their minds to something totally different.

"Oh-ho," Marius said. "Gerri's got a date!"

"Lightning could strike!" Bert yelled. "It's about time, too!"

Lightning could strike? Wasn't that a line from that movie with Brad Pitt, *Meet Joe Black?*

"Stay open," Anthony Hopkins tells his daughter in the helicopter. "Who knows? Lightning could strike."

I got goose bumps.

"What's his name?" Charly asked.

"Uh . . . *Joe,*" I said, blushing.

"And what does *Joe* do?" Ole wanted to know.

"He's a, uh, bigwig at, uh, well, they manufacture . . . scythes and things like that," I said.

"They make swinging tools to cut grass and hay by hand?" Marius asked.

I shook my head. "More like the old-fashioned type of . . . blades."

"Solingen knives, probably," Bert said. "Maybe you can pocket us a couple of good sushi chef's knives. By the way, who's doing the appetizer tonight?"

"I am." Marta yawned.

"Hey, you guys—should we just skip the soup course?" Caroline asked, yawning, too. "I mean, otherwise this is going to take forever. And it would probably work well if we just toss the veggies into the pan to steam on top of the tenderloins. Then we'd combine those courses, which would mean fewer dishes to wash."

"Fine by me," Marius said, also yawning.

Ole exchanged a meaningful look with Mia and me, and looked around for the corkscrew. We held our wineglasses out to him in silence.

The next day, my mother put an end to my brooding over *how* when she entrusted me with disposing of her collection of sleeping pills. I could hardly believe my luck. If I'd had any doubts about my plan, they completely evaporated once I held the shoebox. It was clearly a stroke of fate that they landed in my hands just as I was preparing for the end of my life. Why else would a mountain of sleeping pills materialize just then, and so obligingly?

Now that I was holding the solution to all my problems in my hand, I could plan my *date with Joe*—that sounded much nicer than *suicide*—in peace. I even bought myself a new dress just for the occasion.

I'm typically a fairly frugal person, but now I felt I could blow my money on whatever I wanted without any guilt. It was also important to me that I'd look good when someone found me. And this dress was sheer madness: tight fitting without the stuffed-sausage effect, low-cut without looking tacky, and blazing red, a color that looked exceptionally good on me.

Even the saleslady had said it was "to die for," and she didn't know how right she was.

Unfortunately I had yet to find the right shoes. Initially I considered forgoing the purchase since I was going to be supine when someone found me, but then I spotted these gorgeous red sandals decorated with paste-jewel butterflies. And even though they were pricey and I could hardly walk on the stiletto heels, I bought them all the same. I wasn't going to need to walk in them at all. They made my ankles look wonderfully thin, and they would do that nicely even when I was on my back.

I also bought two bottles of extremely expensive vodka. One for rehearsal and one for opening night. The true artistry would consist in keeping the sleeping pills and the alcohol in my stomach without throwing them back up. And that was going to require a certain amount of preconditioning. I got out the alcoholic beverages in my apartment, arranged them on the table, and decided to drink them all, little by little, every night. That would raise my spirits a little, while simultaneously disposing of clutter and building up my tolerance to alcohol.

I had chosen the following Friday for my date with Joe, but my own apartment was no place to kill myself. After all, I had to have a little consideration for Hilla and the kids. So I reserved a double room at the Regency Palace with a view of the Rhine for a cool 320 euros a night. Breakfast included, but I wouldn't be needing that, obviously. And the best part was that I wouldn't even need to pay the bill.

But I had a lot to do before then.

On Sunday night I got right down to work, training with two bottles of red wine that Uncle Korbmacher had given me for my thirtieth birthday. I wandered through my apartment holding my glass of wine in one hand and a garbage bag in the other, trying to picture my apartment through the eyes of those I would be leaving behind so I could get rid of anything I didn't want them to see. The first thing I threw away was the vibrator Charly had given me for my birthday. It was too horrific imagining my mother finding that. Or my aunt. Plus, it was a creepy item that didn't resemble its human inspiration at all—unless there *were* men out there with dual neon-colored pricks. What the second one was good for, I had yet to discover; to be perfectly honest, it was still in its original, unopened packaging. I suddenly but briefly felt guilty as I stuffed it into the garbage bag. Charly had said it was quite expensive, one of the best on the market, a limited edition, but it was way too late now to sell it on eBay or anything. I didn't toss the garbage into my building's Dumpster—it might occur to someone to search it. Instead I ditched it in the trash can at the streetcar stop. Maybe some homeless guy would come across it and enjoy it.

Back in my apartment I stumbled over the canvas bag Licorice had given me. On top lay *Ronina: Huntress in the Dark*, the pilot novel Mr. Adrian had apparently written himself. I really wanted to toss it in the recycling, but curiosity got the better of me, and I began to read. In it, the fledging-vampire Countess Ronina had to protect a human woman named Kimberley from being bitten by a rogue vampire.

It was so unexciting I had to empty a whole bottle of red wine just to keep reading.

My God! This Gregor Adrian should be really happy he had a day job and didn't need to live off his writing. His lack of *talent* assaulted my eyes from every page, although no one could accuse him of a lack of *imagination.*

Quite against my will, I started to consider how the book could be improved. There was pretty much nothing to this Kimberley as a character, and even the rogue vampire had addled motives for wanting to bite *her*, as opposed to biting *anyone* else. There was nothing special about Kimberley at all, not even her blood type. No, the book was short on everything—drama, authentic motivation, and deep emotion. Emotions and feelings like those Leah struggled with in the throes of leukemia . . . Before I knew it, I was sitting at my desk writing a completely new version of *Leah's Path*. I had to admit my original plot picked up momentum through various battles with cutlasses. And there was no denying the new tension in the book just from adding long canines to the mouths of both the hero and antihero.

As for the erotic aspect: There was something titillating about not exactly knowing whether the guy was going to kiss or bite his next victim.

The phone rang in the middle of the night—right as I was concentrating on the vampire-transformation scene, an awkward mix of blood donation and sex. It was Charly.

"I just had a nightmare," she said, out of sorts. "Did I wake you up?"

"No," I said, pouring myself some more wine. "I was just having a perverse sort of nightmare of my own involving lots of blood."

"I dreamed that Ulrich and I will be lousy parents," Charly said. "And when I woke up, I realized that it's true."

"Oh, you," I said. "You two will be fabulous parents."

"No," Charly said. "Last night I smoked a cigarette again. Only half a cigarette, actually, but it was still stronger than me."

"Only half a cigarette isn't that bad," I said.

"And you know what always happens to my houseplants," Charly said. "What if things turn out that way with the baby?"

"I wouldn't worry about that," I said. "A woman rises to her responsibilities."

"I'll accidentally leave him behind in the grocery store," Charly said.

"We'll tie a little bell around him," I said.

"Oh, shit—I feel sick," Charly said. "I think I'm going to puke. But thanks for listening to me."

"No problem," I said, turning back to my manuscript.

The week until my date with Joe flew by. I diligently rehearsed my alcohol performance every night and worked my way down my to-do list, item by item. And I finished writing *Leah's Path into Darkness* on the side because, as you know, Virgos do not like half-finished tasks. What we start, we finish.

That also applied to major housecleaning initiatives.

I kept schlepping bags and bags of garbage out of the apartment. Once I'd started, my disposal craze knew practically no bounds. Household items, clothes, shoes, underwear, knickknacks, pictures, paperwork, bedding, makeup—everything that I didn't 100 percent love had to go. All that I would leave behind would be things that somehow radiated who I was, in an authentic, pure light. And that applied to surprisingly *few* things. Especially when it came to my clothes: I had almost nothing left.

If I hadn't been saddled with neurotic depression, I might have enjoyed this great purge. My apartment looked much bigger afterward, too. The closets were empty, and everything was in its place.

On Wednesdays I always clean Aunt Evelyn's apartment, and even though this time she had me combing the fringes of the Persian rugs and cleaning the oven by hand, the time flew by. If only I'd known sooner how pleasant it was to clean with a vodka buzz!

"Next week we'll be wiping out all the cabinets," Aunt Evelyn said. She always said "we" when speaking about my tasks, but in reality she never lifted a finger and instead watched me the whole time and talked.

"I'm looking forward to it already," I said. I wouldn't be around by next week, after all.

Later when I was back in my apartment, Licorice called to ask how I was coming with the plot summary. I said I'd mail her the completed manuscript on Friday, and she was beyond delighted.

"Fast and reliable as always! And here I was afraid you were going to leave me hanging," she said. "I would really be up the creek without you, Gerri. The manuscripts from other authors I've read so far are horrific. Apparently it's impossible to suck blood on a somewhat higher level."

Licorice wasn't on the list of people who would be getting a good-bye letter from me. I couldn't write a letter to *everyone*, after all. And so—facilitated by the two screwdrivers I had just downed, for training purposes—I took the opportunity to say, "I really, really like you, Licorice. And

I sincerely wish you all the best, from the bottom of my heart."

Licorice took my outburst of emotion in stride. "I really, really like you, too, Gerri. I love working with you."

Wow! How nice! I was so touched I almost starting crying. "See you on the other side," I said solemnly.

"Yes," Licorice said. "That's what we're working toward."

Then my mother called, and I was sure after we chatted that, if she had known this was the last time she would speak with me, she would have said different things.

"I just wanted to ask you quickly what you're planning on wearing to Alexa's party," she said.

"Well, pff . . ."

"Please, not that ancient velvet blazer again. For this occasion you could go buy something new. Hannah—you remember, Hannah who's married to Klaus, Klaus Köhler— she recently wore a very fashionable pantsuit to Annemarie's sixtieth birthday. With a vest under the jacket. It would look terrific on you. I could have Annemarie ask Hannah where she bought it. Then we could go down there together and buy you one."

"I, uh, already bought a nice red dress for myself," I said. "With matching shoes."

My mother didn't say anything for a couple of seconds, apparently dumbfounded. And then she said, "Red? Does it have to be red? Red stands out so much. Very few people can pull red off. I was thinking of a lovely beige. Hannah's pantsuit was beige."

"The dress is very pretty, Mama. It looks great on me. The saleswoman even said so."

"Oh, they'll say anything to unload their merchandise on people. Don't you know they get a commission on sales? How would it be if you borrowed something pretty from one of your sisters?"

"You mean one of Tina's Laura Ashley blouses, or one of Lulu's black suits? No, Mama. The dress is great. You'll see. It cost four hundred forty euros."

"Forty euros? Oh, Gerri. That's so like you, never spending your savings on the right things. I can only imagine how cheap a forty-euro dress—"

"*Four hundred* forty," I said. "And it was marked down from eight hundred."

"I don't believe it," my mother said. "You're just saying that."

I sighed.

"I'm only trying to help, Riluger," my mother said. "You know, wearing nice things can make you feel better about yourself. And if you wear something cheap, people are just going to say it's no wonder my youngest has no husband, the way she's let herself go!"

I sighed again.

"Do you know there are rumors going around in the family that you're not entirely . . . well, normal?" my mother asked.

"I beg your pardon?"

"That you're not normal," my mother said. "You know. *Different.*"

"Different than what?"

"Oh, stop pretending to be dumber than you are," my mother said. "Different. That way. A bit funny. *Wearing comfortable shoes.*"

"*A lesbian?* The family thinks I'm a lesbian?"

"Sweetheart, I don't like it when you use such language."

"Mama, *lesbian* is the proper term, and *different, a bit funny,* and *wearing comfortable shoes* are borderline slurs," I said.

"If people heard you talking that way, they'd instantly think you really were—"

"A lesbian? No, Mama, I'm not. For that I would have to enjoy having sex with women, OK? And therefore actually have to be having any sex. At all. But I'm not having sex, Mama. Not with women or men. Not that it's anyone else's business. No one asks if Aunt Alexa and Uncle Fred are still getting it on."

"Tigerlu!" my mother said, shocked.

"See?" I said. "Such questions are indiscreet and unpleasant, and yet people constantly throw stuff like that into the faces of single women like me."

My mother paused for a couple of seconds. Then she said, "You do remember that Fred had prostate surgery."

"Sorry?"

"I won't say anything more," my mother said. "My lips are sealed. I am the very embodiment of discretion. But you know, Lutiger, if you brought a man at least *now and then* to family gatherings, then you might stop nasty rumors like that. Think of how often Franziska and Diana bring a date to family gatherings."

"Mama, those two show up with a different guy every time," I said. "Aunt Marie-Luise always pretends wedding bells will be pealing the next day, but if you ask me all those guys are probably escorts. Who will they be practically engaged to at Alexa's party, then?"

"Oh, Diana's new boyfriend is a stockbroker," my mother said. "And Franziska is still with the guy from last time. They're getting married in the fall."

"The hairstylist with Elvis's haircut and Goofy's voice?" I asked, a little shocked.

"He's not just a stylist," my mother said. "He *owns* four salons in town. And Marie-Luise made clear to Franziska that at thirty a girl can't be waiting for Prince Charming to come galloping in. One has to make compromises. And a man with four flourishing businesses isn't anything to sneeze at these days. Hey, what did they say at the pharmacy about those drugs?"

"What?"

"My shoebox with the leftover pills. You were going to drop it off at the pharmacy for me."

"Uh, oh yeah, they were exceedingly pleased," I said. "Ethiopia happens to be having a terrible epidemic of insomnia right now, and your sleeping pills showed up at the perfect time."

"Lovely, lovely. Now I have to finish getting ready for my bridge party," my mother said. "I'll ask where Hannah got her pantsuit, in any case. And I'll take a look in the Heine catalog to see if they have anything appropriate for the occasion. I'll call you later."

Under different circumstances I might have tried to protest, but why pick a fight now?

"Sure, Mama. You do that," I said. "And thanks for everything." I thought those would be dignified last words.

"That's what mothers are for," my mother said.

My dear, sweet Flo,

Do you remember that story about those Sioux children we read together, how they spoke to each other and even climbed a mountain in their dreams? Well, imagine, tonight I had a dream where I was talking with my future husband! He had an eagle's feather in his hair and bright, kind eyes. I knew right away he was the right one for me because my heart was beating like crazy.

"Stop dawdling away your time," he said. "Come here to the sacred mountain ash at the foot of Eagle's Mountain and marry me." (He said it in Sioux of course, but somehow I could still understand him!) "Because you and I are meant for each other," he added.

It was a wonderful dream. When I woke up, an eagle's feather lay on the pillow next to me, so obviously I booked the next flight to America. From the time I was little, I've always wanted to marry a Native American. I had just enough time to pack a couple of things (including the beaded headband you gave me, which is just the perfect thing!) and to write you this letter so that you won't wonder why I suddenly disappeared.

My future husband is the chief of a tribe called the Mahpiya, whose name more or less means "living in paradise." His name is Tawicasa, which means "clever handsome man holding his wife's hands." The Sioux always choose their names wisely. I'm so relieved I'm not meant for Tawicasa's brother Sicamnasi, whose name means "stinking feet"—I sure lucked out there!

What I was able to see of the Mahpiya village in my dream

was truly heavenly: a clear blue lake, grasslands, and forest, and behind them the snowy peak of majestic Eagle's Mountain, horses running free everywhere, and bunny rabbits hopping about among the colorfully embroidered tepees. And there were lots of bushes bursting with huckleberries. I also saw a couple of giant turtles. The youngest children in the tribe were riding on them.

As you can imagine, I'm crazy-excited about being a chief's wife, but unfortunately there isn't a telephone in the village, or a mailbox, and no cell phones. So that's why I'll miss you very much. But maybe we can speak to each other sometime in our dreams and share the latest news.

Always eat lots of vegetables.

Love,
Gerri
(whose name starting tomorrow will be Tawicu, which basically means "floating on clouds")

P.S. Dear Caroline and Bert,

Pets are good for the psychological development of a child. They encourage a sense of responsibility and generally strengthen the child's character. Good parents enable their children to have a pet, and Flo is the right age for a bunny rabbit. I printed a couple of articles on this topic that I found online, and they are enclosed for you. I hope very much that you won't deny a good, old friend's last wish.

Please don't give Flo the aquamarine ring until she turns eighteen, or even older. Until she's grown up and psychologically stable, it's better to let her persist in the belief that I'm alive and well in a Sioux village from two hundred years ago. Unlike some people,

I'm no fan of robbing children too soon of all their illusions, whether about the Easter Bunny, Santa Claus, or what the life of a single woman in Germany is like. And happily, it doesn't seem like you two have a problem with that, either; after all, you were able to convince the child of the existence of the Binky Fairy, who apparently needs used Binkies for newborn babies. I mean, HELLO? Gross!

SEVEN

It was a mistake to head back down to the lobby. A huge mistake, in fact. A huge mistake that cannot be made up for. And I did it out of nothing but vanity.

The fact was that I simply looked gorgeous. My hair, makeup, dress, shoes—the whole package was pure fabulousness! Honestly, I'd never looked better. My week of excessive alcohol consumption had helped my figure, because all the drinking had left me too nauseated to eat most of the time. The result was a nice, flat stomach and noticeably thinner face. The dark bags under my eyes made them look bigger. And the hairstylist had added caramel and pale-copper highlights, which looked fantastic.

Here on this last night of her life, she radiated heavenly beauty. No one who saw her would ever forget the vision. It was as though she had been enveloped by a magic spell, making her irresistible and untouchable at the same time.

It would have been the ultimate waste not to publicly materialize alive at least once in this dress. But I allowed myself to go downstairs among the strangers in the hotel, and then for just five minutes. While I was at it, I could throw out the empty packages from the sleeping pills, which I had individually pushed out of their aluminum-foil shells and laid out on the table in rows of five. Next to them stood the bottle of vodka, a bottle of sparkling mineral water, a water glass, and a shot glass.

I had dropped the good-bye letters into the mailbox in front of the hotel beforehand, each nicely in turn. I had spent a small fortune on postage for next-day delivery, there were so many—some of them in thick envelopes. Once I was done, the mailbox wouldn't hold any more mail.

I had made it in time for the six-o'clock mail pickup. It was now seven thirty, and I was dressed to the nines back in my room. All of my last words were safely on their way to their recipients.

Everything was going according to plan. There was nothing that could go wrong.

"I still have some time," I said to my reflection in the mirror. The floor-length mirror was gilded, providing a worthy frame for my form. "I can go downstairs and allow people to admire me a little, and then I will come back up to my room and get swallowing."

My reflection didn't object; instead, it coquettishly stroked its hair and smiled at me. I smiled back. The brilliant red lipstick looked striking on me. I always used to pick fairly subdued colors to avoid drawing attention to my large mouth—but even Julia Roberts and her big mouth wore bright red lipstick once in a while. And if ever I were going to risk doing something bold, then today was the day. . . .

I arrived in the lobby and threw the pill packages into a trash can. There were only two old ladies sitting in armchairs, and they looked as though they had forgotten their eyeglasses at home. And the girl at reception didn't give me a second glance. Two businessmen in suits came through the revolving door, but they both immediately turned left into the bar. They hadn't seen me at all. *Hello! This is your last chance to admire me alive!*

I should have simply turned around and headed back up to my room, but the sounds of a piano were wafting from the bar, and I somehow arrived at the demented notion of savoring one last glass of champagne, to set the mood, as it were. If the businessmen didn't notice me then, sitting on a barstool with my legs crossed, they were hopeless.

So I teetered in my amazing red shoes into the bar—directly toward my ruin, as it turns out, though I didn't yet realize it. Instead, I reveled in the appreciative gazes of the two businessmen, who had found seats at a table opposite the bar. Exactly as I had hoped! With a satisfied smile, I pulled myself up onto a barstool that put me in the middle of their view. *Well. That paid off.* The bartender also seemed to find me fabulous.

"A glass of champagne, please," I said, fluttering my eyelashes a bit.

"Coming right up," the bartender said.

I crossed my legs, smoothed my dress, and looked around. The space was steeped in cool, dim light and was divided into several plush niches. There wasn't much going on, but it was early. The espresso machine was making friendly gurgling sounds, the piano man was playing "As Time Goes By," and there was a couple making out, half-hidden behind a massive dracaena in the corner opposite the businessmen. I didn't mean to look at them, but the way they were making out, I worried their tongues had gotten stuck in each other's sinuses or something—disgusting.

The woman wore a classic little black dress and had red hair and freckles on her bare arms. She looked like Mia, actually. Then the man disengaged his tongue from her mouth, and she laughed. *The exact same laugh as Mia's.*

Wait a second!

Now I could make out the side of her face, and I instantly recognized her. There was no mistake—it *was* Mia.

But the guy she was with was not Ole. He had dark hair and was at least ten years older than she was.

"Your champagne," the bartender said.

No. Impossible. Mia was doing some kind of continuing ed in Stuttgart, and plus, she was happily married. The woman, who had stood and was now cuddled tight under one arm of the man as they walked past me, could not be Mia. *But she was.* She walked past me so closely that I could even smell her perfume.

I opened my mouth to say something, but Mia didn't notice me at all. The man was resting his hand on her behind, and she giggled as she vanished with him through the glass door and into the lobby.

"I'll be right back," I told the bartender, following Mia and the man as far as the door. I watched her talk to the girl at reception, get a key card, and walk toward the elevators, still practically intertwined with the man.

What should I do now? Shouldn't I at least tell Ole about this before going back upstairs and doing away with the only witness to this incident, namely me? Poor Ole thought his wife was taking class after class for work, but in reality she was cheating on him with an ass-grabbing guy who had an anteater's tongue. Oh no!

On the other hand, what business was it of mine? Maybe it was just a one-time thing. Ole might never find out and would go on to grow old with Mia—

At that moment, someone gently touched my arm. I squealed like a terrified piglet.

"Psst," the person said. "It's just me."

It was Ole.

I stared at him as though he were a ghost. But it really was him. His blond hair was as unruly as ever, and there was a faint cloud of dentist smell about him.

"Wh-what are you doing here?" I asked.

"I had dinner back there," Ole said, pointing to a far-removed niche. "I couldn't believe my eyes when you came in the door."

"Yes, but, but, Mia . . ." I stuttered.

"Yeah, Mia's here, too," Ole said. "With her lover."

I blinked at him, my mouth agape.

"Well, I was a little shocked at first, too," he said. "Come on, take your champagne and come sit with me in the corner. Then I'll tell you the whole sad story. The whole sad story of how I turned into a man who goes spying on his cheating wife."

"You, no, that's not . . . I . . . I've got something else planned," I said. Even though Ole was obviously a hot mess, it wouldn't take him long to ask what I was doing at this hotel. And then my plan would be in acute danger.

Ole tried to swipe his hair out of his face. "Oh, I'm sorry. Of course, you have a date. Joe's his name, right? You're probably waiting here for him."

I nodded.

"Oh, OK. I'm sure you've got a dozen things on your mind other than talking with me about my hopelessly screwed-up marriage. I understand." Ole looked as though tears were about to pour from his eyes.

"This really is a bad time," I said unhappily.

"Of course. Absolutely. I understand. It's just that, when I saw you come through the door, I thought it had to be a sign from heaven or something . . . A familiar face! Someone to help me shine bright light on this madness . . . I'm so sorry."

"No, no, it's fine," I said.

"That would have been too good to be true." Ole looked at his watch. "It's only quarter to eight. You know what? I'm just going to sit down here next to you at the bar and get drunk until your date shows up. When's Joe supposed to meet you?"

"Uh, at eight, actually," I said, resuming my position on the barstool despite the chaotic swirl of thoughts in my head. God, how was I going to get rid of Ole? I wished I had never had the harebrained idea of leaving my room at all. "But it's, uh, please don't be mad, but it would seem strange if we were both sitting here waiting for him, you know? I don't think that—"

"Oh, I understand, I understand," Ole said, taking the barstool next to me. "I don't want to spoil your date."

"Good," I said.

"Don't worry—I'll keep my eye on the door, and as soon as your date comes in, I'll act like I don't know you at all," Ole said. "I'll just be some random drunk guy who happens to be sitting next to you at the bar. Another whiskey, please," he continued, turning to the bartender. "A double. Or a triple, if you have that. Neat."

I took a sip of champagne. This really was an irritating confluence of coincidences. The *one* time I'm all set and ready to kill myself, and . . .

Maybe I should just yell, "Oh—there he is!" and storm out to the lobby, then flee up to my room before Ole even gets what's going on. That was the only escape I could think of.

I looked out through the glass door. A group of Japanese tourists was crowding into the lobby. This was my chance to bail.

"Oh, there he—" I began, but right then Ole burst into tears. He rested his head on my shoulder and started bawling. The bartender set the whiskey glass in front of us and shot me a sympathetic smile.

"Oh crap," I said.

"Tha-hat pretty much su-hums it u-hup," Ole sobbed. I let him cry for a while. Once I could feel his tears on my skin through my dress, though, I gently pushed him off.

"Hey, now," I said. "It's not as bad as that. Statistically, at least sixty percent of all women cheat on their husbands. And seventy percent of all men cheat on their wives."

Ole sniffled. "I never thought I'd be one of the sixty percent who are cheated on," he said. "I always thought Mia and I had something really special."

"But you do," I said. "Despite . . . everything."

"Oh yeah? Can I tell you something? This has been going on for years like this! She has been lying to me for years—I'm certain of that now. And stupid me, I never picked up on the slightest clue. And I would still be clueless if I hadn't been jogging past Aachen Pond in Inner Greenbelt Park yesterday morning, where I coincidentally ran into one of Mia's coworkers."

"Ah yes, always coincidentally," I said.

"No, really! I usually stick to the north end of the greenbelt and jog more around City Garden," Ole said. "Anyway, we had a nice conversation, Mia's coworker and I, but that's how I found out she didn't know anything about any continuing ed classes in Stuttgart—and then she asked if I had enjoyed Mia's and my trip to Paris last month."

"Oh? You didn't mention that to us, either."

"Because we didn't go to Paris at all!" Ole yelled. "Mia said she was off doing some more continuing ed, and I stayed home alone . . . Sorry, I didn't mean to yell at you like that."

"It's all right. So, she wasn't in Paris but at another class?"

"No! Don't you see? She's been lying through her teeth to me and everyone else. She tells everyone else that she's with me in Paris, and she tells me that she's taking a class. And in reality . . ."

"Oh," I said.

"Anyway, I went home and pretended I didn't know anything. At that point I didn't really know anything—yet. I thought maybe her coworker was confused, and everything was just a harmless . . . But then Mia took off again this

morning for Stuttgart for continuing education, and so I
followed her."

"All the way to Stuttgart?"

"No!" Ole yelled again. The businessmen at the table
looked over at us with curiosity. Ole lowered his voice again.
"Only as far as the closest parking garage. That's where she
left the car and then went shopping. Lingerie! Dark red!"

"Hmm," I said. "And you kept following her?"

Ole nodded. "Yes, I shadowed my wife like a sleazy second-
rate private eye. I followed her to the women's underwear
section at Kaufhof, and I had to duck behind shelves of bras
to hide. The other customers thought I was some pervert."

"Presumably," I said flatly. "I mean, oh no."

"My dentist office is closed today," Ole continued. "My
receptionist and the dental assistants spent the whole morning calling patients to cancel their appointments. Because
the dentist was out of the office today so he could go spy on
his wife." Ole sipped his whiskey. "What was I saying?"

"What happened after Mia bought lingerie?"

"She strolled through various boutiques so casually I
thought she may have just made up the class in Stuttgart so
she could go shopping in peace. But then, in that café on
Ehrenstraße, she met up with that guy."

"The one from before, here in the hotel?"

"Yes, of course, him," Ole said. "The first thing he did
when he saw Mia was thrust his tongue down her throat. I
didn't even have time to wonder if he were some cousin of
hers I hadn't met before."

"And then?"

"Oh, it was disgusting. They walked hand in hand to the next cab stand and came to this hotel."

"Why didn't they take her car?" I asked. "Or his?"

"I—no idea." Ole looked at me, irritated. "It doesn't matter. I think they were so hot for each other that they didn't want to waste any time, and they started feeling each other up in the cab. Plus, it's a pretty long haul from Ehrenstraße to the parking garage at Kaufhof, and maybe they didn't want to be seen. Anyway, they took a cab to this hotel. Do you know what a night here runs?"

I nodded.

"I hope that slimeball is at least paying," Ole said. "The lingerie was expensive enough."

"How were you able to follow the cab?" I asked.

"In another cab," Ole said. "I was kind of on autopilot, in shock."

"The cab driver must have been really happy, though," I said. "'Follow that car!' . . . I'm sure he's waited his whole career to hear those words."

"And I tipped him ten euros," Ole said. "Mia and that guy got a room and spent the whole morning in there. I was a total mess. I didn't know what to do."

"That's understandable," I said.

"So I sat here in the bar to wait. No idea what I thought I would do here, but my head didn't clear up at all, that's for sure. Then at some point the two of them strolled in here, too. I made myself inconspicuous in my corner, but they only had eyes for each other anyway. She kept letting out this odd giggle the whole time."

"Maybe his tongue was tickling her nose," I said.

"And then you came in," Ole said, ignoring me. "Like an angel in your red dress. I thought I must be seeing things! But I was also relieved. Honestly, I don't know what I would have done if you hadn't come in. I probably would have had it out with that guy and laid one into him."

"No, I don't believe that," I said.

"Eh . . . me neither," Ole said, collapsing on his stool. "I've just been cowering over in my corner, holding my breath. Ridiculous. God, what a pathetic wuss I am."

"You're not a wuss. You're just in shock."

"Yeah, that's true. Luckily you're here now." Ole tried to wipe the tears from his cheeks. "Oh God, this is so embarrassing. Seriously! You're here looking forward to a nice night on the town, and here I am bawling your ears off. It's really—well, I'm embarrassed and ashamed. I'm really sorry."

"It's fine, Ole. How about we hail you a cab outside so you can—"

Ole shook his head. He looked at his watch. "Punctuality really isn't his thing, huh. This Joe guy you're waiting for, I mean."

Ole seemed glued to his barstool like a limpet. I turned to the door. The Japanese tourists were gone. But there was a man standing at reception. I could run over there and pretend he was Joe. But then I noticed his ears stuck out in the most horrifying way, practically perpendicular from his head. Even from a distance they looked dreadful. I didn't want Ole to think I liked men with jug ears like that.

"Mia gets an employee discount at the Lexington," Ole said. "But she couldn't exactly be setting up rendezvous with

121

her lover there. Too bad for her, huh. Hey, can I get some more whiskey? A double and a triple, please."

"The question is why aren't they meeting at *his* house?" I said.

Ole shrugged. "Maybe he lives out of town, far away. Or his place is a pigsty."

"Or, the man is also married," I said.

"Oh my God," Ole said. "What an *asshole.*"

"I assume Mia and he are looking at it as nothing more than an affair. Their marriages are important to them, and they don't want to give them up," I suggested. "If you pretend you don't know anything, everything will stay the way it was, and you'll still be able to grow happy and old together."

"Are you out of your mind?" Ole yelled. "What kind of a sick relationship would we have then?" He looked at his watch again. "Maybe Joe is stuck in traffic. Where's he coming from?"

Straight from hell. With his scythe.

"From, uh, Frankfurt," I said.

"Oh God," Ole said. "Tell me he doesn't have a Hessian accent. I remember the time you said that's a total turnoff for you."

"Yes, Hessian accents are. But no, Joe speaks perfect High German. He comes from, uh, Bremen originally."

"Either way, he's not here yet," Ole said. "It's just not classy keeping a lady waiting. Alone in a bar."

Ole was starting to get on my nerves. "Listen, Ole, I'm happy to wait for him alone. If I were you, I'd go home now."

"Out of the question," Ole said. "I'm not going to leave you sitting here by yourself in a bar, with strange men gawking at you."

"No one's doing any gawking here," I said.

"Of course they are. Everyone gawks. Those two guys over there have been drooling like dogs at you the whole time. And that dress is . . . pretty hot."

"Hmm, thanks," I said.

"Seriously. I've never seen you in a dress like that. Or in shoes like that."

"Oh, these? They're ancient," I said.

"And you also got your hair done," Ole said. "Mia just got her hair done, too. Yesterday." His whiskey came, and he took two small sips. "How old do you think he is?"

"Joe?"

"No, Mia's lover. He looked old, huh?"

"Midforties, late forties, I'd guess."

"Old bastard," Ole said. "He's presumably going through his midlife crisis with Mia. How old is Joe, then?"

"Thirty-five," I said. That was the number of sleeping pills waiting for me back up in my room, wondering where in heaven I was.

"Ugh, where is that guy?" Ole asked. "He could at least call if he's late."

"I left my cell up in my room," I said. "I'd better go get it."

Ole looked at me, dumbfounded. "You got a room here?"

"Um, yes."

"But why? You could have Joe over to your apartment. Or—oh no. Don't tell me you two are having a secret affair yourselves."

"Don't be ridiculous," I said. "You all know about it."

"He's married, then, right?"

"No," I said. "No, no!"

Ole didn't say anything, but it was somehow a pitying silence. The piano man was playing "As Time Goes By" again. That was probably the only song he could play. I wanted out.

"Would you like another glass of champagne?" the bartender asked.

"No, thank y—*Oh, all right.* "Fill 'er up," I said, sighing. I couldn't just go upstairs and kill myself while Ole was sitting here all lovesick and going through hell. I had to make sure he got home safely at least and didn't do anything to himself. "Are you going to wait here the whole night for Mia?"

"Dunno," Ole said.

"I don't think that's a good idea," I said.

"I'm taking suggestions."

"It'd be better to go home and think things over in peace."

"Think about what?" Ole asked. "About what a complete idiot I am?"

"For example," I said.

Ole flagged the bartender for another whiskey. "But I like it here," he said.

All right then. I had plenty on my plate; I didn't need to shoulder Ole's problems as well. Images flashed in my head of my good-bye letters being machine-sorted and organized by postal code. What was I doing down here, anyway? Was I totally bonkers?

"I'm going now," I said with resolve.

"Where to?" Ole stared at me, shocked.

"To my room. I'm going to call Joe."

"No, stay with me, Gerri. Please."

"No, I can't."

"All right, yeah, I get it. Of course you can't. Sorry." Ole looked at his watch. "But I don't think he's coming. That married piece of shit stood you up."

"That may be," I said. "But that's why I want to call him."

"So he *is* married! I knew it. What a piece of shit. He's lying to his wife and just taking advantage of you. A woman like you, downgraded to a mistress. And even then he can't show up on time." Ole bent forward over the bar. "Hey, you," he said to the bartender. "Did you get a load of that? That married piece of shit stood her up."

"He did not," I said, sliding off my barstool. "Would you bill the champagne to my room?" I asked the bartender. "Room three twenty-four. Tip yourself."

The bartender nodded his thanks.

"No, no," Ole said. "It's on me."

"Take a taxi home, Ole," I said.

"I love you so much," Ole said. "You are the loveliest person I know. And beautiful and smart and funny. Joe is way, way beneath you."

"It's too late," I said, kissing him on the cheek. One last whiff of dentist. I almost started to cry. But I had to stay firm now. "*Auf Wiedersehen*, Ole. Everything will be OK. You'll see. And don't do anything stupid."

"No, no. Don't worry, Gerri. I'll call you later when I'm thinking clearly again."

I bit my lower lip and tottered on my high heels over to the door.

"I'll be here if you need me," he called after me.

Dear Mrs. Köhler,

I know that you asked me to call you Aunt Annemarie years ago, but since I already have so many real aunts, I've never felt the need to assume that level of familiarity with you. Especially since I know you've never been able to stand me, ever since I refused to go to prom with Klaus.

That is an old misunderstanding that I would like to clear up once and for all here and now: I did NOT "change my mind at the last minute" and without warning leave poor Klaus without a date. To the contrary. I made very clear both to Klaus and to my mother—more than once—that I would have rather eaten a pound of writhing slugs than go to prom with a boy who (1) always sticks his butt out when he dances, like a duck taking a dump; (2) smells as though he hasn't taken a bath in more than two years; (3) picks his nose and squeezes the zits on his neck whenever the band takes a break; and (4) despite all those characteristics, still finds himself irresistible. You can take credit for No. 4; that took some parenting.

However, that characteristic is also exactly what drove Klaus in the first place to stand outside my door on the night of the prom holding a bouquet of flowers at the same time that Georg Straub was standing outside my door also holding a bouquet of flowers. (As an aside I know you'll enjoy: Although Georg Straub did smell good, he always miscounted the steps for the rumba, and he practically trampled my toes flat during the tango.)

It's not true that I opened the door and started to laugh. It's also not true that I yelled, "Ha-ha, Klaus, you fell for it! What an idiot!"

Actually, I had the shock of my life seeing two boys at once standing outside my door holding bouquets of flowers. Klaus completely ignored Georg and his bouquet of flowers. He casually picked his nose and said, "Are you ready, Gerri?" And was I ready! To sledgehammer some sense into him, that is.

"Klaus," I said. "I have already told you I did not want to go to prom with you." And Klaus said, "But I didn't think you were being serious. Are you coming?"

What should I have done, Mrs. Köhler? I mean, Georg was standing right there. I had to think of him, my *actual* date. How would it have been fair for Georg or me to take the blame for *Klaus's* ignorance? Do you see? My mother did try to bribe Georg to go home, by waving a fifty-euro bill at him, but Georg's parents were already down in their car, waiting to drop us off at the dance. And under no circumstances did I step into that car laughing at Klaus. I was extremely, deeply depressed. And I did not flip Klaus off!

But this story still had a happy ending. How fortunate it was that Hannah Kopuski was somehow ready to step in "for me" at the last minute. It was in her best interest, of course, and that date evolved into a blessing for your whole family, especially Klaus. I heard that Hannah has been showing off in her fashionable beige pantsuit, standing in for someone during your weekly bridge party. But did you know she has a head for business as well? In fact, the night of the prom she successfully negotiated to save Klaus's honor and got my mother to up her fifty to a hundred-euro bill instead.

Have a nice life.

Sincerely,
Gerri Thaler

P.S. Enclosed please find a copy of *Claudia the Night Nurse: On Suspicion*. Juliane Mark is one of my pseudonyms. I'm quite proud of being a successful romance writer; I do not in fact run a transcription service.

EIGHT

The first thing I did back in my hotel room was take off my shoes and jump onto the bed. I was totally rattled.

Until then I had assumed no one I knew was worse off than I was. But I had to admit Ole was in pretty bad shape. It was certainly unpleasant to find out his wife had been lying to him. That the love of his life was cheating on him in a thoroughly despicable way.

On the other hand, it was better to have loved and lost than never to have loved, as they say. Right? And even though he was particularly worse off than I was *today*, Ole still had only a couple of days of a broken heart to get through, while *I* had a whole life of neurotic depression to look forward to. And that was of course much worse.

I mean, dozens of women would stand in line for a chance to pounce on the good-looking blond dentist, once he was free again. But who would ever be standing in line for me?

That's what I'm saying. And that's why it was my right to end my life to stop any further immiseration.

I put my shoes back on and combed my hair. My makeup was still perfect; just my lipstick needed a quick touch-up. It was twenty to nine. If everything went well, I would fall fast and sound asleep by eleven at the latest. Forever and always.

She was like a newly blossomed rose whom no one wanted to pick, whose scent no one wanted to admire. And now she would wilt overnight, and all her petals would go with the wind.

That's what people would get out of this.

Oddly enough, at that moment a molar in the back left of my mouth started aching. I ran my tongue over it. Just what I needed! I'd had that filling replaced last year. By Ole. Then the aching stopped. *Whew.*

I sat solemnly in front of the coffee table where the sleeping pills were arranged, and I poured sparkling mineral water into the tall glass and vodka into the shot glass.

"Here's to you!" I said to my reflection in the mirror. My reflection looked back at me, a bit skeptical.

"Let's get going," I said. "Don't be shy. We've thought through everything in great detail. There is no other way. Things will only get worse, week by week, year by year."

My reflection still looked skeptical.

"Jobless, husbandless, homeless, childless," I said. "And once everyone gets their good-bye letters, we'll be friendless to boot. There is no way back anymore. Lonely, neurotic, depressed, old, and wrinkled—is that what you want us to become?"

My reflection shook its head. All right then.

Let's get started.

I poured the vodka down my throat, exactly the way I'd trained. *Eww, nasty.* And now the pills. I would start with the pink ones, work my way gradually to the light blue ones, and then nosh on the rows of whitish-gray speckled ones.

Between each pill I would take a sip of water, and a shot glass of vodka.

Pill No. 1: Place on tongue, swallow, wash down. Done.

Pill No. 2: Set on tongue—

Someone knocked at the door.

I had not foreseen this in my plan, which is why I sat still on my chair with my tongue stuck out, hoping that the knocking was for the room next door. But it wasn't. The knocking started again, this time louder and longer.

"Gerri? Gerri? Are you in there?" someone called from the hallway. It was Ole. Oh God! No! Here I was, sitting with my tongue hanging out, so terrified I couldn't move.

"Gerri! It's me, Ole!" he yelled. "I know you're in there. Come on, open up! Otherwise I'll get arrested for disturbing the peace. Gerri! I've got to tell you something. Gerri!"

Now I was getting angry. I retracted my tongue, swallowed the pill, and forgot to wash it down.

"Go away, Ole," I said with a dry mouth, but Ole couldn't hear me. He kept knocking like someone possessed.

"Gerri! Open up, Gerri!"

I stood. I had to go get rid of him. Otherwise he would stand there the whole night, knocking and yelling.

"No Zherrri herrre! I am Yushenka. Go avay, orrr I call police," I said through the door.

"Oh thank God, it's you, Gerri," Ole said back through the door. "Come on, open up! I really have to talk to you."

"It's not a good time," I said. "Get lost!"

"What for? I know that Joe hasn't come; I've been keeping an eye on the lobby the whole time. You're alone! Open up; let me in; people are starting to give me weird looks."

Apparently some of them were walking down the hallway outside my door. "Evening," Ole said to them. "Don't worry; I'm not always like this. It's just that my wife cheated on me today, and so I got myself drunk. Not very original, I know, but I couldn't think of anything better. Do you have any suggestions? Yeah, well, wipe that stupid look off your face. You've got a cavity in tooth three on the upper right. I can see it from here."

This was unbearable. If Ole kept verbally accosting hotel guests about their dental hygiene, it was only a matter of time until the hotel staff showed up, and I did *not* want that. I opened the door.

"What took you so long?" Ole asked, pushing his way into the room. "Were you naked?"

"No, I had just . . ." *Oh God! The pills!* I stormed past Ole to the coffee table and swept them into my hand with one swift motion. At least half of them landed on the floor.

But Ole didn't notice at all. He just plopped ponderously onto the queen bed. "I had this brilliant idea when I was downstairs," he said. "While I was sitting there looking out into the lobby, keeping watch for your Joe, I came up with the most genius idea of all time."

"To come up here and sleep the booze off?" I asked, tossing the pills into the drawer of one of the nightstands. Then I bent over and gathered the rest.

"No, something much better," Ole said. "It occurred to me how I could catch three stones with one bird. What are you doing over there? Did you lose your contacts? Wait, I'll help you."

"No! No!" I yelled furiously, dropping all the pills I had gathered. "I don't wear contacts. I'm just picking up, uh, crumbs . . ."

"Is that so," Ole said. "Anyway, you've been stood up by this Joe guy, right? Am I right? And Mia's been cheating on me. The countless ways the fates have somehow brought all of us here, to this hotel. Are you following me so far?"

"They've brought us all here, except for Joe," I said.

"Yeah, yeah. Where is he?" Ole asked. "Let me guess: One of his kids has measles, right? That's what they all say, those married assholes."

"He doesn't have kids," I said, nonchalantly using my foot to sweep more pills under the coffee table. Ole was unlikely to find them; his powers of perception were severely inhibited currently. "And he's not married. But he may be here any moment."

"What?" Ole sat up. "Seriously?"

I nodded. *And he has a black belt,* I wanted to add so that Ole would get lost. But unfortunately getting lost was the last thing on Ole's mind.

"Ha-ha, almost fell for it," he said, plopping back onto the bed. "That must be some traffic jam he's in, at this hour. Hey, listen. You don't need to feel shy with me, Gerri-Berry. It happens to the best and best-looking of us, being stood up and duped hook, line, and sinker."

"Oh, *please.*"

"It's true, it's true. Just look at me! I'd never have thought my wife would be cheating on me with such a butt-ugly guy. I mean, look at me: I really am better-looking," Ole said. "With all due modesty, I really am the best-looking guy around. And I'm a *dentist* on top of that. I'm not the guy who gets cheated on."

"Ole, I know this has been a terrible shock to you, and I'd love to discuss your self-appreciation with you more . . . at another time, though, because now—"

"First listen to my brilliant plan. It'll make you feel better in no time. Do you believe in karma?"

"Ole! I really would very much like to be alone," I said, yawning. Oh no—were the sleeping pills starting to work already?

"Don't blame yourself for some shortcoming or other," Ole said. "It doesn't have anything to do with who you are that this Joe guy is being so rude to you, believe me. You're truly great, and I doubt Joe wants anything more than to marry you and dump his wife, that ballbuster. But it's too late now. His loss. Asshole. Should've given some thought to things sooner. You do always seem to get a bad hand when it comes to guys, Gerri. I have to say. You're kind of a shit magnet, really. You attract guys who have no sense of responsibility and just want to have fun. Guys who only want to exploit your youth and beauty without giving anything themselves."

I laughed aloud.

"Say, isn't there a minibar in this luxury suite?"

"Yes, over there," I said. "But a seven-ounce bottle of Coke costs over seven euros."

"I don't want *Coke*," Ole said, rolling onto his stomach and crawling from the bed directly to the minibar without standing. "I want whiskey. I'm used to the whiskey now. I don't care what it costs. I'm rich. Yup, I'm a rich man. A good-looking rich man! That's probably why that redheaded whore married me, too." He opened the mini refrigerator. "No whiskey. Just red wine and champagne. And beer. *Bleagh.* I'm calling room service. That's the least they can do for you in a place like this. Where's the phone?"

"Could I offer you a glass of vodka?" I said, pouring my expensive vodka into a water glass.

"Vodka's good," Ole said, taking a long drink. "I'll cover the room charge for it, too. Now, pay attention. So, karma izz when nothing happens by accident. And this here," he said, moving his hands around in circles, "iz karma. All this. So the plan iz, while Mia iz off with her love, and your lover iz off with his wife, the two of us, that iz, you and me, will spend the night together. Here in this hotel room. Tonight. What do you think? Izzat brilliant or what?"

"That's—the stupidest thing I've ever heard," I said. "You're acting like a child. It's like you're saying, 'Hey, Mia, I can do whatever you do, too—neener-neener-neener.' Except that your plan doesn't really benefit me in any way."

"Yes it does. You're showing Joe," Ole said. "Don't you see? That'z what he gets for just leaving you waiting. Once he sees that you can effortlessly land a good-looking dentist who drives a Porsche . . ."

"But Joe won't ever know anything about it," I said.

"Well, yeah, maybe not directly," Ole said, scratching his head. "But indirectly, definitely. Karma! There are no coincidences! Don't you see? It's the pince- . . . prince- . . . *principle.*"

"No," I said.

"Come on! It'z not that hard! Tomorrow morning Mia will be downstairs getting her Continental breakfast with her asshole lover, and you and I'll be sitting there, in love and holding hands. And I'll be gently feeding you bites of my orange-cranberry scone. Then Mia will see how iddiz."

"Yeah, I get it," I said. "You want to make Mia jealous. But as I said, I think it's childish and unnecessary. I'm not playing along."

"But think about how *brilliant* iddiz," Ole yelled. "She won't be able to make a scene because she'd be giving herself away. Imagine you're cheating on your husband, and the next morning you find out he's cheating on you, too— same night, same hotel. It'z perfect for a movie, you know?"

"Listen, Ole," I said. "I understand that you're in the mood for revenge. But don't try to tell me it's all about karma and your plan benefits me somehow."

"Well, yeah, maybe not directly," Ole said again, emptying his glass.

"Not directly?"

"Fine, OK. You'll play an uncredited role. But Mia doesn't like you anyway, you know? You don't have anything to lose."

"That's not what it's about—" I stopped talking. "Mia doesn't like me? Really? Why not?"

Ole started giggling. "She thinks you're in love with me. Too funny, right? I mean, *all* women are in love with *me*."

"Um, no," I said, angry. Well, fine, I *was* in love with Ole, but I had truly never, ever let on. "Where did Mia get that idea from?"

"Well, because we sort of used to date," Ole said. "You and I."

"Yes, but only sort of," I said. I hadn't forgotten. "But then Mia turned back up."

"That'z right," Ole said, holding his empty glass toward me. I poured more vodka into it. "Right when things were going so nicely. Typical Mia. She cannot *stand* it when someone has something she doesn't, down to the dirt under their fingernails."

"You didn't have to start dating Mia again when she came back," I said, a little irritated. I remembered the night Ole told me he and Mia were getting back together. At the time my jaw had simply fallen open, I was so surprised. Because I had considered the Mia chapter closed.

"Yes, I did—oh, izza long story."

"Well, please don't tell me now," I said. The night Ole dumped me, I had planned on moving us to the next level by dropping one of the classic lines. Something like "Are you coming up for a nightcap?" But instead all I did was say, "Oh, that's great—I'm so happy for you," and "Of course we can still be friends"—even though I wasn't sure we could. It was a really terrible time for me.

"No, no, I want to tell you," Ole said. "The story needs telling. Why do you think we rushed to get married so quickly, hmm?"

"Because— Oh! Was Mia *pregnant*?" Ole was offering up some all-new insights here.

"Yup," he said. "She said so, at least. But then she wasn't pregnant after all." He puffed the blond strands of hair off his forehead. Temporarily. "And I was really happy, because there was no way I could be sure the kid was mine. See, we had broken up because Mia had fallen temporarily in love with some other guy. That'z the way she iz, Mia. Everything always temporary. I'mana take my shoes off, 'K?"

I shook my head. "I still want you to go. I'm tired." And that was the truth. I was dead tired. Damned sleeping pills. They couldn't be working this fast.

"That'z so typical of you." Ole slipped off his shoes and blinked his eyes lovingly at me. "You think it'd be immoral if we carried out my plan. And you want to keep me from doing something immoral. You're so sweet. Such an upstanding person. Unlike Mia. You're a real angel. God, I'd like to lay one into that Joe."

"And me into you," I said angrily, but Ole didn't hear.

"Know what? I'm going to shake a tower now, and then we can do some spooning all cozy in bed and talk about what a wonderful person you are," he said, already relieving himself of his attire. "Izz too bad I don't have my toothbrush with me. Couldn't plan for everything, huh."

Helplessly, I watched Ole get undressed in poorly coordinated movements and pepper a chair with his things before he turned around to face me, buck naked, and ask, "Can I use your toothpaste?"

"Makeup case," I said, looking away. "But you'll be sorry if you even touch my toothbrush."

"Don't worry. I'll use my finger, cuddlebugs," Ole said, staggering into the bathroom. He'd hardly closed the door when I leaped back to life. I took a deep breath, summoned all my remaining strength, and dropped to the floor frantically gathering pills and throwing them into the nightstand drawer with the others, next to the Bible. Then I counted them. Thirty-one! I'd swallowed two. Where were the two that were missing? One had rolled over to the dresser, but the other was just gone. I couldn't find it anywhere. I swore up a storm. Those pills were my most valuable possessions. They were my ticket to the beyond. I just couldn't swallow them *at the moment,* unfortunately. Ole would notice something was wrong, and then they'd pump my stomach and lock me in the psych ward.

But what else could I do?

What if I pulled myself together, packed everything, and took off before Ole came out of the bathroom? I could throw the pills into my purse, put on my shoes, and sprint to the elevator. I could take a taxi to another hotel and then, without any interruption . . .

I hadn't finished the thought before Ole came sauntering back into the room, a towel around his waist.

"Man," he said. "A shower like that almost makes you feel sober again."

"Ole, Ole . . . if you're sober, then please be a good boy and take a taxi home," I said with another yawn. My body felt like lead, but pleasantly like lead. All the tension that I'd been carrying in my shoulders the past few weeks had vanished.

"I'm not that sober yet, not by a long shot," Ole said. "I'm guessing my blood alcohol is up to point-two by now. Plus, my plan is still great. Mia is going to have such a stupid look on her face. And it'll be a lesson for Joe, too."

"God, Ole. You are such an ignoramus. Keep Joe out of it. Don't you get that he won't ever find out? But Mia will probably take out a mob hit on me or something. Did you think about that? And I don't want anything to do with any of it!"

"Yes, I do get it!" Ole looked at me, innocently. "But can't I be selfish for once in my life? You know this is a one-time opportunity—you can't just pass it by. Mia won't do anything to you. And if she does hire a killer, she'll sic him on me. And you only have to *pretend* we've got something going on."

"Obviously," I said.

"Please, please, Gerri. Do it for me," Ole said, filling his vodka glass again. "I'll handle your teeth for free for the rest of your life. Only the very best ceramic inlays. I mean, you have perfect teeth there otherwise, cuddlebugs. Have I ever told you that?"

"Yes, at my last checkup," I said. "And stop calling me cuddlebugs."

"Sorry, cuddlebugs," Ole said. "I'm saying that only 'cause I'm drunk. And 'cause I always wanted to call you that. Whoa—hold on there, baby!"

My knees had suddenly turned wobbly. Not unpleasantly wobbly, more relaxed wobbly. I plopped down onto the bed.

"You had only two glasses of champagne," Ole said. "Between the two of us, you're the sober one. So you'll have to swat my hand if I have any indecent thoughts. I'm counting on you."

"But I'm too tired to have any indecent thoughts myself," I said, falling backward onto the bed. "Boy, the pink ones work fast."

"Sorry? Hey, you're not going to fall asleep on me now, are you? The night is still young. It's only nine thirty. What about our party?"

I slid my shoes off, unzipped my dress, and wriggled out of my couture while on my back. "Could you hang that over the chair for me, please?" I said, keeping my eyes open with effort. "It cost four hundred forty euros."

Ole picked up the dress and laid it behind him on the chair. "Listen, Gerri. If you're planning on taking more clothes off, I can't guarantee anything," he said.

"Just my bra," I said, my eyes already closing. "Otherwise I can't breathe."

"Me either," Ole said. "Oh wow!" he added as I slid my bra off.

I tried to open my eyes again, but I couldn't. "I'm going to go to sleep now for a while," I said. "And I want you to behave appropriately while I sleep, is that clear?"

"Then pull up the covers," Ole said. "I'm only a man, after all."

I pulled up the covers. God, this bed was cozy. The pillows smelled freshly washed, and when did I ever sleep in ironed sheets?

"You're squishing the mint they left on the pillow," Ole said.

"Turn out the light, cuddlebugs," I said.

"OK, I'll be right to bed," Ole said. "Just another glass of vodka so I really don't pounce on you."

I wanted to say something, but I had already fallen asleep.

Dear Aunt Hulda,

I'm Gerri, the youngest daughter of your niece Dorothea—you remember who I am, the only one who isn't blonde, the one responsible for the Meissen porcelain debacle.

Of all my great-aunts, you are the one I like most. You're also the only aunt I can tell apart from all the others. Maybe because you didn't opt for the standard white curly hairdo and because you still use lipstick and mascara, even though you're well past eighty. And because you have honest laugh lines and you smoke gold-tipped cigarillos. Because you prefer having a proper conversation instead of endlessly bewailing diseases, and because you tell pretty good jokes about Uncle Gustav and Cousin Harry. But maybe also because you don't have a senile great-uncle at your side who goes around patting every woman under fifty he meets on her behind.

Why didn't you ever get married, Aunt Hulda?

"You'll end up like Aunt Hulda" is a saying in the family, actually; people have told me that at least a thousand times. Like the time I pushed Clemens Diederichs into the stinging nettles in first grade because he wanted to kiss me, even though he had eaten a tuna fish sandwich right beforehand. And of course that time with Klaus Köhler . . . It doesn't matter. Anyway, almost every day since I turned thirty I must have heard the words "You'll end up like Aunt Hulda."

Well, guess what? That would be great! You can be sure that I would NOT be killing myself if I knew I could end up like you. As a rich great-aunt with honest laugh lines. I bet men have been throwing themselves at your feet for your whole life. I bet you were practically besieged with offers of exciting love affairs.

And all the magnificent clothes and hats, the giant country homes, and all the wonderful voyages to the Riviera, India, and New York! Under those circumstances, I imagine it didn't hurt as much that you had to forgo children. I would have really liked to have children myself. (Is it true, incidentally, that you once had syphilis, or is that another family rumor, like the one that I'm a lesbian?)

But times have changed, Aunt Hulda. Nowadays women no longer need to choose between all or nothing, money or love, children or career, muscles or brains, adventure or decency— nowadays it seems like the only choices are between Klaus Köhler and *rockinhard12*, or between cow pies and farm slurry, hell and purgatory. And no one, no one pays your way.

So that's why I don't want to keep on living. For those reasons, and because I'm a neurotic depressive and don't want to take drugs that make my hair fall out.

But I do believe in love, Aunt Hulda. I firmly believe in it.

As you may know, there has always been a lot of speculation among my mother, her sisters, and all their cousins about your will and their potential inheritance, which is why we always had to send you postcards from vacations or banal handicrafts for Christmas and thank you effusively for the tights that you always sent on our birthdays. You were supposed to develop only the best impression of us, which is why I was never allowed to tell you what I did for a living. But do you know what? I'm proud of my work. I don't run a "small transcription service," as my mother always says—I write romance novels. No one in the family has ever made an effort to read my books, either; they all claim they read only Franz Kafka and Thomas Mann. But I wonder if you might not enjoy them, so I've enclosed large-print editions of

Sophia's First Kiss and *Angela the Children's Nurse* for you. You should be able to read them even without eyeglasses.

All my love,
Gerri

NINE

When I opened my eyes, at first I couldn't remember where I was. But when I remembered, I shut them again.

Ole was lying next to me in bed; I could smell him even with my eyes shut. A mixture of vodka-whiskey sweat and dentist smell—not nearly as unpleasant as it sounds, actually. Ole wasn't snoring, but he was breathing hard and loudly.

I breathed in rhythm with him for a while.

Nothing was right. He wasn't supposed to be here; I wasn't supposed to be here. Not alive, at least.

I wasn't at all happy I was still alive. Now everything was even worse than before. And my molar was hurting again. Ow.

"Typical," I said softly, sitting up. It was already light out. The drapes were pulled back, and for the first time I took in the truly magnificent view of the Rhine. A barge was slowly moving upriver, its navigation lights already fading in the morning light. The sky was clear and blue. It was going to be a beautiful, warm spring day.

Germany's postal employees had long been at work sorting good-bye letters into mailbags being loaded into Germany's yellow mail vans and onto Germany's yellow mail bikes.

At the thought of mailmen on their morning rounds, I forgot to exhale for a while. *All right. Don't panic!* All was not lost—yet. I slowly leaked the air out of my lungs. If my pills and I could somehow sneak from the hotel and I found a quiet spot to swallow them before Ole woke up, I could still get back on track.

But then another thought hit me like a brick to the head: I had no money to pay for this hotel room. They would arrest me for sneaking out. And they'd search me at the police station and charge me with illegal trafficking in sleeping pills.

I forced myself to exhale. *Things weren't that bad.* I did have my MasterCard. I could casually stroll out of here and pay my bill. Even though in Germany people generally had to pay their credit cards in full each month, by the time the money was direct-debited out of my checking account, I would be long dead and buried.

It couldn't be this hard to kick the bucket, dammit!

At least the tooth pain had stopped again. Cautiously, I rose to my feet. I had expected my head to be throbbing with pain, but I had no pain at all. I felt comparatively well rested, even refreshed. Those pink pills were good—I recommend them without reservation.

I took a step back in horror once I saw myself in the mirror, however. Not so much because I was naked, except for my panties, but because I hadn't wiped off my makeup before conking out the previous night. Mascara and eye shadow were smudged all over my face.

I looked at Ole. He was sound asleep. And no wonder, after everything he'd tossed back last night. Well, fine. Then

I'd be the first to enjoy a shower and would also have a chance to sort out my thoughts.

The warm water felt wonderful. My panic abated a bit. I still had a couple of hours until the first good-bye letter would be opened and the alarm sounded. Apart from Ole, no one knew where I was, and since no one knew what Ole knew, no one would think to ask him where I was. Had I written anyone that I was planning on holing up in a hotel room? I couldn't remember. But if so, they would probably start scouring every hotel in the city looking for me. Should I drive a bit farther out of town? I could catch a cab at Central Station and jump onto the next train leaving town. No matter where it was going, there would surely be a hotel room where I could take my pills. I had thirty-two left; that would have to suffice. The two pills I had taken last night had put me out like a light.

So, yes, I could still make it. Keep calm, get out of the shower, get into some clothes, put the pills into my purse, and then get out of here. Cab, station, train, hotel—done!

I hastily dried off and sneaked back into the room.

"Gerri? Is that really you, or is this one of my dirty dreams?" Ole was up and looking at me with bloodshot eyes.

Shit! Shit! Shit!

"This is one of your dirty dreams," I whispered. "You are still sound asleep. Close your eyes . . ."

"Ugh . . . not so loud . . ." Ole said. "Honestly, my head is about to explode. You don't happen to have an aspirin, do you?"

"Sleep! *Sleep!*" I implored. "This is a dream . . . You're *tired*, your eyes are getting *heavy*, you want nothing more than to *sleep* . . ."

"You're naked," Ole said.

"Because this is a dream," I said.

"Hmm," Ole said skeptically. "You're naked. This is a hotel room. And I'm naked, too." To verify the latter, he checked himself under the covers.

"Yes, yes. Dirty dream. Sleep, Ole. Just sleep, soon the moon will rise. . . ." I murmured.

"Now I remember," Ole said. "Mia and her lover, the hotel, the bar, you . . ."

"It was all just a dream," I said. "Now, if you could just fall back asleep . . ."

"Oh my God," Ole said. "It's all coming back now, and I feel like the wind has been knocked out of me."

"Me, too," I said, plopping down onto my side of the bed, burying my face in my hands. *I must be jinxed!*

"But it serves Mia right," Ole said. "And I won't tell her so, but you're a lot better than she is."

"At what?" I asked.

"Well, in the sack," Ole said. "You're a regular grenade in bed!"

If only, I thought. I mean, geez, I had taken *sleeping pills*—not an aphrodisiac. And I was 100 percent sure that Ole had not laid a finger on me. Well, 99.9 percent sure . . . I had been zonked, after all. But it was sleep, not general anesthesia. I would have woken up if Ole had touched me. At least, if he had touched me *inappropriately*. But he couldn't possibly have. It was miracle enough that he'd even found his way into bed, drunk as he had been.

But Ole was busy constructing himself a new reality. "I always suspected. Mia is basically—she's more just so . . . Well, she's boring. It's not at all true what they say about redheads."

"Ole, I think you're not remembering everything," I said. "You drank a hell of a lot of vodka."

"True, but I do remember everything," Ole said stubbornly. "Every detail."

"Oh yeah?"

"I remember taking your dress off you, no, ripping each other's clothes off and together . . . We also took a shower together, under the shower, and th-then—oh my God, are you crying?"

I peered at him through my fingers. "No. I don't cry. I'm just thinking that our memories of last night are a bit askew."

"What are you trying to say? Wasn't I any good?" Ole scratched his head, embarrassed. "It was the alcohol, Gerri! Normally I'm much better, honest."

"No, I mean, we didn't . . . What are you doing?"

Ole had grabbed the telephone. "I need some aspirin. Actually, a few aspirin. And a toothbrush. A good hotel will be able to send those up, right?"

In fact, the person who answered told him they'd have both items up within ten minutes. "All right," Ole said, smiling at me. "I'm going to grab a shower. And—Gerri? I'm so sorry. Last night I was just . . . well, I was just a shadow of myself."

"Ole, you weren't at all . . . Oh, forget it!" It was wasted effort. Ole would never accept the reality that we had only *slept* beside each other all night, lifeless like two dead bodies.

Apropos *dead:* I could take off while he was in the shower. Even before he had closed the door to the bathroom all the way, I'd jumped up and started scurrying around like a headless chicken. Pills, cab, station, hotel . . .

Where were my clothes? I had to wear what I'd changed out of when I got to the hotel: jeans, my black T-shirt with Kermit the Frog on it, black sneakers. I also had to put my bra back on, before the clothes of course. *Concentrate, dammit!* And the most important thing—the pills. It would take forever to pick them out of the drawer one by one, but I could just dump them right into my bag if I pulled the nightstand drawer out.

Dammit! It's one of those drawers you can't pull out all the way! Why does a luxury hotel have a shitty two-star-motel nightstand! I pulled with all my strength, and *whoosh!* I flew halfway through the room with the drawer. Pills rained down onto the windowsill, and the Bible was catapulted over to the far wall.

The expletive "Goddammit!" passed my lips.

There was a knock at the door. "Room service!"

"Can you get that, Gerri?" Ole yelled as the shower stopped running.

"I can't just now," I said while trying to shove the drawer back in and sweep the pills off the windowsill and bed.

Ole stepped naked and wet out of the bathroom. "I'll get it," he said, opening the door to a young man in a uniform who acted as though it were completely normal to be greeted by a stark-naked hotel guest.

"A package of aspirin and one toothbrush, sir."

"Thank you so much. Could you please charge it to the room?" Ole grabbed his wallet from his pants hanging over a chair and handed the man a ten-euro tip.

I managed to force the drawer back onto its tracks before Ole was done at the door, but the pills were strewn all over the room. I kicked a few under the bed so he wouldn't step on them and start asking me unpleasant questions.

But Ole was totally oblivious to the pills. "I'll be feeling better in no time now," he said, closing the door behind the room service attendant.

"How nice for you," I said.

"Are you angry at me? I would understand if you are. I really haven't acted like . . . a gentleman. I mean, first I bawl your ears off, and then . . . But I'm only a man, and you're a very attractive woman—"

"I'm not mad at you," I said.

"Well, maybe not. But you probably aren't thinking very highly of me right now," Ole said. And, no, I really wasn't. He was stuck to me like a leech. It was impossible to shake him off.

And the clock was ticking.

I stopped listening to what Ole was saying as he got dressed; all I could hear was ticking in my head. Like a bomb. I knew the first mailmen and -women, were already out doing their routes, *tick-tock;* they would deliver mail to one mailbox, *tick-tock,* and the next, *tick-tock,* and the next, *tick-tock;* they were making their way through front yards, *tick-tock,* past biting dogs and signs that read: NO SOLICITORS . . .

"I'm hungry," Ole said.

"Me, too," I said, a bit surprised at myself. Honestly, I was hungry like a wolf. All right, fine. Then we would have breakfast together. There would still be time afterward to gather up the pills, head to the station, and catch the next train for Ulaanbaatar . . . "You want Mia to see us, right?"

"Who's Mia?" Ole asked.

"Geez, Ole. Mia is the woman who broke your heart yesterday," I said, suddenly no longer furious at Ole. He really was having a tough time. No wonder he was acting so weirdly.

"My heart actually . . . feels OK," he said, watching me reapply mascara and my usual clear lip gloss. "Why do women always open their mouths when they do their lashes?"

"Genetics," I said, picking up my bag and scooting two more sleeping pills aside with my foot. "I'm ready."

"You look really nice," Ole said. "But honestly, to look at you, no one would suspect what a *tigress* you can be . . ."

I rolled my eyes.

The breakfast room was a giant, light-bathed conservatory filled with plants of all kinds. My mood temporarily picked up. The buffet was a feast for the eyes. Mountains of exotic fruits, fresh rolls and artisan breads, Belgian and French cheeses, exquisitely arranged German cold cuts and Norwegian smoked salmon, crisp bacon still steaming from the pan, scrambled eggs in croustades, and cute little sausages that smiled up at us. There was coffee and tea in all variations, freshly pressed juices, and classic German *quark crème*—freshly whipped and topped with shaved chocolate, bright berries, or pineapple. The air was awash in marvelous smells.

"This is how I imagine heaven," I said.

"What are you hungry for?" Ole asked.

"All of it," I said. I had to return to the buffet four times until I had amassed everything my heart desired: a plate of sliced pineapple, mango cubes, strawberries, and papaya spears with lime; a glass of orange-carrot juice; a foamy cappuccino; a still-warm German poppy seed roll and a slice of whole wheat toast with butter melting into it; Catalán-style scrambled eggs with shrimp, mushrooms, and parsley; a slice of pungent, nutty Morbier Royal cheese; a slice of stinky Alsatian Winzer cheese; and one of the cute little smiling sausages.

Ole surveyed my selections with satisfaction. "Well, if nothing else I was able to whet your appetite," he said. "Or ... hopefully, this isn't some subconscious compensation for erotic hunger?"

"To tell the truth, I haven't eaten a bite since yesterday morning," I said as I dug in.

"I've got to go see a man about a horse," Ole said with a wink. "I'll be right back. *Guten Appetit.*"

The food was delicious. I leaned back in the comfortable rattan chair and sipped my cappuccino. There were another twenty or thirty guests in the breakfast room, but the big rush was either coming later or already over. There was no sign of Mia and her lover. Well, they presumably had better things to do. But was it better than enjoying a breakfast like this? Honestly, I was going to miss food when I was dead.

Ole was gone a long time. I had already emptied my fruit platter, devoured the toast and scrambled eggs with shrimp, and half of the poppy-seed roll by the time he came back.

"Where have you been?" I asked, taking a bite of the cute little sausage. "I could have gone to Ulaanbaatar and back three times."

"I checked out," Ole said, sounding like he was in a good mood. "Your bags are at reception; the room has been paid for."

"Excuse me?" The cute little sausage fell off the fork in horror.

"You don't have to be so polite. The least I could do is pay for the room," Ole said. "It has nothing to do with what happened between us last night; it's just a need I have to at least cover the bill. For a friend who was there for me when I was . . . in need."

Were those tears in his eyes?

"That's fine, then," I hastily said. "But my things? You packed *everything*?"

"It wasn't that much," Ole said. "I just threw all your things into your travel case from the bathroom."

"But you didn't . . . Did you look under the beds and in the drawers?"

"No. Should I have? Oh, well, if you're forgotten anything, no problem. We can go pick it up later. I hope it's not jewelry or anything valuable?"

"Uh, no," I said. "Just a . . . a book."

"I saw only a Bible," Ole said. "I thought it was the hotel's."

"Uh, no," I said again. "It was mine."

Ole looked at me warmly. "Well, here I am learning yet another new thing about you, Gerri. We'll go pick up your Bible afterward. That won't be a problem in a hotel like this. How is the cappuccino?"

"Heavenly," I said, pressing the sausage back onto my fork and putting it into my mouth. "I think I'll go get another one. And . . . Ole? I'm going to go get the Bible *alone.*"

"Oh, crap," Ole said. "*Mia!* I'd totally forgotten."

"I'm sure," I said.

"No, seriously! She's here! With her Mr. Lovemeister. God, the poor girl. In daylight he looks like an *antique.* A foot in the grave, practically. As though he didn't sleep a wink all night."

"He probably didn't," I said.

"How do I look?" Ole asked.

"Amazingly good," I said. "Where did you get that nicelooking tan, incidentally?"

"They're sitting at a table in the back. Eight o'clock, kittycorner behind you. Don't turn around! Pretend you can't see them."

"I can't see them," I said. "I lack eyes on the back of my head."

"What do I do if she sees us?" Ole asked, agitated.

"This was your plan," I said.

"What plan?" Ole asked, even more agitated.

"The plan that completely ruined *my* plan," I said.

Ole wasn't listening to me. He was staring over my left shoulder at Mia.

I sighed. "Stop staring," I said. "Here. Move into this chair next to me. Then she'll think you can't see her and won't know that you already have."

"OK," Ole said, sliding one seat over. "Now what?"

"Now you just have to wait for some quark crème to come flying over at us," I said. I was a little agitated myself: What would Mia do if she noticed us? What would I do if I were she? I sipped my orange-carrot juice.

"Mustache," Ole said.

"Sorry?"

"On your upper lip. Of juice." He took a napkin and dabbed my face.

"Oh, that's good," I said. "Mia will lose it if she sees that."

Ole dropped the napkin. "Mia can fuck off. I'm not doing this because of her. You've got such pretty lips, have I said that already?"

And then he kissed me. I was a little thrown off guard, but I played along. It was a grand Hollywood-style kiss with all the trimmings. And our performance was Oscar-worthy. I ran my fingers through Ole's blond hair. I had always wanted to do that.

We stopped kissing only because Ole's cell phone rang.

"Wow!" Ole fished his phone from his pocket, a bit out of breath and looking me in the eyes. "It's Mia!" he whispered.

"Great! Answer it," I said.

Hmm, I thought. *That kiss was not bad.* Now I regretted spending the previous night sleeping like a log.

"Hi, honey!" Ole said. "How's the weather in Stuttgart?"

I pretended I needed to adjust my shoe and casually looked behind me as I did. Mia's lover was sitting alone at a table at eight o'clock; there was no sign of Mia. Her lover looked a bit lost, confused even. He was turning all around as though he were looking for someone.

"Oh, things are fantastic here," Ole said. "I'm just jogging around the park." He winked at me. "Last night? Oh, nothing special. I wrote up a couple of invoices, and then I watched TV. And you? Oh, yeah. I understand. Continuing ed is always very tiring. Those conference rooms can get so stuffy. When are you heading home? Do you want to go to the potluck tonight at Caroline and Bert's, or do you just want to go out? OK, whatever you want. Drive carefully, honey. I love you. See you later." He pressed the End button and slid the phone back into his pocket. "How was I? Where is she?"

"I'm guessing she's out in the lobby," I said. "Her lover is still looking all around for her. She apparently saw us and stormed out to call you."

"Serves her right," Ole said. "Be honest, now, Gerri. Look at him: What does he have that I don't?"

Another cell phone rang. But this time it was Mia's lover's phone. He spoke into it and then left the breakfast room.

"Ha-ha," I said. "That was Mia. I bet she told him she can't do breakfast today. Now I almost feel sorry for her. She's in a real catch-22."

Ole gently put his hands on both of my cheeks. "You're amazing, Gerri!"

"Happy to help," I said.

He got ready to kiss me again. But I wriggled out of his hands.

"Hey!" I said. "No one's watching anymore."

"But . . ." Ole said.

"No buts! Your plan worked." I stood. "I have no idea what you've achieved or what will happen next, but now I really have to take care of myself." And the very next thing I had to do was head back up to the hotel room and pick up my pills off the floor.

Except—just one more bite of that slice of Winzer cheese . . . mmm, delicious!

Ole had a hangdog look. "I understand you need some space for now," he said. "This is all just such a fucked-up . . . Well, it's a giant disaster. And then there's Joe."

"Exactly," I said. I picked up another bit of Morbier Royal but set it back on the plate. What on earth was I doing? I had truly wasted enough time eating. I forcefully threw my bag over my shoulder. "Take care, Ole. It was a very . . . interesting night with you. But now I'm in a terrible rush."

And that was the truth, too. As I sprinted out of the room, I assumed the mailman was already dropping my good-bye letter into my parents' green mailbox. I had to get to Ulaanbaatar on the double.

"Gerri, that Joe is no good for you. You always pick the wrong guys," Ole said, but I pretended I didn't hear him.

As I burst into the lobby, out of the corner of my eye I spied a shock of red hair flashing from behind a column, but I didn't look back. I just kept running up the stairs. When I made it to the third floor, it occurred to me that I should have asked for the room key at the front desk, but the door to room 324 was wide-open.

Finally, some luck! I wouldn't have to stop at the desk and dish up some story about needing a key.

I slammed right into a cart full of housekeeping supplies. From behind the cart, a petite, buxom woman was staring at me in surprise.

She had a canister vacuum slung over her shoulder and a feather duster wedged in her armpit.

"Don't vacuum!" I yelled, entirely out of breath. "This is my room!"

"This room is unoccupied," the housekeeper said. "I just finished prepping it for the next check-ins."

"What . . . already? We were gone for just an hour!" I yelled at her. "No way!"

"Did you forget something?" the housekeeper asked.

"Yes, indeed I did!"

"What was it, then?"

"My . . ." Oh, this stupid bitch! How could she not have noticed vacuuming up thirty-three sleeping pills! *Plop-plop-plop* . . . But what should I do? Rip her vacuum from her shoulder and slice open the bag?

The housekeeper looked at me, shaking her head, and slid the cart past me, the vacuum still over her shoulder. I stood in the room, my arms hanging limply at my sides. I had lost. My ticket to the beyond had vanished up a vacuum hose.

And throughout Germany, mailmen and -women were half-done with their routes.

Dear Tina and Frank,

Just a quick note to be extremely clear: My will is in no way contestable. I want Chisola to have the pearl necklace, the laptop, and the iPod—without any debate and without giving the child a guilty conscience. As far as I'm concerned, Arsenius and Habakkuk can each buy themselves a pearl necklace, laptop, and iPod with your money—but first give some thought to why you favor the boys so much over your daughter and what such long-term preferentialism can lead to with respect to siblings (like us!).

And another thing: There may be cows with eating habits similar to those of your family, but among members of *Homo sapiens,* it is not generally normal to consume foodstuffs that have already been chewed. And if you two are wondering why no one ever eats the salad at your house, this can be traced back to a comment by Tina last summer. And I quote: "Yes, this bowl was really worth the price. We use it for just everything—a salad bowl, pudding bowl, foot bath, and even a puke bowl whenever the stomach flu is going around." Well, then. Any other questions?

I might have written more on the topic of "Good Behavior and Manners in Children," but I still have five more good-bye letters to write, a hotel room to reserve, and an undercounter refrigerator to defrost.

Love,
Your very busy Gerri

TEN

Of course, I couldn't just board some train without any sleeping pills. I mean, what alternative was there? It's not like I could ever go back home. I couldn't return anywhere once everyone had read the letters I had written.

And, boy, what I had written!

To Aunt Evelyn, for example. If she finds out that I'm not even dead, then she'll strangle me to death with her bare hands. And Volker and Uncle Korbmacher were probably not exactly thrilled to learn that Volker is not Uncle Korbmacher's son, DNA-wise. Evelyn certainly wasn't.

And that Adrian guy at Aurora. I was fairly certain I recalled describing my breasts to him.

Oh my God!

What had I done? And what should I do now? I needed a good hiding place. But where? I couldn't think of a single person's house where I could still show my face.

"Gerri-Berry!" Charly said. "What a nice surprise! Hey, Ulrich, set another place. Gerri's come for breakfast."

"Has your mail come yet today?" I asked.

"Yes, it just came," Charly replied. "I got a package from Babyland. Full of cute little clothes. And lanolin for my nipples. I already unpacked it and tried it out. Hey, why do you have your travel bag with you?"

"Well, um . . . I can't go back to my apartment," I said. "My aunt would beat me to death with a crucifix."

"What's the old bag's problem now? Did you forget to polish the stair landings?"

Ulrich, wearing only boxers, patted me on the shoulder. "Mornin' there, old buddy. Coffee?"

"Yes, please," I said, slumping onto one of the wicker chairs surrounding the old kitchen table. A package striped in baby pink and blue was sitting on it, and two letters lay on it—one from me.

"That's good. Charly's been drinking only fennel tea lately," Ulrich said.

"Ugh, you would, too, if you were as nauseated as I've been," Charly said, taking the wicker chair next to me. "'Morning' sickness is a complete lie, incidentally. I've been sick the *whole* day long, every day."

"Me, too," I said, staring at my letter. I could snap it up and eat it. I had done that once in school, with a note that Charly had slipped me in Latin class.

"Hand over the note, Ms. Thaler," Mr. Rothe had bellowed. "Hurry up! I'll count to three. One, two . . ."

On "three" I pushed the note into my mouth. There was no other way out, because the note had read: *Rothe is a sadistic neo-Nazi beer-bellied asshole*—and that was the truth, too.

"Do you remember the time I saved you from Mr. Rothe by eating that note, Charly?" I asked. "He made me write a hundred times: *A proper German girl does not use paper as a foodstuff.*"

"Yeah, that guy was really into medieval methods," Charly said. "He couldn't have been more than forty at the time. It makes me think: My kid could still end up having him as a teacher, too. That would *not* be good. Hey, what's this? A letter from you, Gerri? For me? You could have called." She laughed.

My heart sank. Final defeat. "You know, Charly, last week I was on a bit of a vodka binge . . . Maybe just read it later?"

But Charly excitedly extracted the letter from its envelope and unfolded it. Her eyes darted back and forth down my lines of text. "Why are you writing . . . Well, yeah, that is true . . . No, rust *is* a disinfectant . . ." She giggled, and then her eyes suddenly welled up—I'm assuming that was the point where I had written she was the best thing that had ever happened to me and I wished her daughter would have a friend like her. "*Oh!* Ulrich, Gerri wrote me the sweetest love letter. Oh, Gerri, that's so sweet of you."

I bit my lips.

"You always come up with such lovely, original ideas . . ." Then she wrinkled her brow; she had apparently reached my postscript. She read the last couple of sentences aloud. "'I'd rather have a root canal without anesthesia than listen to Charly singing "Over the Rainbow." Which is why you should please not suggest singing "Ave Maria" or something at my funeral. Under no circumstances do I want to give people reason to laugh as they are standing beside my grave.' *Gerri, what is up with that?*"

Ulrich looked at me in shock. "Gerri!"

"I . . . I . . ." I didn't know what to say.

Charly looked furious. "Is this true, Ulrich? Did you really say that?"

"Um, yeah, well, maybe . . . kind of . . ." Ulrich said. "Gerri . . ."

"You couldn't have meant that!" Charly said.

"Well, fine. If you ask me directly, then I did mean it, a little," Ulrich admitted. "But ask Gerri why—"

"Yeah, what do you mean I can't sing?" Charly said, interrupting him. "I'm much in demand as a performer. I've . . . I've got tons of gigs lined up. Next weekend I'm singing at another wedding, for instance. Do you know how many 'Ave Marias' I've sung in churches? And how many times I've sung 'Saving All My Love for You' and 'Candle in the Wind'? I can't even count how many anymore."

"That's true," Ulrich said. "But that's not why Gerri . . ."

"Haven't you ever noticed that you sing at every venue only once?" I said, looking at the floor. "No one books you twice."

"Well, yes. Because I primarily sing at weddings, and people don't get married that often," Charly said. "Same for funerals. Ulrich, *you* remember how I almost got that recording contract, right? That wasn't just *any* label! They had the biggest stars under contract, and they wanted *me*!"

"Yes," Ulrich said. "But that was before they heard you sing."

Charly was speechless.

"I'm sorry," I said.

"Yeah, me too!" Charly said. "Ten years I've sunk into this career, and only now it's occurred to anyone to tell me I can't sing? What great friends I have."

"Of course you can sing," I said. "Just not well."

"Not well enough, you mean! Here I am, thirty, without a profession."

"You have me," Ulrich said.

"You shut your mouth," Charly snapped at him. "Neither of you have the first clue about music; you're both totally unmusical."

"But so are you," I said.

"And you be quiet," Charly snarled at me. "Some friend! You don't need to write me a letter to tell me something like that! And don't you worry—I will not be singing at your funeral! I'll be dancing . . ." She faltered and looked at the letter again. "What is all this crap about the funeral . . . ? And why are you giving me your rose pillows?"

I looked at the floor again.

"*Oh my God!*" Charly said.

"I knew something was wrong the minute you came in," Ulrich said. "You had that hangdog look on your face."

"Gerri?" Charly looked at me wide-eyed, her hand over her heart. "*Please* tell me that you wouldn't."

"I would," I said. "I almost did. You have no idea."

"*Please tell me that you wouldn't,*" Charly repeated, this time admonishingly.

"I'm sorry. It wasn't supposed to go like this. I had planned it down to the last detail. But then housekeeping at the hotel vacuumed up all my pills." I started to cry. "And now everyone has gotten the good-bye letters I wrote, and I have no idea what to do!"

"If anyone here should be crying, it's me!" Charly yelled. "You couldn't possibly have thought of doing that to me! I'm pregnant! Did you think even *once* of me?"

"I . . . but . . . hey, I'm still alive," I said.

"Thank God," Charly yelled as she nearly crushed me to death in her hug. *"Thank God!"*

It took an hour for me to tell Charly and Ulrich the whole story, and during that time Charly had to jump up and vomit seven times—five dry heaves and two proper goes.

I stopped crying as much as I could, and I talked around the philosophical issues relating to my disaster. I also didn't include all the details about Ole and me—for example, I didn't mention that we had both been more or less naked— I just told them how he had unknowingly kept me from swallowing the pills and how he had unwittingly ensured that the pills landed all over the floor and were vacuumed up.

Although Ulrich was particularly interested in the whole thing about Mia and Ole ("So that redheaded bitch was actually having an affair?"), Charly—despite her nausea— grasped that the Mia and Ole thing was just a side plot and the thrust of the drama was yet to occur.

"So, at this moment, all of your friends and family think that you have killed yourself," she said.

"No. Just the ones who have gotten a letter from me," I said. "Although that *is* a lot of people."

"Your parents?"

"Mmm, yeah."

"OK, have you taken complete leave of your senses?" Charly yelled. "They're going to have heart attacks! You call them right now and tell them you're still alive."

I shook my head. "I can't," I said. "My mother will kill me."

"But that's what you wanted," Ulrich said.

"You *have* to," Charly said. "You know I can't stand your mother, but she really does not deserve this." She jumped up and held the phone out to me. "Go on. Call."

"I don't dare," I said.

"You call them," Ulrich told Charly. "Gerri isn't of sound mind right now, don't you get that? She can't make decisions for herself. She really meant to do it. Otherwise she wouldn't have sent all those letters."

"I can't believe she really would do it," Charly said. "She just wanted . . . She just wanted to shake us up a little. It was a stupid, spontaneous idea, right, Gerri?"

Ulrich shook his head. "That's not how Gerri is, Charly. She always thinks everything through, in minute detail. *She needs help.*"

"I'm not getting locked in the psychiatric ward," I said. "If that's what you mean!"

"Of course not," Charly said.

"Well, that's where you ought to be," Ulrich said. "For your own safety. To keep you from throwing yourself in front of the next train or something."

"But I'm not the Anna Karenina type; I'm the Marilyn Monroe type," I protested. "I need *sleeping pills,* and right now they're all inside the vacuum bag on the shoulder of a housekeeper at the Regency Palace. So I'm not in any acute danger."

God, how stupid I had been! I should have seized the vacuum bag and dashed to the train station. Then I would now be sitting in a private compartment, sorting the pills from hotel filth, clump by clump, pill by pill. That might not have been pretty, but it would at least have been a step forward.

"OK, I'm calling your parents," Charly said. "So we can prevent an even worse disaster."

"I'll be in the bathroom while you do that," I said.

"Under no circumstances," Ulrich said, grabbing me by the elbow. "There are scissors in there."

"I'm not the hara-kiri type, either," I said, looking longingly over at the chopping block on the sideboard. "I wish I were."

Charly had already dialed my parents' number. "Yes, good morning, Mrs. Thaler. This is Charly, Charlotte Marquand. 'That harlot Charlotte'? Yes. Listen, Mrs. Thaler, in the event that you have opened today's mail . . . Oh, you haven't yet? Good, then you probably should not open today's mail . . . Yes, a letter from Gerri, exactly. You shouldn't open it because—well, Gerri has played a stupid . . . Well, the letter is a stupid joke. *No . . . do not open it!* Do *not* read it. Dammit, why aren't you . . . Gerri is fine, really . . . Yes, she's standing here right beside me. Yes, I don't know why she did that, but . . . Well, she *is* right—you really did always say mean things about her hair . . . Don't read any further. As I was trying to say, the pills ended up in a hotel's . . . She's standing right here, hale and healthy . . . Yes, but Klaus really was *totally* a creep. No one with any sense . . . not with a ten-foot pole . . . No, Hannah Kopuski was still reading those Pony Camp books when she was sixteen, and she used to doodle *I love Black Beauty* on her folder—*hello?* Please listen . . . Yes, I'll tell her, although right now is not really the best time . . . But maybe you should . . . *Mrs. Thaler!* You had better starting making phone calls now . . . All the people Gerri sent good-bye letters to . . . so that people don't panic . . . Yes, I can understand you . . . No, I'm sure Aunt Hulda won't take you out of her will because of this . . . but . . . It's a perfectly respectable profession; you can be proud of her. My mother would jump for . . . but . . . Oh God. Stop talking now." Finally, my mother paused for Charly. "Do you know what? It's no wonder Gerri suffers from depression! You are a terrible mother, and I've always wanted to tell you so."

Charly hung up and threw the phone at Ulrich. "That stupid cow thinks only of herself! At least we don't have to worry she'll have a heart attack or something. She's mad as hell at Gerri."

"I'll bet she's not the only one," Ulrich said. "What in heaven did you write everyone, Gerri?"

Yeah, what in heaven had I written everyone?

"I have *got* to get on the train for Ulaanbaatar now," I whispered. "I need to hide somewhere."

The phone in Ulrich's hand rang.

"*Please* hide me!" I said.

"Gerri, I think it'd be better . . ." Ulrich started.

"Please!"

"But Gerri, mood disorders aren't a joking matter. A psychiatric intervention—"

"She can stay in the nursery," Charly said, interrupting him. "I can keep my eye on her there, day and night."

"Thank you," I said. "Thank you, thank you, thank you!"

Everything was quiet in my aunt's building. We sneaked from window to window, ducking under each one, and tip-toed our way up the fire escape. My heart was beating out of my chest, and my hands were shaking so much that I was having a hard time getting my key into the lock.

"I don't know why I'm doing this to myself," I whispered. "If Aunt Evelyn catches me, everything's out."

"But you need your things," Charly whispered back. "If I had come alone, they'd have me arrested for robbery. And when she sees you've gotten your things, your aunt will be relieved you're not dead after all."

"You don't know my family," I said.

Once I had managed to get the door open, we saw that someone had already come to go through everything. Aunt Evelyn, in point of fact. She was sitting at my kitchen table with both of her hands deep in my jewelry box.

She was at least as startled as I was. I stood, rooted to the floor and blinking at her, my aunt blinking back.

Only Charly's nerves remained intact, and she said, "Hello! Don't let us bother you. We just wanted to pick up a few things. And don't worry; this isn't Gerri's ghost. It's Gerri, in the flesh."

"I can see that," Aunt Evelyn said with mild disgust. "Dorothea already called and told me you were merely in-dulging in an ungodly joke at our expense. I myself didn't believe it for a second."

"I-I'm sorry," I stuttered. "I-I didn't want—"

170

"You're putting your mother through hell," Aunt Evelyn said. "She has to call everyone everywhere and explain that you are too feebleminded even to manage swallowing a stack of sleeping pills."

"Hey now," Charly said.

"When Aunt Hulda finds out about this . . ." Aunt Evelyn said.

"What are you doing in my jewelry box, then?" I was torn variously by shame, anxiety, and rage.

"Nothing," Aunt Evelyn said. "But one thing is clear: This is no longer your apartment. You gave notice. And the way you did so, you waived any right to live here."

"But these are still Gerri's things," Charly said. "And Gerri's jewelry."

Aunt Evelyn snapped the box shut. "Are you two trying to insinuate that I'm interested in this cheap junk here?"

"It sure does look that way," Charly said.

"Hmm. You didn't find what you were looking for, huh?" I said, taking a step toward Aunt Evelyn. I knew exactly what she was up to. "The aquamarine ring and pearl necklace weren't in there, were they?"

"Nonsense! Although I *am* entitled to them," Aunt Evelyn said. "You know that perfectly well."

Charly had decided to ignore Aunt Evelyn. She retrieved my giant suitcase from its niche and tossed it onto the bed. "Boy, Gerri. You don't have that much stuff left in here!" she said, looking around. "What on earth did you do with everything?"

"I mucked it out," I said without taking an eye off Aunt Evelyn.

"I feel really sorry for your mother," Aunt Evelyn said. "To be punished with a daughter like you. An ungodly changeling, I always said."

Rage was slowly gaining the upper hand. "Stop calling me a changeling, Aunt Evelyn!"

"Oh, I don't mean anything by it," Aunt Evelyn said. "You were always so hypersensitive. Take yourself a bit less seriously, why don't you."

"Did you read up any on the topic of changelings in my biology textbook, Aunt Evelyn?"

"You're referring to the outrageous insinuations in your letter?" Aunt Evelyn said, crossing her arms. "Even a blind man can see that Volker is Reiner's son. His hair, his bow-legs, his nose. In case you thought you could sow some seeds of discord here, I'm sorry to disappoint—you've wasted your venom."

"You need to understand it, Aunt Evelyn," I said, taking my laptop off my desk.

"Mendel had no idea what he was talking about," she said.

Charly opened the dresser drawer. "You want a couple of pairs of panties still, right?"

"Only the pretty ones," I said.

"There are only three," Charly said.

"Yes," I said, regretting having thrown out all the skin-toned tummy-control panties, which had cost me a small fortune.

"The apartment will need to be cleared out immediately," Aunt Evelyn said. "And it'll need a coat of paint as well. It's so lovely of you to have left it in such a mess and saddled *us* with all the work to clean it. And you still owe us rent for the next three months."

"That's it! Just hold on right there," Charly said. "Your niece just tried to commit suicide, and instead of being glad she's still alive . . ."

"Oh, that's all just show," Aunt Evelyn said. "So she can be the center of attention for once. It's like that time she intentionally destroyed the Meissen porcelain. I've known this child since she was born. I know what she's capable of."

I'd had enough. "Do you know if Uncle Korbmacher read my letter?" I asked. "Or Volker?"

Aunt Evelyn didn't answer. She said, "All these years we've taken you in with us here, and this is how you thank us!"

"So I take it the answer is no," I said. "I would be hesitant to show it to them, if I were you as well. Although, if Volker were paying attention in biology class, I'm certain he'd have stumbled across the issue of his eye color. He may have repressed it or something."

"You really want to destroy a happy family, don't you, with your disgraceful and false accusations?" Aunt Evelyn's eyes were positively glowing.

Charly, who had stuffed everything her fingers could get ahold of into the suitcase, paused and looked at me expectantly.

"I don't want to destroy a happy family," I said. "But I don't want to pay the next three months' rent or do any renovations here. If you insist on those things, then I will insist on giving Uncle Korbmacher a little tutoring in basic genetics. Or maybe Aunt Hulda."

"That's blackmail," Aunt Evelyn hissed.

"If I were to say that you had to pay me a thousand euros a month, *that* would be blackmail," I said. "And you can let me in on your secret. Who was the lucky guy?"

"Disgraceful!" Aunt Evelyn said.

Charly zipped the suitcase shut and heaved it from the bed. "We'll pick up the rest tomorrow," she said.

"I'm guessing Uncle Fred," I said. "Based on the color of his eyes, he would be a good match."

Aunt Evelyn didn't utter another word.

Dear Britt,

I must unfortunately decline the invitation to the class reunion because next Friday I'm going to be dying from an overdose of sleeping pills and thus cannot attend.

I'm sure you are burning with questions about what I've been up to since graduation so that, as usual, you can pretend to be more of a luminary than you really are. But that's fine; I have nothing to hide!

I'm unmarried, have no boyfriend, and haven't really had sex for years. I've been renting a studio apartment, I dropped out of my German literature program at the university after only one semester, and since high school graduation I've put on just shy of ten pounds. All of my friends are happily married and/or raising enchanting children. I drive a fourteen-year-old Nissan March, I already have four gray hairs, and at night I love watching Jane Austen movies on DVD. Once a week I go and clean my aunt's house. And for ten years I have been writing romance novels for Aurora Publishing. My pseudonyms are Juliane Mark and Diana Dollar, although they have dropped in popularity at the moment. My current assets total 498 euros and 29 eurocents. In addition, I have neurotic depression and won a Beatle. Satisfied?

Incidentally, I was NOT the one who dipped the ends of your braids in paste and stuck them to the back of your chair, even though that's what you told Mr. Rothe with such credibility. Despite all my protestations of innocence, I ended up having to write a hundred times: *A proper German girl does not envy the hair of another.* And you sneered at me all the while through your crocodile tears. As though I would ever wish I had limp seaweed hair like yours! Nonetheless, I won't be giving up the name of the *actual* guilty party today—solidarity to the grave!

Sincerely,
Gerri Thaler née Gapingfrogsmouth

ELEVEN

At the base of the spiral staircase outside, Johannes Paul was sitting in his red pedal car, blocking our way off the fire escape.

"Ge-he-rri-hi? Is it true what my mama said?"

"No, definitely not. Garbage is all that comes out of her mouth," Charly said. "Step aside, St. Peter. These aren't the gates of heaven, after all." She giggled at her joke, but the look on Johannes Paul's face didn't change.

"My name is Johann Pa-haul. Petrus is my brooo-hother. Ge-he-rri-hi? Is it true what my mama said?"

"Hey, are you deaf, Mr. Hurdy-gurdy?" Charly asked. "We need to get past!"

"What did your mama say then?" I asked.

"She said you don't love Jesus," Johannes Paul said.

"But . . . I do love Jesus," I said, fairly vehemently.

"Drive your stupid car to the side, though, or I'll drop this laptop on you," Charly said. "That will be expensive for your mama!"

"But Mama says you made Jesus very sad," Johannes Paul said as he slowly rolled backward. "What did you do that made Jesus sad?"

"I—I . . . Jesus isn't sad," I stuttered.

"Exactly," Charly said. "He's a lot tougher than you think. And he's generous, too. You can tell your mama that."

"What did you do-hoo?" Johannes Paul said.

Hilla appeared at the kitchen window. "Dinner, Johannes Paul," she said, giving me a cool look. Charly ignored her entirely. "It's hard for a child to understand that someone might just throw away the wonderful life Jesus has given her. Honestly, it's hard for us grown-ups to understand as well."

I had an urgent need to defend myself. I just didn't know how.

"My life is not that wonderful," I said. "In fact, it's a . . . It's a horrible life. But I don't hold Jesus responsible for that."

"Your life comes from God's hand, but what you do with it is up to *you*," Hilla said.

"Well, maybe fifty percent," I said.

But Hilla put her hands to her hips. "Horrible? *Horrible? You call your life horrible?* You're healthy, right? You have a roof over your head and always enough to eat, right?" she yelled with unexpected spirit, and righteous fury sparked from her eyes at me. "Do you know how many people are suffering in this world? How many people live in countries riddled with war, hunger, and poverty? How many people wish they had a healthy body? You are sinning against God if you can't appreciate how well things are going for you."

I bit my lip.

"You know, you're getting on my nerves," Charly said to Hilla, pulling me by the elbow. "Self-righteous religious wacko! Do you know how much money your kids are going to have to pay for therapy when they're grown up? When you say things like 'You're making Jesus sad when you fight.' 'You're making Jesus sad when you make noise.' 'You're making Jesus sad when you pee your pants.' If anyone is sinning around here, it's you! You just can't see it for yourself. Come on, Gerri. Let's take off before she starts spraying holy water everywhere."

I cried in the car.

"Hilla's right," I sobbed. "If everyone who's worse off than I am committed suicide, the overpopulation problem would be solved in one stroke."

"Of course there are always people worse off than you," Charly said. "'Eat your vegetables; children in the Third World would be glad to have anything to eat at all.' 'Don't whine about your scraped knee; think of the people who don't have any legs at all.' 'Don't cry that your cat has died; poor Ekaterina Lemuskaya lost her husband, sons, and daughters at the Massacre of Vladivostok.'"

I guess I hadn't read the paper in a while. "Who is Ekaterina Lemuskaya, and what is the Massacre of Vladivostok?"

Charly sighed. "No idea. I just made that up. All I'm saying is that there's no standard for unhappiness. Unhappiness is relative."

"Poor Ekaterina Lemuskaya," I said, weeping bitterly at her harsh fate, even though she didn't exist. And then my molar started throbbing again.

Not everyone was angry at me for still being alive. A couple of people were even glad. At least according to Ulrich, who handled most of the phone calls that weekend. My sisters called, Caroline and Bert, Marta and Marius, Aunt Alexa, and Cousin Harry. They all wanted to tell me they were glad I was still alive. That's what Ulrich claimed, at any rate. I couldn't muster the courage to take the phone and silently shook my head whenever he held out the receiver to me. I just could not talk to anyone. I was completely and utterly ashamed. And I was fairly certain that neither Aunt Alexa nor Cousin Harry had wanted to say something nice to me. Probably not Lulu and Tina, either.

"Gerri will call back later," Ulrich said, taking notes like a good secretary. Every so often he would give me a little summary: "Lulu is asking whether you still have the e-mail address for someone called *rockinhard12* and if twelve means what she thinks it means. Tina wants to know what batteries the MP3 player takes, and Cousin Harry said your verse of the song at Alexa's party won't come between Franziska's and Uncle Gustav's but after someone named Gabi, who ended up accepting last minute."

I spent the whole weekend sitting or lying on the couch in Charly's practice room—the future nursery—staring at the wall or the ceiling. I left the blinds down and couldn't tell whether it was night or day. It didn't matter, either.

I would never have thought it possible, but I was doing much worse now than before the suicide. Before the *failed* suicide, I mean. So much for good planning! I really had to take my high opinion of my organizational skills down several notches. Good planning always somehow allowed for the unpredictable; that should have been clear to me. And I should at least have had a plan B.

At least the tooth pain had stopped again.

I stared at the ceiling some more. A couple of years ago, Charly and I had insulated that room with empty egg cartons so that Charly's singing wouldn't disturb the neighbors. The cartons looked a bit strange, tightly packed together and stuck over every bit of the walls and ceiling. Charly had spray-painted them, alternating dark mauve and cream white.

"I suppose it'd be practical to leave the nursery insulated for noise and keep the egg cartons up, but if I were you I'd think about redoing the room minus the cartons," I said when Charly came in again at some point, plopping down beside me on the couch.

"You mean maybe redo the walls and ceiling in light blue with little clouds?" Charly asked. "Yeah, I've already been thinking about that. I guess I'm going to be doing most of my singing in the bathtub now anyway."

"I'm really sorry, Charly. I know how much fun singing is for you. I shouldn't have spoiled it for you." I sighed.

"Well, there are many others ways to have fun," Charly said. "And I have to admit, you're right: I'm not really even a mediocre singer. I might have admitted it to myself much sooner if only someone had said something. But that's how people are. They don't tell each other the important things. I think you've actually set a good example by being so honest with me. I called my dad and told him he needs to do something about his bad breath."

"I bet he wasn't exactly thrilled," I said.

"No, but once he gives it some thought, he'll be glad I said something. Everyone could smell it, but no one gave him a chance to change it—and that's not fair, you know?

We shouldn't always protect ourselves from the truth. Gerri, won't you eat something?"

I shook my head.

"Are you just spending all this time in here thinking how you can do it again?" Charly asked.

"Not the whole time," I said. "The rest of the time I keep trying to remember what all I wrote and to whom."

"Don't you have all of that on your computer still?" Charly asked. "Or did you delete all of it?"

"Of course I deleted everything," I said. "I deleted, cleaned out, and threw away almost everything. I wanted only the *real* things to be left, you know?"

"Makes sense," Charly said. "There is an upside to that, though. Now you've gotten rid of all the dead wood in your life, and you can start everything fresh."

"Without a job, without money, and without an apartment," I said. "And with everyone mad at me."

"The only people who are mad are your whacked-out family. And in terms of a job, you can look for something else with another publisher," Charly said. "You know, it might be true that I can't really sing, but *you* can really write."

"Yes, but I have no *way* to," I said. "And after insulting my editor in chief with a three-page letter, I'm fairly sure I've spoiled my last, teensy-weensy chance of publishing again." I slapped my hands over my face. "Plus, I kind of thought he was nice."

Ulrich opened the door and peeked in. "Caro and Bert are here," he said.

"I don't want to see anyone," I said, but Caroline was already squeezing past Ulrich and dramatically dropped to her knees in front of the couch to hug me.

"Gerri, oh my God, you nearly scared me out of my mind, I'm so glad you didn't go through with it, I would never have forgiven myself for not noticing anything was wrong, I always thought you were happy, you're such a cheerful, wonderful person, and everyone likes you, especially my kids, who love you, what do you think we picked you to be Flo's godmother for, I've always been so reassured imagining you taking care of her if something were to happen to us, oh, Gerri . . ."

"I'm sorry," I murmured.

"Here, your ring," Caroline said. "It is amazingly beautiful, and it's lovely that you intended it for Flo, but I would prefer you give it to her in forty years or so . . ."

She slid the aquamarine onto my ring finger.

"And what about the rabbit?" I asked. "In forty years it'll presumably be a bit late for that."

Caroline sighed. "Well, I'm the one who always ends up doing all the work . . . but we do have enough space, and Florina really is a pretty responsible girl . . . So, yeah, I think she'll be getting her rabbit."

"There's something, at least," I said.

Bert was leaning against the doorframe. "Ulrich says you lost your job. Why didn't you say anything? My company is always on the lookout for someone for the office. They'd pay at least as much as you got writing, and probably more."

"That'd be . . ." I said, choking up. "Thank you."

"And as far as men go—God, Gerri, you are a pretty, funny, brilliant woman, and you will find someone soon enough," Bert said.

"Exactly," Ulrich said.

"*You* didn't want to marry me," I said to Ulrich.

"No, you didn't want to marry *me*," Ulrich said.

"Yes, because you didn't want to marry *me*," I said.

"As long as you're single, you should be enjoying your freedom," Bert said, interrupting us. "Having a family and mortgage to worry about all the time isn't always all that, anyway. Once in a while I think I'd give up everything just to be able to sleep in on Sunday."

"Bastard," Caroline said. "That's typical male thinking there. But of course there is some truth to that, Gerri. Look how much fun you can have as a single woman—remember Bridget Jones."

"Bad example," Charly said. "She ended up with Colin Firth."

"But only in the movie, not in the book," Caroline said.

"Yes, but think about all the marriages that don't work out," Bert said. "And you may not have heard yet, but Mia and Ole's marriage is on the rocks big time."

"Really?" Charly asked.

"Yes," Bert said, nodding. "Ole spent last night at our place and dropped a few obvious hints. Mia—"

"That floozy," Caroline interrupted.

"—has been cheating on him," Bert continued. "And Ole's record isn't exactly clean, either. God, that guy really looked shattered. I've never seen him like that before."

"And, he also got a fright when we told him about Gerri," Caroline said. "His face turned white as a sheet."

"That's true," Bert said. "He asked at least five times if we were totally sure, and he wanted to know all the details."

"You don't say," Charly said. "And where was Mia?"

"Home in bed with a migraine," Bert said. "Evidently exhausted from her continuing ed class."

"She's a bitch," Caroline said. "I always said so. But now we have to get going; we were able to get a babysitter for only one hour." She kissed my cheek. "You take care, Gerri, and you two watch her closely."

"We will," Charly said, resting her hand on her stomach. "Whenever I'm not puking."

"Ha-ha," Caroline said. "Puking is pure child's play compared to what's in store for you."

I would have preferred to sit on the couch in Charly's apartment forever, but it was already clear to me that this would not be possible. I had only three options, none of which I liked one bit: I could try again; I could check into an institution; or I could somehow keep living.

On Sunday night, Ulrich came into my room with a note and read it aloud to me: "Your mother has called to let you know that you should be on her doorstep at no later than eight o'clock tomorrow morning, or else your time as her daughter will have passed. She wants to know if you have the slightest inkling of the hell she has been going through because of you. If she has to answer the phone one more time to answer for your tasteless and cowardly escapades, she'll have to be checked into the hospital for heart problems."

"Good," Charly said. "That's where she belongs, if you ask me."

"Her message continues by saying that the least you could do is come answer her phone yourself and explain your behavior to callers," Ulrich says.

"Oh, *fuck*," I said.

"You don't need to go," Charly said. "Let the old bag have her temper tantrum."

"But you don't know her. She's *serious*," I said. "She'll refuse to ever lay eyes on me again."

"So what? Worst case, she can disinherit you, and then you won't get saddled with various ceramic leopards. *Oh, how awful*," Charly said sarcastically.

"But my mother is right. I really am acting like a coward," I said.

"I don't think so," Charly replied. "I think you've been kind of gutsy. Writing all those letters and then staying alive . . ."

"Gerri didn't stay alive intentionally," Ulrich said. "God, Charly. How often do I have to explain it to you?"

"Yes, it was; yes, it was," Charly said single-mindedly. "You two are underestimating the power of the subconscious! It's always stronger than we are. And Gerri's subconscious wanted to live! It wanted some brouhaha! It wanted action. It had had enough of all the fake polite shit."

"Oh, great," I said. "And now I have to take the heat for all that, too. I hate my subconscious."

But maybe Charly was right: Although I would have preferred staying hidden on the couch, my subconscious woke me up early the next morning and dragged me out of bed. It really did want some brouhaha.

At eight o'clock on the dot I rang my parents' doorbell.

My father opened the door. He looked somehow tired and a bit older than usual.

"Hi, Papa," I said.

"Hi, Gerri," my father said. His face didn't move. He didn't move to hug me or kiss me the way he usually did. "Your mother is in the kitchen."

"You know it's not me standing here before you," I said. "This is my subconscious."

My father's face still didn't move. "Your mother doesn't want to see you. She just received a flower delivery. From Aunt Hulda."

"Oh," I said. "I would have thought you had already let Aunt Hulda know that I didn't . . . Should I leave then?"

"Don't you dare!" my mother bellowed from the kitchen. "She should come in!"

"Come in," my father said.

"Aunt Hulda was away for the weekend!" my mother yelled from the kitchen. "I told—I implored her housekeeper to destroy your letter, but that Polish trollop pretended not to understand me . . ."

"I'm sorry," I said. The part of my personality that evidently loved brouhaha slinked all the way back to the *sub* part of my subconscious. I stood there alone, as conflict averse as ever.

"Oh, be still," my mother said from behind the kitchen door. "Now. You are going to call Aunt Hulda yourself and explain everything. Have you understood me? Her number is beside the phone."

FOR EVERY SOLUTION, A PROBLEM

With a stony expression, my father set one of the dining room chairs next to the telephone in the foyer for me and then disappeared into the living room.

I dialed Aunt Hulda's number.

"Flukmann rzeszidiensz," someone said on the other end of the line. That would be the Polish housekeeper.

"This is Gerri Thaler. I'm Ms. Flugmann's grandniece. Is Ms. Flugmann at home?" It was still early in the morning, but I was somehow craving a vodka. Sadly, all the alcoholic drinks were in the kitchen, and that's where my mother was. She was probably pressing her ear to the door to make sure I was doing my job.

"Yes?" It was the cultivated, youthful voice of my elderly great-aunt.

I choked up. "This is Gerri."

"Gerri?"

"Gerri, the youngest daughter of your niece, Dorothea."

"Dorothea?"

I sighed. "I'm the Gerri who is responsible for the Meissen porcelain debacle, Aunt Hulda."

"Oh, *that* Gerri. Thank you for your nice, and most original, letter, darling," Great-Aunt Hulda said. "But I thought you had already killed yourself. Oh, perhaps I read something wrong. Unfortunately, I've already sent some flowers to your mother."

"Yes, I know. Thank you very much. Um . . . so, it turns out that I'm still alive, and I wanted to tell you that . . . my mother, in any case is very . . . She would still like . . . So, of all her sisters she is really the . . ."

"Oh, stop your blathering!" my mother hissed from behind the kitchen door. I fell silent.

"Of course you're still alive. Otherwise you couldn't very well be calling me, isn't that right, darling?" Great-Aunt Hulda paused. I listened as she lit one of her cigarillos. "How did you want to do it?" she asked. "And won't it be hard to try again, now that everyone knows what you're planning?"

"I . . . well, I had wanted to take some sleeping pills," I said. "It would have been a dead sure way to do it. I had thirty-five pills, but I lost them—under circumstances I would prefer not relating at the moment."

"Lost them?"

"A hotel housekeeper accidentally vacuumed them all up."

"Oh, I see. I understand, darling. That was of course a turn of bad luck," Great-Aunt Hulda said. "And you weren't able to ad lib?"

"No," I said.

"Well, it's all so *unsavory*, isn't it. And whenever you need a poison mushroom, there's never one around." Could Great-Aunt Hulda be giggling? "Are you planning to try again, darling?"

I didn't know the answer myself. Did I want to try again?

"Say you're sorry," my mother hissed from behind the kitchen door.

"I'm sorry, Aunt Hulda," I said.

"But what for, darling?"

"Well, that I . . . that you . . . got that letter," I stammered.

"Oh, please, darling! It was a nice change of pace! And thank you for all the books. Normally I don't read material like that . . ."

"Of course not," I said, bitterly. Everyone only reads Franz Kafka and Thomas Mann.

". . . but I do like the covers. The way this woman here is bending back in her nurse's uniform. Very lithe, really. And the young man has an incredible upper body. And how gloomy he looks. It's delightful. I think I'm going to browse through it a bit right now. *Arrivederci*, my darling."

"Uh, *sì. Arrivederci*, Aunt Hulda."

"Done already?" my mother yelled from the kitchen. "What did she say?"

"She says hello," I said. "Can I go now?"

"Out of the question!" my mother yelled. "You are going to sit at that telephone all day and take calls. You got us into this mess, and it's only fair that you get us out of it."

"Why don't you just connect an answering machine?" I suggested.

"Because that will just make things worse," my mother said. "Then I would have to call everyone back . . . No, no. You're going to personally explain to people directly that it was all a big mistake and that I didn't have anything to do with it."

"You mean a mistake in the sense of . . . uh . . . ?"

"In the sense of . . . Dammit, you can come up with something!" my mother yelled. "I have my reputation to think of."

I made myself comfortable on the chair, hoping that the phone wouldn't ring at all. But unfortunately it rang right away. The first caller was Mrs. Köhler, Klaus Köhler's mother.

"I knew instantly it had to be a nasty joke," she said when she recognized whom she had on the phone. "You always had an odd sense of humor."

"Say you're sorry," my mother hissed from behind the kitchen door.

"Sorry," I said.

"You should apologize to Klaus," Mrs. Köhler said. "The way you trampled his feelings! It's unfortunate you're unlikely to ever have a son of your own; otherwise you would sooner or later learn how much a mother's heart aches, sharing in her son's heartbreak . . . when someone robs him of his illusions that life is fair!"

"But my letter explained how things really happened, Mrs. Köhler!" I said. "*Klaus* was the one who robbed *me* of my illusions!"

"My sweet girl," Mrs. Köhler said, making perfectly clear that she found me in no way sweet. "Whichever way you look at it, it will always be a stain on your life's story, the way you had dates with two different boys for prom. But I always warned Dorothea: The girls who start puberty early, the little floozies, they're the ones left on the shelf later on."

What, and the smelly nose pickers are the rising stars of tomorrow, or something? I was not a floozy! And I did not start puberty early at all. At sixteen I still hadn't gotten the hang of using a tampon. But what was the point of telling Mrs. Köhler all about that?

"Say you're sorry!" my mother hissed from behind the kitchen door.

"Sorry again," I said, hanging up. "Why does Mrs. Köhler think I won't have children, Mama? Is she also under the impression I'm a lesbian?"

"To have children, one needs a *husband*," my mother said from behind the door. "And after what you've done, *no one* will have you anymore. No one who has even *half* his eight senses about him. Can you imagine how glad Klaus is that he passed on you? Oh, I am so completely and utterly embarrassed."

Eight senses? Klaus Köhler has eight senses? Seeing, hearing, tasting, touching, smelling (actively), smelling (passively), nose picking . . . but what could the eighth sense be?

The next caller was Aunt Alexa. "Oh dear, Gerri, my child! You're at home? I thought your mother would never let you cross her threshold again!"

"Yes, but only into the foyer," I said.

"Say you're sorry!" my mother hissed.

"Sorry, Aunt Alexa," I said.

"But what for?" Aunt Alexa asked. Oh, right. I hadn't written her an insulting letter.

"Sorry I destroyed the Meissen porcelain," I said.

"Oh, forgiven and forgotten," Aunt Alexa said. "I've always told Dorothea that her parenting mistakes would catch up with her at some point. Anyway, Gerri. My Lord. That is not how one does things! At most, one *leaves* good-bye letters somewhere in the event of decease, but one does not mail them *in advance*! I hope my Claudia would never be so foolish."

She was impossible, like all my aunts. But she was right: It really was completely incompetent of me. If I hadn't mailed the good-bye letters, I wouldn't be saddled with any of this trouble now. In addition to all the trouble I was having before.

"Did Aunt Hulda call?" Aunt Alexa asked.

"She sent Mama flowers," I said.

"Oh, really?" She gave a hearty laugh. "And does she know that you got the sleeping pills from your own mother?"

"No," I said.

"Well, then I'll be sure to share that tidbit with her right away," Aunt Alexa said, hanging up in a good mood.

The third caller was Gregor Adrian from Aurora Publishing.

"Thaler residence," I said.

"Good morning. This is Mr. Adrian from Aurora Publishing," he said in a warm baritone. "Gerri Thaler worked for us. Are you related to Gerri Thaler?"

I couldn't say anything. My knees had suddenly turned to Jell-O. Good thing I was sitting.

"Who is that?" my mother hissed from behind the door.

"Hello? Are you still on the line?" Adrian asked. I grunted a confirmation. "Well, we at Aurora would like to express our condolences and . . . uh . . . Well, Gerri was a really wonderful person—"

"But you didn't even know her." The words just escaped my lips.

There was silence on the other end of the line for a moment, and then Mr. Adrian said, "Maybe not especially well. But well enough to say she was a gifted author."

"Ha-ha-ha!" I laughed. "Then why did you discontinue the Norina series? Why didn't you make her an offer to write for Lauros? Hmm?"

"Because—well, unfortunately I'm not personally authorized to make decisions like that on behalf of Lauros," Mr. Adrian said. "Plus, I'm new here and had no way of knowing . . ." He choked up. "I know it's a bit early, but . . . um . . ." He choked up again. "Have the funeral arrangements been made yet?"

"Not at all," I said with a chip on my shoulder.

"Sorry?"

"Not at all! Because I'm not actually dead, Mr. Adrian."

More silence, this time much longer.

"*Gerri?* I mean, Ms. Thaler? Is that you?"

"Yes," I said defiantly.

"So you're not dead?"

"Correct," I said. "Which does not mean that I wouldn't like to be." The cringeworthiness of this moment was beyond my ability to exaggerate.

"And—so, what is the deal with the letter and everything? Was that just some kind of, uh, PR stunt?" Mr. Adrian asked.

"No, it was no such thing," I snarled. I didn't know why I was so mad, now of all times, and at him, of all people. "I just had some bad luck, OK? As usual! Bad luck is woven through my life like a red thread. Do you think I would have written you a letter like that if I had thought I would ever run into you again?"

Again there was a moment of silence on the line.

"Presumably not," Mr. Adrian said.

Neither of us said anything for a while.

"What did I write you, actually?" I asked sheepishly.

"Don't you remember?"

"I was drunk," I said. "And I wrote a lot of letters."

"I see," Mr. Adrian said.

"Say you're sorry," my mother hissed from behind door.

"Sorry," I said mechanically.

"For what, exactly?" Mr. Adrian asked.

"What are you, some kind of sadist?" I yelled. "I don't re-member what all I wrote you—but I'm sorry for it and take it back, OK?"

"OK," Mr. Adrian said. "So you *don't* think that my writ-ing is lousy and empty and absolutely bereft of meaning or that my plot was absolute trash?"

"Um . . . actually, yes, I do think those things," I said. "But I'm sorry for saying so. And, um, for everything else I wrote as well. Is Licorice going to be in trouble for giving away secrets?"

"I get the impression you really have no idea what you wrote," Mr. Adrian said.

"No, I don't. But I know what Licorice told me. Have I gotten her in trouble?"

"No," Mr. Adrian said. "This can stay between you and me."

That was really nice of him. "Thank you. Is she angry at me for killing myself?"

"Did you write her a good-bye letter as well?"

"No."

"Then she doesn't know anything," Mr. Adrian said. "She has the morning off today. Listen, Gerri. I read your manuscript. I've got to say, I think it's good. It's really good—in fact, it's *great!*"

"Thank you," I said, taken aback. *He had accidentally called her by her first name, and for inexplicable reasons this sent her heart racing.*

"I also think your critiques make a lot of sense," Mr. Adrian said. "You really understand how to develop characters and shape plots."

"As I said," I said.

"So . . . I would actually like to publish *Leah's Path into Darkness* as the first Ronina novel," Mr. Adrian said. "And that's why I've called, as a matter of fact. I wanted to get permission for posthumous publication and figure out who would be getting the royalties."

"Yes, well, that would really be a bit premature," I said, imagining how my parents would have reacted to this phone call if I had swallowed the sleeping pills. *Our deepest condolences, and may we publish your daughter's vampire novel? You will be able to afford such a beautiful casket with the royalties.*

"Uh, yes, I realize that," Mr. Adrian said. "But I also wanted to know right away if . . . you were OK."

"What if I had actually been dead when you called?" I asked.

"Well, I'd had the thought you may not have taken enough sleeping pills to do the deed," Mr. Adrian said, now sounding a bit irritated. "Or that someone had found you in time or something."

"But . . ." I began.

"Stop saying *but,* child!" my mother hissed out of sheer habit from behind the door.

"The royalties will go to me, in any case," I said. That would at least bring my checking account back into plus territory.

"Good," Mr. Adrian said. "I'm glad we've resolved that issue. We can discuss everything else later."

I didn't want him to hang up. "Would you have come to my funeral?" I asked softly.

"I'd have sent a wreath of flowers," Mr. Adrian said, and hung up.

Dear Harry,

Please excuse the delay, but I've had so much to do preparing for my suicide. Below please find, finally, my verses for the song at your parents' silver wedding anniversary:

Alexa had to land a man
holla hee holla hoe
Hence her fling with Fred began
holla hee-ahoe
Beemer, poodle, kid, and house
holla hee holla hoe
She's as happy as a mouse
holla hee-ahoe

Whoa, now someone's got it better
holla hee holla hoe
The knife she holds has met its whetter
holla hee-ahoe
Pointing at Fred's prostate gland

holla hee holla hoe
Isn't life now something grand
holla hee-ahoe

With love in D major from your cousin,
Gerri

P.S. I'm sorry for that time I told you that eating soap could make you fly. But I was little at the time myself and had no idea that years later you would still be stealing soap from bathrooms everywhere to gorge on. I mean, you were *nine years old* when you got high on soap and jumped from Uncle Gustav's garage! Honestly, I'm amazed even today how you managed to get a doctorate in business administration with such aptitude.

TWELVE

My mother let me leave her house later that afternoon only after the very last of her sisters, bridge friends, and aunts had called. (To the best of my knowledge, I hadn't written any of them, but somehow I had to apologize to all of them anyway.)

Although my mother marched past me at least three times as I sat by the phone (on her way to the bathroom, for example), she never looked at me and never spoke to me. She issued only occasional directives from behind the kitchen door. She also didn't offer me anything to eat or drink.

After school got out, my sister Lulu called. "Hey, what are you doing home? I thought Mama would never let you cross the threshold again."

"Well, she did, unfortunately," I said.

"While I have you on the phone: First, I'm glad you're still alive. Second, your suspicions regarding Patrick didn't check out."

"Then everything is grand," I said.

"Yes," Lulu said. "Patrick and that guy you picked up . . ."

"Rockinhard12."

"Yeah, the pervert. Well, the two of them don't have anything in common."

"Only their looks," I said. "Maybe they're astrological twins. That's apparently a thing, you know."

"Don't be ridiculous," Lulu said. "You were just pro-jecting!" Whenever Lulu used jargon with me, she always enunciated very clearly and slowly. "*Rockinhard!* You always managed to attract the most disgraceful guys. And *online!* The first thing I told you was that the only guys you were going to find online were crazies and perverts. And now hand the phone to Mama. I need to talk to her about something."

"OK, but not too long. Great-Aunt Elsbeth hasn't called yet," I said. "I don't know what for, but there is some urgent need for me to apologize to her."

I also apologized to my mother.

"Mama, I'm sorry," I said once neither of us could think of a single other person who might call.

"You're not getting off that easy with *me*," my mother said. "You need to *think* before you act."

"And what if I were dead now?" I asked.

"That would be just as bad," my mother said.

Well, that was something.

Before I left, I looked for my father and found him in the backyard. He was planting zucchini starts in the raised bed.

"Papa? Are you not talking to me, either?"

"What do you want to talk about then, Gerri?" He still had his face of stone on. "It's not funny, you know?"

"I didn't want to hurt anyone," I said.

"That's ridiculous," my father said, glaring at me with sudden rage. "How can you take your own life without hurting someone?"

"I thought that the two of you wouldn't take it that bad . . ." I felt stupid as tears started pouring down my cheeks again. "Things haven't been going that well for me lately, Papa. You two weren't the only ones who had planned a different life for me. I had, too. Plus, I evidently have some kind of psychological inclination toward neuroticism and . . . I worked my butt off trying to fight it, but in the end it was the only way out."

"We don't always get the life we planned on having," my father said. A vein was pulsing out of his forehead, which normally appeared only when he lost a game of tennis. "I definitely had never planned on my youngest daughter trying to take her own life."

"Like I said, I didn't want to hurt anyone," I said.

My father pressed his lips together.

"And to be honest, I don't think any of you would really have missed me," I said. The words just burst out of me. *Aha, there it was rearing its head again, my allegedly brouhaha-loving subconscious.* "I can't ever seem to do anything right for you. You and Mama are embarrassed about the color of my hair and my job; you're embarrassed that I'm not married. I know I was supposed to be a boy. You wished for a son four times, and you only got daughters. Each time the disappointment was greater, most of all with me. So it's true you don't get everything in life that you wish for. You ought to be satisfied with what you've got, too."

I had talked myself up into such a rage that I had stopped crying. My father was apparently so surprised that he was unable to respond to me.

"Well, at least you have grandsons," I said, turning and leaving.

"Look who's here," Charly said, opening the door to let me in.

Ole was waiting in the living room for me. He looked at me very seriously, his eyebrows drawn together. I had never seen that look on his face before. Normally he looked at me as though I were the little baby Jesus in the flesh, with big, beaming blue eyes.

Well, fine. By all means. He wasn't the only one giving me dark looks these days. I was getting used to them.

"We need to talk," Ole said.

"I don't want to talk with anyone," I said, walking around him to go into Charly's practice room. I just wanted to cry my eyes out, loudly and torrentially among all the egg cartons.

Plus, I didn't look that great. My hair was unwashed, I didn't have any makeup on (there wasn't any point—I kept crying so much that everything just kept running), and I was wearing a T-shirt borrowed from Charly that read: FUCK YOURSELF.

"She's just come back from her parents' house," Charly explained. "Was it bad, Gerri-Berry?"

I didn't want to, but I started crying before I got to the door of the practice room.

"Assholes," Charly said. "Instead of being glad you're still alive and wondering why you tried to—"

"Why did you try to do it, Gerri?" Ole asked.

"Well, I *didn't* do it," I said. "That's exactly my problem."

"So you had only checked into that hotel because you wanted to check out?" Ole asked.

"Leave me alone, Ole," I said, trying to close the egg-cartoned door. "You have enough problems of your own, so let's not get all mixed up in that."

Ole stuck his foot between the doorjamb and the door so I couldn't close it. "I just want to clear up a couple of things," he said.

"There's nothing to clear up," I replied. "You were just in the wrong place at the wrong time."

"The right place at the right time," Charly said, correcting me. "If it weren't for Ole, you'd be dead today."

"Yes, and that would have been nice," I said.

Charly put a hand on Ole's shoulder. "She still needs a couple of days. You should probably come back later."

"Yes, I will," Ole said. "But I still have a couple of questions, is all. What's up with that Joe guy, then?"

I didn't say anything. I just squeezed Ole's shoe harder with the door. "Did you do it because of him?" Ole asked.

"God, Ole! 'Joe' is just a, whatchamacallit, an, uh, sarconym," I said.

"What?"

"An acropolis!"

"Huh?"

"An acronym," I said. "God, how should I know what it's called!"

"Anonym," Charly suggested. "Pseudonym. Metaphor. Personification."

Ole frowned. "I still don't get it."

"You guys invented Joe yourselves," I said. "At the cooking party one night, you all just made up a date that I was supposedly going to have, and I liked it: a date with death. Like that Brad Pitt movie."

"*Meet Joe Black*," Charly said. "Slow as hell. Except for the sex scene."

"So there is no Joe?" Ole asked.

"Yes, there are tons of Joes," I said, irritated. "But I don't personally know any, no. Now go home, Ole. I want to be alone."

But Ole's foot stayed stubbornly stuck in the door. His foot was in a beautiful, expensive, hand-sewn Italian shoe, too, and it was undoubtedly suffering from its poor treatment. "Where did you get the pills from?"

"They were given to me," I said, sinking hard into Ole's toes with my foot. He didn't even remotely wince.

"Why did you come down to the hotel bar? What did you want there?" he asked.

"To have a final glass of champagne," I said. "Yeah, I know. It was really stupid. But it happened. Now please go!"

"Unbelievable!" Ole said. "To think if I really had taken a cab home . . ."

"You saved Gerri's life," Charly said warmly.

"Well," Ole started, smiling weakly, "I guess so. But if I had only noticed something wasn't right, I'd have more to be proud of than merely being in the right place at the right time."

"I'll be eternally grateful to you in any case." Charly kissed him on the cheek, and Ole was temporarily distracted.

I seized the chance and pushed his foot out of the door-jamb, then slammed the door shut.

"Hey!" Ole yelled. "I'm not done yet!"

"Let her be," Charly said. I could hear every word, de-spite the egg cartons. "Gerri's going through a lot right now. And you are, too. I'm sorry about everything with Mia. Did you and Mia talk about it?"

"It's all very complicated," Ole said.

One might say that, yes.

"Is she in love with someone else?" Charly asked.

"How should I know?" Ole asked. "We didn't talk about the other man."

"But she knows that you know she's been cheating on you, right?"

"No idea," Ole said. "I have no idea what Mia thinks. Like I said, it's all very complicated. Mia and I haven't been talking much lately."

"But . . ." Charly began. "Well, if it were me, I couldn't stand not talking it out. Something like this has to be re-solved. I mean, you are married to each other, after all."

"I know," Ole said. "But that's why I'm here."

"What does Gerri have to do with you and Mia?" Charly asked. "Oh . . . I get it! Because Mia thinks you and Gerri have got something going on."

"Like I said, I have no idea what Mia thinks," Ole said. "And I also don't know what Gerri thinks."

Gerri also doesn't know what she thinks, I thought, leaving my listening post behind the door to lie down on the couch.

A moment later Charly came in.

"Ole's gone," she said. "He's acting oddly, too."

"He thinks we had sex," I said curtly.

Charly sat beside me on the couch and asked, "Huh?"

"I mean he was so drunk that he couldn't tell what was a dream from what was real," I explained. "When he woke up naked next to me the next morning, he just filled in the blanks."

"How is it he was naked?" Charly asked.

I shrugged. "He didn't have pajamas with him," I said.

"But someone would know whether he had sex or not," Charly said.

"You'd think so, huh? Remind me again about that guy when you were afraid you might be pregnant that time you fell asleep drunk on his couch? What was his name again, Seppel?"

"His name was Kaspar," Charly said. "And that was different. I blacked out."

"Well, Ole probably blacked out, too," I said.

"But you told him it was all bullshit," Charly said.

I shrugged again.

"He didn't believe me." I sat up. "Charly—I can't stand this anymore. I would rather check into the psych ward than subject myself to a single other person's scrutiny. Plus, it'll be warm and dry there, and they'll feed me."

"Nonsense," Charly said. "You know, when all is said and done, I think you've come out ahead. You've told people what you *really* think of them. And the wheat is finally separating from the chaff, as they say. Now you can focus only on people who truly mean something to you, and who love you."

"But I've embarrassed myself in front of them, too," I said.

"*Embarrassed*—how old are you? Embarrassment is something for teenage girls," Charly said.

"That Mr. Adrian from the publisher called my parents' house today," I said. "He's the guy I wrote saying I thought that he was sexy and that his girlfriend wasn't good for him and that I can't hold a pencil under my boobs. You wouldn't be embarrassed in my shoes, then?"

"No," Charly said. "All those things are the truth."

"But I don't even know the man," I said.

"Whatever. That makes it even less embarrassing," Charly said. "What did he want when he called?"

"He wanted to send a wreath to my funeral and ask whether he could publish my vampire novel posthumously."

"But that's terrific!" Charly yelled. "You've got a job again!"

"I said *vampire* novel," I repeated in as derisive a tone as possible.

"Do you have a copy of it?" Charly asked.

I pointed at the laptop. "In there. *Leah's Path into Darkness*. But don't read it if you're sensitive to blood."

Charly was enthralled with the idea of Leah. After she flipped the laptop open and double-clicked the file, her eyes devoured eighty pages in less than forty-five minutes. I sat across from her the whole time, amazed. She was engrossed, truly engaged in the thrill of the story. At one point she even started nibbling on her fingernails, which she usually does only at the movies.

"It's terrific," she said when she was done. "My God, that was exciting. How does it continue? Will Ronina and Sir Amos get together?"

"Well, that's the question in each novel," I said. "I modeled them a bit after Clark Kent and Lois Lane. Or Remington Steele and Laura Holt."

"Oh, yeah, I can see that," Charly said. "That unknown element does add to the drama. When will you be writing the next one?"

"Charly, I don't write vampire novels. This is nothing but trash!"

"But exciting trash," Charly said. "Very exciting. And since when do you have highbrow literary aspirations? I mean, acting like Young Werther and all his sorrows the way you have been is a far cry from becoming the next Goethe. Quite apart from the fact that I always found Young Werther repulsive. All that self-pitying drama about Charlotte. If I were you, I'd hoof it right on over to that Mr. Adrian and tell him you *will* write these for him."

"Hmm," I said. "But this series is going to be full of all kinds of outrageous gimmicky bullshit—"

"So what? You tell him you'll write within your own parameters: no outrageous gimmicks, and more money. What do you have to lose?"

"Hmm," I said again.

"Come on! If he's going out of his way making phone calls just to buy the rights to a novel by someone he thinks is dead, then he must *really* be into it. You know, I always love your novels, honestly, but this Ronina stuff isn't just romantic—it's also *exciting*. Thrilling. And somehow crazy, with all the bad guys and strange weaponry and magic portals," Charly said. "So, without prejudging the other novels, I can tell you this: *There is something to this.* Just imagine what would happen if the rogue vampires broke into Dr. Poulsen's hospital and stole his supply of blood. And what if Nurse Angela were really a vampire and Chief Goswin got bitten by a werewolf . . . God, you could easily turn practically any of your previous romances into a vampire story! *Transform,* I mean."

Charly might be on to something. It had been easy enough to rework Leah, after all.

Charly's brainstorm continued. "How many novels have you written in the last ten years?" she asked.

"Two hundred forty-one," I said. "*Leah's Path* was two hundred forty-two."

"There you go," Charly said. "A bottomless barrel of source material. You just sprinkle in a little vampirism between the lines—"

"Plus, I have them all backed up on CD-ROM," I said.

Charly laughed. "You kept those CD-ROMs but ditched all your panties. You are one crazy little neat freak, Gerri. What—did you want us all to think you wore only skimpy little thongs? By the way, I'm curious—what did you do with your vibrator? The one I gave you for your birthday?"

"Oh, that . . ." I scratched my head. "I'm sure Aunt Evelyn made off with it."

"Oh, I *knew* it!" Charly yelled, seeing through me. "You totally ditched it! Anyone who won't admit wearing panties won't admit having a vibrator! Do you have any idea how expensive that was?"

"Gerri Thaler. I have an appointment with Licorice," I said.

The receptionist frowned. "With Ms. Karisch?"

"Yes. And please don't tell me you don't call her Licorice, too. In secret, at least," I said.

The receptionist slowly shook her head.

"Seriously? Li-ly-Ka-risch?" I said. I looked at her incredulously. "Well, you must be some kind of saint or something if you weren't already calling her Licorice."

"We call her Tweedbutt," the receptionist said reluctantly.

"Tweedbutt?"

"All the nicknames around here have to do with people's butts," she said. "The nice ones have *butts*; the less-nice ones have *asses*. Boneyass, Stripeybutt, Thunderass, Leatherass—unfortunately, the asses are in the majority."

"Wow! Well, that's . . . What's the new editor in chief's nickname? Mr. Adrian?"

"Tightass," she admitted.

"He probably is one of the less-nice ones," I said regretfully.

"He's not that bad, actually, but newbies are always asses to start out with," the receptionist explained, picking up the phone. "I don't know why I just told you all of that! Ms. Karisch? Gerri Thaler is at reception for you."

Licorice came down a minute later and led me back up to her office.

"Champagne?"

"No, thanks. The last time is still too fresh," I said.

"But it did spur a splendid performance. I'm really excited about *Leah's Path into Darkness*," Licorice said. "And The Boy is, too. I have to give him some credit; he immediately tossed out the crappy story he had written and is releasing yours as the first novel in the series. Where is he?" she said, looking at the clock.

"I thought we were meeting in his office," I said.

"In that glorified cubby?" Licorice laughed. "Don't be silly! Are we supposed to spend the whole meeting standing around? Let me tell you—that isn't a good starting position to negotiate a higher advance or royalties from."

I apparently looked taken aback, because Licorice added, "Well, come on, girl. That's what you wanted this meeting for—right?"

"No, it's about . . . You mean I could ask for more money?"

"Of course!" Licorice said. "A hundred euros more per novel, at least."

Someone knocked at Licorice's door, and Mr. Adrian came in. I would have liked a glass of champagne after all, if for nothing else than to have something to hide my face behind. Because my face was turning red, even though I had run through this moment a hundred times back in Charly's practice room specifically so I would *not* turn red.

"The trick is simple," Charly had said. "You're not allowed to think about what you wrote him in your letter."

But it was much harder not to think about something than one might think. You haven't thought about an armadillo in several months, I bet, right? And certainly not of an armadillo wearing a bikini and smoking a cigar, right? But if now I say, "Don't think about a cigar-smoking armadillo in a bikini," what is the next thing you do?

That's what I'm saying.

"Good morning," Mr. Adrian said, holding out his hand. I tried to shake his hand and look him in the eyes as naturally as possible while not thinking about the fact that he knew that I thought he was sexy. And I still did. Even though he was shorter than I had imagined, having only seen him seated before. He was a good inch or two shy of six feet. Much shorter than Ole in any case.

"I'm glad to see you so *lively* today," he said. *Did he just wink at me?* I straightened my Kermit the Frog T-shirt, annoyed I hadn't worn something else. But whatever. I had thrown out all my old stuff, and Charly had practically nothing I could borrow for the day—that wouldn't get me arrested, that is.

"Would you like a glass of champagne?" Licorice asked Mr. Adrian.

"Are we celebrating something?" Mr. Adrian said as he turned away from me and toward Licorice, allowing me to check which sense of "tight" people had in mind when they called him Tightass. As I thought! They were evidently *not* referring to his handling of money.

"Yes! We've lined up Gerri for the Ronina series, and we have a terrific first title already in production," Licorice said.

"All right, then. I'll have a glass," Mr. Adrian said.

"Let me run and get clean classes from the break room," Licorice said, squeezing her Tweedbutt through the door. "Gerri, will you be having some as well?"

"No, thank you. I'm trying to cut back," I said.

"*In vino veritas,*" Mr. Adrian said.

"Yes, but I was drinking vodka, not *vino,*" I said. "And writing all sorts of things that I did not mean."

"Then it's good you don't remember what you wrote," Mr. Adrian said, looking—if I'm not mistaken—at my breasts.

Although it was technically impossible, I turned even redder.

Licorice returned with glasses and uncorked the bottle of champagne. "The novel is wonderful, isn't it?" she said. "If things continue like this, even I might become a vampire fan. Gerri, are you busy working on the second title?" She raised her glass. "*Prost!* To your health, and to Aurora's new best-seller."

"*Prost*," Mr. Adrian said.

"Not so fast," I said. "I am prepared to write for this vampire series, but only if we rework the series' backstory and supernatural details first."

"Agreed," Mr. Adrian said. "As I told you on the phone, I think your suggestions for improvements make a lot of sense. You can talk to Ms. Karisch about all that so she can include those points in her presentation at our next meeting of series managers."

"No, you've misunderstood me," I said, laying a plastic binder on the table. "This is the reconception of the entire vampire series. It draws very little from the first concept. I reworked all the characters, created a good dozen new ones, constructed a story arc for the entire series, and structured the whole thing into subseries of ten books each, which can be continued indefinitely. There is a thirty-page glossary and a reference sheet titled 'The Ten Golden Rules of the Vampire World,' which should make things easier on the series' authors and help us avoid jarring continuity errors with different writers working on the series."

Licorice and Adrian stared at me, both equally flabbergasted.

"I know the whole thing sounds a little highbrow," I said. "But after I researched all this online, I realized there is tremendous sales potential here. You were right that vampires are really taking off now. And we want our vampires to bite their way through the mediocrity of the current market and stand out nicely, correct? So that's why I've struck Ronina's speaking bat, Java, for instance. A speaking animal belongs more in the stories from the kids' comics division."

"Java can't speak in the conventional sense; she can *communicate* only with Ronina," Mr. Adrian said.

"Please!" I said. "Ronina has mastered an incredible body of skills: telepathy, kung fu, telekinesis, healing—does she really need bat language, too? By which I mean, no. As far as I'm concerned, Java can remain a tame exotic pet, but he cannot play a leading role in snooping out the villain."

"Hmm," Mr. Adrian said, picking up my binder and browsing through it, his mind not yet made up.

"I urgently need a job, but I can take on this series only if it strives at least for a *certain* level," I said. "Otherwise I'll have to pass on it and find something else." I pulled a second binder out of my bag and set it in front of him. "These are plot outlines for the entire first subseries. You will get another two hundred thirty novels from me, provided the readers like them."

"And what do you want for that?" Mr. Adrian asked.

I watched Licorice pinching herself in the arm as though she wanted to make sure she was not dreaming.

I took a deep breath. "I actually don't want a fee per book; instead, I want a share of all sales."

That threw Licorice and Mr. Adrian for a loop. They both looked disbelievingly at my binder.

"But that's . . . that's rather . . . that's not the usual way it's done," Mr. Adrian said.

I shrugged. "Think how much you're going to save by not having to sign a dozen untalented authors under separate contracts. And if the books don't sell well, there is no risk for you."

Mr. Adrian blinked at me. I tried not to be distracted by his green eyes but to look back at him as naturally as possible. I had worked hard over the past week, and with Charly's help I had transformed all ten of the Children's Nurse Angela plot outlines into Ronina plot outlines.

Angela's new name was Belinda, and the handsome blond hospital chief, Dr. Goswin, was after her because (a) he preferred mortals with type O blood (especially during a full moon) and (b) he wanted to leverage Belinda's close friendship with Ronina to force Ronina to get in the way of the machinations of senior nurse Alexandra, who was running a flourishing black-market trade in the hospital's blood-bank reserves and thus supporting the renegade vampires behind the scenes. Fortunately, the chief resident was still around—Dr. Orlando, who as usual brought order to chaos and turned out to be a supremely talented cutlass fighter, upon whose chest Belinda could rest her head at the end of every adventure. No one would recognize Belinda as

Angela, but I could still recycle whole passages almost verbatim from the Angela story. It was all going to be a walk in the park.

"If you're not interested, I'll pitch it elsewhere," I said. "As you have already observed, vampires are the latest craze."

"We've actually used an arrangement like this before," Licorice told Mr. Adrian. "With the Colt series. That was long before your time, of course, but the series creator and authors got a share of all sales."

"In this case I'm not the inventor, of course," I said modestly. "I merely, shall we say, made improvements."

"How much do you want?" Mr. Adrian asked.

"Five percent," I said.

Licorice and he looked at each other. Then Mr. Adrian nodded slowly. "I'll need to discuss this with management," he said. "And read your plot summaries. How were you able to write them so fast? I mean, you've had . . . a *lot* else . . . going on lately."

"Gerri is a genius," Licorice said.

"Hmm," Mr. Adrian said, giving me a penetrating look.

"Take your time," I said, trying to look as penetratingly back at him. "By next Friday, let's say? I'll need to have your decision by then." I grabbed a pen and notepad out of my bag, and wrote Charly's phone number on it. "You can reach me at this number."

"But I have your phone number, Gerri," Licorice said.

"No, you don't. I, uh—I've moved for the time being," I said.

Mr. Adrian smiled at me. "Did you write your landlord a good-bye letter?"

Did he know how nice he looked when he smiled? The left corner of his mouth curled up in three little wrinkles, with even more little wrinkles at the corners of his eyes.

"Not all people are equipped for the truth," I said. "Some take it very poorly when they find out what others really think of them."

"I can imagine," Mr. Adrian said. "Although I suppose it depends on how much those opinions matter."

"What are we talking about?" Licorice asked, confused.

Dear Mr. Rothe:

I don't know if you remember me, which is why I'll give your memory a little boost here just to be sure: Gerri Thaler, class of '98, AP Literature/Composition. Although I had the misfortune of having you as a teacher from seventh grade onward (alternately in history, Latin, and German), I don't assume that you ever actually knew my name. This is because you always addressed me as Little Miss, Miss Smarty-Pants, Miss Know-It-All, and Miss Stare-in-the-Air. We had a lot of names for you as well, but you would be interested to hear only very few of them.

In any case, I'm the one who always *earned* an A+ in German but to whom you always gave a B- because you didn't like my interpretations of Goethe, Schiller, Hesse, and Grass.

Now that the end is nigh for me, I find myself wanting to sum up my life. To my own surprise, I genuinely have quite a bit to thank you for. For instance, I would never have grasped the difference between *effect* and *affect* if in seventh grade you hadn't had me write *A proper German girl may not effect an affect for effect* a hundred times on the blackboard.

And then, of course, there was the memorable sentence *Nam in dando recipimus,* "For it is in giving that we receive." I had to write that a hundred times when Britt Emke helped herself to my pen from my desk and wouldn't let go of it until I threatened to slug her over the head with my Latin book. Unfortunately, that was the instant you entered the classroom and immediately sided with Britt. Why did you always do that, incidentally? Because she had a face like a proper German horse? Because she could shed tears on command, while I could only grind my teeth in rage? As though I had given her that pen! It was in fact a gift to me from my great-aunt Hulda and one of the only gifts I had ever truly liked because it wasn't a scratchy pair of wool tights or something: There was a little railroad inside the shaft of that pen, and the train would come and go as you tilted the pen back and forth. I still have it today. It's a good thing you don't know how I got it back because otherwise I would have had to write *A proper German girl may not plunge the nib of her fountain pen into another.*

Sincerely yours,
Gerri Thaler

THIRTEEN

Flo opened the front door for us. "Did you bring us anything?"

"Why aren't you in bed?" Charly asked.

"Because I'm not tired yet," Flo said. "And because I got permission to wait up until you came." She hugged me rapturously to say hello and once more after I slid a little sticker of a unicorn into her hand. "You're the best in the whole world, Gerri!"

"If I had brought you something, would I be the best in the whole world?" Charly asked enviously.

"No," Flo said. "But second best."

"Go to bed," Charly said.

"Tonight is the full moon, children basically never sleep then, better get used to it!" Caroline said as she came out of the kitchen to give hugs and kisses all around without one period in her stream of speech. "Charly, you poor thing, you're still puking all the time, aren't you, ha-ha, well, the first thing I told you was that it's no picnic, Ulrich, you haven't shaved, you look like a Berenstain Bear, Gerri, it's so nice you're here, you look wonderful, is that a new T-shirt, Severin, let go of her earring, I got salmon—no ahi steaks, you're not supposed to buy them anymore because of overfishing and pretty soon all the tuna will be dead because the young ones aren't getting a chance to get big anymore and reproduce, and they don't have anything left to eat, either, Severin, I said let go, because we're catching all the smaller fish, too, it's just terrible, sometimes I'm embarrassed to be a human, the salmon is from an organic fish farm in Ireland, so we can eat it with a good conscience, I thought maybe we could have it with a creamy dill sauce and tagliatelle, those are quick to cook and filling, plus, the kids like that, too, Marta and Marius had to bring both their kids along tonight, their babysitter canceled, Ole and Mia are already here, please not a word that we know their marriage is on the rocks, Ole swore us to total secrecy, so pretend everything is normal, Flo, please go back up to your room now, I think Odette wants to put the Sleeping Beauty dress on Pocahontas."

"She's crazy!" Flo exclaimed, running up the stairs.

"Good trick," Charly said in praise.

"Only works on girls," Caroline said, lifting Severin up onto her hip and clearing a path for us through the mountains of clothes, shoes, and toys by kicking everything to the right and left of her.

I suddenly was too afraid to keep going, but Charly grabbed me by the elbow and said, "Come on! There is nothing you have to be embarrassed about."

Oh, Charly! What would I do without her? This morning she'd had her last official performance as a singer: She had sung "Ave Maria" at a wedding at St. Agnes—the second-largest church in Cologne after the cathedral—and Ulrich and I had sat in the last row and listened. We listened not only to how Charly sang but also to what the other wedding guests said about it.

"Heavens! Who hired *her*?"

"She must be related to someone."

"No wonder the bride's mother is crying."

"*Thank you*," Ulrich had whispered into my ear. "It was really high time for someone to put an end to this whole nightmare."

"My pleasure," I had said, although my heart bled because Charly had been singing all the wrong notes with such pure, fervent joy.

"Chest out, head high," she now said, and I did as she commanded. There really wasn't any reason to be embarrassed. Not in front of my friends.

It was a Saturday evening superficially like any other; we cooked and tried to ignore the noisy children as much as we could as we talked. But at the same time, things felt quite different. For one thing, Marius and Marta kept giving me strange looks and speaking to me slowly with exaggerated clarity. For another, Ole was avoiding looking at me, while Mia was stabbing me to death with her eyes.

I actually considered standing on the kitchen table and offering an explanation: "I am *not* using psychiatric pharmaceuticals, and I *never* had anything going on with Ole. I swear on my life."

But I was too afraid. Plus, although I hadn't had anything going on with Ole, I was starting to regret that more and more—because Mia obviously blamed me for the impending demise of the relationship, anyway.

I was vaguely aware that Mia wanted me to notice her, and I couldn't take it anymore, so I finally took the bait once we were all sitting at the dining table to eat.

"Well, how was your continuing education class last week, Mia?" I asked, taking a bite of smoked-salmon pasta. Flo had squeezed her way as usual onto my lap and had me feeding her as though she were still a baby. I loaded a fork with a bite of food for her.

"Boring as ever," Mia said. "While you apparently had a fairly exciting weekend."

"Mia!" Marius hissed, but Mia pretended not to hear the hissing.

"Open up, here comes the train," I said to Flo.

"I'm curious, Gerri. How was it?" Mia leaned a bit forward, her red hair gleaming like fire in the light of the lamp. "You tried to take sleeping pills, but something kept you from doing that. Do you mind if I ask what that was? Or who?"

"Mia, stop," Caroline snapped at her. "I'm just so glad she didn't do it. And remember, there are children present!"

"But I'm interested," Mia said. "In Gerri's shoes I would be glad someone was interested. It's better than pretending nothing happened. Right, Gerri? So, why don't you tell us how it was."

"Normally, people prefer asking why," I said, sending another fully loaded "train car" into Flo's mouth.

"Oh well, if you *really* had wanted to do it, that's something that would make complete sense to me," Mia said. "I mean, you live in a miserable studio apartment in a building owned by your awful aunt, you write embarrassing soft-core porn, and you have a butt big enough for two."

"Mia, have you gone completely batshit?" Bert asked. "Gerri doesn't write porn! And what way is that for one friend to talk to another who has just tried to . . . You know what she's just been through."

"The nerve," Marta snorted at Mia.

"If you look at things objectively," Charly said, "Gerri's life is not one bit worse than yours or mine."

"What are porns?" Marta and Marius's daughter Odette asked.

"Now see what you've done?" Caroline said to Mia. And to Odette she said, "Sweetheart, porn means exciting stories about ponies."

"It's too bad you don't write porns, Gerri," Odette said with genuine regret.

It occurred to me that no one was defending my butt. My butt really wasn't above average in size—just to be clear. Recently it had gotten smaller, in fact. I was hardly eating anything.

"Oh, I apologize, Gerri. I didn't mean to step on your toes or anything," Mia said with exaggerated gentleness. "I'm sure you had your own good reasons, which are no one else's business."

"Shut your trap, Mia," Ole said. And Mia did just that, at least until the children had finished eating, been excused from the table, and were back to their regular rowdy play— during which every five minutes one of them would get hurt and come running back into the dining room in tears. I stretched my legs, which had fallen asleep under Flo's weight, and stole some glances at Ole. He looked furtively back. I would have smiled at him, but then I would look at Mia and stifle the smile just in time.

Mia got up and sat down on the chair that had become available next to me. She slid up close, which wasn't necessary.

"This whole time I've been thinking how I would go about planning it, if I wanted to kill *myself*," she said softly. She had chosen a good time for her attack: Charly was busy helping Caro clear the plates, Marta was helping Odette's little brother, Odilo (yes, I know—those names are right up there with Arsenius and Habakkuk) get a Lego out of his nose, and everyone else was absorbed in conversation. The only person who was watching us, with worried eyes, was Ole, but from the other end of the table he evidently couldn't hear what Mia was saying.

"I might book a nice hotel room, put on my nicest clothes, and maybe call up someone I'd had a crush on for a long time," she said.

Ah, way to cut right to the chase. She was fishing. *Fish away!* I thought. I obviously had the upper hand since, first, I knew *what* she knew and, second, I knew she couldn't let on *that* she knew it, unless she were to admit she hadn't been at a continuing ed class but had instead joined her lover at Ole's and my hotel. And third, nothing had gone on between me and Ole in the first place.

"Is there someone you've had a crush on for a long time?" I asked Mia. "I mean, you are married, after all!"

"No, no. You've misunderstood. I was trying to put myself in *your* shoes," Mia whispered. Her pale, light blue eyes had tiny pupils, despite the meager light. I thought her eyes looked a little creepy; I made a mental note of this look for Ronina. "I was thinking what I would do if I were *you*. And *I* would have called the guy that *you* have had a crush on all the while. And then I would have cried up some sob story that I was about to kill myself, and naturally he would have dropped everything to come and keep you from killing yourself."

"But that would have been rather dumb of you," I said. "Because then you wouldn't have been able to kill yourself anymore."

"That's exactly it," Mia said. "Did you know that thirty percent of all suicide attempts are nothing more than attention-seeking behavior? These people don't want anything other than to get the love and affection they think they deserve."

"Ah, did you research that online?"

Mia nodded. "And you know what? I think that's exactly how it was with you."

"That at least explains your lack of sympathy and concern," I said.

"I have to say I think that trick isn't half-bad," Mia said. "Underhanded, true. But effective. How could the guy you've had a crush on so long resist you, standing there so unhappily, batting your doe eyes at him. And never underestimate the effect of letting a man feel like he's your savior. And before you know it, you're lying in bed with the guy."

"I don't know, Mia, but I think the effort for all that would be overkill, just to land someone in bed," I said.

"Many men can't be seduced so easily," Mia said. "Married men, for instance."

I had to laugh. "But who would be so stupid to throw herself at a married man?"

Mia studied me seriously. "More women than you think, Gerri. You may not believe it, but even Ole goes astray from time to time."

"Ole?" I looked over at him. He looked uneasy, a bit as though the chair cushion under him were glowing hot. "Not Ole!"

"Yes, it's true," Mia murmured. "He doesn't know, but a girlfriend of mine saw him last weekend with another woman."

"Maybe it was his cousin?" I suggested. I was finding this whole conversation funnier and funnier.

"No," Mia said, leaning forward slyly. "My friend saw Ole and his lover at a hotel. Having breakfast. Making out."

Mia must have been thinking I was the ultimate bitch, since I hadn't even faintly blushed upon this revelation. "No, I don't believe it. Not Ole! Your friend must have confused him for someone else."

Mia shook her head. "She's one hundred percent sure."

"And when did this allegedly transpire?"

"Just last weekend," Mia said, her pupils now as tiny as pinheads.

"Oh dear! You poor thing!" I said sympathetically. "When you were away at a continuing ed thing! That's really just—in such poor taste. What does he say about it?"

"He doesn't know I know yet," Mia said. "I wanted to . . . wait, for a little longer."

"Do you think it's serious?" I asked.

Mia studied me for a while. Then she said, "I think that's pretty much impossible."

Oh, really? What a brazen bitch. "Then everything should be fine for you," I said. "I just don't understand why you haven't confronted Ole with your friend's discovery; you could have found out the whole story by now."

"Maybe I will," Mia said. "I would have done it sooner if all this whirlwind about your near-suicide hadn't cropped up. Will you be giving it another go?"

"You know, I think I've gotten plenty of attention, love, and affection for the time being," I said.

"Aren't you interested in what kind of woman this other woman is?" Mia asked.

"You mean Ole's lover? Of course I'm interested," I said. "I just thought it might cause you more pain talking about it."

"No, not at all," Mia said. "My girlfriend says she's a fairly nondescript, insipid woman."

"Well," I said with a warm smile, "that's what I would have told you, too. Who wants to hurt her friend's feelings unnecessarily by meticulously describing what a real hottie the other woman is? It's bad enough that he's cheating on you, you know?"

"No, *really!*" Mia said. "My friend said for the life of her she cannot fathom what Ole sees in her."

"There's no accounting for taste when it comes to love—" I said.

"Love!" Mia snorted. "But I said it wasn't serious!"

"Hmm, then it must be—animal attraction?" I said. "Even better. Then it'll run its course and be over with faster."

"Yes! Ye-e-es!" Marta had finally squeezed the Lego tail light out of Odilo's nose and was holding it in the air triumphantly. Odilo staggered off, obviously relieved. He often got things stuck in his nose, and Marta couldn't always get them out. Just before Easter, Odilo had pushed a hat to a Playmobil fireman up his nose, and that one had to be removed in the ER. Marta also swore that two Barbie shoes had recently gone missing up Odilo's sinuses.

"We had better get going," Marius said, looking at Bert, who had fallen asleep sitting with Severin on his shoulder, which happened almost every Saturday.

"Yeah, us, too," Ole said, jumping up. "Are you coming, Mia?"

"I've just been having a nice talk with Gerri," Mia said.

"We'll talk some more another time," I said, indulging in a thin smile. "I'm excited to hear how things go."

"Me, too," Mia said.

Ole frowned.

During the general chaos of getting ready to leave—kids being hunted down through the house to get their coats on, Bert waking up and searching in vain for Mia's jacket—Ole unexpectedly grabbed my arm.

"You and I need to *talk*," Ole said.

"If I were you, I would talk with Mia first," I said. "Because she thinks that I lured you to the hotel to keep me from committing suicide. She would readily believe you if you just told her you had no trouble resisting the temptation of my fat ass."

"But that's not the truth," Ole said.

"Well, the truth-truth is just as harmless," I said. "But Mia is operating under some serious misconceptions! So what are you waiting for? You're holding all the aces."

Bert triumphantly pulled Mia's jacket out from under a red parka and a pair of rubber boots and handed it to Mia. Marta had managed to catch Odilo and was holding him tight under her arm. He was desperately roaring and thrashing.

"Monday at half past noon at Café Fassbender. Please be there!" Ole said so softly that he was practically mouthing the words.

Mia took his arm and blinked seductively at him. "I'm looking forward to bed, honey. Aren't you?"

Ole reflexively pulled his arm away from her, and Mia shot me a final look that said, "I'm calling a hit man the second I get home."

That would be fine by me. My only preference would be that she not hire some second-rate bungler but someone who could off me quickly and painlessly.

My mother called the next morning.

"It's Sunday," she said when I answered.

"I know, Mama," I said courteously.

"Supper will be on the table at twelve thirty exactly," my mother said. "I thought I'd do a German springtime classic: plaice filets with lemon, steamed asparagus, and boiled white potatoes with butter and parsley. I don't want you to be late; otherwise the fish will disintegrate in the pan."

I was a little surprised. "Mama, are you telling me that you want me to come to Sunday supper?"

"What else!"

"And you don't want to serve me my plate out in the foyer and otherwise ignore me?"

"Don't be silly," my mother said. "So twelve thirty on the dot. And wear something appropriate; Patrick is bringing his mother, and I want us all to make a good impression. We owe that to Rigerlulu."

Ugh, things were definitely getting serious if Lulu dared admit her future mother-in-law into our leopards' den and familiarize her with the whole family and its foibles—including Arsenius's and Habakkuk's table manners, which would take anyone some getting used to. Lulu's previous relationships had mostly ended after two months, the longest after three, and I couldn't recall ever having met a single potential mother-in-law. Lulu had to be pretty sure about their relationship to dare taking that step.

Well, I was glad for Lulu. The only weird thing was that some pervert who looked exactly like my sister's future husband was running around out there.

"I'll see you then, child." Because of the special guest, my mother had evidently decided to gloss over the fact that she was actually livid at me and never wanted to talk to me again.

It was hard to find anything appropriate to wear, since most of my things had found their way into various charities' curbside donation bins during my cleanup operation, and Charly's closet unfortunately contained little of what my mother would consider "appropriate." After separating out all the pieces that had the words FUCK and SHIT emblazoned across the chest, the choice I had was pretty much between a

T-shirt that read I WANT TO HAVE YOUR BABY, LUKAS PODOLSKI under a picture of Cologne's handsome left-footed footballer and sometime underwear model, and a sheer white blouse.

"Everything else is waiting to be washed," Charly said apologetically, holding a black leather corset up to me.

"No," I said. "Better the T-shirt with the skull on it."

"But that one has a giant hole in the armpit," Charly said.

In the end I wore the sheer blouse because Charly said that, over a pretty snow-white lace bra (a little scratchy, but classy, which is why I hadn't ditched it), the blouse looked elegant and trendy.

Ulrich made a catcall when I emerged from the bathroom. "Wowza, old buddy!" he said. "Good pick. You never know when you might run into a single guy."

Charly ribbed him with her elbow. "You look very—presentable, Gerri-Berry."

"I don't know . . ." I said. "Can you see my nipples?"

"Yeah, baby," Ulrich said. "Enormously presentable. Who's the lucky guy? Don't you think it's a little early for dating again? I think you might do better to stabilize psychologically before . . . Ouch!"

Charly jabbed him again.

"My sister's future mother-in-law is coming to my folks' house for Sunday supper today," I said, looking down at myself, undecided.

"Oh, of course," Ulrich said. "Well, it's exactly the right outfit for that."

"Chest out, shoulders back, head high," Charly commanded. "And don't let them walk all over you, do you hear? All of this can't have been for nothing."

"What do you mean?" I asked.

"All of this bucket-kicking business," Charly said.

Patrick's mother was a petite, unprepossessing woman with short gray hair, ghastly eyeglass frames she must have picked from the bottom row on the rack, and a multicolor floral blouse that somehow looked beige. As she respectfully took in the decor of the dining room, she said, "Oh, I love what you've done in here." With that comment she had won my mother's heart forever.

"A very simple woman but a heart of gold," my mother later said in the kitchen as I was helping her plate the food for serving. The others were sitting in the living room, chatting. "An impossible blouse, though, the poor woman. But when would she have had time to develop fashion sense? She started cleaning houses so her son could go to college. And now she's proud that Patrick has found himself such a clever and beautiful girl like Geritilu: a schoolteacher from a good family."

"And blonde," I said.

"And blonde," my mother repeated. "Their children will be so cherubic. More sauce, Tirigerri, but only on the asparagus. Your blouse incidentally is dreadful! Everyone can see your bra. Didn't I expressly say you should wear something appropriate? If I ever ask *one* thing of you . . ."

"I'm sorry," I said. I should have worn the Lukas Podolski shirt.

"Oh, please," my mother said. "You did it intentionally. You've always been like that—you refuse to fit in!"

Supper was delicious, as always, even though Arsenius and Habakkuk spurned both the fish and asparagus and conducted some very unappetizing experiments with their potatoes. But everyone was the way they always were, except my father didn't deign to glance at me. He was probably still mad about what I'd accused him of last Monday.

Chisola had taken the seat next to me, and she gave me a shy smile. "Here's your MP3 player back. You're still going to need it yourself."

"You can keep it, Sissi," I said. (Sissi was my secret name for her, which was better than Chissi, as my mother sometimes called her: Nicknames do not always help things.) "For it is in giving that we receive."

"But you're going to stay alive now, right?"

I sighed. "Presumably," I said.

"Asparagus tastes like spew!" Habakkuk yelled.

"Fish tastes like poo!" Arsenius rhymed. How fortunate we were they hadn't been triplets. Otherwise the potatoes would probably have . . . Let's not go there.

"Habi! Arsenius! What will our guest think of us?" my mother said. *Guest,* singular. Patrick apparently was already part of the family.

"Oh, it's so lovely having a big family," Patrick's mother said. "I always wanted siblings for my Patrick"—here, she sighed—"but it wasn't to be."

Ah, so Patrick did *not* have a twin brother trolling around the Internet under the name of *rockinhard12*. Pity.

"We're missing one of Tigerlu's sisters," my mother said. "My second-eldest daughter lives with her family in Venezuela. Her husband is a diplomat, and our Gertirika works as an interpreter for the foreign ministry. She speaks three languages."

"Oh, how wonderful. What delightfully talented daughters you have," Patrick's mother said, turning to Tina. "What do *you* do, then?"

"I'm a stay-at-home mom, currently working at full capacity," Tina said with dignity. "But once the twins are out of the woods"—God, when would that day come?—"I'll go back to my teaching job at school."

"Another schoolteacher," Patrick's mother said, impressed, and my mother nearly burst with pride. But when Patrick's mother turned to me, my mother's hands rushed faster than a lightning strike to hold up the bowl of potatoes to her.

"A second helping?"

"No, thank you," Patrick's mother said. "The meal was exquisite. Like in a restaurant. Normally I'm not able to indulge in something so fine."

"Now, Mama! As though you can't cook!" Patrick's mother was apparently a little embarrassing to him.

She turned to me again. "And what do you do, my dear?"

My mother leaped up and began hectically clearing the plates. "Won't you help me get dessert ready in the kitchen, Luriger?"

"Oh, and there's dessert as well," Patrick's mother said.

"Now, Mama! Don't pretend as though you never get dessert," Patrick said.

"Gerri is an author," my father said loudly. My mother froze with a stack of dishes in her hands. Everyone else stopped to look at my father, aghast—especially me.

"An author!" Patrick's mother repeated. "Oh, that's wonderful. What do you write? Would I know any of your books?"

"I . . ." I started, but my mother dropped a fork onto the tile floor, and I fell silent.

"My favorite book of hers is *Claudia the Night Nurse: On Suspicion*," my father said. "Quite exciting, to the very last page."

If I had had a fork in my hand, I'd have dropped it as well.

"I also enjoyed *A Rose for Sarah*," my father continued. "That one is very tender and emotional."

"That sounds delightful," Patrick's mother said. "I'll have to pick up one when I have a chance."

"I'd be happy to lend you my copies," my father said. "If you promise to take good care of them."

"Of course I will," Patrick's mother said.

Mr. Dietmar Mergenheimer
Moltkestraße 23
50860 Cologne

Dear Dietmar aka Max, 29, NS/ND, shy but up for any kind of fun,

While doing some tidying around the house, I came across our old letters and thought of you. Our first and only meeting didn't go that well, unfortunately, and perhaps you're wondering even today whether something happened to me in the ladies' room.

I apologize that I just left you sitting there. (I bailed through the back door.) But I was honestly shocked that your name is not really

Max, that you are not really 29 years old, and that you are not really shy. I had assumed that you were in fact up for any kind of fun, however, but based on the letter that you sent me after our first and only meeting, even that proved untrue. (Sorry I didn't reply to your letter, but I didn't want to add fuel to the fire!)

Let me be honest, Max or Dietmar. That is just not right! You cannot pretend to be ten years younger than you are when you actually look five years *older* than you are. And if your name is Dietmar, you cannot be a Max. I also have problems having to be a Gerda and not, say, a Chloë. But sometimes that's just how things are: Our names are a part of us. I admit that it's hard to come across as sexy on paper or in an e-mail when your name is Dietmar, but how would it be if you went by D-Mar or something instead? Or maybe just go by your last name. "Hey, I'm Mergenheimer." Well, all right. That sounds kind of . . . Fine, it sounds like shit. But what I wanted to drive at here is that someone generally comes across much better if he's authentic and honest. Which is why I've enclosed a copy of a novel for you. It features a fairly unattractive protagonist who ends up earning the love of a terrific woman simply because he's honest, authentic, and above all very, very sexy. So read *The Summer Laura Found Love*, and then you'll know basically everything you need to know about men and women.

Good luck in your search for a girlfriend.

Yours,
Gerri Thaler

P.S. The five-euro bill is to pay for the macchiato that you had to pay for me when I bailed on you in the café. Sorry again.

FOURTEEN

I really don't know what has gotten into your father," my
mother said in the kitchen.

"Me either," I murmured.

"We never talk about your 'professional' activity around
here," my mother said. "Why did he have to start doing that
today, of all days?"

"Maybe he thought Patrick's mother likes to read romance novels?"

"Mmm, maybe. She is a simple woman, I guess." My
mother clicked her tongue. "Only one peach per plate,
child! And center them on the plates. Drizzle the raspberry
sauce clockwise around them—for heaven's sake, stop pretending to be dumber than you are."

I was almost glad that everything between my mother
and me was back to how everything used to be.

"I hope you'll at least wear something appropriate to
Alexa's silver-anniversary party," she said, using a chopstick
to draw pretty patterns of raspberry sauce and cream around
the peach slices.

"Mama, I don't think I should go to the party now that
everyone has gotten my good-bye letters," I said.

"Oh, you mean because of Evelyn and Korbmacher?" my mother asked, arranging the next two dessert plates. "Evelyn already called me to complain about you. She says you have some crazy notion that Volker can't be Uncle Korbmacher's son because of his brown eyes."

"That's right," I said.

"Well, I would say you've hit the bull's-eye on that one," my mother said.

I looked at her dumbfounded. "I wrote it only because I'd had it to here with her condescension. And because she always calls me a changeling."

"Pride goes before a fall," my mother said. "I told her I can't help it if my children paid close attention in biology class."

"You said that?"

"You can never be mad at someone for telling the truth," my mother said, drawing a perfect spiral around the current peach. "I said I suspected it was Harald, that guy she used to work with, and she got very quiet."

"Not Uncle Fred?" I asked.

"Hmm," my mother said. "That would be another possibility, yes. An even racier one, I'd say. In any case, you can move back into your apartment any time. She rescinded your notice. Here, take these two plates out for Arsenius and Habakkuk."

I must have been gaping, because the next thing she said was "Please don't go out there with such a feeblemind-ed look on your face, child. I would like Patrick's mother to have a good impression of us."

Although I was confused and completely thrown by my parents' behavior, a warm and previously unfamiliar feeling took possession of me—which took me a little while to identify: This was how it felt to be loved by one's parents. Well, in this case, loved by them in their weird, special way.

It was a good feeling that made me forget my other problems for a while.

Only as I was walking to my car an hour later and someone grabbed me by the arm did my problems fly back at me.

"What's with all that shit you wrote in your letter to Lulu?" someone hissed behind me while shaking me like a sack of flour. "She started snooping around in my e-mail and checking what Web sites I've been visiting."

"Oh, *that*! I'm sorry, Patrick. It's just that you really are the *spitting* image of a guy who goes by *rockinhard12* I once had a less-than-pleasant date with, and I thought Lulu should know."

"You can't prove anything!" Patrick said. "Too bad, huh?"

"Um . . . that's not what I was trying to do . . . Do you mean to say that you . . . Hey, you're hurting me!"

"I'm not going to let you ruin things for me, you bitch!" Patrick said. "Just because you're one of those fucked-up women who can't handle a one-night stand. First you look for someone online to fuck you, and then you get all mad when he doesn't turn around and marry you! I can't even remember you, but you bitches are basically all the same."

"What? Hey, now Patrick, you listen here . . ."

"I don't care what you tell her, I'll deny everything," Patrick said. "She believes me more than she does you."

I should have known: It's not possible for two people to be so similar. Astrological twins, my ass!

"So, message received?" *rockinhard12* asked with a final squeeze of my arm. "Just be glad you've had the pleasure of my drumstick between your thighs, and leave it at that!"

And on that note he spun and walked back down the street to my parents' driveway, where my sister and his mother were waiting for him in the car.

I couldn't stop trembling. What did that asshole dream about at night? I'd never have touched his drumstick, not even with a pair of tongs. *Oh God, eww!*

But once again it just goes to show how small the world really is.

Driving back to Charly's, I rubbed my arm and wondered how it could be possible that I immediately recognized *rockinhard12,* but he had completely forgotten me. Either I really was the nondescript, insipid woman Mia claimed her girlfriend said I was, or *rockinhard12* had gone on dates with so many women that he had completely lost any and all perspective. I imagined a whole string of women at the café, or wherever his meetups took place, notifying him of their disinterest in his drumstick the way I had, and Patrick lobbing the same insults at them he had lobbed at me as he absconded without paying for his coffee. It was amazing that he had apparently gone out with enough women who had actually . . . Oh God, no, honestly. The thought was just too repulsive.

I'd rather my thoughts dwell on Aunt Evelyn than on *that.*

"Good news," I said when Charly opened to the door to me. "I can move back into my apartment."

Charly looked disappointed. "Back into that horrific hovel? Are you nuts?"

"Charly, I can't live here at your place forever," I said.

"One week!" Charly yelled. "You've been living here for only one week. And it's been nice with you here, hasn't it?"

"Well, yeah. But you and Ulrich . . ."

"Ulrich likes to have you around, too. Isn't that right, Ulrich? You don't want Gerri to move back into her awful aunt's building, right? Into that oppressive, tiny attic closet!"

"Ulrich used to live in that oppressive, tiny attic closet himself," I said. Well, he used to *lie around* in it, at least.

"I don't think it's a good idea to move back to the place where unhappiness began," Ulrich said. "Why don't you just take your time and look for something better, old buddy? You can stay here until you've found something."

"Exactly," Charly said. "You're earning a lot more now, so you can afford something much nicer. Close by!"

"Well, it's not a sure thing with that job," I said. "And finding a new apartment can take a while, especially in Cologne."

"No matter," Charly said. "That's right, isn't it, Ulrich? It doesn't matter to us."

"That's right," Ulrich muttered.

"We love you very, very much," Charly said. "Isn't that right, Ulrich?"

"That's right," Ulrich muttered again.

I was actually quite touched and started crying again. "I love the two of you very much, too," I said.

"Good," Charly said. "Then please don't ever kill yourself again. Do you hear?"

It was my duty to tell Lulu about Patrick's assault—what she might do with that information was her business. Honestly, the fact that Patrick had been horning around the Internet as *rockinhard12* and found it necessary to have women touch him in cafés—*ew, ew, ew!*—was not what I found so bad. Everyone had some kind of blemish on their past, after all, but Patrick hadn't actually crossed the line until he had spoken to me that way. He was a disgusting, sexist, lying asshole.

So I called Lulu and told her about it.

"Lulu, I have confirmed that Patrick and *rockinhard12* are one and the same person," I said straight out. "He admitted it to me himself just now."

"I know what you two were talking about," Lulu said coolly. "Patrick just told me."

"Really? Well, now that surprises me. Because he told me that he would deny everything and that you would believe him over me anyway."

"Gerri," Lulu said. "You're my little sister, and I love you, but you're going too far now. It's one thing to find Patrick attractive and flirt with him, but it's quite another thing to tell such awful lies to break us up."

"What? I would never flirt with that guy. Are you crazy? I have no idea what he's told you, but it's really . . ." The idea was enough to make your hair stand on end, it was so outrageous. I could only laugh. But just briefly. "You know, Lulu, honestly? Patrick is a total asshole. He used to pick women up online and lure them with his rockin' hard line into bed—God only knows how—and now he won't even own up to it."

With all the excitement, my molar started aching again.

"Stop it," Lulu said. "I know you're going through a tough time right now, Gerri, but this is just—*sick*."

"Yes, sick of *rockinhard12*," I said. "He couldn't even remember me, he's been out with so many women. He didn't even know if I was one of the women he's actually been in bed with or merely one who's given him the brush-off. And it can't have been very few women, either, because his 'take a feel' line in the café was really beyond the pale."

"I'm hanging up now," Lulu said in her best teacher's voice. "I'm not mad at you, OK? But I just want to end this conversation now."

"I bet he isn't anywhere near twelve inches, either," I said, but Lulu had already hung up.

"And he probably is more the soft-rockin' than rockin' hard type," I said to myself.

Charly laughed when I told her. She said, "Your sister is a grown woman, and if she wants to keep that slimy Web weirdo around, then that is *her* decision alone."

So, fine. That had been resolved. The only thing left was the secret meeting with Ole.

My tooth was still hurting as I sat waiting for him at Café Fassbender the next day. The tooth had ached on and off the whole time since it started hurting, but it was to the point I couldn't pretend it was some mysterious pain and not the actual tooth.

Even so, I added a lump of sugar to my macchiato as I nervously looked around to see if Mia might be lurking somewhere ready to shoot me with a poison dart. It was a beautiful May day, and I had managed to get us a table outside along the gray-cobblestoned pedestrian street just across from the Romanesque Basilica of the Holy Apostles.

Ole came charging along, only five minutes late. His dentist office was two blocks away.

"A little boy wouldn't open his mouth," he said, out of breath. "His mother had already been to three dentists with him, and he hadn't opened his mouth for any of them. But I managed to do it. Am I good, or what? Sorry I'm late. I really wanted to be on time. You look great, by the way. Did you do something with your hair?"

"I washed it," I said honestly. I had totally planned on doing myself up a bit, but all I could find to wear were my jeans and the I WANT TO HAVE YOUR BABY, LUKAS PODOLSKI T-shirt, so I didn't put much effort into other primping.

"Too bad I'm not Lukas Podolski," Ole said. "But seriously—aren't I better-looking than him?"

"This is Charly's T-shirt. I also think it's meant *ironically,*" I said. "Podolski is too young for us. Or rather, we're too old for him." My tooth was really hurting now. I involuntarily put my hand to my cheek. "And—did you finally talk to Mia?"

Ole nodded. "It's all over."

I forgot my tooth for a moment and spontaneously grabbed for Ole's hand. "Ole, I'm really sorry. So the thing with Mia's lover is serious?"

"No idea," Ole said. "We didn't talk about him."

"You mean Mia didn't want to talk about it?"

"I didn't want to," Ole said. "I didn't even ask her about him. You know, I don't care a rat's ass about that guy."

"But he's still the reason your relationship is falling apart," I said. "Don't kid yourself!"

"No, I'm not," Ole said. "We shouldn't have gotten married in the first place—that's clear to me now."

"Aren't you being a bit hasty? Not two weeks ago you were a happily married man . . . Ouch!"

"What's wrong?"

"Oh, this tooth," I said. "It hurts. Pretty badly."

"How long has it been hurting?" Ole asked.

"A couple of days," I said. "But it keeps going away on its own—until now."

Ole stood up. "Come on!" he said. "Let's take care of that right now." He waved the waitress over and paid for my macchiato, and I didn't protest. "It's been six months since your last visit anyway."

"Maybe it'll stop hurting again on its own," I said, but Ole had already taken me by the arm and was guiding me through the tables and out into the street.

"Which tooth is it?" he asked.

"Bottom left, the second-to-last molar. I think. Actually, it hurts everywhere."

"Mmm-hmm," Ole said. "That's the one we did the root canal on last year."

"Yes, that's right!" I said. "But getting back to Mia—does she at least know *she* was why you came to the hotel, and not me?"

"No," Ole said. "I didn't even get to bring that up. On Saturday night she had hardly gotten into the car before she said, 'I know that something's going on with you and Gerri, but I'm ready to forgive you. We'll start again, from the beginning.'"

"So far so good," I said. "That would have been the moment when you should have said, 'It's not because of Gerri but because of that old bastard you were French-kissing.'"

"I told her it's not that easy," Ole said. "And then Mia went postal. She hurled some pretty nasty insults at me for always working and never being interested in her, for having sex so rarely—and when we do, then it's dead boring—for spending all our free time talking about teeth, and for committing the ultimate betrayal by having an affair and with someone like you, with an ass as big as a circus horse's."

"And that would have been the moment when you should have said, 'Hey, shut up, you bony-assed liar. Who's been secretly meeting married men in hotels, you or me?'" I said with increasing rage.

"But I didn't," Ole said. "I told her your ass is absolutely topnotch and that I get a hard-on whenever I think about it."

"Oh," I said. "Well, that's . . . of course . . . Have you gone totally apeshit?" I yelled.

"No, but Mia has," Ole said. "She yelled, 'You'll see soon enough what you've sown,' and once we got home she packed a bag and yelled, 'Don't even try to stop me!' although it's not like I was planning to. Then she stormed out and into her car and zoomed off."

"To her lover's place! Well done, Ole!"

"To her parents', in fact," Ole said, correcting me. "Her father called me first thing yesterday morning to have a 'serious talk' with me. He said it wasn't 'particularly classy' to have an affair with someone from the same circle of friends, and he asked if I had any capacity to 'think with my head instead of my dick.' But he added I could find Mia at their house if I ever came to my senses again."

"What kind of family are those people?" I said, honestly stunned. "He actually said *dick* to you? That would definitely have been the moment when you should have said, 'Hey, father-in-law, ask your daughter about the dick whom she met last Friday at the Regency Palace. And that's just the tip of the— Oh God, my tooth is really hurting!"

"We're here," Ole said, pushing the door to his office open.

"I thought you would be out of the office longer than that, Doctor," the receptionist said.

"Yes, but Ms. Thaler here has acute pain. Please write her in for one o'clock, and send Lena in." Ole winked at me and disappeared behind one door while I walked through another door into the treatment room.

"Your insurance card, please," the receptionist said. I handed her my card; she swiped it and handed it back.

"You're lucky," she said. "The doctor is booked through the end of next month!"

"You think I'm lucky?" Well, my definition of lucky looked a lot different. I hated unplanned procedures like this. I liked to prepare myself for a few days before a visit to the dentist, both mentally and physically.

As I sat back in the dental chair, the pain abruptly stopped. "I think it's gone," I said, trying to stand. "I guess I'll be going."

"Stay put. That's how it always is," the gracile blonde dental assistant, Lena, explained as she tied a bib around my neck. "It's the adrenaline. As soon as you're home, the pain will start up again."

"All right, let's take a look," Ole said. In his white jacket he looked like the incarnation of Chief Goswin. (When I invented him, I hadn't met Ole yet—but Ole really did look amazingly similar to him.) I spent another moment admiring how well the white went with his blue eyes, tan skin, and fair hair, and then he flipped the chair back so my feet were in the air, and he pushed a massive lamp right into my face.

I reflexively shut my mouth and eyes. Eventually I opened them again.

"Very nice," Ole said as he used a metal hook to tap around on my teeth. It turned out not to be the same molar that I'd had the root canal on. That one had hurt so much I nearly went through the roof. This time it was the very backmost molar, which had never even had one filling. Although they were straight and white, my teeth weren't particularly good, despite the total ban on sweets through my childhood. Thank you, Mama!

"It's actually not a big deal," Ole said as he pressed two gauze pads into my cheek. "It's only a tiny little pit-and-fissure cavity. We don't even need anesthetic, do we?"

"Yesh! Wishout adeshetish I wo'd we awo to ake it!" I yelled, muffled by my cotton-filled cheek.

"Atta girl," Ole said, his drill already buzzing away. "Now where were we?"

"Adeshetish! Adeshetish!" I waved my fists wildly in the air.

"Oh, yeah, right," Ole said as the drill ate its way into my sore tooth. *That noise!* "Mia moved out, and her father thinks I don't have my dick under control."

Surprised at those words, his assistant let go of the saliva ejector, which slid halfway down my throat. Apparently, the latest updates on the boss's private life had not gotten around yet.

"Ghghghgh," I said.

"Sorry," Lena whispered.

"I'm going to have to see a lawyer in the next few days and go through what I'll have left after the divorce," Ole said, drilling right into the center of the pain.

"Ow!" I yelled, trying to sit up. "Adeshetish!"

But Ole gently pushed me back into the chair and kept drilling. He had cured me once and for all of my fantasies of the two of us making passionate love on this dental chair. Like I said—a fantasy. And neither a drill nor a dental assistant showed up in my fantasy.

"That should do it," Ole said just as I thought I might pass out. "You were very brave. I probably won't actually be out that much money; the loan for the office is big cash, and we obviously don't have kids. I'll probably have to pay for the condo, but I can manage that. No, no, don't get up—now we'll do the filling. A bit more, Lena. Yes, just like that. As far as I'm concerned, Mia can have the condo. But then she would have to pay me. Ha-ha—I'd like to see with what. The woman blows every eurocent she earns on shoes."

A puff of cold air from some tool hit the exposed nerve of my tooth.

"Ow," I said, worn out.

When I was finally raised back to sitting position and had rinsed out my mouth, I said, "That hurt! Why didn't you give me anesthetic?"

"It turned out great," Ole said. "Lena, you can take a break for ten minutes."

"Do you always do it that way?" I snarled at him once Lena was out the door. "You could hear me screaming!"

"But the pain is gone now," Ole said, removing the bib from my neck. "And nothing is numb!" He gently wiped my lower lip with the tip of his gloved thumb. "If I were to kiss you now, you would feel everything."

"*If,*" I said. "But after a torture session like that I'm really not in the mood for kissing. Ole, I don't think it's right you're leaving Mia in the dark about why you two are breaking up."

"But you are the reason," Ole said.

I looked at him, dumbfounded. "I am not!"

"Yes you are," Ole said.

"Nonsense! Mia has been cheating on you, remember?"

"I love you, Gerri," Ole said.

Charly held an ultrasound image right in front of my face the minute I came through the door. "There! Your god-child! Or, well, somewhere there in the middle."

"Cute," I said, distracted.

"What do you mean, cute?" Charly said grumpily. "You can't even make anything out yet! Somehow I thought technology had come along enough that nowadays you could clearly see if the baby was sucking his thumb or not. I'm kind of disappointed, honestly. I've been looking forward to this image for weeks, and all I have is a shot of my uterus, a black hole in space. And then the cheap paper they printed it on! It's like a grocery store receipt."

"Charly, it's very early in the pregnancy. The baby doesn't even have thumbs yet."

"Still," Charly said, wiping tears of frustration from the corner of her eye. And then suddenly her whole face lit up. "But now to the really good news of the day: Your fairy godmother at the publisher called for you. They want to meet you for a business lunch the day after tomorrow, at the *Beethoven*. I took the liberty of accepting on your behalf."

"Oh? And who are 'they'?" I instantly perked up.

"Well, the publishing pooh-bahs you're wheeling and dealing with, *businesswoman*," Charly said, beaming even more. "I'm so proud of you!"

"Thank you, Charly. That's nice of you," I said. "But let's not jump the gun. They may want to turn me down."

"Nonsense," Charly said, taking my hand and doing a little circle dance with me. "Why else would they invite you to the Beethoven?"

She was right again.

"Don't look so skeptical. Just be happy," Charly commanded.

All right, fine. I could probably be a little bit happy. "I don't have anything to wear, though," I said after being happy for two seconds.

"I'll lend you something, I'll lend you something," Charly sang. "You see? Life is good! It pays to hold out." In her exuberance, she knocked a stack of papers from the chest of drawers, and they shot across the wood floor. "Oh, yeah, your Aunt Evelyn dropped off your mail, and your sister called, too."

"Which one?" I looked through the stack of letters that Aunt Evelyn had brought. Shit! My credit card bill! And a letter from Dietmar Mergenheimer, aka *Max, 29, NS/ND, shy but up for any kind of fun.*

"It was Lulu," Charly said. "Snooty as usual. You should call her back."

"Ha," I said. "Maybe she's unmasked Patrick finally!"

But that wasn't the case.

"Mama says you don't want to move back into your old apartment. Is that true?" Lulu asked.

"Um, yeah," I said. "I'm going to look for something else."

"So you could move out basically right away, right?"

"Yes," I said hesitantly. "I don't think Aunt Evelyn will be raising any big stink. Why?"

"Because I have an apartment for you," Lulu said. "Patrick's apartment, in fact. If you take over his lease and if the landlady says it's OK, of course."

"Where is Patrick moving?" I asked, a bit slow on the uptake.

"He's moving in with me," Lulu said. "My apartment is bigger and closer to my school and to Patrick's company. Plus, he's here practically all the time anyway, and it's stupid to be paying double the rent. We could be saving the money for something better."

"Lulu? I would really give some serious thought to—"

"Do you want the apartment or not?" Lulu asked gruffly. "It's very nice, nothing spectacular, but it's in Südstadt downtown, just south of the medieval center and close to tons of pubs and trendy shops. One bed, one bath, separate entry, kitchen, balcony. Third floor. At street level there's a cheese shop. The landlady and her partner live on the second floor, and a young couple, both students at the university, live on the fourth floor. The rent is OK, it's in perfect condition, the courtyard in back is nicely planted with a small lawn, and all the residents can use it."

"It sounds nice," I said. "But . . ."

"Patrick has to give three months' notice, but if the landlady agrees you could move in on June 1."

"Well then," I said. "When can I take a look at the apartment?"

"Tomorrow afternoon after school's out," Lulu said. "I'll pick you up at Charly's, at three. And Gerri? Please be nice to Patrick."

"Lulu, you're starting to sound like Mama," I said.

"I've just grown up, is all," she said. "You might try some growing up, yourself."

"It's one thing after another," I said under my breath. But actually, I was feeling pretty good. The job thing was promising, my tooth didn't hurt anymore, and if I could find a new apartment, I wouldn't have much left to complain about. Who'd have thought?

"The apartment of that pervert? Fuck that," Charly yelled when I told her.

I shrugged. "If it's nice and more or less affordable, I'll take it," I said. "I could hire a feng shui expert to go through the apartment and smoke out the pervert's chi with some incense or something."

"But then you'd have that pig to thank, and then he'd have that to lord over you," Charly said. "And plus, what's the rush? Why not take another two or three weeks to plan your move? There's nothing wrong with living here for a little while longer."

"There's a lot wrong with that, Charly," I said warmly. "Besides, Patrick's not doing me a favor—I'm doing him one. Otherwise he'd have to go through the whole rigmarole of finding a tenant to take over his lease, and if he couldn't find anyone, he'd have to pay for three more months' rent."

"But we have so much fun together! And once you're living on your own again, you might start coming up with stupid ideas again. I can keep an eye on you here. . . ." Charly had tears in her eyes. That was typical of her lately: one minute dancing and laughing, the next suddenly sobbing in misery. But that was the pregnancy hormones, no reason to worry. "I hope it's an ugly shithole," she said. "Where the other tenants listen to Xavier Naidoo all day and have a mynah bird that can imitate the sounds of a landing airplane. At the original volume."

"You do not, Charly," I said. "I think I'm on a lucky streak right now, actually. Oh, and by the way—Ole loves me."

Charly did a double take. "Of course he does. We all love you. We need you. Our lives would be sad, tedious, and empty without you. We—"

"No, no," I said. "Not please-don't-kill-yourself-again love; he *love*-loves me. In the classic, romantic sense. Mia moved in with her parents, and Ole won't go back to her because of me. He says, at least."

"Well, that's some encouraging news," Charly said, beaming again. "Congratulations!"

"Hello?" God, what was wrong with everyone? Somehow everyone kept skipping over whole chapters—everyone but me. "This is setting off all kinds of warning bells. The poor guy doesn't know what he's saying."

"Well, Ole really isn't the type who just casually says, 'I love you,'" Charly said, again doing a little dance but without me this time. "It's finally clicked for him; we've been waiting for him to figure it out for years! Caro will do somersaults of joy. And now you want to find a new apartment to live in by yourself, of all times? What a waste—think about it. You'll have just moved in when you decide to turn around and move in with Ole. Oh, I really hope he'll be able to hold on to that great condo of his in the divorce. Those supertall arched windows are simply incredible."

"Are you high, Charly? Don't you see how crazy this all is?" I shook my head. "Ole is all rattled and confused. He has no idea what he's feeling. He found out only a couple of days ago that his wife has been cheating on him. He needs therapy to work through his shock first."

"Sometimes we just need a little impetus in our lives to sort through our emotions and make some long-overdue course corrections," Charly said. "People don't need therapy for that. You like him, too, though, right?"

"Of course I like him," I said. "Very much, in fact."

"Well, there you go," Charly said. "Then just enjoy that you're finally getting what you want. Plus, sex in a dentist chair! You'll have to tell me all about it!"

I blushed. "Did I ever . . ."

"Yes, Gerri-Berry. You did." Charly laughed. "You were pretty drunk that night. And in exchange I told you the

super-embarrassing story about Leo Kernmann in the bathroom on the airplane."

"Oh, I don't remember that at all."

"Good, that's what I was hoping," Charly said. "Some
things are better kept to oneself."

"I was in Ole's dentist chair today," I said. "Believe me
when I say I wasn't thinking about sex." I had even slightly
turned my head to the side when Ole tried to kiss me right
after his declaration of love.

"Sorry, Ole, but this is all going way too fast for me," I had
said.

Ole had looked a little disappointed. "I understand that
you . . . It's only been a week since you . . ." he said. "But you
feel it, too, right? Between us. There is this special bond . . .
and that's the reason for all these coincidences that brought
us together at the hotel. A magical night . . ."

"Ole, I have told you now a couple of times—nothing
happened between us that night! I had taken sleeping pills,
and you were drunk. There wasn't anything magical about
it except for what you imagined, all in your pretty blond
head."

"I may not be able to remember all the details," Ole admitted. "But I do remember one thing very clearly: My feelings for you are not imaginary."

I studied him for a while, very skeptically. He looked delicious, with his serious blue eyes, his contrarian hair that
he couldn't keep out of his face, and his becoming white
jacket. If I had been born under another more passionate
sign of the zodiac, I likely would have pushed aside my reser-

vations, thrown myself into his arms, and pressed my cheek against his broad chest. But you can't escape your own skin. And we Virgos are born skeptics. We live by the motto "If it sounds too good to be true . . ."

"Have you been going to a tanning salon?" I asked him.

Ole sighed. "I get that you need time, Gerri. You haven't had the best experiences with men."

He was right about that. But I hadn't had the best experiences with him, specifically, either. It's not exactly a feeling of exaltation to fall in love with someone and then watch him marry someone else.

"First you need to . . . go and figure out what's up with you and Mia," I said as I walked to the door of the treatment room. "I refuse to be the reason for your divorce. That is not fair to me."

"I can wait!" Ole called behind me.

Ms. Gerri Thaler
Dornröschen-Weg 12
50996 Cologne

Dear Gerri,

Thank you for your letter. I was surprised to hear from you, since it's been almost two years since you left me sitting at that café. At the time I ended up having a rather unpleasant conversation with the waitress and manager because I refused to pay for your macchiato. Ultimately I convinced them and didn't have to pay, but they banned me for life in return. That wasn't a very nice experience, as you can imagine. But let's forget about that.

What you wrote in your letter gave me a lot to think about. I did end up meeting quite a few other women, some even prettier than you. But only one wanted to get to know me better. *Jessica, 24, sexy, natural blonde.* But Jessica's real name is Hildegard, and she's forty-three. She is a real blonde, but of course she's also fat. Or at least plump. She's very nice, but I had always imagined my future wife differently.

Now that I've read *The Summer Lara Found Love*, maybe I'll give Hildegard another call. It's true, as Lara noted, that a sexual connection with someone else is ultimately conveyed by things other than appearance, age, and name. The way Lara slowly but surely fell in love with Nathan was an exciting read. And I really liked the end when Nathan landed that asshole Torsten a right hook to the chin so hard he fell back into the buffet table and pulled down all the Meissen porcelain. The author really understands love.

I'll wrap this up then, and maybe go and call Hildegard. She has a nice last name: Catz. I could call her Pussy. What do you think? On that note . . .

Yours,
D-Mar Mergenheimer

P.S. If things don't work out with Hildegard, would you be interested in getting together again? I could give you back your five euros.

FIFTEEN

Patrick's apartment was even nicer than I could have hoped. In the entry and bedroom I especially liked the practical *built-in* closets, which are so rare in Germany.

"I sanded them and painted them white myself," Patrick said. I noticed he kept avoiding looking me in the eyes. Maybe he had remembered he still owed me for a cappuccino, but maybe he was just generally embarrassed. I made sure never to be alone with him in a room, because I was a little afraid of him. I had gotten some nice blue-and-green bruises at the spot where he had grabbed my arm and shaken me.

The whole apartment was done in black-and-white. The tiles were done in a chessboard pattern; the floorboards had been stained with a white stain; the walls were white; the built-in kitchen was all black, with high-gloss cabinet fronts and stainless-steel countertops; there were black-leather sofas, white bookshelves, a zebra-skin rug on the floor, and framed black-and-white photographs hanging on the walls.

"Perverted," whispered Charly, who had insisted on coming with me.

I honestly thought it was pretty cool. And the balcony was extremely big for Cologne. I could set a table and chairs out there, and there would still be room for a chaise longue. Or a hammock. Oh God, how had I held out all these years without a proper balcony?

The landlady was a nice woman around fifty who ran the cheese shop on the ground floor with her partner, a woman about the same age. Charly had conspicuously raised her nose in the hair and sniffed as we had walked through the corridor to the apartment's front door, but the scent of cheese didn't bother me a bit. I love cheese. And the scent wasn't noticeable inside the apartment. The most important thing was that the landlady didn't object to letting me take over Patrick's lease. She said I could move in on June 1. She also didn't want to see proof of employment; she thought it was perfectly reasonable that I didn't really have that kind of thing as a freelancer.

The only problem was the deposit of three months' rent. I didn't have enough credit left on my MasterCard to cover that.

"I'll lend you the money," Charly said, generous as always. But she didn't have any money, either, and whenever she did talk about money, it was actually Ulrich's money. And I really could *not* take Ulrich's money.

"It's not necessary," Lulu said. "Papa said he'd cover the deposit."

"Well, well!" Charly said.

"What?" I asked Lulu in disbelief. I was pretty close to fainting. During my first and only semester at the university, my parents had stopped giving me any money at all. Not even at Christmas or on my birthday. On those occasions my mother preferred to supply me with things she thought

I urgently needed. Such as winter coats, sweater sets in gray-flecked angora wool, and the AutoJuicer 2020, which pressed unpeeled fruits and vegetables into healthful beverages at the push of a button.

"Just take it," Lulu said.

"I don't want charity," I replied.

"Shut up," Charly said.

"You would have to buy the kitchen," Patrick said. In Germany, you typically take the kitchen cabinets and appliances with you when you move, so a built-in kitchen like his was unusual—and expensive. "I would need at least three thousand five hundred for it."

"Patrick!" Lulu said, reproaching him. "You know Gerri has no money, and she's my little sister."

"But the kitchen cost me almost nine thousand," Patrick said. "And even that was a bargain because I got a monster discount on it. The refrigerator alone ran me . . ."

"Patrick!" Lulu said. "We're family now. In a family people don't wangle each other out of money."

"The kitchen is hideous anyway," Charly said. "It's like a set for a Frankenstein movie. And you'll be able to see every fingerprint on that glossy finish. I wouldn't pay one eurocent for it."

I thought the kitchen wasn't bad at all. To be honest, I thought it was terrific. The apothecary-style slide-out pantry storage; the dazzling, massive American-style refrigerator that extended from the floor nearly to the ceiling; the awesome gas cooktop . . . At last, I could host our Saturday-night cooking parties in my own kitchen. And Flo, Gereon, and Severin could sleep in my bed, in the separate bedroom.

The bedroom wasn't that big, but with the built-ins it looked quite spacious, and I could set up beds for Marta and Marius's kids in the living room, if need be.

"I am going to have to take those bookshelves, though," Patrick said. "They're designer pieces, and I have to sell them off because they won't fit in Lulu's apartment."

"eBay," Charly said. "I hear you're a rockin' hard salesman when it comes to the Web."

"I can't do it that fast," Patrick said, shooting Charly a withering look. "And storing furniture costs a small fortune."

"It's not that easy making one apartment out of two," Lulu sighed. "Each of us has to give up a few things; that's just how it is. I'm giving up my favorite sofa, for instance. Do you happen to want it, Gerri?"

"For free?" I asked. Lulu loved her aubergine silk neo-baroque sofa more than anything. It had gilded lion's feet, and the back was embroidered with a golden crown. She'd had it in front of a wall painted lavender next to a chest of drawers from Ikea that she had pepped up with some napkin decoupage. Napkin decoupage was one of Lulu's hobbies. Patrick's black-leather couches were going to look a bit odd in her apartment.

"Of course for free," Lulu said. "I don't need it anymore, after all." I didn't have to think for long: It would bring me untold pleasure to give away the old red couch from my attic studio. As it would giving away my old kitchen. Maybe Aunt Evelyn could find someone in need to donate them to through church.

"All right," I said buoyantly.

The landlady brought in the paperwork, and we all sat at Patrick's glass dining-room table to sign the various instruments of German bureaucracy. Patrick signed an early termination agreement, and I signed a bridge lease for the remainder of his lease as well as my own new lease. Charly insisted that Patrick also issue me a handwritten gift agreement for the kitchen.

"So that you won't try to wangle money out of Gerri for it," she said. "When Lulu doesn't happen to be listening!"

"We're family now," Lulu said again. "A gift agreement really isn't necessary."

"Trust, but verify," Charly said. "I'm always rockin' hard about things like this."

"It's fine by me," Patrick said, evidently bored.

On the street in front of the building's main entrance, Patrick had one more chance to speak to me alone while Charly and Lulu were asking the landlady about her secret for the lushly blooming geraniums on either side of the cheese shop's door.

"I warned you, *bitch*," he said. "She believes me over you any day."

"That's true, unfortunately," I said. "Incidentally, you and I never actually hooked up, asshole, so stop calling me bitch. You were angry I didn't want to touch your rubber tip, and I had to pay for your cappuccino after you hurled a series of rather ugly insults at me."

"That's why I've given you my kitchen," Patrick said. "I think that makes us even, you b—." He didn't finish the word but added, "Frigid cow."

Yes, he was right about the even part. I had come out ahead. For a kitchen like that and this awesome apartment, I was happy to be called a frigid cow.

I had never had a business lunch at an elegant restaurant like the Beethoven, but I did know that one does not show up at a place like that in an I WANT TO HAVE YOUR BABY, LU-KAS PODOLSKI T-shirt. So I took my MasterCard, ignoring the fact that my checking account was in the red, and bought myself some new clothes, including panties. It was a good feeling for a change to be wearing something that wasn't see-through, ripped, or inappropriately emblazoned with the faces of soccer players/underwear models. The light-weight pale-gray pants and short-sleeved sweater may not have been exactly peppy, but they looked classy, flattered my figure, and were not likely to get wrinkly or creased. Before getting into the car, I checked my rearview mirror to make sure there was no lipstick on my teeth or a curler left in my hair. (That was always happening to Charly. She had spent half of Caroline and Bert's wedding with a curler on the back of her head. I'd discovered it only after getting curious as to what everyone had been giggling about.) I also took the gum out of my mouth; it was sometimes hard to get rid of gum without swallowing it once you were at a restaurant.

The radio weatherman had forecast storms that would temporarily put an end to our warm spring weather, but it was still dry, which justified wearing my fantastic new shoes: retro black slingbacks that were amazingly comfortable giv-en the height of the heels.

The Beethoven was a beautiful restaurant, at least from the street, and when I looked between the mullions of the window I was amazed how many people were having lunch there in the middle of the week.

As always, I was punctual to the minute and wondered if I shouldn't walk around the block one more time to avoid being the first to be seated. That looked so overeager, and I wanted to come across as a little cool. Plus, I didn't know whether Licorice had reserved a table.

"There you are already," said a warm baritone next to me. It was Mr. Adrian, in jeans and a green polo that perfectly matched the color of his eyes. I was pretty sure that a woman had picked that shirt out for him, a woman who had looked deeply into his eyes. Maybe his mother, though.

"It's nice that you're so punctual," he said.

"I always am," I said. "It's my sign of the zodiac."

"Virgo," Mr. Adrian said.

I nodded, surprised. "Are you a Virgo, too?"

"No. I'm Sagittarius, the archer."

"Do you like being a Sagittarius?"

"It doesn't matter to me," Mr. Adrian said, holding the door into the restaurant open for me. "I don't believe in astrology."

"Me either, actually," I lied, trying to remember whether Virgo and Sagittarius were a compatible match. I would have to look that up online the minute I got home. The waiter led us to a corner table set for two.

"Just the two of us?" I asked before I could bite my tongue.

"Ms. Karisch sends her regrets," Mr. Adrian said. "Family matter."

"Oh," I said. "But nothing bad, I hope."

Mr. Adrian shook his head. "What are you in the mood for? Everything on the menu here is delicious; it's just that the portions can be a little on the small side."

I studied the menu. "International cuisine" evidently entailed a menu mostly in languages other than German. "What is abalone again?"

"I think those are like sea snails," Mr. Adrian said.

"And *émincé*?"

"Thin slices of meat," Mr. Adrian said. "Braised in a sauce."

I shot him an astonished look. The guy seemed to know a few things. I wanted to test and see what else he knew.

"Scoparolo?"

"Cheese. A sheep's milk cheese." Mr. Adrian raised one eyebrow and studied me over the top of his menu. "Did you really want to know, or is this a quiz?"

"Chiffonade?"

"That's, uh . . . I don't know," Mr. Adrian said.

"Well, you still had a good run. Do you often dine at fine eating establishments, then?"

"Yes," Mr. Adrian said. "But I also like to watch those cooking shows on TV."

"I love those, too." I was unable to keep from beaming at him. "Cooking is truly exciting. My friends and I get together every Saturday night to cook together."

"Wow, I love parties like that," Mr. Adrian said. "We used to do that sometimes, too. We'd cook or play cards . . . But now almost all my friends have kids, and somehow . . ." He fell silent.

"Yes, when they get kids, they get kind of strange, don't they?" I said sympathetically. "But what can you do? You can't go out and find new friends just because the old ones have kids, you know?"

"But you also can't spend all your time with nothing but happy families," Mr. Adrian said. "No human being can take that."

"Sometimes I feel as though I'm from another planet," I said. "Or worse yet: as though the world has kept on turning but I'm stuck in place."

"Exactly," Mr. Adrian said. "My friends always claim they're envious, but in reality they only pity us singles."

"Yes, I'm always getting appointed godparent, almost like a vicarious—" I paused. "But you're actually not single," I blurted out, and then blushed. "I mean, uh, sorry . . ."

"You mean the fling with Marianne? I didn't realize everybody knew about that until I got your letter." Mr. Adrian rubbed his nose bashfully. I immediately forgot my own embarrassment.

"But an office affair like that can never stay secret," I said in a motherly tone.

"No, I guess not. I've ended it, in any case."

"What? Because of me?" I said a bit too loudly, blushing a darker shade of red. "Because of my letter, I mean? Because of what I wrote . . . about, uh . . ."

"Yes," Mr. Adrian said. "Because of what you wrote. And because it was a pathetic, superfluous affair anyway. Do you remember what you wrote?"

I shook my crimson head. "Only vaguely." I'd have liked to ask him what was pathetic and superfluous about the affair, but I lacked the courage. I guessed Marianne Schneider left her boots on during sex or something. Pathetic and superfluous.

The waiter came to take our order, giving my face time to return to its normal color. When we were alone again, Mr. Adrian took a large envelope out of his briefcase and handed it to me. "I brought you a proposed contract under which you will get five percent of net retail sales of the Ronina series. Payment will be made semiannually. That's why I added a clause providing for a six-month advance so that you won't have to wait until February for your first payment. The advance will be paid out fourteen days after the contract is signed."

"Then show me the dotted line," I said, trying to seem all casual. Oh my God! Contract! Advance! Money!!! Now I might be able to pay the deposit on the apartment myself without robbing a bank or taking my father up on his offer. "Due to unforeseen expenditures, my account is unfortunately in the red at the moment," I continued. "How much is the advance then?" I opened the envelope and took out a stack of heavy paper covered with double-spaced lines of text. My hands tried to tremble, but I refused to let them. I was a pro. Or on my way to becoming one.

"Take your time and read it through," Mr. Adrian said. "Under this contract you are not only gaining certain rights but also assuming certain obligations. Are you sure you're up to it?"

"Of course." I didn't understand a word of what I was reading; I impatiently scanned the pages, searching for the number that might bring my account back into the black. When I finally found it on page three, I nearly squealed aloud. *"Twenty-four thousand euros!"*

"Well, the advance is half of that," Mr. Adrian said. "It's based on an estimate, of course—although we very much hope that Ronina will be pulling in even more money. Much, much more."

Now my hands *were* trembling. "Twenty-four thousand euros a year. I've never earned that much before!"

Mr. Adrian raised an eyebrow. "It's all relative, Gerri. Don't forget. First, you're going to have to pay taxes on that; second, you'll have to submit two manuscripts a month; and third—have you ever calculated what your hourly wage works out to be? I'm pretty sure only Peruvian asparagus pickers earn less."

"But it's a clear improvement," I said. "And I really *love* doing it."

"I nonetheless want to be sure that you're up to this," Mr. Adrian said.

"All right, listen up," I said. "I wrote for Aurora for ten years, two novels a month, and I submitted every single manuscript on time, if not early. With no copyediting errors and ready for production."

"Yes, I know," Mr. Adrian said. "But, uh, in the interest of the publisher, I have to make sure that you won't try to kill yourself again. Because then we would have a serious problem."

"Well," I said. "You can never be entirely sure. I mean, I might also die from bird flu or get hit by a garbage truck. And that could happen to you, too. Lightning can strike anyone, anytime."

"So you won't be trying to kill yourself again?"

"Um, no. Not for the time being," I said.

"Good," Mr. Adrian said. I waited for him to ask why I had wanted to do it, but he didn't.

"I'm not neurotic depressive," I said. "I just had a prolonged rough patch. Love life, work life, other life—there had been no prospects anywhere. But that's changed now."

"I'm happy for you," Mr. Adrian said.

"Not that *everything* is great now," I added. "It's just—gotten better."

"In all areas?"

"Sorry?" I asked.

"Love life, work life, other life," Adrian said, repeating my list.

I thought for a moment. "Yes," I said. "You might say so."

The food arrived, and it was delicious. Chiffonade, incidentally, apparently refers to fresh herbs and leafy green vegetables cut into long, thin strips added to broth. Mr. Adrian ordered the cream of asparagus soup with wild garlic to start and halibut for his main course. I would have loved to try his food, but I lacked the courage to ask. But my guinea fowl was excellent. We didn't talk a lot during the meal, but I didn't care. It was a pleasant silence.

"How did you know that Virgos tend to be punctual?" I asked over dessert.

"I didn't know that," Mr. Adrian said.

"But you *guessed* my sign," I said. "Before we came in, outside the front door. Don't you remember? You commented on my punctuality, and I said it was because of my sign, and then you said—"

"I know what I said," Mr. Adrian said. "I had noted that your birthday is September fourteenth is all."

"Oh." I took my last spoonful of strawberry parfait. *Oh?*

Mr. Adrian leaned back in his chair. "An espresso?"

"Well, how do you know when my birthday is?" I asked.

"No idea. Maybe from looking through your old contracts, or maybe it was on Ms. Karisch's calendar. Photographic memory. Espresso?"

"Yes, please." How odd, though. I was pretty sure that Licorice didn't know my birthday, and my birthday had never been listed in my previous contracts. Otherwise Licorice wouldn't have been so surprised by how young I was.

I looked Mr. Adrian directly in the eyes. He looked away.

"OK, OK," he said shyly. "I googled you."

"Me? My birthday is listed somewhere online?" I was a little flattered. How nice—he'd *googled* me. He wanted to find out about me. The idea of googling him had never occurred to me. Hmm . . . I definitely had some catching up to do at home.

"It was on your high school's home page," Mr. Adrian said. "It also listed your final GPA and your AP classes."

"Surely that information is protected under the Data Protection Act," I said.

"Yes, it definitely is, in fact," Mr. Adrian said. "Personally, I would sue my school if they were to disclose my GPA publicly. But in your case—three-point-eight, that's rather good."

"It would have been better if my neofascist cue ball of a teacher, Mr. Rothe, hadn't screwed up my final grades with a ridiculous curve," I said. "So mine was by far the worst GPA that anyone in our family has ever graduated with. Apart from my mother, of course, who never graduated from high school at all. But she was still disappointed I wasn't in the top three percent of my class, the way Tina, Rika, and Lulu had been. Those are my sisters. They're all just better at everything than I am. They're blonde, smart, and married. Or at least engaged." I fell silent. I hoped that hadn't sounded bitter and envious.

"I've got two brothers," Mr. Adrian abruptly said.

I smiled at him. "Is it just as bad?"

"One has a PhD in nuclear physics and was on the German rowing team at the Seoul Olympics, and his kids all play violin and piano; the other took over my father's company and married a fashion model. My parents are very proud of my brothers."

"And not of you? But you're—"

"*I* sit in an old storage room at Aurora," he interrupted. "Which, naturally, no one is allowed to find out officially. My parents always say, 'Our Gregor works as a manager in the publishing industry,' but the word *Aurora* itself is taboo."

"That's crazy," I said. "How old are you?"

"Thirty-four," Mr. Adrian sighed. "And every Sunday I still have to make an appearance at my folks' house for supper."

I bent forward. "Me too! And mainly just so they can nitpick and nag me to death. Have you ever thought about moving away, maybe to another city?"

"Oh, definitely," Mr. Adrian said. "I studied in Britain for two years."

"There you go! Then your parents would—"

"While my brother was working as a guest lecturer at Oxford," Mr. Adrian interrupted.

"Hmm. I'm getting the impression that your brothers are tough acts to follow," I said. "But there's no way they are as good-looking as you are!" I uttered that last comment with full confidence of victory.

"Alban did some modeling while he was in college," Mr. Adrian said. "And four weeks ago Nikolaus was voted 'Europe's Hottest Scientist' in some online poll."

"They got stuck with names like Nikolaus and Alban, though," I said, because I couldn't think of anything else to say. "And I'm sorry, but I just can't imagine that they're better-looking than you. Why didn't *you* do some modeling in college? Whatever Alban can do, you can, too."

"Too short," Mr. Adrian said. "I'm only five eleven. My brothers—"

"You know what?" I interrupted. "I don't want to hear one more word about your brothers! If *I* say you're the best-looking guy I've come across in years—no, the best-looking guy whom I have *ever* come across, then you can simply take my word for it. And I know *a few* good-looking guys."

"But you've never seen my brothers," Mr. Adrian said. "All of my old girlfriends used to end up with crushes on them. At least, the girlfriends whom I dragged to my folks' house for Sunday supper."

"Including Marianne Schneider?"

"I did not introduce Marianne to my family!" Mr. Adrian said in horror. "She would never have wanted to go, anyway. I think I mentioned that was just a meaningless fling."

"You said 'pathetic and superfluous,'" I said, correcting him.

The waiter came and took our espresso order.

"How is it that all of your sisters are blonde but you aren't?" Mr. Adrian asked once the waiter left again.

"My aunt Evelyn thinks I'm the mailman's daughter," I said. "But actually I'm the only one who takes after my father instead of my mother. He has brown hair, brown eyes—"

"But your eyes aren't *brown*," Mr. Adrian said, bending forward. "They're more like—caramel sauce held up to the sun."

Hmm, that was a lovely description. Better than "amber," which is what people usually tell me. "My sister Tina has the same eyes, but with her blonde hair they somehow look nicer," I said to conceal my embarrassment.

"You know what?" Mr. Adrian said, laughing. "I don't want to hear one more word about your sisters."

I would have bet my new contract that none of his brothers had as nice a laugh as he did. I couldn't help but laugh with him.

The espresso came, and so did the end to our business lunch, which I was deeply sorry about. But Mr. Adrian had to get back to his storage room, and I had to go to Charly's house, where she had a bottle of champagne waiting for us to celebrate my contract. And I wanted to stop by and visit my father on the way.

"I really enjoyed this," Mr. Adrian said outside, in front of the restaurant. He held out his hand so oddly that I couldn't decide whether to shake it or high-five it. I didn't do either.

"I did, too," I said, suddenly a bit anxious. "Thank you so much for inviting me. Good-bye."

"See you soon," Mr. Adrian said.

Once I was a few steps away, he called after me, "Wait!"

I went back to him with excitement in my eyes.

"I think, um, I was thinking, now that we're kind of working together and all, that we can drop the formal Mr. stuff and just call each other by first names," he said, a suggestion that in German culture marks the start of a true friendship—or something more.

"All right," I said. "Although I like *Adrian* better than *Gregor*. Especially since I named that vampire Gregor in the Ronina book."

"As long as we drop the titles and can be . . . friends," Adrian said, "I don't really care *what* you call me."

My father put his face of stone back on when he saw me. "Gerri, what a surprise. It's not even Sunday. Come in, your mother is at bridge. Can I make you tea?"

"Lulu said you wanted to pay for my deposit on my new apartment, Papa," I said. "I came over to tell you that I can't take the money. Even though it was very nice of you to offer."

"It has nothing to do with niceness," my father said. "I already electronically transferred the money into your account last week."

"Really, Papa. I can manage fine on my own. I've *always* managed fine on my own."

"Oh, my baby girl. Two weeks ago you tried to take your own life," my father said. "That is *not* what I call 'managing fine' on your own."

I blushed. "Yes, but apart from that . . . Well, at the moment things are going quite well for me. I signed a new contract with Aurora today. A contract that gives me huge royalties. They're advancing me twenty-four thousand euros the first year alone."

"That works out to two thousand, gross, per month," my father said. "That's not exactly swimming in money. Especially when you consider how little you're saving for retirement. Coincidentally, twenty-four thousand is exactly the amount I just transferred into your account."

"What? But the deposit on the apartment is only—"

My father raised his hand. "It's exactly the right amount of money you're entitled to," he said. "I should have given it to you long ago."

"But I don't want—"

He interrupted me again. "I paid about twenty-four thousand euros for each of your sisters to go to college. You dropped out after one semester and paid your own expenses from then on. It's only right and proper that you get the money now."

That made me cry, annoyingly. "Even though you were so angry at me . . . I'm so sorry, Papa. I didn't even write you a good-bye letter."

My father made a motion as though he wanted to hug me, but then he took my hand. "I have spent the last few weeks thinking a lot about us, and you. I blame myself for allowing this to happen. What you said out in the backyard the other day was true: We've never shown you how proud we are of you. I was angry at the time that you dropped out of school, since you're just as smart and talented as your sisters. All these years I've been thinking you're throwing your life away—"

"Not everyone can become teachers and interpreters," I said.

"That's true," my father said. "Plus, I think your novels aren't half-bad! Really. I found myself forgetting that my own daughter had created everything in the story, and I was truly gripped. You might even try writing a *literary* novel sometime."

"Papa . . ."

"Yes, sorry. That's not how I meant it. How about a novel about a young woman who wants to kill herself and sends good-bye letters to everyone she knows?"

"First I have to write thirty-two vampire novels," I said. "Vampires are really taking off, you see."

"Well, your aunt Alexa will be glad," my father said. "She's one of them."

The Thaler Family
Hasenacker 26
51068 Cologne

Dear Mr. and Mrs. Thaler:

I would like to offer my sincerest condolences on the passing of your daughter, Gerda. Gerri and I were in the same homeroom in school from fifth grade onward, and we were very close. Unfortunately, we lost touch in recent years (I moved to Bavaria to major in special education at the University of Munich, then after graduation I worked with handicapped children until I got married, moved to a large estate, and had my own two children: Luise, age 4, and Friedrich, age 1), so I was, sadly, completely unaware of Gerri's problems.

Oh how I wish she had come to me; there were so many times in school that I helped her out of one mess or another. But now it's too late, and all that is left to assuage us, the bereaved, are the poet's words: "It is hard to lose someone, but it is a comfort to know he was well liked."

I also take comfort in a quote by the nineteenth-century Austrian writer Otto Leixner von Grünberg, "Giving solace is an art of the heart; it often consists in loving silence and silent sympathy." My heart and thoughts are with you.

Sincerely yours,
Baroness Britt von Falkenstein, née Emke

SIXTEEN

A re you still feeling sick all the time, poor Charly, I got something for you that used to help me a lot, and it has no side effects, Ulrich, please go shave for once, you look like a bear, hey, you look fantastic, Gerri, are those shoes new, I got lamb, but they didn't have any eggplants that I could be sure weren't genetically modified, Severin, stop that, you're not a dog, come on in, Marta and Marius are already here, please don't make any stupid comments about her swollen ankles, she'll start crying and won't stop, it's really high time for this elephant baby to be born, Ole's here, too, without Mia, they've officially separated, but I'm sure you knew that already, I can't say I'm sad about it . . ." Caroline said, holding her usual Saturday-evening welcome monologue, and we fought our way through the mountains of toys and clothes.

Flo and Gereon had been in bed for an hour already, although Flo was just awake enough to accept the gift I brought her, a barrette with a glittery pink dragonfly on it, and hear me whisper, "You're really the best," before she fell asleep.

"We drove down to the Siebengebirge mountains today," Caroline said, explaining why the kids were asleep already. "We hiked almost nine miles, all the way to the castle ruins at the summit of the Drachenfels. We're all pretty pooped out, although Severin isn't since he spent the whole day sitting cozy in his carrier on Bert's back."

"Which means Bert will probably be falling asleep by nine thirty tonight," Ole whispered into my ear.

"Hi," I said to him, a bit embarrassed. I hadn't spoken to him since my dental procedure on Monday.

Ole flashed me his most charming Chief Goswin–style smile. "Hi, you," he said. It sounded very tender. *Too* tender, really, to my ears.

"Is Mia still staying with her parents?" I asked to bring us both back down to earth a bit.

"Yeah. She stopped by to pick up a few things and used the occasion to accost me again. Verbally, I mean."

"And I hope you took that opportunity to ask her what she found so great about the old fogey she was with at the hotel?"

Ole shook his head. "There's no point. Because then she'll think we separated because *she* had an affair."

"But that *is* the reason, Ole."

"No, it's not," Ole said stubbornly. "And eventually I hope you'll understand that as well."

"Now, would you two mind julienning the vegetables for me?" Caroline said, tossing two zucchinis at Ole, who caught them adeptly. Caroline winked at me and gave me a meaningful smile.

"Fantastic shoes," Marta said.

"Thank you. They're new," I said.

"They look just great," Marta said, and then she started to cry. "Imagine my fat feet squeezing between those straps! What I wouldn't give to have slender ankles again. Or perky little breasts. I really can't understand why someone like you—"

"Marta!" Caroline snarled.

Marta sniffed.

"Oh, Marta. It's just temporary," I said. "Your feet will look normal again soon enough." Although, truth be told, I could hardly imagine that, the way Marta's feet looked inside the giant, worn-out Birkenstocks she had borrowed from Marius.

"I know, I know," Marta sniffed. "And they're just my feet, and . . . Well, breasts get even bigger while you're nursing."

"And that's because you're going to be holding a beautiful baby in your arms," I said.

"Exactly," Caroline said. "So stop with the crying and dice up these onions for me."

"But how am I supposed to stop crying if I'm dicing onions!" Marta protested, and all we could do was laugh.

Bert put in an old Gipsy Kings CD and turned the volume up louder than usual, since the kids were in an unusually deep sleep from the mountain air they had been breathing all day. The rhythm was catching, and soon we were all dancing through the kitchen, slicing vegetables and shaking our butts, stirring the pots and snapping in time with the music. Severin cooed happily in Bert's arms. Even Marta relaxed and ventured a spin on her swollen ankles.

"Still can dance, little elephant," Marius said, dancing around her once, which took quite a while. Marta laughed.

Someone knocked at the side door to the kitchen. We apparently hadn't heard the bell ring at the front door.

"Who could that be?" Caroline asked.

Bert sambaed his way to the door and came back in with Mia at his side.

"Hi, everyone," Mia said. She looked good, as always, maybe even a bit better than usual. She had on a light blue summer dress that brought out her eyes and her wonderfully slender figure. I was pretty sure that it was brand-new, as were the matching sandals on her feet.

Everyone stopped dancing, although the music kept playing.

"What are you doing here?" Ole asked.

"I thought tonight was our weekly cooking party," Mia said. "I didn't say I wasn't coming, did I, Caroline?"

"No," Caroline said.

"Why are you all so surprised to see me, then? I was here last week, too."

"Stop it, Mia," Ole said.

"Stop what?" Mia threw back her long, shiny red hair.

"Would you like something to drink, Mia?" Bert asked.

"Yes, please," Mia said. "I actually had a bit to drink at home before I came over, but I'm definitely not planning on sobering up. So bring on the hard stuff."

"I hope you didn't drive over, then," Ole said.

"Oooh, are you worried about me? Are you afraid I might I ram into an overpass support or something?" Mia asked. "You're into suicide victims, I hear. Isn't that right, Ole? Doesn't that turn you on?"

"Mia," Caroline said. "I think it would be better if you . . ."

"What?" Mia snarled at her. "If I would get lost so you guys can have your little party here without me? What would you say if it hadn't been Ole but Bert who had gone to bed with Gerri, hmm?"

"Shut up," Ole said. "I'm calling you a cab now."

"It's a fine mess you've made, Gerri," Mia said. "Tell me, how does it feel to have someone else's failed marriage on your conscience?"

"Leave Gerri alone," Caroline said. "She can't help it that Ole and you have grown apart."

"Grown apart!" Mia said, laughing. "I see you haven't gotten the latest news flash. Don't you know that Gerri and Ole have been fooling around?"

"That is absolutely not true," Charly said.

"You two should really keep your marital problems—" Marius started, but Mia cut him off.

"You should probably not butt in, asshole! Or should I tell Marta how often your hand has happened to land on my ass and how you're always staring down my blouse?" She looked over at Marta and made a contemptuous grimace. "You are all so hypocritical!"

"If anyone here is a hypocrite, Mia, it's you," Ulrich said.

"And why is that, then? Because I've pretended these Saturday nights weren't half as tedious as they are?" Mia asked. "I'm going to let you all in on a big secret: Last Friday when Gerri allegedly tried to commit suicide, she actually spent a passionate night of love with my husband at the Regency

Palace. And I know that because a girlfriend of mine saw them both there. Making out in the breakfast room the next morning."

"While you were off taking a continuing ed class in Munich, right?" Charly said.

"In Stuttgart," Mia replied, correcting her. "Yes, that's right. Ole, incidentally, does not dispute this, my dear *friends*. He admitted he's in love with Gerri."

"I am," Ole said. "That's no secret."

Caroline put her hand over her mouth and said, "Oh!"

"Yes, *oh*," Mia parroted. "And that's why I moved out. But I'm sure you don't find that upsetting in the least, now do you, Caroline? After all, you've spent *years* trying to get Ole and Gerri together, and you never forgave me for snatching him up. But now the tables are turned. Your dear, sweet, innocent Gerri lured Ole to the hotel with her suicide plan . . . And you all still feel sympathy for her, treating her with kid gloves. So go ahead, side with her. I suppose it doesn't matter that she's destroyed my life. The main thing is that our dear, sweet, beleaguered Gerri is doing OK again."

"Now just hold on right there, Mia!" Charly said. "We know it wasn't your girlfriend who saw Ole and Gerri together. It was *you*!"

"But she was in Munich," Marius said.

"Stuttgart," Marta corrected.

"She was not," Ulrich said. "She got a room at the Regency Palace that night with *her* lover."

"Oh!" Caroline, Marta, and Marius said in chorus.

Mia looked shocked.

"And not for the first time," Charly said. "She kept telling Ole she was at whatever her latest continuing ed class was, but each time she was having a rendezvous with her lover."

"Some wrinkly old bastard," Ole said.

"He isn't old," Mia snarled, having quickly overcome her initial shock. "And he's ten times better than you in bed! You are so clueless! You're a total loser."

"Then go be with him," Ole said. "What are you waiting for? I don't want you anymore anyway."

"No, because now you've got Miss Fatass here," Mia said. "If I had known that's what turns you on, I'd have happily packed on a few extra pounds for you."

"I honestly don't understand one thing that's going on," Caroline said.

"Me either," Marta said. "Mia and her lover were at the same hotel as Ole and Gerri?"

"No!" I said.

"Yes," Charly said. "But all Gerri was trying to do was kill herself undisturbed. She is absolutely innocent. Ole had clued in that Mia was cheating on him, and he followed her and her lover to the hotel. He *coincidentally* met Gerri there, who was consoling him because he was in total shock."

"And drunk on whiskey," I said.

Mia laughed, although she looked a bit unnerved.

"It was fate," Ole said. "Providence. Karma. Whatever you want to call it. Of all the hotels in the city of Cologne, somehow it was that one. Anyone who thinks it was only a coincidence has no idea what they're talking about."

"Huh?" Marta said. "Can someone explain why Gerri was at that hotel at all, and how it is that she met Ole there?"

"Karma!" Bert and Marius said as though from a single mouth.

"Actually, we can all be grateful to Mia," Ulrich said. "Because if she had really gone to some continuing ed thing, Ole would never have ended up at that hotel, and there would have been nothing to keep Gerri from committing suicide."

"Wow," Marius said. "That is some story."

"I still don't get it," Marta said. "How did Ole know that Gerri wanted to commit suicide? And why were they making out over breakfast?"

"He didn't know," Bert said. "He was just at the right place at the right time."

"Because of Mia," Ulrich said.

"Karma," Caroline said.

"To Mia!" Bert said, raising his glass. "To Mia, who saved Gerri's life by having an affair!"

"To Mia," Ulrich said festively.

"To Mia," Marius said.

Mia shot toxic glares around the room. "You can all fuck off," she said, tossing back her glorious hair. "You are all complete assholes!"

And with that she stormed out of the kitchen. A second later the whole house shook as Mia slammed the door.

"*Auf Wiedersehen*," Caroline said.

"I still don't get why you were making out over breakfast," Marta said.

"Because Gerri had a carrot juice mustache on her upper lip and such a sweet mouth," Ole said.

"Because Mia was *supposed* to see us doing that," I said, correcting him. "And she did see us."

"Brilliant," Caroline said.

"Have you really been feeling up Mia's ass?" Marta asked with an ominous look at Marius.

"There's nothing to feel," Charly said.

"That's true," Marta said, and then she started to cry.

"I hope you're happy now," Ole said outside after the party broke up. Charly and Ulrich were already waiting in Ulrich's car for me.

"What do you mean?" I asked.

"Mia finally knows that I know she cheated on me," Ole said. "That's what's been bugging you the whole time, after all."

"Yes, it was," I said. "Still, I guess we could have spared Mia that embarrassing scene."

"But that wasn't my fault," Ole said. "Ulrich and Charly started it."

"Because it was *wrong* to let Mia blame me for your breakup," I said.

"But you *are* the reason," Ole said.

"Why am I having more déjà vu?" I sighed.

"Because we had this same conversation a couple of days ago," Ole said. "I love you, Gerri, and I want to be with you. What's so hard to understand about that?"

"Ole, it's—I'm sorry. I just can't take this seriously," I said. "I mean, you really need to ask yourself where your feelings are coming from so suddenly! Were you in love with me four weeks ago?"

Ole looked uneasy for a moment. Then he said, "Basically, yes. I just didn't know it yet. And even if I didn't know it, what's wrong with suddenly and unexpectedly falling in love with someone?"

"Nothing," I said. "I just think the timing is a bit unfortunate. It took you all of six hours after finding out your wife was cheating on you to fall in love with the first woman you crossed paths with. You can call it karma if you like, but you can also call it a panic response, projection, or even an act of defiance."

"Why can't you ever let anything positive into your life?" Ole asked. "Just *once*, Gerri, jump over your shadow. Your destiny is right here, ready for the taking, and you should seize it. Believe me—anyone would be glad to be in your shoes."

"What are you talking about, Ole?"

"Do you think I'm full of myself? Women just like me; that's how it's always been. Tall, blond, good-looking dentists rank highly. And nothing has changed about that just because Mia has problems with sex and intimacy and went looking elsewhere. Who knows, maybe it's early menopause. But whatever it is: You won't be able to find anyone better than me. Isn't that clear to you?"

"I could find someone *more modest*," I said. "I mean, hello? You seem to think very highly of yourself!"

"There is no place for modesty at a time like this," Ole said seriously. "Think about it, Gerri! I'm the best thing that will ever happen to you, because I see you the way you are—with all your wonderful qualities and funny little quirks. And I love you for them. I will spend my life waiting on you hand and foot, and everyone will envy you."

I would have loved to find out what my wonderful qualities and funny little quirks were, but instead I said, "Well, how about I take a bit more time to get clear on *my* feelings?"

"How much time?" Ole asked.

"No idea, Ole," I said.

Ole bit his lower lip for a moment. "I'm not going to wait forever," he said. "I don't want to waste too much more time."

"I'll have to risk it," I said.

"You're being stupid," Ole said. "You're really stupid!"

"God, thank you very much," I said. "Is that one of my wonderful qualities, stupidity?"

"Maybe you should give some thought to how it makes me feel when you keep rejecting me and doubting the sincerity of my feelings," Ole said.

"But I've been doing that the whole time," I said.

"We're made for each other, Gerri," Ole said. "We have the same group of friends, we enjoy the same things, we have the same interests, and we're a good match in bed. What more do you want?"

"Dear, sweet Ole. We have yet to determine if we're a good match in bed because *we did not have sex!*" I said, enunciating the last few words very slowly and clearly.

Ole was silent for a moment. "What about our kiss?" he asked. "You can't tell me that you didn't feel any tingling when we kissed."

"Hmm," I said. The kiss had in fact been very nice. But pretty much all kisses are, right? As long as you're not kissing someone you dislike, or someone who jams his tongue down your throat, then there's always that special tingling. Or usually there is. So, at least 50 percent of all first kisses are nice. Maybe 45. But that's a high rate, in any case.

Ole misinterpreted my silence and laughed with satisfaction. "Think about it overnight," he said, kissing my cheek and walking off to his car. It was a black Porsche Carrera; Ole called it his dentist car, and Bert, Ulrich, and Marius all burned with envy for it. I watched him skillfully maneuver out of his parking spot and speed down the street.

"Gerri! He's gone, you can get in now," Charly called from Ulrich's car.

I climbed into the backseat. "Sorry," I whispered.

"No prob," Charly said. "It was obviously an important conversation, so it needed to take as long as it needed."

"Did you two hear everything?"

"Only after Charly rolled down her window," Ulrich said.

"And Ole is right, Gerri," Charly said. "Why are you letting all your doubts screw things up with him? And why are you spending so much time being all wary and overanalyzing things? You should seize happiness with both hands and hold on tight."

"Nonsense," Ulrich said. "Gerri's right. Ole's feelings really did come on all of a sudden. If Mia hadn't been cheating on him, Ole would still be with her today. And if he were really serious about Gerri, then he wouldn't be putting all that pressure on her to make up her mind quickly. He would be letting things run their course."

"Plus, it's not about Ole's feelings," I said. "It's about *mine*!"

"But you like Ole!" Charly said.

"Yes. And once upon a time I was also in love with him. But that was years ago!"

"You cannot seriously be telling me that you don't have a crush on him anymore," Charly said.

"Charly, I have crushes on Robbie Williams and Giovanni di Lorenzo and David Beckham," I said. "Even on Ulrich, at least sometimes."

"Hey, thanks, old buddy," Ulrich said. "If you want, I'll start walking around in my boxers at home as long as you're staying with us."

"But—" Charly started.

"Leave her alone," Ulrich said. "If it's serious between Ole and her, then she has all the time in the world to figure that out."

"Unless it's too late," Charly said. "And then she'll starting thinking about committing suicide again, and no one wants that."

"We've got two cover mock-ups back from the graphics department, and we need your opinion," Licorice said on the phone.

"*My* opinion?"

"Yes, honey. Didn't you read through your contract? You have a veto on the covers, and you're going to need it, too, because one mock-up has Ronina looking like Madonna in the eighties, in an aerobics outfit to boot, and the other mock-up is overflowing with more blood than there was at the Battle of Watergate. So stop in on Monday, and I'll introduce you to the folks in graphics."

"OK," I said, resolving to find out what the Battle of Watergate was.

Wow! I had a contractual veto on the covers. This was revolutionary! Now my protagonists might have the same hair color on the cover as they did in the stories! "Is your, uh, family matter, uh, I mean, I hope it wasn't anything bad," I said.

"What do you mean?"

"Well, you weren't able to attend the business lunch last Wednesday," I said.

"Oh right, *that*," Licorice said. "Yes, I really needed to take a day off, and I thought it might do you and The Boy some good to be alone. Did you know he's not dating Ms. Schneider anymore?"

"Yes," I said. "It was just a pathetic, superfluous affair."

"I'm not sure if she sees it that way," Licorice said. "Anyway, that breakup seems to have agreed with him; he's busy hauling his stuff out of the storage room and moving into the corner office."

"Oh," I said. "I guess he has a hard edge after all."

"Mmm, not really," Licorice said. "That office has been empty ever since our colleague had that nervous breakdown. But it's a start. Have a good weekend, Gerri. We'll see you on Monday."

"I'm looking forward to it," I said, meaning Monday and not the weekend. Because my weekend was shrouded entirely under the shadow of Aunt Alexa's silver-anniversary party.

The week had gone by in a flash. I talked to Ole on the phone about forty times, wrote fifty pages of the second Ronina novel, and helped Patrick and Lulu with their move. And that was mainly because I was rather interested in seeing how Patrick's brushed stainless-steel CD shelves looked next to Lulu's napkin decoupage chest of drawers.

Patrick handed over the keys to me on Thursday night after we had gotten Lulu's sofa into my apartment and Patrick's couches out.

"Is that everything?" I asked skeptically.

"Of course," Patrick said. "What are you afraid of? That I'll sneak in at night and rape you?"

"Um . . . yes . . ." I said.

Patrick grimaced. "You don't have anything to worry about, sweetheart! Someone like you I would fuck only in an emergency."

Obviously, Lulu was out of hearing range during that exchange—whenever she was listening, Patrick was always sweet as sugar to me. Once he even called me little sister.

"You could try to meet him halfway," Lulu suggested at one point. "He's making such an effort with you."

"I'm sorry, Lulu. Just this once it turns out I know more about something than you do: That guy is and will always be an asshole."

"Which didn't keep you from taking over his apartment and kitchen, however," Lulu said. "You should be ashamed!"

"I did think long and hard whether our arrangement is morally defensible," I said. "And, well—yes! Yes, it is."

I had the locks changed on Friday morning. The landlady was a little surprised about it, but obviously I covered the cost in full and explained it had to do with feng shui and the apartment's chi. In addition to the new locks, I also had a new security bar installed behind the door. And then I drove to my parents' house.

My mother had ordered a pantsuit for me and insisted I stop by to try it on.

"I've already told you I have a dress," I said.

"A *red dress!*" my mother said. "I have not forgotten. Probably with spaghetti straps and so tight someone can see your panty line."

"No," I said. "It's a great dress, really."

"Well, this is also a great pantsuit," my mother said. "It's exactly the same one that Hannah wore to Annemarie's six-tieth birthday. Slip it on quickly for me."

I sighed and did her bidding. The pantsuit was beige, which made me look pale, and it hung off me like a sack.

"I don't understand," my mother said. "It's EU size forty-two! Stand up straight!"

"I'm size thirty-eight, Mama," I said.

"Really? Usually I have such a good eye for sizes, and you are the fat one in the family. Ah, well, no matter. They have twenty-four-hour customer service. If I call right now, we can have the size thirty-eight here by tomorrow afternoon."

"Mama—" My cell rang. I could see on the display that it was Ole. *Again.*

"No, no talking back. It's important to me that you look presentable tomorrow because everyone will be giving you some extra-close scrutiny, you can count on that," my mother said. "I want you to be able to stand there with your head held high. And me too! I hope you haven't forgotten what an awful position you put me in, a mother whose daughter tried to take her life . . . Go and answer it, child. That thing is making a terrible noise."

"Hello?"

"Hello, my beauty. I just wanted to see how you're doing," Ole said.

"Who is it?" my mother asked.

"I'm fine. I'm at my mother's house at the moment," I said.

"Have you told her about me?" Ole asked.

"Ole, there's nothing to tell," I said.

"Hurry up!" my mother said. "Can't you call back later? We've got things to do!"

"Gerri, you're really starting to go over the top," Ole said. "Shall I remind you how many offers I've gotten from women this week to take Mia's spot immediately? With all the benefits and privileges?"

"I'm betting every single one of your office assistants," I said. "How many is that?"

"Ha-ha, could someone be jealous?" Ole asked.

"Cell phones are such a vulgar habit," my mother said. "They really ought to be banned. Being reachable anywhere at any time—it's just dreadful. And people typing away at all those SOS messages. Habakkuk and Arsenius have even started at it already."

I sighed. "Ole, I have to go. I'll see you Saturday at Caroline and Bert's." I hung up and put the cell back into my bag.

"Finally! Now, do you have shoes that will work with this?" my mother asked. "Plain black pumps would be good. Your hair looks like it's in good shape for once, I must say. If you blow-dry it over the round brush, that will work. And if anyone asks where you're currently living, then please don't say you're living with that harlot Charlotte. You know what everyone will think then—ugh, and Charly has that tattoo on her arm . . ."

"Mama! No one will give a second thought to the fact that I'm temporarily staying with my *married, pregnant friend* and her husband."

"Ha, you have no idea how people are," my mother said. "There's no end to the filth in people's minds, you know. Speaking of which, based on unconfirmed rumors, I've heard that your cousin Diana and her stockbroker boyfriend have apparently broken up. But like I said, I haven't been able to confirm these rumors yet." My mother sighed. "So you'd better be prepared to be the only one tomorrow night who shows up without a significant other. I'm glad that Rigerlulu won't have to come alone this time, at least. Alexa is green with envy because Patrick has a master's degree, while Claudia was only able to land a midlevel civil servant who started training right out of high school. When I told her how much money someone can earn in eye-tea, all the blood drained from her face, she turned so pale."

"What's better—someone in eye-tea or a dentist?" I asked pensively.

"Silly question. A dentist, of course," my mother said. "At least then people know what you're talking about. But dentists are hard to come by. You should stay realistic."

I couldn't keep the fantasy at bay of driving up to the hotel hosting Alexa's party, and Ole and me stepping out of a Porsche Carrera together and onto a long red carpet leading to the lobby. The jaws of my aunts and great-aunts would hang agape at the magnificent sight, and once they heard he was a *dentist,* their teeth would chatter in shock, and my mother would be so proud of me that she would forget to harp even once on my red dress . . .

"And get your nails done," my mother said. "You're not still chewing your nails, are you? You know you shouldn't do that."

Mama, I chew where and when I want, and I will not wear that boring pantsuit! I wanted to say, staring my mother resolutely in the eyes. But I just couldn't do it.

Back at Charly's, I was so angry with myself I could have banged my head against the wall.

"*Someday* I have got to find it in myself to stand up to her," I moaned. "But whenever she's right there in my face, I always buckle. I'll probably just sweat myself to death tomorrow in that beige monstrosity."

"Hey, now. Where is my little revolutionary?" Charly asked. "The Gerri who sent out those subversive good-bye letters? The Gerri who conquered the most handsome dentist in Cologne with her charm and has been keeping him at arm's length, drooling? The Gerri who has wrought havoc in the vampire novel industry? The Gerri whose first act after moving into her new apartment was to change the locks?"

"You mean the Gerri who will be freezing her ass off in a red dress tomorrow night to make an appearance at Aunt Alexa's anniversary party?"

"That's the one!" Charly said. "You go get her and give this wussy Gerri the boot! Head high! Stomach in! Chest out! Fists ready!"

"All right," I said, grabbing my phone and giving my mother hardly a chance to get a word in. "Mama, I want to thank you for your help, but I will be wearing the red dress."

"Don't be ridiculous, Rigerlu," my mother said. "The pantsuit in the smaller size will be delivered tomorrow; I'll send your father over with it."

"But I—"

"It's a gift from me. No, no, there's no need to thank me—that's what mothers are for. Oh, someone's calling on the other line. I'm sure it's Evelyn. Can you believe my holier-than-thou sister actually tried to negotiate with your father about the rent for your old apartment *behind my back?* She is such a greedy, money-grubbing woman. I explained to your father she just cannot be trusted, what with her track record of provinciality."

"Provin— Oh, you mean *promiscuity.*"

"Yes, whatever," my mother said. "If you don't know a Latin word, Gerri, just go ask Lulu. She knows all of them. I have to go."

I hung up.

Charly held one thumb up in the air. "You really gave it to her!" she said.

"If I'm going to put on the red dress tomorrow, I'm going to have to start getting drunk at least an hour beforehand," I said. "Maybe I should dribble some wax into my ears, like Odysseus's crew did for the Sirens. Then I won't be able to hear my relatives insulting me and my mother nagging me, and I'll be able to spend the whole evening with a relaxed smile on my face."

"Oh, Gerri-Berry. Just stay home, put your legs up, and watch a DVD with me," Charly said.

"But that wouldn't exactly be revolutionary," I said.

"It'd be a quiet revolution," Charly said. "I think that's allowed."

Dear Gerri,

Mama says we should rite you that were glad you didn't kil yourself and that we love you.

But we think its totally roten you left all the good stuf to Chisola and not to us. if you kill yourself again pleas be Fare. You can give the necklass to Chisola but we want the computer and the iPod and at least some mony to by a nother iPod because were twins and we need too of everything.

Your loving godsons,
Arsenius and Habakkuk

PeeS. We'll also take the TV if nobuddy else wants it.

SEVENTEEN

I'm proud to be able to say I didn't need to drink any courage as I slipped into my red dress on Friday night. I stood there, stone-cold sober, touching up my bright-red lipstick, blow-drying my hair (over the round brush, but not enough to make my hair look *too* big), and then sliding my feet into the amazing red-butterfly sandals. I listened, stone-cold sober, to Charly's and Ulrich's compliments; I left their apartment stone-cold sober; and I arrived at the Lexington stone-cold sober. But once there I immediately wished I hadn't been so goddamned brave and had tossed back a few shots of vodka after all.

"Look, Heinrich. There's Gerri!" my great-aunt Elsbeth yelled the moment I entered the hotel lobby after I had failed to take up a timely hiding position behind the monstrous fountain there. "The Gerri who's responsible for the family's Meissen porcelain debacle and who tried to *kill herself* last week."

Needless to say, Great-Uncle Heinrich and everyone else within earshot looked over at me.

"But not because of the porcelain, Aunt Elsbeth," I said. "Also, that was over twenty years ago."

"I'm not your aunt Elsbeth, I'm your aunt Adelheid," said Great-Aunt Elsbeth and/or Adelheid. I already mentioned that they all look alike. "You look good, child. Have you put on a few pounds?"

"No," I said.

"But you carry it well," Great-Uncle Heinrich said, clicking his tongue and pinching my waist.

"Is it true that you write . . . erotica for the . . . reading matter one buys under the counter?" Great-Aunt Adelheid asked.

"They aren't sold under the counter," I sighed. "You can get them at any newsstand. And at the grocery store. It's not porn."

"Oh, yes, times have changed," Great-Aunt Adelheid said with a small laugh. "Nowadays one offers the filthiest material for sale *anywhere*, and even to minors. Hmm, you remind me somehow of my sister Hulda, when she was young. She had a penchant for the scandalous, as well. Did you know she used to be a striptease dancer? She would be up on the *stage* with only those little tassels on. How do those stay attached, anyway? Perhaps double-sided tape?"

"I don't believe that," I said.

"No, I shouldn't believe it, either," Great-Aunt Adelheid agreed. "There's surely another trick to it."

"I meant that I don't believe that Aunt Hulda was a striptease dancer," I said.

"It may also be that I saw that in a motion picture," Great-Aunt Adelheid admitted, gently taking my arm as we walked from the lobby up to the party. "At my age it's difficult to keep the memories straight. Oh, I'm very much looking forward to the party this evening. Such tasteful festivities are more and more infrequent, regrettably; I hear young people nowadays prefer to have their festivities in their *living rooms*. Can you imagine anything more uncouth? But it's much more celebratory in a fine hotel like this. And it's so delightful to see everyone again. I'm already at the edge of my seat to meet your sister Lulu's fiancé. One hears only the best things about him. Your cousin Franziska is not marrying that coiffeur after all, I heard. Thank goodness; he had such a terrible hairstyle, didn't you think, Heinrich? Dreadful. Like a skunk."

"Franziska is single again?" My mood temporarily lifted. Maybe I wouldn't be the only person without a date tonight. I looked around the hall to see if Mia might be around; she was assistant front-desk manager at the Lexington, and I had prepared myself inwardly in case I ran into her. (Which had been another argument against the boring beige suit and in favor of the sexy red dress.) But I couldn't see her anywhere. I could only hope today was her day off.

"The Hall of Mirrors is wonderful," Great-Aunt Adelheid said. She continued to hold my arm firmly as we walked up the wide marble steps that led from the lobby to the stately corridor leading to the hotel's two elegant event halls. "But the Crystal Hall next door is much more beautiful. Unfortunately, it had already been booked for another event. Poor Alexa tried everything to switch, but the other party must have been ridiculously stubborn. And they're only having a seventieth birthday—there won't even be dancing."

"Oh no . . . is there dancing again tonight?"

"Of course, my child. The Viennese Waltz, exactly as it was at Alexa's wedding all those years ago. When you pulled down the porcelain. I shall never forget the din of all the crashing. Do you remember, Heinrich? Really nothing survived intact, most incredibly. Only a single milk pitcher. I wonder what became of that piece? Incidentally, Hulda won't be here this evening. She preferred to fly to Sardinia tonight." She paused and then whispered, "Accompanied by a man young enough to be her *grandson*."

"I thought he was her nurse," Great-Uncle Heinrich said.

"Nonsense," Great-Aunt Adelheid said.

We had made it only halfway up the marble steps when I saw my mother in a lilac-colored gown not too far down the corridor. She was standing at the huge double doorway leading into the Hall of Mirrors, my father, and Lulu and Patrick, on either side of her. Lulu was wearing a black pantsuit that, apart from the color, was identical to the beige one.

Suddenly I lost all my courage, untangled my arm from Great-Aunt Adelheid's grip, and said, "Oh no, I forgot something. You go on ahead, Aunt Adelheid."

Great-Aunt Adelheid grasped the banister tightly. "Now where is that child scurrying so fast?"

"Maybe she suddenly came up with a good idea for some porn," Great-Uncle Heinrich said.

I hastily stumbled back down the stairs. Had I gone completely out of my mind? If I drove home now and quickly changed into the beige suit, I could be back before Uncle Fred gave his speech and opened the buffet. And then I could spend the rest of the evening in peace and quiet, standing in the corner drinking myself silly.

But on the second-to-last step I tumbled directly into a man who kept me from falling but was staring at me, horrified. It was Adrian.

"What in heaven are you doing here?" he asked.

I stared back at him, at least as horrified. He was wearing a suit and tie, and unless I'd lost all my faculties, his wavy dark hair that usually looked a bit tousled had been parted and slicked back in an eighties/Pierce Brosnan look. Despite all the hair gel, however, the waves curled outward on one side and inward on the other.

"Oh no!" I said. "*Please* don't tell me you're Cousin Franziska's new boyfriend! That's more than I can take!"

"I can confirm with certainty that I am not," Adrian said. "I'm quite unfamiliar with Cousin Franziska. And you— you're not here with Cousin Martin? Tall, thin, IQ of 180, slightly balding?"

I shook my head. "Unfortunately, no," I said with a sarcastic smile.

"Thank God," Adrian said. "Martin's girlfriends are always skinny with thick glasses and look like they cut their own short hair. I suppose that's better for him than coming alone, but between you and me his unending string of four-eyed dates always makes me feel better—even though they usually have PhDs or a National Order of Merit cross because they donated their egg cells to science or something."

"You're here for a family party, too?"

"Yes," Adrian said. "In the Crystal Hall."

"Oh, the seventieth birthday party," I said.

"That's right," Adrian said. "My father."

"We're next door in the Hall of Mirrors, celebrating Aunt Alexa's silver wedding anniversary," I said. "With a small string orchestra."

"We've got an a capella band and a magician."

"We've got a five-level wedding cake," I said. "With silver fondant!"

"My uncle is going to recite a three-hundred-verse poem," Adrian said.

"We're all going to sing rhyming verses we had to make up, to the tune of 'Holla Hee Holla Hoe,'" I said.

"My mother is going to hold a long, formal speech in tribute to my father and his three wonderful sons. She will praise Nikolaus to the skies, shed tears of joy for Alban, and then sigh and say, 'Last but not least, our youngest, Gregor, who once again hasn't quite managed to tie his tie correctly,' and everyone will chuckle."

"My aunt and uncle will be dancing a waltz, and everyone has to dance along," I said. "I presume I will yet again be the only single woman at this party, and the only single man will be my great-uncle Augustus, who will be ninety-three in two months. So I will have to hold his urostomy bag while we dance."

"OK, you won." Adrian laughed.

"Hmm, your tie really *isn't* tied correctly," I said.

"I know," Adrian said. "I looked in the Yellow Pages, but they don't list any emergency tie-tying services."

"Let me help you," I said.

"How do you know how to tie a tie?" Adrian asked skeptically.

"Oh, my mother taught us," I said. "She thinks it's something a proper German girl should know how to do." I carefully loosened the lumpy tie-like formation at his neck and smoothed it out. "We got to practice on my father. He had his tie tied four times every morning. He had to get up fifteen minutes earlier to make time for it. But it paid off. See? A perfect knot."

Adrian touched his neck. "Oh God, you're an angel! I bet my mother won't know what to say about me in her speech now."

"I'm sure she'll think of something else," I said. "If I were your mother, I would comment on your hair."

"What's wrong with it?"

"It looks so . . . oddly brushed," I said, studying the asymmetric waves.

"Oh, my mother *likes* it this way," Adrian said.

"You're sure?"

"Weren't we just talking about you?" he asked.

"Tiluri? Is that you?" someone called from behind me, up the steps.

"Oh no!" I said without turning around. "My mother."

"The lady in purple?"

"Lilac," I said.

"Lavender," said my mother, who was now standing next to me, intensely exuding the scent of Calèche. "We lucked out, child! Your cousin Diana came alone—Marie-Luise says the stockbroker is sick in bed at home, but we all know they've broken up! Why are you standing out here still? Everyone is waiting for you inside."

"I just . . . I-I wanted . . ." I stuttered.

"She just wanted to quickly say hi to me," Adrian said. "Good evening, Mrs. Thaler, I presume? Dr. Gregor Adrian. Gerri and I happened to run into each other here. My family is having a party in the Crystal Hall tonight."

"Doctor?" I repeated, perplexed, as my mother shook his hand.

"I'm pleased to meet you," she said, studying him as closely as she does the bell peppers at the grocery store before setting them in her cart. "Are you Lurigerri's dentist?" At that point my heart stopped beating temporarily, because I briefly thought my mother knew about Ole and me.

"Or her gynecologist?" she continued, and the unavoidable image in my head of Adrian performing a gynecological examination on me turned my face as red as my dress.

"I hope she's healthy?" my mother said. "Recently her health has been a bit . . . shaky . . . Oh no. I hope you're not a *therapist*." At that point I would have turned even redder, but it was impossible to increase my redness from maximum.

"I'm not a medical doctor. My doctorate is in art history," Adrian said. "Unfortunately."

"Oh, how interesting," my mother said. "My second-youngest, Tigerlulu, has a doctorate in literature. She teaches high school, actually. Where do you know Riluger from, then, if I might ask?"

"Uh, sorry—who?" Adrian asked.

"She means me," I said, my cheeks glowing as I recited a silent incantation at him, *Do not say it! Do not say it! Do not say it!*

"Oh, we know each other from . . . from the museum," Adrian said with a frown.

I rolled my eyes. Adrian apologetically shrugged.

"From the museum?" my mother repeated. "Oh, of course. You're an art historian . . . But what has Lugerri been doing at a museum?"

"Uh, sorry—who?"

"She means me," I said, despairingly.

"Oh, Gerri often comes to the museum for research," Adrian said.

I lowered my forehead into my palm.

"For her historical novel," Adrian continued.

"I see," my mother said, taking my arm as though she meant to arrest me. "It was nice to meet you, Doctor, but unfortunately we have to go now. My sister places great value on punctuality, and Gerri still needs to stand for the guest book photograph at the door. In that dress, of all things. I knew you would try to make a fool of me. What did I ever do to deserve a child who never, ever listens? And what kind of lipstick is that? Are you a brake light or a young lady?"

"A brake light, Mama," I said. As she pulled me up the stairs, I looked back down at Adrian, over my shoulder. He smiled and held both thumbs up. God, he looked so cute with his hair done in that ridiculous way.

"Maybe we can meet up again afterward! After my waltz with Uncle Augustus," I called out.

"Yes," Adrian said. "I think I'll be needing to get a bit of fresh air more than once tonight."

"Nice man," my mother said. "Married?"

"No," I said.

"Light in the loafers?"

"He's not gay," I said, rolling my eyes.

"Well then," my mother said. "Maybe you should be going to the museum more often."

The wait for the buffet to start dragged on and on, like chewing gum you keep chewing well after its flavor runs out. Plus, my place card had me sitting between Great-Uncle Augustus and Great-Uncle Heinrich, so I spent the wait being pinched alternately on the cheek, waist, or thigh. Uncle Augustus would have pinched me elsewhere as well, but when he tried I thwacked him hard on the hand with my soup-spoon.

"Ow!" he said. "The young should indulge the old!"

"The next time I'm using my fork," I warned him.

Sitting opposite me were Tina and Frank with Chisola, Habakkuk, and Arsenius. Tina was wearing the same pant-suit as Lulu, except in a light brown.

"Hungry, hungry!" Habakkuk and Arsenius were yelling, drumming their forks on the table. Beforehand I had handed them two iPods—pedagogically perhaps not the smartest move, but I did have the money at the moment, and they had been right in their letter. The sheer surprise of the gifts had shocked them into being good for at least fifteen minutes after that. I had to give them credit for not asking about the TV or computer.

But now they had reverted to their former wild state.

"It's bedlam in here!" Great-Aunt Adelheid said two places away from me. "Children nowadays no longer learn proper deportment. When we were little, our parents would strike us with a stick if we could not sit still."

Arsenius and Habakkuk found this highly interesting. They asked Great-Aunt Adelheid for details. She told them how her teacher had once hit her so hard over the head that her blood ran to the floor down her legs. Arsenius and Habakkuk were enthralled.

"And when did that supposedly happen?" Great-Aunt Elsbeth (at least, I *think* it was Elsbeth) asked from the other end of the table.

"Hmm, nineteen hundred . . . Well, it may be that I saw that in a motion picture," Great-Aunt Adelheid said.

"Your dress is terrific," Tina said to me. "It looks really good on you. Have you lost weight?"

"A little maybe," I said.

"I would have preferred wearing a dress, too," Tina said. "But Mama insisted on this pantsuit . . ."

"It doesn't look bad," I said.

"It's just too bad it's the color of poop," Habakkuk said, and Arsenius roared, "Like diarrhea! Mama pooped her pants! Mama pooped her pants!"

Uncle Augustus rummaged in his suit pocket for a piece of paper. "My verses," he said. "I can't see without my glasses. Could you read them to me, my dear grandniece?"

"'Hark, whose song is drawing near, holla hee holla hoe,'" I began. "'Can it be her voice I hear, holla hee-ahoe.' Uncle Augustus, these are the original lyrics to the folk song; you were supposed to write your own."

"I know, I know," Uncle Augustus said. "But I couldn't think of anything."

From inside my bag, my cell phone played Mozart's *Jupiter* Symphony.

"That nitpicker Harry won't let me up onstage at all," Great-Uncle Gustav said, chiming in. "And I love to sing so much. It's really unfair. I know so many lovely folk songs, and I sing like Hans Albers in an old fifties movie. Women used to worship me when I sang."

"Where is that lovely music coming from?" Great-Aunt Adelheid asked.

"From Gerri's bag," Tina said. "Gerri! We were supposed to turn off our cell phones."

I took the phone out of my bag. "Yes?" I whispered into the phone.

"Hello, my lovely *Liebchen*. What are you doing right now?" Ole asked.

"That Harry wants to boot me out! He doesn't want me to steal the show," Great-Uncle Gustav said. "Harry and his silly piano playing!"

"Ole, this is a bad time. I'm at the Lexington at the anniversary party I told you about, and cell phones are banned here on pain of death," I whispered.

"At the Lexington . . . ? Have you run into Mia?"

"No, not so far," I said. "But I have my pepper spray with me, just in case."

"How can a handbag produce such lovely music?" Great-Aunt Adelheid asked. "I'd like to have one like that myself, Heinrich. Ask Gerri where one can procure such a thing."

"Charly said you signed a lease for a new apartment. Is that true?" Ole asked.

"Yes, that's true. It's an awesome apartment right in Süd-stadt, near all the pubs and boutiques," I said. "Didn't I tell you about it already? I got the keys yesterday."

"No, you didn't tell me about it," Ole said. "You must have forgotten somehow. Don't you think that's a bit odd?"

"What's odd about it?"

"Well, everyone knows that you're moving into a new apartment except for your boyfriend?"

"Ole, you're not my boyfriend. You're my *friend,* and that's all . . ."

"What do you want a new apartment for, anyway? You can move in with me—right now!"

"Thanks," I said. "But no thanks."

"Gerri, this game—all this playing for time—it isn't dignified," Ole said.

"Ole, I'm not playing for time!"

"You've left me hanging for weeks now—what game are you playing?"

"*Joe Millionaire,*" I said, but Ole didn't laugh.

"I don't want anything other than a clear answer," he said. "Do you love me, or don't you love me? Do you want to be together with me, or don't you?"

"I really do love you, Ole, but I . . ."

"Gerri!" Tina hissed. "Put that thing away! Aunt Alexa is marching this way!"

"Uh, you know . . . Right now I can't really . . ." I whispered, hiding behind Great-Uncle Heinrich for cover.

"Yes or no?" Ole said. "You can say only yes or no. It's not that hard."

"And what was the question again?"

"Gerri! Don't push it!"

"Please, Ole, I—"

"Do you want to be together with me or not? Yes or no?" Ole asked.

"Did someone at this table forget to turn off his cell phone?" I heard my Aunt Alexa ask.

"Ole . . ."

"Gerri's handbag can perform music," Great-Aunt Adelheid said.

"Yes or no," Ole said.

"At the moment, I guess no," I said. "I'm so sorry. I don't have a gun held to my head."

"OK," Ole said. "I guess you just want to keep playing games."

"You wanted an answer!" I said, but Ole had already hung up. I threw the phone back into my bag, just in time so that Aunt Alexa didn't see it.

"I don't want to hear one more peep out of your handbag," she said sternly.

"Like mother, like son," Great-Uncle Augustus whined about Aunt Alexa, still upset about Harry. "You know Harry doesn't want to hear a peep out of me, either. Even though the young should indulge the old."

"We can invent a verse for you to sing, Uncle Augustus," Arsenius suggested. "Habakkuk and me are great at making rhymes. *If I had a zit that hurt, holla hee holla hoe, I'd want to have you see it squirt, holla hee-ahoe.*"

"And then something with poop," Habakkuk suggested.

"Not bad," Great-Uncle Augustus said. "It's just a pity I don't have any zits. Now think of something that rhymes with *artificial urinary sphincter.*"

That kept Habakkuk and Arsenius busy for quite a while.

"You know what?" I said, having had a great idea. "I'll give you my verses, Uncle Augustus. See, I printed them out at such a large point size that you should be able to read them even without glasses." Apparently my verses were only half as bad as I had thought, because Cousin Harry had already included them in his printed program, uncensored. Idiot.

Great-Uncle Augustus was touched. "You would do that for me? Give me your moment of glory? You really are an angel, grandniece."

"Yes, I know," I said. "But that's not an invitation to pinch my thigh."

"Pshaw," Great-Uncle Augustus said. "That hadn't even crossed my mind. Are we two assigned to dance the Viennese Waltz together afterward?"

"It looks that way, Uncle Augustus," I said.

"The buffet is open!" Uncle Fred announced, and Arsenius and Habakkuk leaped up and sprinted to the front.

"Take only what you like," Frank called after them, knowing he would have to eat their leftovers otherwise.

"You'd better go with them," Tina said to Frank. "Otherwise they'll start with dessert again, and Aunt Alexa will lecture me about their upbringing."

At the last big family party, Arsenius and Habakkuk had devoured one huge ice-cream bombe intended to feed twenty people between the two of them. That wouldn't have been so bad in and of itself, except they later vomited half of that back up. I won't tell you where in case you happen to be eating right now.

I waited for the first buffet wave to finish, and then Chisola and I went up and got our plates. The one positive thing I might add about these formal family fests was that the food was traditionally excellent and copious.

"I'll show you what you definitely should try when you're at a party like this," I said. "A lot of these things don't look appealing at first glance, but they taste delicious. And other things you can safely ignore altogether."

"I can't eat anything because of my stupid braces anyway," Chisola said.

"Oh, you poor thing. How long do you need to wear them, still?" I asked.

"Four more months!" Chisola said. "At our last class party, I got some spinach leaves stuck in them and didn't notice. And ever since then the kids have been calling me spinach piehole. No boy will ever want to kiss a spinach piehole."

"Oh, I wouldn't say that. The older boys get, the more important food becomes to them," I said.

"Gerri?" Chisola looked up at me with her big eyes. "Mama says that you used to be ugly when you were a kid, too. Is that true?"

"No," I said. "No, but your mama was ugly! She had sticky-out ears that stuck out even through the perms she used to get all the time in those days. And she always wore blouses and jackets with shoulder pads in them that made her look like a steroid-doping prizefighter."

"Do you think maybe I'll be pretty, too, when I'm older?" Chisola asked.

"I think you're pretty *already*, Sissi," I said. "And once those braces come off, you'll feel even better—I bet then the boys will finally see how pretty you are. But it's really important to sit and stand up straight. You have to throw your shoulders back, raise your chin a bit, and look people right in the eyes. Head high, chest out—see? Like me.'"

I rammed my plate into Lulu, who was holding up traffic as she stood with Cousin Diana next to the huge platters of steaming prime rib, pork roast, and turkey. Chisola giggled as I hastily picked a slice of smoked mozzarella off Lulu's jacket.

"Hi, Gerri. You look fantastic," Diana said. "Is that because of the museum director I hear you've been seeing?"

"Sorry?" Lulu asked.

"My mother was tearing up as she told me the rumor," Diana said. "Is it more than a rumor?"

"Just a rumor," I said. "I don't know any museum directors."

Diana sighed. "God, what an annoying family we are, constantly inventing random stories and butting into one another's personal lives. That guy Nick I've been seeing? He and I really had a terrible relationship. Any other mother would have been glad to hear I had finally dumped him. But my mother sobbed. 'A stockbroker, child! You'll never find another one like that!'"

"Yeah, it really takes guts to show up alone at a shitfest like this," Lulu said.

"It's all well and good for you, Lulu. You've got that— what does your fiancé do again?"

"IT," Lulu said. "We've just moved in together. Patrick is really great. I'll introduce you when he passes by again."

"No rush," Diana said. "And Franziska was saying she'd sooner chop off her own hand than subject herself to this pack of wolves without a date at her side. I'm excited to see who she shows up with."

"I saw her before with a good-looking guy," Lulu said. "Mama says he's a veterinarian."

"And where did she come up with him so quickly, I wonder?" Diana said. "No, no, that's just another rumor." She looked around. "Where is Franziska, then? I haven't seen her tonight yet! They seated me next to Cousin Claudia and her auditor boyfriend, and opposite us we had a panorama of all eleven of Cousin Miriam's kids."

"Five," Lulu said.

"Four," Chisola said.

"Whatever," Diana said. "Miriam taught them to *tick-tock* like a clock, so whenever she said, 'But Diana, you're over thirty now, can't you hear your biological clock ticking?' all the kids would say 'tick-tock, tick-tock,' like that crocodile in *Peter Pan*. Oh, there's Franziska! She's in back, with your parents!"

"Patrick and I are seated with Volker and Hilla and their kids," Lulu said. "We said grace twice even before the buffet started. They have this odd way of droning on and on, don't they? And did you know that Hilla is pregnant again?"

"This time it'll be a Benedikt or Franziskus for sure," Diana said. "Oh my God, I don't believe it!"

"What it is?" Lulu asked.

"There! That guy next to Franziska!" Diana said.

"The vet?"

"Vet my ass!" Diana yelled. "I know that guy!"

"Where are they?" Lulu and I craned our necks to see.

Diana laughed. "And boy, do I know him. My sister picked up that guy *online*! And that guy, of all guys!"

"Where? Where?" Lulu and I said, all excited. We hadn't located Cousin Franziska and her new boyfriend yet.

"I'm laughing my ass off," Diana said. "That guy is a total sleazeball! *Rockinhard13* or something, that's his username. Can you believe it? I met him last year on DatingCafé.de."

Lulu and I both stared at her.

"Oh, don't give me those horrified looks, you two!" Diana said. "I was in a really, really dry spell just then, and online dating is a perfectly legitimate way to meet men nowadays. And not all the guys were losers like *rockinhard13*."

"Twelve," I said softly. I finally spotted Cousin Franziska in the back of the hall talking to my parents. Patrick happened to be standing next to them.

"Thirteen, my ass," Diana said. "He was totally average—six at most. The thirteen thing was just a bait and switch. I'm seriously laughing my ass off! This can't be a coincidence. First he catches me, and now my sister!"

Lulu turned as white as a ghost. "I think I'm going to pass out," she said.

"I'm sorry, Lulu," I said.

"Will you guys excuse me for a second? I'm going to go over and say hi to him," Diana said. "I'm dying to see his face!"

"He may not recognize you," I called her after her. "His memory isn't that good."

"Oh my God," Lulu said. "I think I'm going to throw up."

Dearest Gerri, My Grandniece,

Since we won't have a chance to see each other at Alexa's anniversary party, regrettably, as I will be setting off on travels, I wanted to be sure to answer in writing the questions you had for me in your letter.

First of all: I am glad that you decided to keep on living. Life is a great adventure, darling, and problems are nothing more than opportunities to show what you can do. Show them, darling. You are young and beautiful and full of imagination—I would change places with you in a heartbeat if I could.

I was never married because the man whom I loved was already married. To a woman who was so ill that under no circumstances did we want to add to her many troubles. I didn't want a different man (even though there were others)—he and I were like Spencer Tracy and Katharine Hepburn: a secret couple who shared true love for each other but who could never share this love with anyone. And unlike Spencer and Hepburn, we couldn't even star in motion pictures together. But I never regretted my fidelity to this man. He died more than twenty years ago, and his ailing wife is still alive today.

I think it is extremely reasonable for you to wait for true love— do not let this family and our idiotic panic mongering lead you astray: You need never settle for second best. Never. Try to get what you love; otherwise, you will be forced to love what you get.

I enjoyed your novels very much, and the ladies at the retirement home were enthralled, as well. Have you written others? If so, we would all love to read some more. I do think it's too bad that they are printed on such cheap, thin paper—which is why I asked a friend of mine to retype them word for word, print them on handmade, deckle-edged paper, and rebind them. Enclosed please find a collector's edition of the Angela books, with gilt edges and bound in fine red Morocco leather. I have no doubt that in this format your books would find their way to a different audience. Perhaps you can suggest as much to your publisher.

Inspired by reading your books, in fact, I have started to do some writing myself, slipping in a few things from my own experiences. If you would be so kind to have your editor read my enclosed manuscript, I would be very grateful. I have called it *Forgotten Days on the Riviera*, but that is only a working title. If they like it, I can supply more. If they find the love scenes too risqué, they are obviously welcome to abridge them.

To you, my darling grandniece, I offer my wishes for a wonderful life from now on, and always remember: Losing your heart is the most beautiful way to find out you have one.

Your Great-Aunt Hulda

P.S. Please accept this check as a gift, and buy yourself a couple of pretty hats or anything else you like. Although they are not surefire methods, I also recommend getting a convertible and/or a dog. Both considerably simplify breaking the ice with the male sex. And both make life without a man more bearable.

EIGHTEEN

Lulu didn't throw up. (She did later, however, but that was after a bottle of scotch.) In the bathroom, she scooped gallons of cold water onto her face with her hands, but she did not cry. Not even a single tear.

"I'm genuinely sorry, Lulu," I said. "I didn't want this for you."

"It's not your fault," Lulu said. "You tried to warn me."

"You know, I think those rockin' hard days may be long behind Patrick," I said, although I would have preferred not rising to the asshole's defense. "I'm sure he's changed. And he really loves you."

"He's a lying sack of shit," Lulu said. "I can't believe how calm and cool he denied knowing you."

"Well, he had also totally forgotten me," I said. "It wasn't just an act."

"Because you were only one of unimaginably many," Lulu said. "Like Diana."

"Come on, now," I said. "Unlike Diana, I didn't verify in advance whether his metrical claims were true. All that happened between us was he called me a frigid cow and stormed out of the café. And I had to pay for his cappuccino."

"I've been so blind," Lulu said, splashing on more cold water. "I'm sorry I didn't listen to you, Gerri. And all the things I said to you . . . How could I?"

"It's fine," I said. "I would honestly have preferred it if Patrick really did have a doppelgänger walking around."

"What am I going to do now?" Lulu asked.

"Well, I have no idea, either," I said, suppressing all my spontaneous answers. "But sometimes when you love someone, you can overcome misunderstandings like this . . ."

"Are you crazy?" Lulu snarled at me. "I'm supposed to stay together with a lying sack of shit like that? You don't think that might be a bit beneath me?"

"Yes, it *is* beneath you," I said. "But think about . . ."

"What, then? The fact that I'm thirty-two? The fact that my mother is going to have a hissy fit when she finds out I'm single again? The fact that my whole family will treat me like a leper?"

"For instance," I said.

"Pff," Lulu said. "I really don't give a shit. But unlike you, I won't be turning straight to suicide once things get tough. I'm going to hang that guy out to dry—I don't care what Mama says!"

"Good," I said, relieved. "You have to kick him out of your apartment right away, though. Do you hear? And then change the locks, the way I did."

"No! I can't do that," Lulu said. "If I kick him out now, he'll just move back into his old apartment. His lease runs technically through the first of the month."

"But he can't. I've already moved in and changed the locks," I said triumphantly.

"That doesn't matter: Legally he's entitled to stay in that apartment until the first of next month!" Lulu said, rubbing her eyes. "The way German leases work, he could even sue the landlady . . . so I can't let that happen."

"Lulu, I don't need the apartment! Make a clean start: Throw him out."

"No way," Lulu said. "He's not getting off that easy with me." She straightened up. "How do I look?"

Like an employee at Feldmann's Funeral Home, I wanted to say.

But I actually said, "The way you always do, except your face is a bit damp. Do you want some makeup? I've got some in my bag."

"Thanks," Lulu said. "I definitely don't want anyone noticing anything."

"You won't be able to keep the act up until the first of the month," I said.

"Ha, you must not know me well," Lulu said. "I'm going to keep *everything* up, even his cabbage soup diet." She straightened her top and took a deep breath. "And now you go back out there and pretend nothing is wrong. Run a misinformation campaign on Diana about astrological twins or something. I'll come out soon."

Waiting for me outside the bathroom, leaning on the banister and holding a hand-rolled cigarette in his hand, was Adrian.

"You smoke?" I asked.

"No," Adrian said. "But I'm seriously considering start-ing. This is actually a joint I bummed off my sixteen-year-old nephew."

"Ha! Now we've got evidence!" I said. "That your broth-ers aren't so perfect after all, I mean."

"My brothers are, just their kids aren't," Adrian said.

"Yes, because of all those violin lessons," I said. "In your shoes I'd love nothing better than to rub my brother's nose in the fact that his child rearing obviously leaves something to be desired."

"I had to promise not to squeal," Adrian said.

"Too bad. Did your mother give her speech already?"

Adrian nodded, unconsciously rolling the joint between his two fingers.

"Uh-oh . . . Was it bad?" I asked sympathetically.

"Oh, no. This time it went all right. It's just that at the end she made a sort of public appeal for someone to find me a wife. 'Our Gregor is about to turn thirty-five, so per-haps one of you knows a nice young woman who might take an interest in him.'"

I laughed. "That's classic. Now you'll be having a whole slew of women calling you up over the next few weeks."

Adrian laughed, as well. "And what about you? Did you dance with the urostomy bag?"

"Not yet," I said. "But it's been plenty exciting already!" I was glad we were finally talking comfortably, like friends. I smiled at him.

Lulu came out of the bathroom. "I said you should go on ahead," she said, annoyed.

"I think you put too much rouge on the left," I said.

Lulu rubbed her cheek. "Is that better?" Then she noticed Adrian and looked him up and down. "Who are you? Franziska's veterinarian?"

"No," Adrian said. "I'm, uh . . ." He looked at me for help.

"Good grief," Lulu said. "You don't know your name?"

"This is Gregor Adrian," I said. "He's the editor in chief at Aurora. His father is having his birthday party in the Crystal Hall next door. Gregor, this is my sister, Lulu. Normally she's a little nicer, but she's just broken up with her fiancé and is in a bit of shock."

"I'm not single *yet*," Lulu said. "Not until the first of the month. Hey, is that a joint?"

"Yes," Adrian said.

"Can I have it?"

"Sure—here you go."

"Thank you!" Lulu tossed the joint into her clutch. "For later. See you, Gerri. I'm going back in now."

"Head high, stomach in, chest out," I said, and Lulu marched off.

My bag played the *Jupiter* Symphony again.

"Your cell!" Adrian said. "You've still got yours! They frisked us when we arrived to make sure no one smuggled one in."

"Do you want to borrow mine?" I fished my phone out of my bag.

"Do you have any good games on it?" Adrian asked.

"Wait, let me answer this. Hello?"

"I've thought it over," Ole said. "It's never going to be."

"What do you mean?"

"I mean us," Ole said. "You and me!"

"Yes, we cleared that up previously," I said.

"But you weren't being serious," Ole said. "I know you."

"You do not, unfortunately."

"Oh, yes I do, Gerri Thaler. I know you like the back of my hand. And I know that you're going to be sorry once you're thinking clearly again."

"You may know my teeth, Ole, but as for the rest . . ." I gazed toward Adrian, who had turned around to look over the banister and down the corridor at the people coming out of each of the parties. "Why do we keep having this conversation?" I asked Ole.

"Because I'm waiting for an answer, have you forgotten?"

"I gave you my answer, have you forgotten?"

"But that wasn't an answer you had thought through very well," Ole said.

"That's exactly the problem," I said. "You're not giving me any time to think."

"Because there's nothing to think about," Ole said. "You have to decide things like this with your heart."

"Well," I said, looking over at Adrian. In the light of the massive chandelier, his smooth hair had taken on a reddish glow. And despite more combing, the waves of his hair still curled inward on one side and outward on the other. I suddenly had an irresistible urge to sink both my hands into his hair and give it a thorough tousle.

"'Well'? That's all you have to say?"

"You're probably right, Ole," I said pensively as I looked at the back of Adrian's head. "If I loved you, I would know it. And I would be getting those strange twinges in my stomach just from the sight of you. And I would always want to be near you and protect . . ."

Oh my God. How could I have been so blind? Those *were* exactly my feelings.

But not for Ole.

"You're saying you don't love me?"

"Not in the way you'd like," I said. "We can still be good fr—"

"Don't say it!" Ole yelled at me. "Do not say it!"

"That we can still be—?"

"I told you not to say it!" Ole roared so loudly that Adrian turned around and raised his eyebrows at me. "I'm coming over there, and then we can talk this through finally! You don't know what you're saying."

"Ole! Don't you dare come down here!" I yelled, but he had already hung up.

"Who was that?" Adrian asked.

"A—my dentist," I said, and my heart skipped a beat when I looked Adrian in the eyes. "Shouldn't you be going back in? I'm sure they're already missing you."

"You, too," Adrian sighed. "I mean, your family."

"Yes, I have no doubt they are. I'm sure that Cousin Hilla wants to lecture me about Jesus again; Great-Aunt Elsbeth wants to inquire about the 'porn' that I write; and Aunt Marie-Luise wants to refute the rumor she's heard by now that I'm seeing a museum director. Oh, and my great-uncles will undoubtedly want to know what exactly a lesbian does with another woman."

Adrian laughed. "The rumors that I'm gay were finally snuffed out with reports I had been seen with a prostitute."

"I'm guessing that was Marianne Schneider," I said, and then quickly put my hand over my mouth. "Sorry. I just thought because of all the leather she wears . . ."

"Yes, exactly," Adrian said. "The rumor was she was a dominatrix."

"I could go in there with you and attest that you're not into S-M," I said. "But I'm worried a vampire novel author isn't exactly what your parents had imagined for you."

"Listen," Adrian said, "I think by now they're in such despair they would have accepted even a real dominatrix. So they would be positively enraptured with you."

"But I didn't even graduate from college," I said. "And I'm not a model, either."

"Believe me, they'd be delighted if I had a girlfriend like you," Adrian said. "But what would your family say about your dating the editor in chief at Aurora Publishing, Germany's leader in romance fiction?"

"'Oh, Aurora!' they'd say. 'Don't they publish those awful pulp rags people buy under the counter?' On the other hand, they'd say, 'She's thirty now, and look at her hair color—she's never going to be able to reel in a dentist now, anyway.'"

"Is a dentist good?" Adrian asked.

"Yes, the only thing better would be a baron or count with a large estate." I said. "Do you really have a PhD in art history, or did you just invent that?"

"I really have one," Adrian said. "I've just never made much use of it until now. I was so relieved to get the job at Lauros. And now that I'm the editor in chief at Aurora, my pay isn't half-bad."

"Yes, but your job doesn't have that much to do with art history."

"Now don't you start browbeating me, too," Adrian said.

"I'd be the last to do that," I said, a little startled how affectionate my voice sounded. "I'm relieved you got the job at Lauros, too. Otherwise we would never have met."

"Yes, that's right. That's been the best thing about that job so far." Adrian took a half step toward me and said, "With an animalistic grunt, he pulled her toward him and kissed her wildly, and desperately."

"What?" I instantly stopped breathing because he was standing so close to me.

"It had taken him so long to realize that she was the only one who could unlock his soul and allow his body to experience true ecstasy," he said.

"Really?" Now my knees turned to butter. I had to use the banister to hold myself.

"She was the light in his darkness," Adrian continued.

"Oh, shit. Did I write that? It's . . . it's horrifically trashy!"

"But this is the good part," Adrian said. "He carried her in his strong arms to his bed, dropped her onto the bearskin there, and . . ."

"Oh my God, I remember," I said. My nipples were as hard as two little pebbles.

"Ever since I read that scene, I've been dreaming of doing the same with you." He gently stroked a strand of hair out of my face.

"This is a hotel," I said, sounding as though I had just run the hundred-meter. "They have *rooms* here!"

"With bearskins?" Adrian asked. His mouth was now so close to my face that I could smell his breath. He smelled of strawberries.

"We'll have to give some thought to the bearskin," I said.

"Are you sure that—oh no, who are they?"

Habakkuk and Arsenius had abruptly materialized next to us, having apparently been dispatched in search of me. "Gerri! Grandma says you should come back in because we're going to sing now. Should we tell her that you want to stay out here kissing instead?"

"Yes," I said. "I mean . . . no! Tell her I'm coming."

Habakkuk and Arsenius disappeared.

"Come on, let's get out of here," I said, taking Adrian's hand and leading him to the stairs out.

"But you just said—"

"I said I'm coming," I said. "And I'm about to do just that."

Adrian stood there frozen for a moment and then pulled me to him, kissing me . . . and, yes: wildly, and desperately. I pressed myself so closely against him that not even a thin page of pulp fiction could have slid between us.

The kiss lasted a classic eternity, and afterward we held hands and ran down to reception.

"A king room, please," Adrian said. "With hot tub, if possible."

My legs buckled when I heard him say that. I was only just able to keep myself upright by grabbing hold of the edge of the counter. "Not the *hot tub scene!*" I whispered.

"Let's see how far we get," Adrian said. I was infinitely grateful that Mia wasn't the receptionist who handed us the room key and watched us with a raised eyebrow as we walked over to the elevators, our arms wrapped tightly around each other.

"Tilugerri! This is really totally beyond the pale! Where in the world have you been?" my mother yelled. "Uncle Augustus had to sing for you, and Diana had to dance with him, and something horrid happened with his urostomy bag . . . and then some young man showed up and claimed he was your dentist and had to speak with you right away!"

"Oh no!" I said. Ole! I had totally forgotten about him. "Where is he now?"

"I have no idea," my mother said. "Lulu and Patrick took care of him. We thought you would be back at any moment! Where have you been?"

"I . . . had forgotten something at home," I said, tracing my lips with my finger. They were sore from kissing. "How long was I gone?"

"Over two hours!" my mother yelled.

Adrian and I would have stayed away longer, but we knew we had to take a break.

"For health reasons," Adrian had said, and I resolved, the next chance I got, to do some online research about whether excessive orgasms were bad for one's health.

"If we sneak back downstairs now, maybe they won't notice we've been AWOL," Adrian said. "We'll chat for an hour or two with aunts and cousins, and then we'll take off and meet back up here."

In principle that had been a good idea; it's just that my disappearance had not gone unnoticed.

"That is so typical of you," my mother complained as she sat down with me at a table. "Oh, there are Lulu and that dentist. Is he married?"

"Yes, but separated," I said.

"Then sit up straight," my mother hissed.

"Hi, Gerri," Ole called out to me. "Nize party. And thizziz great scotch. Me and your sizzer have already emptied a whole bottle. Know what? Lulu wants to come have me do her teeth."

"Lulu never usually drinks alcohol," Patrick said, vaguely disgruntled. Lulu held a glass up and said, "Oh, shuddup you, you eye-tea!"

"Luriger!" my mother said.

"*Prost!* Everybody, toast with me! To thiz wonderful, wonderful day in May," Lulu sang. "Mama, did you know that Gerri and thiz handsome blond dentist were *almost* a couple?"

"Yeah," Ole said. "I waz ready to give her my heart, plus the passenger seat in my Porsche. But the only thing Gerri said to me waz that line with the f-word in it . . ."

"I did no such thing," I protested.

"You did so," Ole said. "You just brushed aside my feelings without a second thought."

"She did no such thing," my mother said, backing me up. "I'm sure this is a misunderstanding. Say you're sorry!" The last bit she said to me.

"Sorry," I immediately said. It was a Pavlovian reflex at this point. Resistance was futile.

"Now'z too late," Ole slurred. "I warned you. There'z a limit to how much abuze even I can take."

"And that's why you came all the way downtown?" I asked.

"Yeah! You don't tell a girl something like that on the phone," Ole said. "I know how to jehave like a bentleman."

Lulu laughed. "Yeah! Thaz right! Life punishes those who delay."

"Too bad, so sad!" Ole said, laughing as well.

"Well, then, it sounds like we've resolved everything," I said. "I really hope that we can be f—"

"There!" Ole yelled. "There iddiz again! The line with the f-word."

"'We can still be friends,'" Lulu said. "God, I hate that line, too!" Ole and she doubled over in laughter onto the table, where they had sat down opposite my mother and me.

"But I know you've never heard that line yourself, with your looks," Ole said once he had calmed back down. "I bet men are alwayz throwing themselves at your feet!"

Lulu squealed with laughter. "Yeah," she gasped. "Boy, do they!" And then she bent closer to Ole and whispered something into his ear.

"Oh, until the first of the month," Ole giggled. "Maybe my broken heart will be mended by then!"

Lulu raised her glass. *"Prost!"* she said, looking at Patrick. "Go on, Eye-Tea. Drink."

"I can't stand by and watch this," Patrick said, standing up. "If you'll excuse me, I'm going to go over and chat with your father. He's sober at least."

"I don't mind in the leazt," Lulu said, which Ole found so funny that he nearly tipped out of his chair with laughter.

"Patrick's right," my mother said. "Ritilulu, I'm so embarrassed for you!"

"I'm embarrassed for you, too," Lulu said. Now she looked as though she might pee her pants from laughter.

"I had no idea you have such a super-nice sizzer, Gerri," Ole said.

"I have three super-nice sisters, actually," I said, standing and trying nonchalantly to add some distance between him and me.

"Where are you going?" my mother asked.

"I just remembered I forgot something else," I said.

"You can—" my mother started to say, but then she also stood to follow me. "Tirilu! It's enough that one of your sisters is making a complete laughingstock of me here, but *you* will behave appropriately now! Oh no, here comes Alexa! Don't you say one word about your drunken dentist! We'll say we don't know him."

"Where were you during the song, Gerri?" Aunt Alexa asked. "I missed you."

"Oh, Uncle Augustus was so sad he couldn't sing that I handed my part over to him," I said.

"Oh, what a good girl," Aunt Alexa said. "Marie-Luise says you've been dating the curator at a science museum. Do you think that's the right thing to be doing so soon after your suicide attempt? I would think it's not the healthiest thing to put your delicate psychological state through right now, dating a taxidermist."

"No, no," I said, ignoring my mother's wild gestures to stop talking lest she slit her own throat. "Gregor is an art historian. He doesn't work at a museum but in publishing. I

336

would have liked to introduce him to the family tonight, but he happens to be celebrating his father's seventieth birthday in the Crystal Hall next door."

"He's one of the *Adrian boys*?" my aunt asked. "That filthy-rich couple from the society section in the paper? The university professor and engineer?"

"Yes, that's them," I said. "Gregor is their youngest."

Aunt Alexa's mouth hung agape. My mother's as well.

I took the opportunity to flee. "I just have to rush over now to meet him," I said. "See you later!"

As I stood outside the double doorway to the Hall of Mirrors, I toyed for a moment with the idea of going next door and bailing Adrian out of the Crystal Hall. But that wasn't necessary. He was already standing in the corridor waiting for me, leaning on the banister to the marble steps leading back down to the lobby.

"That was fast," he said. "I thought we agreed on a one-hour break."

"Oh, you know . . . I'm actually feeling quite rested already."

"Me too," Adrian said, smiling at me. His hair now looked the way it usually did: I had taken the opportunity upstairs to tousle it thoroughly.

Lulu and Ole came tumbling out of the hall side by side. "Ugh . . . I think I really do need to throw up now, Gerri!" Lulu cheerfully called at me.

And Ole said, "I'll hold your hair back for you. The sign of a true gentleman iz he doesn't let a girl puke all alone."

"No way you're watching," Lulu said. "There are things a girl has to do by herself, my mother taught me that." She slammed the bathroom door in his face.

"I can wait," Ole said, leaning on the door. Calling down the corridor to me, he said, "Well, I won't be there next time to save you from suicide, Gerri. I hope you get that."

"There won't be a next time, Ole," I said, taking Adrian's hand and walking down the steps with him.

"Who's that?" Adrian asked, but only after we were nearly all the way back to the lobby.

"That's, uh . . ." I said. "That's Chief Goswin."

"Ah," Adrian said. "Does that mean I need to go over there and lay a solid left hook into his chin?"

"Not necessary," I said, pulling him toward the elevator. "Let's skip that part."

The last thing I saw before the elevator doors closed behind us was the completely floored face of the scheming redheaded head nurse Alexandra standing behind the front desk.

AFTERWORD

The plot and characters in this story are purely fictitious. Any resemblance to real persons, living or dead, is pure coincidence and completely unintentional.

As usual, I would like to thank all the people who have given me their support: my sister Heidi for her imaginative brainstorming; Silke, Sigrid, and my tireless, wonderful mom for "baby"-sitting; Elke Hurtz and Ednor Mier for their valuable help with research; my colleagues at the Association of German-Language Romance Writers (DeLiA) for their many inspiring postings and suggestions for staving off acute writer's block (cleaning windows really does help!); Eva Völler for her e-mail messages, which made me laugh so hard I nearly spit my nettle-and-Bach-flower tea all over my keyboard on a daily basis. (My keyboard is now hypoallergenic, doesn't have any outbreaks anymore, and it likes itself just the way it is.)

My fattest thank-you must go to the world's best editor and captain of Bastei Lübbe's soccer team, Claudia Müller, who has shown a great deal of patience, humor, and commitment. She was unflappable even when faced with my minor panic attacks, such as when I forgot to make a goody bag for my kindergartner's first day of school. "If it weren't for the last minute," Mark Twain once wrote, "nothing would get done." I have firmly resolved to deliver my next book punctually, at the last minute.

It is traditional in Germany for parents to go all out for their children on the first day of school and hand-make them massive goody bags (actually shaped like cones) filled with school supplies and candy; we call them *Schultüten*. The one we made was not as beautiful as the one I'd always imagined, but we turned out something award-worthy despite all our limitations (all thumbs, and a child who had very specific expectations of the thing). It was shaped like a "Dangerous Dragon with Glitter, Not Girly Glitter but Magic Glitter." Contact me if you're interested in assembly instructions.

Writing a comedy on the subject of suicide was a weightier enterprise than I had previously assumed it would be. In no way is it my intention to make fun of depression, people suffering with depression, and people who commit suicide, nor is it my intention to trivialize the subject in any way whatsoever.

While I was working on this book, I found myself identifying so closely with my heroine that I started writing goodbye letters myself. And then the book surprisingly ended up done, so I never needed to send them out. Here are a few excerpts:

Elke—I was young and needed the money.

Mr. Fischer—Boxwood is not even remotely a cemetery plant, and you can shove your blue spruce!

Renate, Barbara, Janine—I'm glad you exist.

Mike—You can kiss my ass.

Chrissi—I may be fat, but you're stupid.

Bernhard, old buddy—I miss you.

Frank, Lennart, Mama, Werner, Heidi, Harald, Florian, Benjamin, Leonie, Dagmar, Biggi, Rosine—I love you.

— Kerstin Gier, Summer 2006

ABOUT THE AUTHOR

 Kerstin Gier started writing women's novels in 1995 when she found herself with a fresh teaching diploma in hand but without steady work. She is best known in the United States for her Ruby Red Trilogy, and her first book, *Männer und andere Katastrophen* (*Men and Other Disasters*), was recently made into a movie starring actress and singer Heike Makatsch. Her subsequent books have enjoyed great popularity in Germany as well. Her novel *Das unmoralische Sonderangebot* (*The Immoral Deal*) won the 2005 Best German-Language Romance Novel Prize from the Association of German-Language Romance Writers (DeLiA).

Kerstin Gier, born in 1966, now works full-time as a freelance writer in a village near Bergisch Gladbach, Germany, where she lives with her husband, son, two cats, and three chickens.

ABOUT THE TRANSLATOR

Erik J. Macki worked as a cherry-orchard tour guide, copy editor, Web developer, and German and French teacher before settling into his translation career. This was probably inevitable, as he has collected grammars, dictionaries, and language-learning books since child-hood—and to this day is not above diagramming sentences when duty so calls. A former resident of Cologne and Mün-ster, Germany, and of Tours, France, he did his graduate work in Germanics and comparative syntax. He now trans-lates books for adults and children full-time, and he has pub-lished translations of Mirjam Pressler, Jutta Profijt, and Sara Blædel, among others. He works from his home in Seattle, where he lives with his family and their black Lab, Zephyr.

F GIER, KERSTIN 12/13
For every solution, a problem/